Falling From Heights

a novel

CHRIS F NEEDHAM

CANADA

Library and Archives Canada Cataloguing in Publication

Needham, Chris F.
Falling from heights : a novel / Chris F. Needham.

ISBN 978-0-9739558-1-1

I. Title.

PS8627.E43F34 2007   C813'.6   C2006-905619-6

Printed and Bound in Canada

Now Or Never Publishing Company
11268 Dawson Place
Delta, British Columbia
Canada V4C 3S7

nonpublishing.com
Fighting Words.

*For putting up with so much,
and making do with so little,
this book, too, is for Lori.*

A "high" typically involves numerous phases. The initial effects are often somewhat stimulating and, in some individuals, may elicit mild tension or anxiety which is usually replaced by a pleasant feeling of well being. The later effects usually tend to make the user introspective and tranquil. Rapid mood changes often occur. A period of enormous hilarity may be followed by a contemplative silence. Many users report that they have some control over the degree to which they are involved in the subjective effects and that, when necessary, they can "come down" and perform normally. . . . The ability of subjects to "come down" at will has not been adequately explored experimentally.

—*LeDain Commission's Report for the Canadian Government Inquiry into the Non-Medical Use of Drugs,* 1972

Royal Heights

JUNE, 2002

One quick conversation with his father. That is all it took to remind Jeremy Jacks why exactly he had abandoned the West Coast entirely almost two years before. Not quite ten hours prior to this telltale encounter, he had received a phone call from his father at his small studio apartment in Toronto, explaining how his brother Robert, an army reservist, had suffered a terrible parachuting accident while on a weekend training mission in Wainwright, Alberta. Apparently, according to their father anyway, Robert's parachute had become entangled with that of a Corporal Sidhu shortly after exiting the aircraft earlier that afternoon, and the tangled mass of chutes, cords, and confused yet dutiful soldiers had culminated their thousand-meter freefall by slamming as one into the hard, sun-baked earth. This was perhaps appropriate, or so at least Jeremy decided at the time, as he had spoken to his brother that very morning, and had himself characteristically refused to fall into line. Robert had called, not surprisingly, to inform him that their father was in trouble again.

"What'd he do now?" Jeremy asked, heaving what he believed to be the appropriate sigh, the same sort of sigh he always heaved when it came time to contemplate either member of his immediate family. In answer, Robert held his breath momentarily, the same sort of breath he always held before releasing something that was not quite truth, yet not quite false enough to be tagged an outright lie.

"Beat the shit out of the pay-parking machines at the hospital."

"The pay-*parking* machines? What the hell for?"

4

CHRIS F NEEDHAM

"What do you mean what for? Listen, loser, you know god-damned well—"

"But I thought he wasn't, you know, drinking anymore."

Again Robert held his breath, thereby gaining the crucial advantage, at which point he very calmly informed Jeremy that their father was in fact totally and completely sober—as if there were any other kind. "And hey, he's been asking about you too," he went on.

"And?"

"And he wants to know when you're coming home."

"Oh fuck, Robby, I don't know. . . . I'm pretty settled in out here and—"

"He wants to see you though."

Wincing, Jeremy asked what for.

"Again with the what for. Well I don't know, Jer. Conceivably because you're his son though."

"Well can't I just talk to him on the phone?"

"Sure you can, if you want to be an absolute prick about it. Thing is, he wants to *see* you though."

"What's he doing, dying? Christ, he is dying isn't he. Oh that's perfect. Just fucking perfect."

"Easy, buddy. He just misses you, that's all."

"Avoiding him are you, Robby?"

"No, *you're* avoiding him, Jeremy. *I* see him all the time."

This was true, Jeremy knew, but he was not about to let the subsequent guilt get the best of him, or worse, back to Robert, the reigning paragon of Jacks family protocol.

"So what's the problem then," Jeremy said. "I mean, besides the obvious."

"Well I haven't been getting over much lately. . . . Linda, hey, she took off for a while."

"She *left* you? *Why?*" For a moment Jeremy thought he would be unable to bear it should Robert, because he was Robert, tell him he had cheated on his wife again, an admission that would require Jeremy, because he was Jeremy, go out and get a belly full of booze for breakfast.

"No big deal, believe me. A little breather, that's all. So anyway, with work and all—"

"Oh what the fuck ever," said Jeremy. "School's out for summer break."

"You're missing the point here, pal."

"Yeah, well, tell him I'm busy. Tell him things are going pretty well out here in old Tor—"

"For crying out loud, Jer, your father's in jail."

Jeremy laughed. Such maudlin appeals always brought an abrupt chuckle, for their father had been incarcerated how many times before. "And hey, if you're so all of a sudden concerned, why don't you get him out?"

"Because, asshole, I'm in Alberta with the army right now. Remember Bob File though? Constable Bob? Yeah, well, Bob said he won't release Dad until you come get him. You explicitly, he said."

"I'm touched. Really."

"Don't be. Bob says one more stunt like this and Dad'll have to do time. Contempt of court or something like that and—"

"He actually said that? *Time*? Christ Almighty, the old man's nearly seventy god-damned years old."

"Hey that's what I said, but Bob said the judge is pissed. Told me to tell you that."

"Yeah, well, I'm pissed too, Robby—tell him that."

And that was how the conversation ended for Jeremy, placing familial thoughts and misgivings more or less out of mind until his father himself called with the unfortunate news of his brother's incredibly unfortunate demise. Jeremy booked the first flight available out of Toronto, arriving in Vancouver just after two A.M. local time. It did not even occur to Jeremy to ask his father how he had gotten himself out of jail until he saw him standing there in the reception area, alone behind a barrier of awkward formality, a prisoner serving time. He looked tired, the deep vertical seams bisecting his cheeks threatening to draw deeper all the time. Hardly out of line for a seventy year-old standing alone in the middle of an airport in the middle of the night, mind you, but still Jeremy could not get over it: Jon Jacks had become an old man.

Shaking Jon's large, scar-crossed hand, Jeremy immediately asked about the funeral arrangements, military or otherwise, as it was such an important part of the truncated family dynamic that neither father nor son display any symptoms of genuine affection much of the time.

Looking eligible to have taken the fall himself, Jon rubbed his weary red eyes and shook his tousled-haired head. He then started into a long tremulous sigh no doubt meant to offer some semblance of sad stability to the moment, but which caught up in his throat instead; therein it formed another grade of wretchedness, a cough this time, disturbing and painful, and he managed to say at length, "They're flying him home in a week's time."

"Why so long? An investigation or something?"

"No, no investigation. He won't be fit to fly till then."

"Jesus," said Jeremy, imagining, despite himself, the sorry state of his brother's corpse. Ever since he had first heard about the accident, he had been going over their final conversation, dissecting it, correcting it, continuing it, saying goodbye over and over again.

"Jesus," he repeated, breathing hard through his nostrils.

His father nodded grimly, no doubt compiling a laundry list of grievances against that particular deity. "Doctor so-and-so in Edmonton says slight compression of the spine. Estimates a four-to-six week recovery time."

"I—I don't understand."

"What's not to understand?" said his father, the whites of his eyes clouded to the waterline. "He'll be up and jumping again in no time."

Jeremy took one unsteady step back. "He's *alive*?"

"Well of course he's alive. Why wouldn't he be alive? That poor son of a bitch East Indian corporal broke his fall."

"You're joking."

"No I'm not joking. Why would I be joking? Of course the East Indian corporal didn't make it out so well."

Friday, June 30, 1972

Dear Mom & Dad:

Today has been somewhat stimulating, I guess, buzzing around buying long underwear, etc, trying to get organized and ready to sail into jail by 3 PM. Two unexpected bonuses: 1) The sky *isn't* falling, though your last phone call seemed to suggest as much; and 2) Gold's Luggage called on behalf of Air Canada (I filed a damage suit after my flight back from Vancouver; they didn't really do it much harm, but your old suitcase had just about bit the biscuit by that time), and I explained to the old codger that both shells had been crushed, and that the skin was ripped in countless places, so without further ado he invited me down to the Queen Street store to pick out a brand new bag—the fool. Despite his grumbling protestations, I decided to move up the line ever so slightly, to a soft-side jetliner in avocado green with black trim. It's a $55 bag (he reluctantly allowed $45 on the old one) so I paid the $10 + tax difference and now have a beautiful new bag that holds *tons*. I won't have to worry about the sides crushing now either. I bought two pair men's socks (warm ones, as the hospital air conditioning is supposed to be quite chilly), one bra, four panties and the aforementioned long underwear—I'll worry about looking sexy and feminine again when I'm finally paroled in October.

Checked in at 3:30 PM (taxi was late picking me up, but we really had until 5 anyway) and met the nine other girls on our ward. Lorna, unfortunately, has been placed in the other group. Kind of strange, you know? I guess we just sort of assumed we'd be embarking on this adventure together, but that's okay. This girl from Spain, Maria, is in my group, as well as Anne, an old friend of Mike & Lorna's from Saskatoon. Actually they're all quite nice, and I'm looking forward to making some female friends, as all of mine, with the exception of Tracey, Ruth and Lorna, seem to be men. Should be interesting.

It has been gradually settling in that we are indeed in a hospital, in a ward, in, what, something of a fishbowl of sorts. We have our own little dining area from which the food trolley arrives and departs, our own lounge w/TV and hi-fi, our own washer & dryer and iron & board in a large laundry room, and we buy our snacks and treats from the nursing station down the hall. We choose our day's menu the day before, just like you would in a hospital. It looks like there won't be much variety though: similar to the Y in taste and tedium—you know, bland, allegedly nourishing institutional food—but that's okay; I didn't come here looking for a gourmet chef anyway. Food will cost about $2 per day, which is fair enough when you think about it, otherwise you'd have all sorts of folks just looking for a place to hit welfare for three months, and that is definitely *not* the idea here. For the first few days we'll be subsidized by the Foundation, until we've learned how to weave correctly. We use plastic coinage, just like money (all ten of us have been assigned different coloured chips, so Birdie Cormack's can be spent by Birdie Cormack only) and they advanced me $5 today, plus supper free at 5 o'clock. Urine sample bottles were passed out for first thing in the morning—no liquids after 12 at night—a practice to be endured twice per week, as well as blood samples. The experiment will develop over a period of time, with new surprises to be introduced along the way. There are literally millions of tiny adjustments to make—have you any idea?

July 1, 1972

Happy Canada Day. God bless the Dominion. Awoke early this morning with throat, eyes and nose as dry as the Prairie Dustbowl. Actually, they call this a dust-free purity controlled air system—our clothes won't get dirty, and neither will our hair and hides, except from actual body perspiration, and the temperature remains constant(ly freezing) at all times. On the bright side, the air seems relatively dry, and therefore a nice change from all that rain out in Vancouver. But alas, where are you my sweet Toronto pollution?

Started to learn how to thread a loom today—très compliqué—but not really: you can't ride a bicycle the first time either. There apparently comes a time when you can do it quite naturally. I shall be weaving in my sleep by the end of the week, I'm sure.

The staff here (too many good looking guys!) are very quiet, pleasant and helpful, but *silent*. They all but blend into the woodwork. I'm not kidding; you hardly even notice them there. Every half-hour, around the clock, they patrol the ward, scribbling down little notes as to where you are, what you're doing, etc—doesn't bother me a bit—if you're in the can they just call your name and you answer, and that's it.

The girls are great fun—we'll all get along fine—and at least one aspect of our respective situations is identical: none of us will ever again be living in precisely the same set of circumstances as we are right now. Quite interesting, really. I can see how we're going to become quite the tight family unit in here.

I shall be having an EKG and EEG at some point in the next few days. In one of the tests (which one I'm not exactly sure) they'll stick twenty little pins into my head, all of which are hooked up to an enormous graph machine, and attempt to translate from the resulting scrawl how (if) in fact my head actually works. Don't you wish you could read EEG charts, Mom?

Had a lovely sauna tonight at 7 PM—it will be quite nice to have that to change the atmosphere now and again—and we also got out to the courtyard from 3:30–4:30 this afternoon. The whole idea of specific, regulated times is that we don't have any contact with people from the outside world. This is a hundred-bed hospital, and fairly large in staff and outpatient numbers, so these seemingly innocuous little escapades require quite the detailed arrangement, let me tell you.

July 2/1972

I'm finding that the famous five-hour sleeper is going to be sleeping a heck of a lot more in here. I guess the cool air does it, or something. It's so peaceful in here, and quiet, except when the hi-fi is going, which is most of the day in the big lounge—what a racket.

Dr. Miles (head of the study and a psychiatrist/scientist) and Dr. Congreves (same qualifications but Miles' assistant, collaborator and slave, or so it seems) met with us last night to answer any questions we might have concerning the experiment. A strange pair, these two. Classic Crusoe-Friday dynamic, as it were. In another life I see them squatting on their haunches in the dark, there on the beach between them the scattered remains of a neglected and slowly dying fire, each man dressed in soiled loincloth, long stringy beard and thick cloak of distraction, one berating the other over a slight miscalculation concerning the influence of the winter solstice on the rapidly approaching tidal wave. Of course they would not and will not tell us anything that might precondition us, i.e. *when* and *if* anything green will be introduced into our barren little lives. Their main point was that the "evening walk" will not be permitted till early in the morning (5–7 AM), ostensibly because we're girls, and because of the area of the city we're in. I suppose that's valid though. And anyway, it's the nicest time of the morning, so I really don't mind at all. We're to be "escorted" of course, so no worries of our being in danger of any sort.

Would you please keep my letters intact and in order? I want to be able to read them again when I emerge again in October. Probably twice a week you can count on receiving daily notations and thoughts and the like, so don't be surprised if they wander off the mark a little bit. Who knows, maybe someday someone else will want to read what I have wrought. Speaking of which, I didn't call Winifred, so you can show them to her, but no one else.

All my love, Birdie

JULY, 2002

Robert returned home a few days later—walking with the aid of a cane, yes, but walking nonetheless—and indeed, contrary to initial reports, he was not at all dead. And although Jon of course had nothing to do with the accident, Jeremy would never put it past his father to at least contemplate such a scheme. He really was a wily old man, and as Constable Bob File had informed Jeremy by way of his brother, getting himself in too much trouble again. If nothing else, at least Bob had seen fit to have Jon released upon hearing of Robert's near fatal accident. And so, for the time being anyway, Jeremy decided to stay and see what could be done for them, expecting really nothing in return, salvage paid being of course proportional to the helplessness of the vessels being saved.

Together Jeremy and his father tried to get limping Robert into his now vacant, incessantly leaky condo—as mentioned, Robert's wife had taken a recent leave of absence from their relationship, taking with her their three year-old daughter—but with his various minor injuries, together with everything else presently falling apart in his life, they thought better of it and decided to install him in his old room at his father's house, the very house Robert and Jeremy had grown up in. This way no one, especially the press, would be able to bother Robert until he had more or less convalesced and felt ready to face the world again. His accident had captured a normally fractured national attention. What with the existing War on Terrorism humming along under its own impetus, and the so-called friendly-fire incident in Afghanistan of late, in which four Canadian soldiers had been thoroughly obliterated by the five-hundred pound bomb dropped from one of their American ally's planes, Canadian military stories were eagerly sought after by Canadian news agencies these days—especially those stories featuring tragic accidents—and if there had to be a happy ending to the story, so be it, we would all just have to grin and bear it anyway. This way, though, no one could get to Robert. Not with father Jon dutifully entrenched at the front gate.

The Jacks house, an unremarkable split-level affair common to these and most other North American middleclass parts, stood halfway down a steeply sloping street ending in a brief cul-de-sac, the street itself situated near the bottom of a neighbourhood known vaguely, to some of us anyway, as Royal Heights. Royal Heights is part of the municipality of Delta, North Delta to be precise, which, as the name implies, stands atop the flood plain of the powerful Fraser River where it crashes headlong into the Pacific Ocean, bringing with it the broken mountain remains of the interior of the province and the attic of time. And while 'South' Delta lays claim to the nutrient-rich farmland of the lower elevations, the foundation of its population still white milk-fed farmers and their whiter soymilk-fed families, with a few tribes of steadfast Native Indians and the stubborn and retired wealthy clinging to the waterfront fringes, 'North' Delta holds mostly to the higher elevations of ancient glacial moraine, a hodgepodge of aging, oddly homogeneous homes connected one to the others via the elevated arteries of power lines and the underground gossip and general malaise of their inhabitants. Dogs bark in faraway lots. Sirens scream nearby. A feeling of dread hangs suspended in the air; a seething desperation; a silent scream of cast-aside dreams and endless days of drudgery. As a measure of patriotism, people hang Canadian flags from their assorted roofs and garages. As a measure of economy, they shop at the not too distant Wal-Mart and, occasionally at least, at Zellers, the recently arrived Punjabi population devoting themselves largely to the latter along with their own assorted mysterious shops. In general, North Delta attracts the imminent mediocrity of the middleclass and any recently arrived Indo-Canadian immigrants. Actually, like much of the West Coast, North Delta is a relatively newly settled region, and the recent wave of immigration makes it that much newer all the time. Of course anxiety, as a rule, accompanies the risk of any rising tide, and the grumpy incumbents, those few white folks whose great-grandfathers colonized the area themselves all of a century before, decry these plagues of unwashed and their seeming unwillingness to better integrate themselves, while at the same time wanting for all the world to keep them as far away as possible, preferably back where they came from—on the other side of the world, if feasible. Every time a new family of Punjabis arrive, a vast nasal whine goes up from the steadily dwindling ratio of remaining Caucasians, a muttering of angry regret and hopeless despair. "Oh no, not again," they say, recalling realities that never were. North Delta is rife with racial tension. People literally hate each other there.

And yet I suppose it was nice enough. Three blocks and two streets up the hill from the Jacks residence stood the Royal Heights United Church, and four blocks beyond that, though no one liked to talk about it, the rapidly deteriorating Royal Heights

Shopping Centre. It was here that, after enduring several long difficult years of unemployment after inexplicably aborting a longer albeit far more difficult career as a salmon boat captain, Jon had poured his meagre lifesavings, any and all profits still lingering from the sale of his boat, and a sizeable loan into a largely unsuccessful stint as a video store owner-operator. Still, he managed to scratch almost six years out of that venture, and that mall, before the Punjabis moved in and took over it all, obliterating his already minimal income stream and sending him reeling back to the workforce once more, where he would settle in temporarily and irritably until at last forced into mandatory retirement from his part-time parking attendant post at Surrey Memorial Hospital. Truth be told, though, Royal Heights was not all that much of a mall. Not anymore. Since the Punjabi population had moved in to capture, over the previous decade or so, increasingly impressive stretches of the adjacent commercial and residential landscape, the mall, and its various tenants, had suffered immensely to be sure. Not that this suffering could be blamed solely on the Punjabis, as they had done, and continued to do, their very best to integrate themselves to the North American brand of capitalism via their own variety of local stores and restaurants, but simply that the Royal Heights Shopping Centre resided on Scott Road, that perpetually shifting mix of strip-mall monotony and miserable race relations, not to mention consensus dividing line between the arguably tolerable municipality of North Delta and the sinking city of Surrey. "The line between consent and rape" was a slur Scott Road was more often than not subjected to. Now I do not want to go into too much detail here, but suffice to say that Surrey, at least North Surrey, anywhere within a drive-by shooting of Scott Road, was not the place one wanted to raise one's children, not if one had any choice in the matter at all. Of course it was not the same back when the Jacks brothers were children, but then what suburban neighbourhoods were? And their father's house, despite the fact it stood rather effectively removed from this wholly inhospitable environment, nevertheless lay less than seven blocks away as the bullet flies, leaving their father with an

incessant soundtrack of wailing sirens and squealing tires to keep
him awake and increasingly embittered throughout the night.
And Robert's ill-fated condo, due exclusively to Robert's ill-fated
foresight, stood smack on the corner of Scott Road and whatever, not three blocks from that tragic husk of failed entrepreneuri-
alism and a father's sovereign dreams, that sad and shattered strip
mall still known to some of us as Royal Heights.
POSTED BY LUCY @ 1:46:13 P.M. 4/2/2007   0 COMMENTS

                                                        July 3, 1972
Dear Mom & Dad:
All sorts of excitement around here today. Had my first belt
accepted, and as they have us weaving on the most primitive of
handlooms to such an extremely strict set of standards, that's quite
the accomplishment, believe me. The loom requires a great deal
of concentration and agility to handle at first, and your belt must
meet their criteria exactly in order to be passed, no exceptions.
Depending on how tight your tension is on the strings (the loom
is restrung for each belt) you must over-weave by a certain
amount to allow for shrinkage when you finally cut the belt off.
It's all terribly complicated, but I won't bore you with the details
just yet. One of the nurses just laughed and said we'd be whip-
ping them off like nobody's business by next week. Yeah, right.
   On a more, what, electrifying note, I was hooked up to the
EKG today—nothing to it—but the EEG was something else
entirely. First they measure your whole head off into twenty little sections marked with black wax pencil (Phrenology maybe?
Or something like it anyway.) then stick electrodes into your
head and ears, and turn the machine on and bingo! all sorts of
waves come pouring out on the tickertape. I felt just like the
stock exchange. They can apparently tell by the readings if you
have any sort of brain damage or impending tumours or other
such pleasantries, i.e. if you happened to fall out of a certain
homemade highchair when you were a kid. Brain-eye responses
are measured with the aid of a strobe light, as well as respiration

and deep breathing responses, bringing the total test time to approximately thirty minutes—a lovely little half-hour pit stop to be repeated six more times over the course of the experiment. All these little experiences I hope to be able to put into a book one day. (As I write this, it strikes me suddenly, if abstractly, that for writers and weavers vaguely similar rules apply. But then I'm not a writer, at least not yet, so you'll have to endure these yarns of wool for now.)

July 4, 1972

Slept in this morning till noon for no particular reason, except that we watched TV till about two last night. Still, I managed to weave five belts this afternoon, all of which passed, praise Allah, so I made a whopping $12.⁵⁰. Had a shower and washed my hair— we'll all have slight dandruff from the dry air, but it'll disappear as soon as we're out again in October. What else . . . Oh yes, urine and blood samples were taken again this morning—minor sacrifices to the great god of bodily fluids lingering somewhere beyond these sterile, whitewashed walls. Have I mentioned that everyone here has aching muscles? Even mine are sore, a symptom that will disappear soon enough, we're told. Still, I've been conducting yoga exercises in the corridor, with special emphasis on sore back and arms. And thank the Lord my fingers are so strong from piano and guitar. I'm not suffering too much, but believe me, some of the girls sure are.

Can you imagine ten women locked up together on a Friday night in the middle of downtown Toronto? What a riot. I've never laughed so hard in my life. The girls are great fun, and of course we get very giddy at times. Watched a decent movie on TV tonight—"The Glass House" by Truman Capote, about a professor in prison. We could all relate already. Still I have to wonder how really close to the book they kept it, as it seemed a little overwrought in parts, but then maybe that's just Capote.

Thanking my lucky stars I'm not in Ottawa right now, what with that terrible thunderstorm and all. Lucky for us the weather really doesn't exist here in the fishbowl. Don't worry, we can partake of it all via the windows, but it really doesn't register because the climate is always the same here in the hospital. I haven't felt any desire to go out yet, and I'm not going to until I really feel the need, you know? It's a most interesting situation, really . . . I'm surprised how easily we've fallen into the routine, and gotten used to each other (terrible catchphrase that: "used" to each other) and the staff. I feel almost as if I've always lived here—I never felt that way at the Y—whether with the ladies or the actual building, though, I'm not entirely sure. I think the comforts make all the difference though. Little things like no dust bunnies in the corners, no concern about theft, and no overly chlorinated matron or Y-type personage relentlessly hovering about, ready to pounce at the first sign of perceived misbehaviour (the staff here don't seem to care one way or the other)—even the fact that it's a small number of us, all one family at the dinner table, is somehow very cozy, very warm—I miss that. Although I suppose that hardly characterizes the spirit which has recently taken possession of the Cormack family firm, now does it?

July 5, 1972

Up at 7:30 this morning for breakfast, then off to work—had three belts polished off by noon or thereabouts. My timing's down to about 80 minutes per belt now, and when we really get into gear after another week or so, I'll be able to weave one every 20–25 minutes. That's about the limit apparently, this according to the nurses anyway, but the first belt took me all day, so I'm definitely improving. Yesterday, at my request, the resident shopper, a funny little camel named Stan (comes equipped with his very own hump and everything) bought me a plastic laundry pail, which I'm going to keep filled with water and standing in my room, so that should help moisturize the air a little.

Listened to the "Goon Show" on FM radio today with Peter Sellers and co. Very British, very funny—it's a rerun from the 50s but really outrageous, and of course we'll laugh at anything in here. I think I now know why all my friends are male—chicks are crazy—fun though, and an education in itself, even if further evidence of the impending apocalypse perhaps already well underway.

Here we are, Thursday morning, up at 8 o'clock for a stretch, a yawn and, after pumping out the required blood and urine samples, a bowl of Red River cereal to start things off with a bang. Then it was off to the belt factory for the remainder of the day. How Dickensian my sorry existence has become, eh? My timing is now down to one belt per hour, including stringing, so I made an eye-popping $25 today. Felt very satisfying, though, I must say. And to make things easier to keep track of, rather than having thousands of plastic chips rattling around in your sock at the end of the experiment, they let you cash in every $50 worth to the nursing station, where they keep a little bank book. We've made great advances in our weaving ability since that first dreadful belt on Monday too. Needless to say, the time will now pass more swiftly, now that we can see a reasonable improvement in our earning power.

How to explain the experiment? Each day we learn a little bit more about what (and how) the medical staff is studying. Our group has seen nothing as yet, and truth be told we may not throughout the entire experiment. Perhaps we're the control group and Lorna's is the experimental—I really don't know. Anyway, they come around to monitor us every half-hour or so, but strangely enough it doesn't really bother me, perhaps because it's so impersonal, so objective—anything they observe is just that: an observation; a statistic; so much data to be collected. You see what I mean about the fishbowl though. It's like living behind a wall of glass with the entire world looking in on you, watching your particular reality unfold.

Good morning Mom & Dad—happy Friday. We've been here one whole week now. Got up at seven this morning, had a shower and washed my hair—felt great—then gobbled down some cream of wheat cereal and grapefruit juice to start the day. I then proceeded, with comparative ease, to polish off ten *perfect* belts. Far out, eh? Tomorrow I'm going to go for twelve, with any luck. I'm sure glad I'm not allergic to wool though. If I were, I'd be sunk.

A completely different set of staff came in with the 7:30 shift change this morning, and here in the fishbowl these new arrivals are very much strangers in our midst—a somewhat awkward phenomenon, like having surprise houseguests, or a large family of noisy immigrants moving in down the street (wink, wink). What will they be like? Can you trust them? Will they like you, and more importantly, your belts? Remembering a host of new names (in three shifts, that's twelve new nurses, orderlies, psychiatrists, psychologists or whatever) presents an enormous new challenge in itself.

I'm beginning to realize just how much I'm going to learn from this experiment, about human beings, about their relationships, and how I'll maybe be able to use it as fodder later on. All good writing comes through experience, they say. . . . It's like holding a tiny segment of life under your microscope, Dad, and seeing many things you couldn't under ordinary circumstances.

The ladies are outrageous—we laugh a lot, and are even quite silly at times, but underneath we're beginning to let down our hair and really get to know one another. We're a very diverse group of course, with plenty in common, but with most interesting personal circumstances. I shall speak of them all from time to time, but I'll start with the one girl who has impressed me the most, Maria from Spain. Tall, slim, blond, about 21—looks like Ingrid Bergman in a way, less the willingness to weep all the time in order to get her way. I really like her. Last September she left for Europe, where she met an English friend in Greece, and together they travelled all throughout the Mediterranean, living in a kibbutz (state commune) in Israel for the better part of three months, and the rest of the time touring through various parts of Africa and the Middle East. Her friend has since returned to England, and will be coming over here in October; Maria having continued on to Canada (obviously) to enter into the experiment

with her friend Shirley—a cute wee girl very much like Aunt
Zelda in appearance, only this kid's an absolute riot, believe me.
She seems very quiet, and you barely know she's in the room—
that is, until she drops one of her little "gems" and the whole
group breaks up with gales of laughter. Maria and Shirley share
the first bedroom, opposite mine, and we get together and chat
from time to time.

Must get this off to the mailman.

Lots of love, Birdie

July, 2002

Putting off the effort of any sort of exercise, reclining in dull
observation instead in one of two identical green deckchairs
located at the far rear edge of his father's backyard, Jeremy gazed
out over the ravine at the narrow tract of almost too-blue sky
thereabouts. Being as it seemed an almost meteorological necessity that it rain profoundly each and every time he so much as
glanced in the direction of his running shoes, Jeremy took the sky
for what it was: a favourable omen of favourable conditions for
one to shake off any extraneous poundage acquired in recent
lethargic weeks and months. Not that his need for caloric restraint
was in any way one of vanity; it was, in truth, of the economic
variety. His financial situation being what it was in those days—
having hit a low point, where it now seemed determined to
remain—his various forms of credit all but depleted, he could
scarcely afford the calories the ever-increasing obligation of obe-
sity implied, let alone any new clothes to match an ever-
expanding waistline. Therefore he ran, or tried to run, every
second day, and in running kept the middling sins, those somehow fraternal twins, portliness and poverty at bay.

"Hey fag, how's the back?" he asked, following with interest his
brother's limping journey around the shallow end of the peanut-
shaped pool. Actually, a quick word on the pool seems only
appropriate here. Their father had had it installed some five years
before, some five years *after* both Robert and Jeremy had moved

out of the house seemingly for good. I suppose he thought a pool might entice his offspring to return, or in lieu of an out-and-out homecoming, at least give them reason to stop by here and there. As far I know, Jon himself never used the pool. He cleaned it, yes, and he maintained it, even upgrading it from time to time (for instance, installing an impressive and altogether expensive solar-panelled heating system on the roof of the house), but he never actually *swam* in it. No, it was more on an ornament of sorts. A totem. A peanut-shaped shrine to departed but not forgotten sons. Still, it was nice to look at. And it did offer their father something to work on in his spare time. That is, when not decking over what little yard remained green and wild to him here at the start of the new millennium. It was common knowledge amongst the Jacks boys that their father had no friends. Now in truth he had been, for most of his life, a friendly enough fellow— one might even say amiable—but then for years now he had not allowed this amiability to take root for anyone outside his immediate family. No, for strangers (and by broad definition that included both neighbours and relatives) he had managed to deck over the more agreeable aspects of his personality years ago, spending his many off-hours knee-deep in the ritual skimming of his pool, lost in abstractions of a semi-aquatic nature, hatching some new plot, Jeremy thought, against what would have to be considered human evolution in general.

Anyway, Jeremy was sitting in the backyard, putting off the effort of a run, calling his brother a fag and asking how his back was coming along.

"Sore, little brother, sore," said Robert, lowering himself gingerly into the shaded chair alongside Jeremy's out there in the sun. At twenty-nine, and approximately twenty minutes older than Jeremy, Robert was, less the accident, at the height of his formidable power. And as solid with muscle as he had become in recent years, especially through the chest, shoulders and arms, he was somehow resembling less and less his father, perhaps echoing some long lost relation on his mother's side. Robert and Jeremy never really knew their mother. Or rather, they knew her, but only in the way abandoned sons recognize a certain hoof print across the heart of an abandoned father. However, they certainly know *of* her, mostly by way of fragmentary eulogies delivered occasionally and reluctantly their way over the muted jingle of some annoying television commercial. Her name, they were told in just this way, was Virginia, and according to their father, she had died of complications stemming from a heart attack suffered exactly forty-six hours after wedding her second husband on a beach somewhere in the middle of the Mexican Riviera. The exact whereabouts of her grave, however, remained something of a mystery, as prior to Jon's aversion to television in general, and commercials in particular, they received no real information on her at all. Then, suddenly, in their teens, when their father opened his doomed video store and subsequently refused to watch so much as one more second of television, they stopped talking about her altogether. And so it comes as no surprise that the demise of these two phenomena, Virginia Jacks and television, specifically commercials on television, are tied closely together in their memories now, a point that, however fascinating, has little or nothing to do with our actual narrative unfortunately.

And anyway, Jeremy looked nothing like his mother. No, he resembled his father in almost every conceivable manner. Still, as brothers, he and Robert looked well enough alike, which was really no surprise considering the circumstances of their earthly arrivals. One noticed immediately how in fact their faces shared the exact same features, even if Jeremy's seemed to be arranged over a slightly larger playing field. And yet it was not as though his face were exceedingly lengthy. On the contrary, it was just that, in comparison, his brother's seemed slightly abridged, as though all the necessary players, however prepared, had apparently deemed it necessary to prolong the huddle indefinitely before dispersing to their respective positions on the field.

Robert retrieved a can of root beer from the pocket of his robe, popped it open, and offered his brother a drink. Jeremy accepted, tilted the can back, and handed it back finished by half, as requested. Falling further into the comforts of routine, Robert asked his brother how much he weighed—Jeremy told him, and returned the favour immediately. This was quite the right thing to do when sharing a root beer in your father's backyard, in my opinion.

"You know it's a miracle you're alive," Jeremy observed, bridging his hand across his brow to better shield his eyes from the sun. "Don't know if I've mentioned that."

"I know," Robert said. "And you have." He left it at that, and so Jeremy shifted his attention out over the ravine, following the erratic movements of squirrel tails and bird wings amid the short-cropped, chainsaw-topped trunks of the nearby cedar and spruce out towards the enormous leafy dome of the ancient maple tree beyond. Robert did not seem overly eager to discuss his accident, at least not yet, and as Jeremy did not want to push him on the subject—after all, a fellow soldier and friend had actually *died* breaking his fall—he changed the subject entirely, piloting the conversation in the direction of more hospitable waters, if recently estranged shores.

"Talked to Linda?"

"Just now actually," Robert said, aiming his root beer in the direction of the house and by extension, Jeremy supposed, the telephone thereabouts.

"So, what, she's given you some sort of open-ended sentence?"

"Seems so anyway."

"Strange . . ."

"What's *strange*," Robert said, in a complicated voice Jeremy did not recognize, at least not right away.

"Just that an accident of this magnitude, you'd think it would galvanize rather than destabilize, is all I'm saying."

"Yeah, well, you don't know what it was like before she left."

"That bad?"

"Pretty fucking bad," Robert said. "After Stephie was born, Linda and I . . . well we weren't intimate for a long time, hey."

In a book, Jeremy thought, I would offer some sort of condolences here. Some sort of look suggesting a brotherly understanding—an understanding by association, as it were. Yet he could not bring himself to do it. And so he avoided looking at his brother altogether, if for no other reason than Robert should feel he meant anything particular by the exposure.

"Where's she at?" he contrived to inquire of his hands instead.

"Ted and Lauren's."

"Ted and Lauren—Hansen?"

"They got an extra room," Robert explained, frowning down at his slippers. It was common knowledge, at least in this yard, that Robert's special slippers always made him feel less tired. But not today. And so he struggled to his feet to move awkwardly toward the railing of the deck overhanging the ravine. "Remember when we built this fucking thing?" he said, tapping the deck with his cane. "That was fun."

"Yeah it was," Jeremy agreed, standing up alongside so that they might lean out over the railing together. Some forty meters down the ravine's aggressively descending tree-studded slope, though hidden, ran the audibly attendant stream. "Listen, you can hear the river."

"Of course you can hear the river."

For some reason Robert and Jeremy had always referred to the stream as a river, perhaps because for them, in their childhood, large portions of which had been spent at play here in the ravine, a river it very much had been—relative to their size, I mean. Or perhaps because that was what they had always imagined it could be, given the appropriate opportunity. And anyway, all rivers start off as streams at some point, so in a way, I suppose, it was, if only partially and in theory.

"Look, you can still see our old fort down there. Or what's left of it anyway."

"You know, at one point I was going to build my daughter a fort," Robert observed after a short pause, holding his head at a strange angle. He moved it with difficulty, indicating that his back and neck were still causing him some measure of discomfort and pain. "Same place as ours was, hey, in the crook of the maple tree there."

"So why didn't you?"

"Don't know," he shrugged. "Maybe I will."

"Not for a while yet," Jeremy said, indicating the cane.

Robert frowned down at his cane, then at the treacherous plaid slippers loitering about alongside. "Not for a while, no."

Together they spat out over the railing, watching the two elasticizing globules plummet into the crowded green underbrush below.

"So how long?"

"Sorry?"

"How long you out for?" Robert wanted to know.

Jeremy shrugged. "No offence, but if I'd known the truth about what happened, I probably wouldn't have come out here at all."

"Writing?"

"Not right now, no." He paused. "Anyway, I'm thinking of staying the summer. Maybe longer, I don't know."

"That'd be all right. Try not being such a dick to Dad though, all right?"

"Yeah, well, we'll see how long each of us can stand the experiment. Check this out though." Together they watched their father, in an outfit perfectly suited to the task, a bright yellow T-shirt and a pair of transcendentally lime green Bermuda shorts to be exact, slowly engineer his descent of the sundeck stairs. Fortified by the proximity of his sons, and the conviction that he had raised two rather good ones, there had returned a relative spring to Jon's step in recent days, and he sailed along at a kind of dignified slant until finally reaching the bottom of the stairs, whereupon he suddenly and somewhat surprisingly revved up the engines and all but sprinted the final few steps to the pond and his collection of hungry, colourful, impatiently waiting Koi. Almost all of Jon's comings and goings of late, by movements as natural as the tides themselves—that is to say, grudging—took place in that space between the raised shore of sundeck door and the vast ocean of air extending out from the far rear edge of the artificially reclaimed backyard below. The effort by which these outings were undertaken, which may or may not be successful depending on the undertaker's state of mind at the time, where the vast majority of problems went unseen and unchecked well below the waterline, had eroded between Jon's eyebrows a deep and serious trench. And yet there was always something strangely fluid suggested by his actual stride, even aquatic, as though he were separated only by air and a few billion years of evolution from a would-be amphibian's primitive limbs and a splendid sea level view of some coveted beach environment. Still, most if not all of what this nautical manner of movement implied remained completely lost on his sons. This was due to the fact that, while they were at least tenuously aware their father had some sort of semi-dignified seafaring past, they tended to associate his character more with the periods that immediately followed—that is, those of a long shambling unemployment proceeding, by a series of unremarkable tacks, towards ill-fated video store ownership. Their collective attitude towards the truth had always been rather flexible, and therefore more like their father's than Jeremy cared to admit, and so it came as no surprise that he had long ago capped his father's dubious list of talents with the ability to do absolutely nothing for regular and extended periods of time.

And yet despite all this, and despite himself even, Jeremy smiled at his father, just managing to turn away in time before Jon could accuse one or more of his sons of making fun of him in some way, as he surely would and as they often did. And so he winced instead. At the thick foamy mattress of white bread his father was about to stuff into his mouth, and at the deep spread of margarine oozing out from between his freshly minted, preposterously white teeth. What inevitably followed was a horrific sneezing-coughing fit. Jon Jacks, it can with certainty be said, had become at some uncertain point entirely allergic to bread. And though it could be argued that real honest to goodness grain was nowhere to be found in that bleached slab's long list of ingredients, sneeze and cough he most definitely did. Taken suddenly with an odd gasping roar of sorts, commencing with a long cascade of moist flushing coughs, he progressed steadily through a trembling choking fit that ended inevitably with his hawking into a balled up wad of tissue an oyster of truly inordinate size. They had at first frightened and then amused his sons as youngsters, these seemingly random sneezing squalls, often announcing their wet and violent arrival before Jon could make the necessary, however inadequate, leap to the nearest Kleenex box.

"You think he's all right?" Jeremy asked, recently returned from his tour of his father's not-so-personal habits.

"He's fine. You're fine, aren't you, Dad."

"What's that?" their father somewhat absently asked, despite the fact that, unbeknownst to all, even himself perhaps, he had for some reason been following the conversation with excruciating interest. Presumably he said these things automatically, as notwithstanding a still strong instinct for self-preservation, Jon Jacks felt he no longer understood, nor did he ever again expect to understand, exactly what was going on in any particular situation he happened to find himself in. Back in his younger, more energetic days, for purposes of pleasure there had been no substitute for heated debate, but now, nearing seventy years of age, Jon felt it was all he could do simply to keep pace with what was being said around, or in this case, about him. And yet the kinds of things he assumed he was hearing now, albeit in snatches only, were exactly the sort of persecution he expected and secretly hoped for from his sons. He smiled at them both, wagged an accusing finger intended to mean absolutely nothing and, having raised inactivity to something of a virtue, returned to postponing whatever it was he thought he had not been doing before this latest tidal wave of mucus had arisen from his lungs.

"Oh yeah," Jeremy said at length, "just so you know, I'm having lunch with Bob File tomorrow."

Robert surveyed his brother suspiciously. "What for? Dad?"

Jeremy nodded while watching their father putter about the pond. "Wants to have a little chat, I guess."

"Bob fucking File," Robert mused. "He and Jody, they're married now, huh."

"Well then it's a good thing you got to her when you did," Jeremy replied with a laugh.

Robert's crowded features consolidated further, then corrected themselves to the expression of one who is, after all, in the right.

"What do you know about it?" he demanded.

Jeremy shrugged. "Just the really disappointing stuff."

"So who else knows?"

"Who else knows what?" Jon asked, pivoting about in his curious and deliberate way. Neither of his sons answered, and so he stared at them, paused, even shook his head a little, but in the end did nothing, as though any display of actual interest here would be surplus to the question's true nature.

POSTED BY LUCY @ 7:28:03 A.M. 4/3/2007   0 COMMENTS

Saturday, July 8, 1972

Dear Mom & Dad:

Got your wee note yesterday—sounds like that storm wave really hit your area too. There was a fair amount of rain down here, enough that the cars were spinning up and down Spadina Crescent on their summer tires. The address you used is just fine—

> Birdie Cormack
> West 4073, 33 Russell Street, Toronto

—so your letters will reach me directly, without exciting Lloyd Beatty et al of the Bobcaygeon Post Office, so keep them coming if you don't mind.

A few aches and pains still cropping up from the weaving, especially around the nape of the neck and between the shoulder blades. You know how you feel after you climb the radio tower, Dad. Well try doing that every day—you'd be sore for the first while too, until the necessary muscles developed in time. Goal today is twelve belts—hope I get them done. This evening we'll be writing psychological tests for a couple of hours at $5 per test. . . . Makes for a nice break in the evening anyhow.

Love, Birdie

P.S. No, I haven't heard anything yet from G. Not that I'm worried though; they're busier than ever out there with D.M.A.W. and besides, she's never been all that proficient at the art of correspondence anyway. Just so you know, though, I started a letter to her this morning, which I hope to get into the mail in the next few days, so I should (hope to) hear back in a couple of weeks or so. In the meantime, please relax. If there's one thing we know about Ginny it's that your fretting about her won't do anyone any good.

JULY, 2002

Jeremy met Bob File for lunch at the Dairy Queen on Scott Road, opposite the Royal Heights Shopping Centre where, not three days before, an eighteen year-old named Sukhvinder Rai had mysteriously disappeared while purchasing a Peanut Buster Parfait. Having been positively identified entering the Dairy Queen, the account of her movements thereafter becomes largely that of hearsay, as Miss Rai and her boyfriend, a twenty-one year-old Indo-Canadian named Paul, had apparently just gotten into a fight, or rather, continued with one from earlier that day, at the conclusion or intermission of which she had promptly removed herself from Paul's friend's father's brand new Lexus and walked hastily and rather angrily away. And now, nearly seventy-two hours later, with her whereabouts still unknown, and the boyfriend, the very boyfriend for whom the parfait had evidently been intended, no longer considered a suspect but in some vague capacity actually aiding in the investigation, the police were hoping for the best but naturally anticipating the worst, especially in light of the veritable rash of racially motivated acts of violence that had come to pass in and around Royal Heights in recent years, months, and even days.

Unaware of any of this, as he was unaware of the vast majority of significant current events, Jeremy gazed out the window of their booth and thought about other, more abstract things. The window afforded him a nearly perfect view of his father's failed video store, at present a fruit and vegetable stand, and the various empty windows of the various other empty enterprises, some waiting to be reborn under Punjabi rule, and others enduring a seemingly indefinite exile—echoes of a chronically marginal economy no longer viable somehow. Even 7–Eleven and the twin kitty-corner Esso stations had long since pulled stakes and moved on, their absence measured in magnitude of graffiti and length of wild grass having long since infiltrated their mutually sad and sagging lots. A felt reproof to such quitters, the little Silver Moon convenience store was still making a go of it though—that is, if having to resort to a barricade of metal bars for your windows and padlocks for your bicycle stands was still considered making a go of it—but alas, the Burger King was no more. How, or more importantly, *why* the Dairy Queen had not followed, or at the very least been fallowed, for no less than the foreseeable future, was certainly a point worthy of discussion, and that was exactly what Bob and Jeremy opted for as soon as they sat down that day.

"How's work?" Jeremy asked once that subject had quickly and thoroughly exhausted itself. The figure limping out of the distant pub could not under any circumstances have been his father, but at least it relieved him of the somewhat painful notion that the mall was entirely uninhabited now.

"Not bad," said Bob, forced to herd his words around a considerable mass of Brazier burger. "Only back for the summer though," he added after an enormous swallow. "Not sure if you knew, but I just completed my first year of law school."

"Good for you. How was it?"

"Wonderful, Jeremy. Law school was wonderful."

"I meant how were your grades, asshole."

"Oh, right. Seventh, I think."

"Seventh? Really? Out of how many?"

"Two-twenty," Bob answered matter-of-factly, frowning down at the sorry state of his food. "Fuck. Too much mayo. Explicitly asked for no mayo. Did you not hear me ask explicitly for no mayo?" He shot the clerk an angry look, but to no avail. "Anyway," he resumed, "now that I'm back at work, come out for a ride-along sometime. Seriously though. Show you Slurrey and North Delhi here like you've never seen 'em before. Show you some dead guys too. Y'ever seen a dead guy? Well you should. Good for your writing. Good grist for the mill. Should've seen this ol' gal we found last week," he said with a chuckle. "Ancient. Scabs all over. Picked at her scabs too, see, so you can imagine just how really bad they were."

Jeremy winced and said that, severely scabbed-over or not, he had no desire to see a dead person up close. In that capacity at least his imagination was more than ample enough.

"Fair enough, but you're missing the point. Neighbours in the suite below, see, they notice this peculiar stain coming through the ceiling. Sort of this pink, plasma-like tinge. Enter the landlord, and in turn, Delta's finest. Enter me. Well, turns out our bird upstairs has been dead for like a week. Lying there in her ratty old shit-filled underwear, catheter dangling out her cunt, three fingers deep if you know what I mean."

Wincing again, Jeremy asked Bob to stop.

"Wait, gets worse. Guts have all liquefied, see—now she's literally bloated with the junk—and it's poured out her rectum, soaked through the mattress, and started working its way down through the ceiling. That's how come the neighbours. That's how come me. Anyway, we go to move her, and the poor thing bursts open like a piñata. Liquefied guts everywhere. Can't imagine the stench. Nothing compared to death from head trauma though," Bob reflected, shaking his head. "Tell you what, there ain't nothin' in this world like the smell of brains."

"I'll have to take your word for it," Jeremy said.

"For instance, take the other day," Bob continued. "Pickup T-bones the trailer of this left-turning semi. And okay, fine, I find the driver's head back there in the bed of the pickup, in all probability right where it ought to be. Thing is, it's empty. No brain, see. Can't find the fucking brain anywhere. So I look inside the cab of the truck and there's his spinal column, intact, sticking up out of his neck like a Pez dispenser, but still no sign of brain anywhere. So I follow the smell," he said. "Believe me, nothing like it anywhere. Awful. Just awful. And I'm smelling it, and smelling it, and what do I find out there a good ten yards in *front* of the truck? The brain. Full and intact. Lying there on the pavement just like that. See," he said, "way I figure it, force of the impact must've ripped off his skull like a mask"—here Bob leaned forward to thoroughly diagram his theory with his hands—"and deposited it there in the back, then shot the brain forward, employing the spinal column as some sort of, what, catapult-like device."

Bob nodded with satisfaction at the image, with its various working parts, now floating disembodied between them. It is, admittedly, quite a sight, Jeremy thought.

"Best part, though, was the sign on the side of the semi trailer. 'West Coast Movers: *We take a load off your mind.*'" Bob chuckled wickedly to himself. "Anyway, that's how come I have to get out, see. I'm sick of it. Sick of the *smell*. That and getting the finger from East Indians every day as well." He paused, seemingly reading something into the alphabet of French fries before him. "How's your brother?" he asked after a time.

"He's, uh, all right," Jeremy rallied, trying desperately, if unsuccessfully, to shake the idea—and this idea of a *smell*—of a disembodied brain. "Improving anyway."

"Miracle that boy's alive, taking a fall like that."

"Yeah, that's what I keep telling him."

Bob laughed at something, consumed a single fry, then dragged a short-fingered hand through his hair a couple of times. He had bleached his hair a poor sort of copper on top, no doubt trying for blonde, Jeremy thought, in an ineffective and somewhat misguided attempt to camouflage the fact that he was slowly and irrevocably going bald.

"Speaking of which, you know he got suspended from school."

"No, I didn't," Jeremy leaned in.

"Yeah, on account he got in a bit of a tussle with the vice-principal."

"He didn't. Tell me he didn't. Fuck me." Jeremy leaned back again.

"Yeah, came back from stress leave and—"

"Stress leave? I didn't know he was on *stress* leave."

"Well he was—is. Anyway," Bob said, "he went in for a visit one day and all his fish had died. Yeah," he added, "they didn't take care of his fish while he was away apparently, so I guess they all died."

"My father gave him those fish," Jeremy reflected. "From his pond."

"Yeah, well, what kind of fisherman keeps fish as pets anyway."

Jeremy had never really thought about it that way, and aiming a bland smile at the large vacant parking lot across the street, reluctantly admitted as much. "Atonement perhaps," he suggested with a shrug.

Bob shrugged too, though not as much. "Seems sort of odd, you ask me. Course your dad's an odd old man."

"He is that," Jeremy agreed.

Bob looked at him, resolved something in his mind, then continued on energetically: "Anyway, your brother, he starts freaking out in front of the class, ranting and raving and all that, swearing and carrying on about these blessed goldfish of his—"

"Koi."

"—these blessed Koi of his, when the vice-principal happens to come along and catch the tail end of this diatribe, and tries to get him to relax. Well Robby, he just pops him one. No warning, nothing. Just turns around and pops him one. And of course he doesn't stop there. No, he starts beating the vice's head against the classroom floor—like this—and all of a sudden, wouldn't you know it, the kids start cheering him on."

"Jesus."

"You're telling me—but wait, there's more. Officer on duty at the school, see, he hears the ruckus and comes wading into the fray, and your brother, well he goes off on that poor bastard too. And now Robby's getting the better of him, the both of them, until the principal himself comes rolling along and all three manage to wrestle him down and more or less subdue him with the taser gun."

"Jesus," Jeremy said again, as he began to entertain the unpleasant notion that yet another member of his family was beginning to lose his grip on reality. His complicated expression bore witness to this, and he sighed tremendously as Bob said—something. The comment was lost, drowned in a mind at high tide.

"Like father like son, I guess," sighed Jeremy at length, pressing hard on his eyeballs so that sparks appeared. "Still, you'd think he would've grown out of getting suspended from school by now," he said to the swirling phosphorescence in his head.

"Exactly," Bob said, his fingers testing absentmindedly the superior bulk and line of his bicep, a habit formed, Jeremy recalled, at some point in his early teens, back when Bob had first become fanatical in the escalating maintenance of his craft. Considered by those who knew him to have been spared the inconvenience of conscience, Bob had, for the longest time, taken extremely seriously his role as bully, managing in the process to all but perfect the technique really, and Jeremy pictured his police work as a practical extension of what had always been an altogether natural inclination if rather disturbing modus operandi.

"Anyway, no one's pressing charges or anything, not now that this whole parachuting thing's come up. Not that I think he'd actually do it on purpose or anything, but . . . well, maybe. Who knows. That brother of yours is capable of anything." Bob paused. "But the kids, hey, they just love him. Can't get enough of him. Think he's the best thing to happen to academia since Marc Lepine, I'm told.

"But yeah," he concluded, "he's back on stress leave indefinitely, I think. Good timing it being summer break and all, but I don't think he's going to be working there again anytime soon. Least not when school cranks up in the fall."

"Christ what a fucked-up family," Jeremy said. He lowered his head into the palms of his hands and shook it steadily back and forth. Finally, with considerable effort, he raised it up again. "I had no idea. Here I thought I was going to be defending my *father* to you, and then you go and blindside me with Robby."

"Sorry," Bob shrugged, testing again, with that familiar series of strokes and pokes, as though searching for some new flaw in the arrangement, the assorted muscles of his chest, shoulder, and upper arm. Biologically speaking, Bob was not really designed to make friends, but then was not really designed to resent this, or anything else. Those who found themselves liking him had no real easy way of telling him, since he seemed to regard both friend and enemy alike.

Jeremy looked out the window, across the busy street to the idle mall and the feeble excuse for a fruit and vegetable stand alone there at the center of it all. "I wonder if he knows."

"Your father? Doubt it. I'd think he'd be pretty upset, right?"

Having digested all he could for the moment, though, Jeremy dodged that subject as best he could. "How's the wife?"

"Jody? She's all right. Wrestling with the big question in life."

"What's that, implants?"

"No, Jeremy," said Bob, "not implants."

"*Ah,*" Jeremy nodded. "Wants kids, huh."

"Well that's the thing—not really. No, she's just, what, struggling with her biology a little." The words sounded strange and more than a little forced in Bob's characteristically steady unassuming voice, which, however quiet, had always commanded the complete attention of whomever it was he was about to beat up. Recent undisclosed strains on his marriage had evidently relaxed Bob's habitual control, as it was not like a File to offer any sort of insight into his love life at all. More awkward still, he was now admitting to having recently started reading the self-published novel Jeremy had sent him some months before.

"Started kayaking too," he added quickly, as though to lessen the impact of what was, for both men, an altogether embarrassing admission. Actually, much the best way of tempering such an uncomfortable confession, when to continue on with it would prove an impossible strain on the friendship, is to bring to light one's recent outdoor exploits. The kayak of course being the natural device of choice to defuse any such difficult situation.

"And so what did you think?" Jeremy suddenly heard himself asking.

"And, well, I'm still working on it," Bob rather guiltily admitted.

"I see."

"No, I really am reading it—honest."

"I understand," Jeremy said, waving off any impending apology.

"No, it's just . . . I mean it's just that it's fairly long and—"

"A whole three hundred and sixty pages, yes."

"Are you sure? It felt like a little, you know, more." Bob sat quietly ruminating as a wave of impatience rolled up over Jeremy. He was trying not to feel rebuked by this. By any of this.

"No, believe me, it was three hundred and sixty pages exactly."

Bob nodded, compelled to agree, while Jeremy gazed in the direction of the massive, sadly moustached cashier currently leaning heavily on her elbows against the counter, scowling balefully at a booth of loud, giggly Indo-Canadian teens. Jeremy's attention unintentionally caught hers, and together they turned their mutual embarrassment to the nearby freezer and the collection of fossilized cakes and logs on seemingly permanent display behind its fogged-up, stand-up, childproof double-doors.

"Anyway, it reads pretty well," Bob remarked vaguely. "Even though, for me, it seems a little, what . . ."

"Lepinesque?"

"Sorry?"

"Misogynous? Hateful towards women?" continued Jeremy with relish. "Yup, alienated damn near eighty percent of potential Canadian publishers, she said."

"Who said."

Jeremy shrugged, "This catty old bitch of an agent I recently signed with. She who shall evidently decide my fate in all matters literary," he said. He was trying to be blasé and light about it, and in doing so managed to fail quite miserably.

"So, what, guys don't read?"

"Do you read, Bob?"

"Believe me, at school that's all I do," Bob said. "But books are just so . . . Anyway, working on anything else these days?" he asked, no doubt concerned he had not explored sufficiently Jeremy's floundering literary career to this point.

"Some short stories, yes."

"Now *I* could read a short story, hey. Something with not too many pages to it maybe—like a script. You know that Vin Diesel's getting like twenty million for his next movie? Imagine that. Twenty million. For one movie. And you know he wrote his first script too, hey. Sure he did. Wrote this script about being a bouncer or something, and now just look at him. Rich." Bob shook his head at the true marvel of Hollywood. "Well at least you don't have to do any real work."

This impression of the writer's life, let alone the self-published writer's life, was so amazingly wide of the mark that Jeremy found it easier to say nothing, simply making a gesture that suggested slight inaccuracy instead.

"So I'm trying to get some cash together for this tree fort I'm building," he said at length.

Bob blinked. "Tree fort, Jer? What are you, like *twelve?*"

"It's for my niece."

"Oh, right. What does your brother think of such faggotry?"

"Robby? Robby thinks it's great." This was something of a lie however. Between the two brothers there was no pretence, and if the thought of building a tree fort spoke specifically to Jeremy's reluctantly admitted deficiencies as an uncle, rather than to his excesses, they both supposed that he had no legitimate business attending to it.

"Why don't you go work with your brother then?" Bob suggested. "You know, just for the summer."

"Oh I don't know, Bob. Maybe because I'm hardly qualified. Generally they require members of the military have at least *some* semblance of formal training in this country."

"No, I meant at the mill."

"I don't understand."

"Your brother," Bob said. "He's on at the feed mill again. Least he was until he hopped out of that plane."

"Are you serious?"

"Far as I know anyway. Apparently—this according to my wife who must've been talking to his wife—he went back and applied when he went on stress leave from the school. Said he wanted the extra money to buy some . . . now what was it . . . oh yeah, to buy your dad some hearing aides."

"Hearing aides, huh. What the hell," Jeremy said.

Bob wiped his mouth, then shrugged, "In the meantime, come out for a ride-along sometime. Seriously, though, you should.

Show you the saddest bunch of hookers y'ever saw. And the saddest bunch of cops, too, I might add. I mean it. Incestuous pricks. And that's another reason why I've got to get out, see. I'm sick of the people I work with constantly trying to fornicate with one another each and every goddamned shift."

POSTED BY LUCY @ 11:30:56 P.M. 4/4/2007   2 COMMENTS

Sun. July 9, 1972

Dear Mom & Dad:

Unlike my digestive tract (more on that later) we keep fairly regular hours here—to bed usually by 11 or 12—but so far this one girl Rosemary and I are the only two getting up early for breakfast, mainly because we're the ones who like the hot cereals and such. I really enjoy the early morning though—the shift changes at 7 o'clock, but other than that things are absolutely still on the ward.

Wrote another psychology test today, which took two hours approximately, and made for a nice break in the afternoon. Also wove ten belts with great ease, so that made me feel good.

The ward has windows overlooking the tree-lined courtyard, and we can sometimes catch a glimpse of the other wards, especially, and most intriguingly, the fourth floor and Ward A. Although we have no verbal communication with the other group, apparently we just happened to catch each other in passing today, and through a primitive yet effective system of sign language managed to learn a little of what was happening over there. The report: having a ball; no grass as yet; top speed weaving, seven belts a day. Of course that makes us feel great, as we're doing much better over here. It all reminds me of a boarding school atmosphere, as if I were thirteen again, and what it might have been like had you allowed me to attend a private school somewhere.

Monday, July 10, 1972

Up early again this morning donating our samples to science—what a way to start the day. Now if only I could get the rest of my plumbing to behave half as nicely we'd really be on our way. Naturally, I've found myself a little bit backed up since my arrival here at the hospital. The usual scenario—don't know if it's the food or the new environment or what—but I'm sure the system will come around soon enough. And anyway, what would a letter from Birdie be without an update on her bowels, eh?

Regardless, feeling quite good—aches all gone now, except for the one that hits between my shoulder blades at around 11 at night after weaving all day. Twelve belts done with ease. Will try for fifteen tomorrow.

Wrote another little test today, this one on "mood." Our "mood" will be tested weekly, but I'm quite certain (unlike her BM's) Birdie's will remain somewhat consistent—confident, peaceful, rested, happy—she is her mother's daughter after all. It is in just this sort of situation that I'm going to find my real inner strength, I'd say. I don't feel cooped up quite like some of the girls do—a few are really beginning to get the blues—as that stems from characteristics within themselves that would flare up from time to time in the outside world too. In fact, our two most boisterous girls, Barbara and Evie, were the first ones to shed a real tear!

Barbara is twenty-three, quite big and floppy if you ask me, and she was, at first, the most vocal member of the group. Countless mentions of all the "hip" people she knows in the Village—you know, namedropping to the nth degree (a real biggie with the Rochdale circuit apparently: knows all the local rock groups "personally")—a champion of the environment and health foods, not to mention the chronic deployment of curse words, but always at the wrong time and at all the wrong things, and unfortunately a very uptight, very insecure person when you get right down to the nitty-gritty. Terribly pathetic way to live, in a fantasy world, spouting whatever half-baked philosophy happens to be popular, whatever happens to be "in." Barbara went to school in New York (the state, not the city) and claims to be in semi-regular contact with several key members of either the Weather Underground or the Velvet Underground (exactly which "Underground" it's somewhat difficult to say, as she grows increasingly vague and irritatingly suspicious whenever pressed on the matter, you see.) which might help explain why on Saturday, having removed herself to one of the little sitting rooms to weave, she threw a regular childlike tantrum when two of her belts were failed, and has been secluding herself generally ever since. Radical leftist revolutionaries and/or overrated rock bands aside, it has been my experience that your average American lacks significantly in the way of social graces. She needs *our* help—somehow the group has to knock that chip off her shoulder, and get her into a better state of mind. It's fall into line or fall, baby. At least that's what we keep telling the swine.

Her roommate Evie is both a joy and an annoyance at the same time. She's twenty-one, fair, and fairly outdoorsy—a true nature girl, she really feels homesick, and misses being outside very much not surprisingly. One of seven children, Evie hails from Peterborough, and she went to work for the Mississauga newspaper right out of high school before attending Columbia University for a year, at which point she decided to give panhandling on the streets of Vancouver a go, and when after six months that didn't "pan" out, hightailed it back to the newspaper in Mississauga, quite unable to figure out what she wanted to do with herself. Seems to be very close to her family—she loves them all "very, very much" and misses her boyfriend (he's in with the Weather/Velvet Underground too apparently)—but she's determined, apparently, to stick it out. Has her job at the paper when she gets out, but I really wonder whether she'll make it all the way through or not. Evie and Barb share the room next to Maria and Shirley, but the four of them don't get along all that well unfortunately.

P.S. Got a surprisingly upbeat letter from G today. I take it you forwarded her my address—thanks for that. No mention of any problems, so maybe you were just imagining something of the sort. Anyway, I believe a couple of quotations are in order:

1) "J Jr. still remembers you each night in his prayers. Over dinner one evening he started chanting 'God Bless the Bird' quite spontaneously . . ."

2) "It was the funniest thing after I was talking to you on Sunday night. I shed a few tears—homesick?—I don't know. Because of everything that's happened, and is happening, I feel a closer tie or bond between us than ever before. Anyway, I would have given anything just to give you a big hug on Sunday night. I'm thinking of you constantly. I'm really proud of you too . . ."

Then I shed a tear this morning because I think Ginny is right: we *are* closer now than we ever were before. I guess there was just too much of an age difference when I was, say, five and she was fifteen, to share more than just a closet.

Anyway, must get this off to the mailman.

Love, Birdie

JULY, 2002
Of his own accord, the taxi driver, a distant cousin on his mother's side of the still missing Sukhvinder Rai (she of the Peanut Buster Parfait), dropped the Jacks brothers off at the base of the wheelchair access ramp leading up to the front door of the bar. And just as Jeremy was about to explain that his brother was not in fact crippled but injured, the painful and rather unfortunate result of a celebrated military parachuting accident suffered while training to protect his, the driver's, ungrateful immigrant ass, Robert cut him off before he could properly formulate the words, paid the driver, tipped the driver, and pushed his brother out. Armed as he was with seemingly miraculous powers of recovery, Robert's physical health was improving dramatically, and now, mere days after leaping out of a perfectly good plane and falling into the dry hard earth, he was ready and eager to make the transition back to ordinary life again. And that meant returning to some of his more favourite haunts. For numerous reasons the Flying Beaver had long been considered one of these, not the least of which was its proximity to nothing—that is, nothing other than the small isolated southern terminal of the airport. Robert's favourite bars were always located in and around small isolated airports. The unique brand of energy he felt in these

places—of possibility; of improvement; of the possible improvement of people coming and going, quite literally carrying on with
their small and isolated lives—that is what attracted him, and not
the abundance of liquor, I would suggest. Robert Jacks did not
drink. Having grown up under the often absent, occasionally violent, always mystifying rule of a quasi-alcoholic father, he had
decided at an early age that he wanted nothing to do with the
stuff, and had held to that promise, more or less, all his life. And
yet, while Robert himself never saw a drink, he took enormous
pleasure in getting his brother blind drunk. Jeremy did not share
Robert's aversion to alcohol. In fact, he never had. And so, long
ago, in cahoots with one Bob File, he had decided to become
something of a drinker himself, if only to spite his dad. Not a
drunk, mind you, but a drinker, slow and steady and deliberate,
focused exclusively on the situation at hand. But regardless of
their particular views on alcohol, and airports, both brothers really did enjoy a good bar. And so it was a natural echo of this
enjoyment that brought them back to the Flying Beaver on this
occasion I relate to you now. That and the fact some teachers
Robert worked with had recently formed a band, and the band
happened to be playing the Beaver that night as well.

It was a Monday night, and though there were still a handful of
tables available, the brothers had always felt more comfortable sitting up at the bar, and thus took up their positions there and cast
about a while. Proximity to the source was crucial, they both
knew, as they had both worked behind a bar themselves, and
therefore knew firsthand the shortcuts taken by bartenders when
it was thought the customer was not around to observe. For himself Jeremy ordered a Crown and Coke, and for his brother an
iced tea, watching each drink's construction closely, knowing full
well the unsanitary conditions bar glassware was more often that
not subjected to. Then they turned around and watched the band.
As usual, especially when the performer displayed even the slightest suggestion of musical talent, Robert sat with his head bowed,
silently respectful, until long after the song had elapsed—typically the length of time it took Jeremy to finish his Crown and Coke

and quickly order another. The Kurt Cobain-aping guitarist proved impressive in his performance, and the keyboardist was no slouch himself, especially with the drummer noticeably absent— a last minute cancellation on the grounds that he did not feel quite capable enough.

"We should have brought Dad," said Robert at one point, resting heavily on his elbows against the bar, his forehead grazing his straw.

"Don't be absurd." In Jeremy's mind, the military life had long ago instilled in his brother a sense of decorum commensurate to his capacity for blunder, one that bled a fair extent into his civilian life unfortunately.

"What do you mean?"

"Yeah, that's good, Robby: bring an alcoholic to a bar. Fuck me," Jeremy mused idly.

"Dad's changed a lot. You don't know."

"Sure, he's even more of a superior prick now."

"No he has," Robert said. "He has changed. There's this sort of, what, method to the madness now."

"There's always been a method to the madness, Robby— perhaps you've heard of it—it's called the drunken rage and vandalism of private property. And the fact he's raised the bar by demolishing one or two pay-parking machines hardly meets the criteria of groundbreaking personal growth, I'd say. Christ Almighty, the man's a menace to society. To which his sole contribution has been a fucking *fish* pond by the way."

"No, I mean his motives are much more . . . considered, I guess would be the word. He's found a sort of higher calling now."

"Oh yeah?" Jeremy laughed. "What higher calling is that? Wild Turkey? Famous Grouse? Or has the old man finally abandoned all those dubious principles of his in order to bless with his presence this so-called 'family' of ours."

"Forget it," his brother waved him off. "Just forget it if you're going to be like that."

"No really, Robby, what brought this on? Yet another instalment in an ongoing series of mid-life crises? Or no. Wait. Our Captain

Ahab's simply out to snare the big white whale of the dreaded pay-parking *Establishment*."

Robert shook his head dismissively. "Like I said, you don't know."

"Yes, well, there's a lot I don't seem to know about this family right now."

"What's that supposed to mean?"

"Oh I don't know. Maybe just the fact I get to have all these clandestine conversations about the two of you now. I mean did you actually think I wouldn't find out? Taking out your vice-principal *and* a police officer right in front of your *students*? Good job, Rob. Real role model material. Totally inspiring stuff."

"Who told you about that? Dad?"

"So he knows then."

"Yeah he knows," Robert said, hanging his head.

"Yeah, well, it wasn't Dad. It was Bob File as a matter of fact."

"Bob *fucking* File," Robert spat. "Well Bob can shut his trap, how's that."

"Like I said, I'm loving all these deep-and-meaningfuls I get to have about the two of you now."

"Yeah, well, you should hear what Dad and I have to say about *you*," Robert shot back, and with that, not surprisingly, the conversation fizzled out, leaving in its wake a moment of irritated embarrassment for both. Robert and Jeremy had never felt all that comfortable delving into the subject matter of their father, let alone each other, perhaps because, with all his complexities and obvious shortcomings, Jon was still the lone foundation their lives had ever known, and to evaluate his conduct, out loud at any rate, might just dispel any remaining magic to be extracted from such a stone.

The band, which apparently did not have a name, took a break at the completion of the next song, at which point Robert waved to the short, half-Japanese keyboardist who did have a name to make his way over to the bar. Harvey Hasegawa, Jeremy was told, was the music teacher at Robert's school. Harvey and Robert shook hands a while, and eventually Jeremy was introduced as Robert's itinerant little brother, a label he actually rather enjoyed.

"Sit down," Robert told Harvey, removing his cane from the stool alongside.

"What's going on?"

"Nothing. Nothing's going on. Just came to have a drink and listen to you play, that's all." Robert waited for Harvey to receive a beer from the bartender before continuing on. "So my brother here's going to come work with me at the mill."

"That so?" Harvey elevated his eyebrows at Jeremy.

"Sure is," Robert said.

Now that was not exactly true. Yes, they had touched on the possibility of Jeremy getting on at the feed mill for the summer, just as, in the same truncated manner, they had touched on Robert's troubles at school of late, but no decision had been reached on the subject, not by Jeremy anyhow.

"Christ, I must have the smallest dick in this place," Harvey announced, apropos essentially of nothing insofar as Jeremy could tell, the grim cast of his features betraying nothing if this in fact were a joke of some sort. Gazing coldly about the place, his concentration ultimately migrated to the enormous pair of breasts with which the waitress had made fast to the end of the bar, at which point the soundness of his observation struck him as worthy of repetition somehow. An admission, twice given, that earned Mr. Hasegawa the expected kudos from his audience. He shrugged them off however.

"Makes no difference to me. Nope, makes no difference at all. By labelling me they're missing what's really unique about me, you know? And hey, you know what I say when I meet a girl? 'I've got a small dick. You got a problem with that?' And you know what? More often than not they don't. Women can be very accommodating that way, I find. At least all the women I meet are."

Jeremy blinked. Robert smiled. "Good ol' Hasegawa and his cock-talk," laughed the latter at once.

"Whatever. Makes no difference to me," Harvey said. "But then hey, speaking of which, how about your brother here, Jeremy. Nothing can kill this prick. Not even falling out of a god-damned *plane.*" He glanced about furtively, leaned in close, and dropped his volume to a near conspiratorial whisper. "I take it you've been filled in on his situation at the school."

"Not really," said Jeremy, amending that quickly with a, "Well sort of, sure."

"Well let's just say he and some of the other members of our staff have some, uh, *issues* to resolve," said Harvey, offering, Jeremy thought, a most generous interpretation of events.

"What sort of issues."

Harvey looked at Robert, gauging whether or not he had already taken the conversation too far. Following the lead of the immediate family, Robert's friends had always had a range of subjects they tacitly agreed not to broach in conversation, and Jeremy could see that Harvey here was no different in that regard. Still, he could imagine that his brother's stress leave, coupled with the notorious fish incident, had proved a hot topic of gossip in and around the staff room in the weeks leading up to summer break. But even Jeremy was not privy, at least not yet, to what had brought the whole situation to a head. Though he was fairly sure it had everything to do with Robert's wife and child having left.

"You know, issues," Harvey said, barely sucking back a smile. This not-so-veiled suggestion of insider information irritated Jeremy somehow.

"That's pretty vague."

Harvey winked, and turned to Robert. "So hey, I've been meaning to ask you, where do you want to go camping this summer?"

"It's up to you," Robert said.

"How about you, Jer? Any suggestions? I'm thinking up near Nelson somewhere."

Looking up from the close inspection of his drink, Jeremy promptly finished it, and slid the glass, empty except for ice cubes, back across the bar as a prompt for replenishment. "How about an internment camp. I hear they're all the rage out there."

Unbeknownst to Jeremy, he often unconsciously imitated his father's voice, and like Jon many years before, was beginning to drink a little too much from time to time, out of boredom, or depression, or both. Caught off guard by this comment, Harvey looked questioningly to Robert, who in warning shook his head almost imperceptibly back and forth. No one spoke for a time, and the flow of Jeremy's thought wavered, ebbed, and changed direction of its own accord. He promptly ordered another drink to further buoy himself.

"And hey, just for the record, my father gave me those fish those fuckers killed," Robert grinned at last, lending some much needed strength to the waning conversation. Robert cared nothing for the good opinions of others, and had, as a result, a great capacity for personal happiness. At this point, then, he was perfectly happy. "Harv, what's wrong?" he asked.

"I think I'm having a heart attack."

"Come on, it's just gas."

Clutching his chest, Harvey winced at Jeremy. "What do you think, Jer? Think a guy like me could be having a heart attack?" he gasped.

Still feeling somewhat adrift, Jeremy had managed, while listening without paying much attention to the recent direction of the conversation, to swallow further quantities of Crown Royal, the effect of which was a growing sense of hostility rather than one of sympathy somehow. "Not likely," he said, dragging a hand free of its task of supporting his body against the bar. "Not a man of your, uh, measure, Harv. And besides, our resident medic here in the white man's ward has already declared it flatulence."

"Yes, well, he would be the expert on that. Hey didn't you write a book?" Harvey asked once the majority of the pain had passed.

"I did," Jeremy said, moving around at moorings, priming his pump with rye in anticipation of the inevitable and uncomfortable discourse on which they were presumably about to embark.

"And what are you doing now?"

"Now?" He glanced at his brother. "Well now I'm packaging fish feed apparently."

"I see. Preserving that crucial writer's anonymity. So, what, I guess neither of the Jacks boys gives a damn about the environment then."

"Sorry?"

"Harvey here's a bit of an idealist," Robert said by way of explanation such politically correct conversation. "A real citizen of the world."

"Hey I've been abroad."

"Yeah to *Mex*ico," Robert said. He shook his head. "Your whole problem, Harv, is that you never developed a healthy respect for firsthand experience. It's true though. Your very existence is a slap in the face to genuine educators everywhere. 'Knowledge is experience; everything else is just information.' Einstein said that, you know."

"Yes, I do know. If you recall, I gave you that calendar. And he also said imagination was more important than knowledge, so there. Your brother here, Jer, he always been this confrontational?"

"He gets it from his mother," Jeremy said. The tide was making in his brain, but his humour still rested deep in the mud.

"Must've. But then get a load of this guy here," Harvey said to neither Robert nor Jeremy, but instead that space there in between, where at this exact moment, accompanied by what one would have to presume was his girlfriend, a bespectacled man of about the Jacks brothers' age dressed in a bright red blazer was about to slide on in. Despite the overt good looks of the girl, the blazer was the real attraction here, especially for someone like Robert, not that that excused his subsequent behaviour even a little.

While the man in the red blazer and his companion stood waiting for the bartender to work his way down the bar, Robert reached over and slipped his hand into the fellow's waist pocket, and thus inserted, left it there to loiter a while.

"Robby . . ." said Harvey.

"Just a sec," Robert said, his arm fully extended, his hand completely immersed in a blazing red blend of nylon and wool. He was grinning up at the man, obviously hoping for some sort of reaction here, but anticipating nothing of the sort to be sure. This was typical of Robert, at least it had been in the not so distant past, if not for the actual procedure, then certainly for the sentiment dwelling in behind it somewhere. In Robert's mind the bright red blazer implied a craving for attention, and so attention was what he was going to provide. That and a little hostility, I probably need not add. The girlfriend, for her part, glanced over, and noting Robert's hand fully inserted in the pocket of her companion's jacket, thereinafter stood quite transfixed, blinking from her boyfriend to Robert and back to her boyfriend, yet refusing to make genuine eye contact with anyone just yet.

Meanwhile, all too aware of the intrusion on his person, Red Blazer stood facing straight ahead, campaigning energetically with his eyes for the bartender to acknowledge his situation, clearly confused at the conundrum he now found himself in. The poor fellow obviously had no idea what to make of this overly large, seemingly normal, obviously disturbed, innocuously grinning man sitting so casually with his hand in his, Red Blazer's, pocket, and so he ignored both Robert and, by extension, Robert's hand, no doubt reasoning that if he just ignored both hook and bait, they might just drift off down the bar of their own volition. Jeremy, though, knew differently. Having seen this sort of thing play out countless times before, he knew that, though Red Blazer obviously thought differently, it was definitely in his best interest to slip away as quickly and quietly as possible. This excruciatingly uncomfortable albeit entirely silent standoff persisted for several seconds, for as much as he did not want to get into any sort of altercation with Robert, Red Blazer obviously had no desire to lose face in front of his girl.

Finally, having taken notice of the unbelievably bright red blazer bellied up to his bar, as well as the collection of limbs making an overabundance of use of its particulars now, the bartender made his way over to take the poor fellow's order. Listening to Red Blazer stutter and stumble through his list of drinks—there must have been a whole crew of his colleagues around somewhere, each decked out, no doubt, in much the same manner—the bartender stared all the while at Robert, and at the unexpected bond between them there. Eventually, unable to perceive any sort of genuine hostility on Robert's part, yet refusing to believe that all was well and good here, the bartender moved away to speak to his manager. Still, though, Robert kept his hand in the man's pocket. It just seemed to belong in there.

"Robby," Harvey pleaded, "that's offside."

"Just a sec."

"Robby . . ."

Just then the manager appeared. "Do you know this gentleman?" he asked Red Blazer, indicating Robert with a curt nod.

"No I *do not*," said Red Blazer, and in truth it was the *do not* that did it. Robert hated any sort of affectation of speech, and the rampant use of italics, intended or not, was just the sort of pretentiousness that sent him off on his more violent combat operations. Capable of channelling enormous energies, Robert Jacks was proficient at many things, none more so though than the visiting of violence upon another human being. Though simply overwhelming an opponent with abuse seems hardly worthy of the term 'proficient' in my mind. One thing he was not was an adherent of any particular style. But those unlucky enough to find themselves at odds with Robert Jacks soon realized, along with everyone else in the room, that to continue on such a course was no longer a very viable option. As a rule, his enormous capacity for violence manifested itself in a wholly unruly and unorthodox flailing of arms and legs, elbows and knees, and even forehead and teeth if need be, so that more often than not his unfortunate opponent(s) simply withdrew his (their) services, cutting losses before absorbing too much injury. The problem with this approach of Robert's is that it only holds in theory. For instance, occasionally, in his youth, he did have the opportunity to come up against those who devoted themselves to destruction just as much as he did, and a few who appeared to devote themselves even more, but it was a rare thing indeed to find that sort of devotion driven by the kind of unrelenting enjoyment that could somehow match his own. Not that some did not test him from time to time, often as not older boys who through continuous training and life experience tended to practice better form. However, these infrequent occurrences served only to increase Robert's taste for fighting, and before long he was the unquestioned king of Royal Heights and various neighbourhoods beyond. Even Jeremy had made the mistake of stepping into that path of destruction once, receiving, for his trouble, a cleanly severed collar bone. But then it was no doubt this ever-ready willingness to fight that got Robert himself into trouble on several occasions. It is difficult to imagine now, as it has been for some time, that he had ever been anything other than a large intimidating specimen of a man, but in his pre-pubescence he was actually rather short and incredibly thin, and considered by most, including his father, to be an altogether fragile and effeminate thing. And of course that sort of construction, combined with that feisty frame of mind, led him into all manner of difficult situations—situations that required, if he were going to survive, some sort of working defence mechanism, however haphazardly inspired. And so, in high school, with the long awaited addition of testosterone and, consequently, attendant mass, Robert Jacks the sporadically storming boy became a veritable cyclone of a man. Still, it took him several years to hunt down and visit retribution on each and every boy, and girl, who had ever been really nasty to him.

"Absolutely not," said Robert with sudden glad familiarity when the manager requested he remove his hand from Red Blazer's pocket. It was not that he held a too high opinion of his own abilities, but simply that he had a good grasp of the likely regarding any given altercation he was to be involved in.

"Why not?"

"Well why should I, really. I mean this guy here"—he indicated Red Blazer with the same curt nod the manager had given—"he's the one who wore the jacket, not me."

"But it's his jacket," the manager said sensibly. "And your hand's in *his* pocket."

This piece of information seemed, quite rightly, I think, all too remote and academic to Robert, who stared vacantly at the manager and said "What?" and it was here that Jeremy knew a fight was more or less underway. Because while it was true that the

Jacks brothers had grown up trying to comply with their father's one rule with regard to combat, namely that it was wrong to start fights but even worse not to finish them, the actual 'start' to the fight, for Robert at least, had always proved a real bone of contention. For Robert, Jeremy knew, the fight had started, in theory at least, as soon as the red blazer appeared on the scene. That it had not actually erupted into the physical world as yet was of no real concern to him. And so it was that, drawing a deep breath, Robert flung himself at once into the mounting riptide of would-be bouncers suddenly gathering in around him, and therein began a stiff-armed flailing at faces, a crawl really, obviously intended to clear a sort of path to the far side of the bar where, moments later, his breath all but exhausted, he arose with an expression of utter surprise that he was still in sight of anyone at all. As for Jeremy, he stood back, absorbed in the very ritual of it all.

To this day Jeremy will not deny that he thoroughly enjoyed watching his brother fight. If you asked him seriously what he thought was wrong with the world, he would probably sigh and go on at length about humanity's penchant for mass destruction and self-corruption or else some other such pap, but in actuality he really did enjoy a good scrap. For in truth, watching his brother go to work was like watching some biblical climatic event take place. And while his standards regarding fighting were much the same as Robert's, he did not feel he was wealthy enough, ability-wise, to apply them as often, or in such a wide range of conditions, as his brother so obviously did. Besides, it did not seem likely that a situation too labour-intensive or time-consuming could ever arise for Robert, whereas Jeremy felt that, for him, there was scarcely any reason to begin if he could not finish his opponent within the first few seconds of conflict. And so, as the camera moved steadily back, rather than finding him readily engaged, it was much more common to find Jeremy as he was now, standing apart and watching his brother with all the rapture and intensity of your typical fight fanatic.

POSTED BY LUCY @ 4:20:00 P.M. 4/5/2007   2 COMMENTS

The Great Grass Experiment
Addiction Research Foundation
33 Russell Street, Toronto, Ontario
July 10, 1972

Dear Ginny:

'Faith begins as an experiment, and ends as an experience.

Time goes, you say? Ah, no! Alas, Time stays, we go.'

Who said that? Who knows. Anyway, hello young lover, way out there in Lotus Land. Here we are in what has got to be, bar none, the most singular and interesting experience I shall ever encounter, and I don't even know where to begin.

Checked in on Friday, June 30th at 3:30 PM to the 4th floor, west wing of the Alcohol and Drug Addiction Research Foundation (better known and henceforth referred to as A.R.F.), bag and baggage, paint brushes and (empty) moneybag in hand. I was presently installed, along with my new roommate, Rosemary Tate (Lorna's in the other group, in Ward A, which is probably a good thing, as quite frankly I'm sick of the bitch altogether) in Room 4073 on Ward B, a high-security floor (elevator doesn't even stop here) with masking tape covering even the cracks on the IBM time-locked doors. We eat all our meals here, weave here, sleep here—everything *here*. The whole place is carpeted, beautifully furnished, quiet, completely dust-free and quite comfortable—we have one big lounge with TV, stereo, etc plus smaller lounges and sitting rooms, so as you can see we are very well appointed—and yet Mom and Dad think I'm completely out of my mind of course. Can you imagine what they think this experiment might do to their precious reputation in little ol' Bobcaygeon? Ah well, what they don't know won't hurt them, and believe me, they *won't* know! Comprendez? Very sterilized letters heading up their way. Of course I still tease them a bit (can't help it; I'm mean) but alas I'm even keeping the fact that I have a roommate secret from them as, well, you know the Cormacks: you build a thousand bridges and dig one clam, they don't call you a bridge-builder now do they.

We are completely self-supporting here thanks to our weaving, and pay for absolutely everything excluding the bed. This means food, shower, radio, TV, walks, sauna, gymnasium, snacks, linen, etc. This may sound strange and even a little harsh at first, but as we are part of an experiment we are providing "data," and therefore every purchase made is recorded by item, name, time, amount, frequency, yada yada yada. It all makes sense when you think about it. On the bright side, things are so incredibly cheap that I shall only spend about $200 throughout the entire hundred-day experiment.

We use ARF plastic coinage (each of us has a different colour: me, why I'm cool mint green of course) just like regular currency. They gave us fifteen dollars for the first few days until we could begin to support ourselves through weaving.

We have pulses taken at 8:15 PM and 9:15 PM, give urine and blood samples every Monday and Thursday, write psychological tests (paid five bucks per test) about twice per week—I've had EKG, EEG, and a host of other quiet horrors visited upon my person lately. All kidding aside, the EEG didn't hurt a bit. Kind of freaked me out, though, know what I mean? Having your head measured and marked off like that is somehow akin to being measured and marked off by the undertaker himself. What a trip.

The ten of us spent the first night just gabbing and getting to know one another, and spouting forth all sorts of nonsense about what we thought was going to befall our lot over the next fourteen weeks or so. Saturday, July 1st we were presented with very primitive handlooms, and shown how to string the fuckers up. I don't know if Mom mentioned it, but an ARF belt must be woven to ridiculously strict specifications, and each belt woven is passed or failed depending on whether these exact specifications are met. It must be between 52" and 54" long, 1¾" and 2" wide, at least 5 picks/inch in tension, utilizing at least two colours of wool yarn (provided free, thank God), tassels must be 5–6" in length on each end and knotted three times (again, ridiculous), sides of belt must be straight and parallel with each other, and if that doesn't kill you, nothing will, baby. (Oh yes, and we're paid a whopping $2.^{50} per belt, so there.) The first belt took exactly one day to make. Ouch. Today, though, I finished fifteen belts, so my timing is improving rapidly, to say the least. By next week I hope to be polishing off 25–30 per day, which would mean weaving about 16 hours a day. Might as well, as I sure as hell can't do anything else in this place.

Can you imagine . . . do you have any idea . . . what it's like to be stuck with ten of the horniest, dirtiest, funniest chicks in the middle of downtown Toronto on a Friday night? What a gas! We have more giggles than a barrel of monkeys (if, indeed, monkeys do giggle, as various recent studies seem to suggest) and it's been eons since I've been to a hen party. Oh yes, I almost forgot. One girl, Maria, even has a tattoo just above her ass.

As the experiment moves along, so does our understanding of its intentions and operations. We are under constant surveillance by a three-shift, twenty-four hour team of doctors, nurses, clinical psychologists and psychiatrists, and every half hour they come around, day and night, solo or in pairs, to ogle you, taking detailed notes on whatever you're doing, or not doing, as it were. Strangely enough, they seem to melt right into the woodwork. You hardly even notice them there. Yes, they do talk to us, and some even smile occasionally (one flirts, but he's *shockingly* unattractive), but as a group they never answer any specific questions about the experiment. However, contrary to what you might imagine, there is very little paranoia, as they are merely in the business of collecting data—purely objective, not personal (except that you are one of the persons). They give you a "sociability rating" (A, B, or C) and measure *everything*: # of ounces of what you eat and drink, the time, the frequency with which you laugh, cry, eat, sleep, shit (admittedly, not much), piss, belch (well maybe not quite *that* much), weave, shower, watch TV, who pays for TV, who argues about what, everything—and yet so unobtrusively that you really don't even notice them there. Can you dig it?

Haven't seen any grass as yet, and believe me, we give them a pretty hard time about that, chanting from time to time, à la football cheers, "We want some smoke! We want some smoke!" but of course they just smile faintly and otherwise ignore us outright. I'm sure they're going nuts just looking after this motley crew. They don't want *any* preconditioning to occur. Stan, the hunchbacked shopping man, well now here's a bit of a character—among his various duties, effectively executing the obligatory role of comic relief—but I shall save him for a later, less garrulous letter.

Now hey, thanks for all the concern, big sis, but really, I'm feeling just fine. My mind is cool—I'm safe, comfortable, a bit stiff from weaving perhaps and a little backed up, but otherwise sailing along at an even keel and completely sans complaints, all right? I know the time is just going to fly by—weaving all day is just such a placid activity—you have no idea how absolutely soothing it is. Don't get me wrong, it's damned hard work, and it pisses me off that we all have aching shoulders and hands, but then it really doesn't matter what I think, now does it.

So what's the ol' rabble-rouser been up to? Any more expeditions to Alaska planned, or is he going to settle down to working his own boat for a change and maybe putting some bread on the table? Joking of course. Everyone out this way is still agog (love that word "agog") with the accomplishments of the mighty Phyllis Cormack, and despite what you may or may not think, Ginny, it really is a good thing your husband's doing, not to mention Uncle John, and more than that it's the *right* thing they're doing—and it's good to know people like that are standing up for this world we're trying so hard to ruin. I must admit I'm glad they took my advice on the name change though. "Don't Make a Wave" was just too cumbersome in my opinion.

Now where was I . . . oh yes, we do all sorts of IQ, sensory response, psychological tests, etc each week, paid $5 per test, and we can sell the powers that be our diary (or a Xerox of it) for $25 at the end of the experiment to help in their "data" collection (the perverts). The experiment itself is headed by a Dr. Miles, a scientist and psychiatrist, and his collaborator and constant companion, a Dr. Congreves, who is also a scientist and shrink. These two are a real riot, believe me. Lifted their routine straight from the transcripts of Laurel & Hardy, I swear. From time to time, they drop by the ward to say hello and ask how things are going, but that's about it before storming off to some remote section of the hospital, debating heatedly amongst themselves as they go. We have absolutely no communication with the other group (Lorna and her nine compatriots) so it looks as though we'll not see them again until October 8th, our last day.

I've been writing my diary in the form of letters to Mom and Dad, but of course they're not getting the full treatment. No, my dear, that burden shall fall to you and you alone, replete with all the gory details to lug around. Anyway, my point is, the parents are going to save all the letters so I can Xerox them to sell, and I'd appreciate if you'd do the same, if for no other reason than I might like to cross-reference them later on in order to extract some semblance of truth from this little experiment in street-drug experimentation. I write the old lady daily, sending off a bundle once or twice a week, and Mom, bless her cotton socks, is writing me directly, so I guess *her* head is in the right space at least. Let me know what she thinks okay? I know we both tend to get censored letters, but it's the best she can do under the present regime, and we know that all the love in the world is sent along with them, so what more can you expect, eh?

Really am weary now—it's 4 AM, and since I usually get up at 7:30, I guess I'd better say bye for now. I feel as though I've been here for days uncountable . . . almost as if I've always been here. Weird, isn't it? What a nightmare. Mind you, it's going to be very nice to wake up from it with four or five thousand dollars cash in my sock, tax-free and well-earned. Speaking of waking, here's some Roethke:

> I wake to sleep, and take my waking slow.
> I feel my fate in what I cannot fear.
> I learn by going where I have to go.

Love, Birdie

JULY, 2002

An hour later, by necessity, the brothers had changed venues, and
cities, migrating north to Vancouver and away from Richmond
and its various bruised bodies and egos still holding out for an
opportunity at reprisal. Despite his recent injuries, none of which,
incredibly, had been aggravated in the tussle, Robert expressed a
not entirely unexpected desire to dance, so of course they ended
up at Vancouver's only guaranteed hotspot on a Monday night,
the true Mecca of the suburban club-going set, the venerable
Roxy on Granville. When they arrived by taxi there was quite a
queue out front, but then Robert spoke with Vic, the veteran
doorman who always seemed to remember him but, inexplicably,
never seemed to so much as recognize Jeremy, and of course they
strolled right in. Robert limped ahead through the crowd, at
home here in the dark and anywhere within sight and sound of
scantily-clad women getting drunk. The bar was busy, and the
band was loud, and the brothers made their way to the back bar
where the staff were more familiar, and more familiarly corrupt,
and therefore willing to negotiate a better contract for all those
involved (excluding, and at the expense of course, of the house).
The fight at the Beaver had come and gone without much real or
lasting damage to any of its principal combatants, barring perhaps
a vague technical awareness on Red Blazer's part that his bar-
going wardrobe would require serious reconsideration at some
point. Robert had fought, and beaten, both bouncers thrown at
him, managing, via a series of seemingly effortless but in reality
carefully constructed tacks, to work his way over to the front door
so that he and Jeremy might make a getaway of sorts. On their
way out, someone—neither brother knew who—standing near
the front door said something vaguely derogatory, earning himself, courtesy of Jeremy, a rapid series of piston-like shots to the
head. Otherwise they exited the premises unmolested. And once
safely outside, having managed to locate a cab, they were halfway
downtown before Robert realized he had left his cane behind.

"We have to go back."

"Not a chance."

"Maybe Harvey'll find it," said Robert, hopefully, a little later.

"Maybe," Jeremy said. "But I doubt it."

He did not bother telling Robert that he had seen Red Blazer hurl the thing into the river out back, as that was just the sort of excuse his brother would need to immediately renew acquaintances with the Flying Beaver, its patrons, and its staff.

Anyway, they ended up at the Roxy downtown as Robert was so determined to dance. As mentioned, other than a scraped knuckle on his primary pitching hand, he had emerged from the incident essentially unscathed. In fact, he seemed to have taken something from the fight with him, having grown in stature, in his brother's mind, one exact measure. And so it was that, two hours of hot sweaty jumping and dancing amid strangers later, Jeremy managed to slip out into the night, jogging unsteadily in the direction of a good late night pizzeria on Robson Street that had bailed him out so many times in the past. It was a nice night out for a jog. The stars were out, a breeze was rising, and the temperature had dropped in concert with the tide. Unfortunately, even as Jeremy tried to pass him by on the sly, Vic the suddenly vigilant doorman selected this particular evening to finally catalogue his face, and in turn collect its counterpart, whereupon he promptly volunteered the information that Jeremy was no longer on the premises, but running hard and heading west.

What a wonderful world it once was. A world in which a white man could go out running in a city at night without fear of being reprimanded in transit. First Jeremy found himself the reluctant quarry of two handsome drunks, each of them young, each of them fast, but in the end they could not catch him, as his was a heart theirs simply could not match. Next he was sworn at repeatedly by a shopping cart-pushing street dweller of indefinite age and race, who evidently mistook Jeremy for a rival worthy of much vocal and heated debate. Thirdly, he was overtaken by an overly enthusiastic bicycle cop. The rotund helmet-clad officer wanted to know where Jeremy was heading in such a hurry, sensing, no doubt, some sort of crime in progress at this point. Eventually, convinced Jeremy was simply hungry and drunk, he grudgingly set him free, but not before entering his own verdict on this already much maligned, clearly misguided performance. And finally, just as he thought he had cleared all impediments in his path, Jeremy heard from blocks behind him the distinct and telltale sound of his name being shouted.

He immediately turned south, then east, doubling back over his route one street removed in an effort to somehow throw his tracker off his scent. Next he cut through a parking lot, chancing a quick backwards glance to confirm his pursuer's presence only once he had made the far side. And there he was, or rather, it, a pedal-powered rickshaw, skidding to a stop at the light, and though Jeremy could make out neither operator nor client for the glare of the overhead streetlight, he knew without doubt the make of at least one mug leering out from beneath that klieg-like brightness.

With an audible groan from its operator, the rickshaw jerked forward across the intersection, bearing down not on Jeremy's present position but the next street over, looking to cut off his escape route entirely. Panicking, Jeremy turned north, thinking, mistakenly, that if he could somehow make the next one-way street his hunters would be unable to give chase. But of course this was not the case. Evidently the rickshaw driver, summarily bored with his evening thus far, had taken it upon himself, no matter what the physical cost, to take this game to ground. Jeremy did not know it yet, but (according to witnesses) with news of his departure, a limping man had come lunging forth from the bar asking any and all within earshot if they had seen another man, very similar in appearance, running hard anywhere particular. Several people had in fact, but to their everlasting credit would not admit it, at least not right away, not until informed that the bastard they were after had run off with the limping man's broth-er's wallet, at which point they could not do enough apparently. And together as one they raised their hands in the direction of unlucky Jeremy's departure, all but sealing his fate, and restating his case to the first available rickshaw operator, the limping man was at once hot on his trail.

Now heading the wrong way down a one-way street in the middle of a busy city like Vancouver could have worked, would have worked, and in reality *should* have worked, if not for the undeniable will, and its devoted driver, bearing down on Jeremy from behind those widespread hornlike handlebars.

The rickshaw skidded to a stop on the sidewalk before him, its front tire narrowly missing his left shoe. And there, in the carriage, leaning heavily over the shoulder of his faithful chauffeur, sat Jeremy's excited sweating brother.

"What the fuck happened to you?"

Trapped, Jeremy was of course compelled to get in, and as punishment befitting his crime, conveyed immediately to the nearest lap dance bar, Brandi's down on Hornby. They took the elevator to the fifth floor, and numerous highballs and several lap dances later, both sources of discomfort funded one after another by his brother, Jeremy allowed himself to be dragged down one flight of stairs to the Swedish Touch massage parlour. In direct contrast to his recently estranged wife, Jeremy thought it no coincidence that Robert went with the first tall thin blonde he could find, limping from reception to the nearest available stall with the worn-down yet dogged resolve of the veteran prize-fighter. As for Jeremy, he took up his customary position in the starkly decorated foyer. Not that he took issue with such an establishment, or with its employees, or even with the services they cheerfully or not so cheerfully provided on a case by case basis, and not because of some harboured indifference to, or general dislike of women that his brother presumed he had, but simply that he considered his now drunk and foul-smelling flesh the last thing one of these hardworking women deserved this early on in the night. This is what he told himself, at any rate. And so he sat and read a book instead, as if, in a brothel, with regards to pleasure, engaging merely in the theoretical were still somehow commensurate to the practical in the heady business of having your bilges professionally pumped out.

"What's that you're reading?" asked the tiny Asian receptionist from behind her big Mexican pine desk, having watched Jeremy wrestle the thin little book from the back pocket of his pants.

"Uh . . . Steve Martin," he said, checking the book's cover to confirm that he was correct.

"As in the comedian?"

"As in the comedian. It's called *Shopgirl*," he added when he could see more information was indeed desired on the subject. "Say, any way you could turn up the lights in here? It's a little difficult to make out the words."

She smiled coolly. "Not that that would have anything to do with all the liquor you've consumed tonight."

Jeremy looked at her appraisingly. "That's right."

Evidently, though, she could not or would not turn up the lights as she made no effort to do so. Against company policy, Jeremy thought, and so decided to let it go.

He returned his attention to *Shopgirl*. Just then three young Indo-Canadian men came barrelling in, not one of which had ever so much as set eyes on Sukhvinder 'Parfait' Rai, and after much fruitless haggling and credit card juggling, they were escorted separately into three separate rooms.

Jeremy returned to his book as the trio swayed drunkenly away.

"So, what, it's funny?" asked the head of the receptionist a little later, floating vaguely disembodied behind the enormous desk.

"Sorry?"

"Your book, it's funny? Like a comedy?"

"Not exclusively, no," he told her, and again found his spot in the book, locking himself into that particular, and particularly elusive, collection of words.

"So then, what, a tragedy?" she continued, refusing to let the matter drop, bored as she so obviously was at this relatively early hour of the night.

"No, this," Jeremy said, indicating their exchange thus far, "*this* is a tragedy."

And so she left him quite alone after that.

Finally his brother returned, limping a little more pronouncedly perhaps but, outwardly at least, no worse for wear. And so, taking leave of Swedish Touch and its garrulous receptionist, the brothers gradually returned to street level. Walking along side by side with no particular destination in mind, Robert employing his brother's shoulder as crutch, they eventually made their way back to Granville Street and its considerable collection of dingy take-out stalls dispensing cheap Indian food and the like.

Suddenly Robert stopped.

"What's wrong?" Jeremy asked, coming to an abrupt halt himself. And there on the sidewalk, in plain sight of everyone, he watched with dismay as his brother unbuttoned his fly and began fishing about in his shorts.

"Oh shit."

"What is it?" Jeremy said.

Right hand fully inserted, Robert levelled a look at a trio of young men walking by before reporting, somewhat ambiguously, "She must've had some in her mouth."

"Say what? What the fuck are you talking about?"

"She must've had some in her mouth," Robert repeated, gesturing over his shoulder. "My Swede back there." And with his thumbs hooked inside the band, he directed Jeremy's attention down the open front of his underwear.

Jeremy leaned in to assess the damage. "Jesus," he repeated several times in disgust. "Jesus Christ, that's terrible."

"Well," sighed Robert matter-of-factly, releasing his underwear with a resounding snap of the elastic waistband, "it's gonna have to be cut out of there."

Jeremy followed his brother into 7–Eleven, where Robert promptly inquired of the aging, forlorn, Indo-Canadian clerk if she might have any spare scissors available. She did, she said, and promptly passed a pair over the counter, then watched with bewilderment as Robert limped back out the door.

"Where's he going with my scissors?" she asked Jeremy, perturbed.

"He's got a little, what, personal grooming to take care of," he explained, inviting her over to the window to see, through the haze of convenience store reflection in between, Robert sitting there on the curb, his head bent hard to the task, carefully trimming a complex web of chewing gum from a matted patch of pubic hair.

Tuesday, July 11, 1972

Dear Mom & Dad:

Well here we are on day number twelve, and what a difference a day makes. Enjoyed my first consistent crap this morning, and wouldn't you know it, but Doctor Congreves shuffles reluctantly into the dining room at lunchtime to deliver the colon-constricting news that, for purposes of the experiment, five of us would be switched for five of the ladies from Ward A. Well you'd have thought the sky had fallen in. We knew it was coming, had even been vaguely warned it was coming, but still found it shocking, to a woman, when it did. The ten of us have become unbelievably close in our short time here. Regardless, Maria, Misty, Anne, Connie and I were to have our bags packed and ready to pass through the IBM-locked door by 3:15 PM, just under three hours away.

There were moans and groans for the first few minutes as we all packed, but pretty soon we had a big farewell party going full swing in the big lounge, with all of us letting loose—tears, laughter, dancing to the stereo, lots of talking and trying not to notice the precious seconds slipping irretrievably away.

We five bid a sad farewell @ 3:20 and passed through to Ward A, our new home for the remainder of the experiment. But what a difference! So very quiet and *sombre*. It sure didn't take us long to see why the big switch had been made. Physically, the two wards are identical, but therein end all similarities. Apparently our group had by some strange miracle hit it off extremely well—very lively, competitive, running the gamut of emotions, but on the whole getting along quite splendidly—while Ward A had a couple of emaciated witchcraft (think Charles Manson) séance-style people continuously bringing the others down. Nothing too provocative mind you, but disturbing, to say the least. Lorna and one other girl were the only ones even bothering to weave more than one belt a day. The rest were just moping and coasting, doing enough for their meals and that's it. No "spirit," eh?

Anyway, Maria, Misty and I were the top weavers (Anne and Connie the slowest) in Ward B, so maybe we can get the ball rolling in here.

Things have settled down now. I have my own room (one of the sitting rooms has a desk and bookshelves too) right across from the nursing station, as does another girl Debbie, a big blonde bird of a woman with bad teeth and massive breasts given to enormous fits of gum-chewing and inopportune laughter—if first impressions count for anything in here, she'll prove to be my nemesis for sure. It's 10:30 PM and I'm heading off to bed. It's been a long hectic day, and I'm getting a little grumpy apparently.

Love, Birdie

P.S. Tracey moved her things back into our apartment on July 1st, and I think Ruth was staying until the 18th or 19th (at which point and with any luck someone else will arrive to take her place) so hopefully I won't have to pay rent for July, August, or September.

JULY, 2002

It was almost three in the morning when Jeremy, having managed to successfully drink himself sober, finally realized that his brother was no longer around. However ironic was this reality in itself, it was certainly not in the least bit remarkable, and in any case he was now in the company of a moderately successful local actor entirely unfamiliar to Jeremy except as, at best, a fringe friend of Robert's, as well as a trio of moderately pretty, morally repugnant twenty-something girls presently a few paces removed and plotting amongst themselves. The girls had not been paying much attention to Jeremy all night, and so it came as something of a surprise when one of the trio, an indiscriminate blonde who had once, long ago, spit at and missed the head of Sukhvinder Rai from a passing school bus, came up and asked him for a light.

"Sorry, don't smoke," he told her, forced to clear his throat, it having been so long now since he had last said anything at all.

"No bother," said the blonde in a strained imitation of un-stoned ease. "Say, where'd your brother go?"

"I was going to ask you the same thing."

"Ah. Took off again huh," she nodded knowingly. Then charily: "I suppose you're expecting his share of the ecstasy then."

"Actually, I think I'll just coast a while if that's okay."

"Suit yourself," she said, pivoting away. "Gav! Hey Gav, are we going or what."

"Yeah sure," Gavin told her. "But hold on a goddamned second, all right?"

Gavin could of course be excused for his current air of hostility, as at that very moment he was involved in a solemn and clandestine conversation with what was, according to the girls, a burly-set, tracksuit-clad member of the local Russian mafia. Not that such suspect affiliation was so very far out of Gavin's line, not so far as Jeremy could tell anyway, but simply that the Russian in question happened to be a very large, very intimidating specimen of his kind. Jeremy tried to remember if he had ever met a Russian before. No doubt he had, he told himself, if entirely unbeknownst at the time, though perhaps not one of this particular calibre, and certainly not one in possession of a weapon. But then that was wrong as well. After all, he had seen several Russian players at several hockey games back in Toronto and, prior to that, here in Vancouver, but then again that had been from behind a barrier of protective glass, and therefore difficult to reconcile with the present context. No, Jeremy was fairly certain this was the first real Russian mobster he had ever willingly encountered, and of course it would happen when his brother was no longer around to provide the required diplomacy or, barring that, some decent backup.

Gavin rejoined the group just as the Russian beat a hasty retreat to wherever it is Russians go whenever they take a break from intimidating the really good, honest citizens of the world. Jeremy stood, feet set wide apart for balance, but not so wide that he might appear as though he were expecting trouble of some sort. Which of course he had every reason to be at this point. After all, it was early Tuesday morning in downtown Vancouver and, due to various mitigating circumstances, he was off to an illegal after-hours nightclub in the company of people he did not like or even care to get to know.

"Well we gotta wait here," Gavin announced to no one in particular, but with a convincing air of authority, canting downward by degrees the bill of his recently acquired Stargate Atlantis baseball cap. "Jer, you get another pill?"

"No, I—"

"He didn't *want* one," interrupted the blonde. That said, the other girls regarded Jeremy, amid a general shrugged confusion, with something akin to distrust—a matter of deeply furrowed, severely plucked eyebrows chiefly—all the while huddling closer together against the wind now tumbling in across the water, a process of perpetual readjustment. Jeremy amused himself with the only somewhat abstract notion that, if somehow reversed, all three women's skirts would not quite cover their bellybuttons.

"He didn't *want* one," repeated Gavin incredulously, stepping up close to Jeremy. "Something wrong? You wiggin' or something?"

"No I'm not *wiggin'*," Jeremy told him, feeling a concrete aversion to Gavin's proximity, let alone his particular application of cologne. "I just don't want any more right now."

Gavin glanced sideways at the girls. Then, moved by a seemingly irresistible impulse, he leaned in close to confess, "That's all right. I've never done the stuff before either. Truth is, the whole idea sort of freaks me out. I mean doesn't it fuck with your spinal fluid or something? Well doesn't it? And anyway, I was just trying to get in with the bitchy one," he admitted, signalling over his shoulder with a conciliatory thumb.

"Stacey."

"That's right—Stacey. Anyway, just so you know," he grinned mischievously, "I went ahead and spit out my second one."

"That so, Gavin? Good for you."

"Aren't you even the least bit concerned?" said Gavin, still grinning, still arching for emphasis one of his own recently trimmed brows.

"Not really. Because hey, you know what? I went ahead and spit out my first one."

For a moment, as Gavin's concerned expression graduated to the reality of his suddenly singular predicament, a strong sense not precisely of panic, but more of apprehensive abandonment, passed visibly over him, and he appeared, quite rightly, Jeremy thought, like a man alone on an island on an altogether unfamiliar mission, the possible perils of which remained largely, frighteningly, undefined.

"So what's happening?" asked the bitchy one, Stacey, having come gradually to the conviction that her night was suffering under the weight of unreasonably elevated expectations. Stacey wore her dyed black hair long, organized parenthetically around her pretty sculpted face, and Jeremy noticed with at once regrettable joy that she had quite obviously been crying again. "Are we going to this place or what?" she demanded.

"We have to wait," Gavin told her, standing once again shoulder to shoulder with his inflated sense of self, having regained a measure of control over his various incumbent fears. "They're going to call me on my cell. Say, where's Robby? He phantom already?"

"Yeah he's gone," answered the last of the girls, a petite, athletic, deceitfully studious and therefore, in Jeremy's opinion, altogether unattractive moron.

"Then what?"

"Sorry?"

"Then what happens after we get the phone call?" said Jeremy, impatient now, one of the many patent disadvantages he found to having so many Russians around.

"Oh then they give us 'the location,'" Gavin told him. "Don't worry though," he hastened to add as the girls wheeled their collective eyes skyward, "it's definitely right close to here.

Somewhere. But hey, ladies, if it'll make you feel any better, feel free to finish my beer."

Jeremy gazed around at the various enigmatic storefronts as Gavin gloomily watched the last of his beer disappear. The academic acknowledgement that in all probability he had family right nearby did little to allay Jeremy's present feeling of escalating individuality in an increasingly alien world. Suddenly, materializing as if from thin air, or at most a sketchy section of the nearby sidewalk which had appeared, initially, from the corner of his eye, to be nothing more than an escalator to nowhere, a comely young prostitute strolled up wearing little more than a sweeping generalization of a smile—a broad, altogether benign affair of the sort common to prematurely developed girls still within a memory's stone-throw of their abandoned high school prom. And for a brief, obscure, yet sentimental moment, Jeremy thought she might have been someone his brother knew, possibly someone Robert had taught in some recent year who mistakenly thought she recognized her teacher here too, but then of course he could not in any way be sure, for just as suddenly the impression passed, as did the girl, and at that moment Gavin's cell phone rang, breaking up any and all illusions he might have had of something familiar, however dubious, at which to make a last ditch grab here. And a few seconds later they were off to the next designated rendezvous, eager to get inside and out of this unseasonably cold July weather.

Together they assembled outside an unmarked metal door. For whatever reason—undoubtedly the almost palpable sense of displaced duty he felt towards his absent brother, to whose own oftrepeated disappearing act he had a longstanding relationship of sorts—Jeremy had decided to stay the course. Gavin knocked once, twice, three times, and at the third knock something happened. The door opened with an ominous metallic squeal, and in the open doorway stood two men—Russians, again, if their tracksuits were any indication—as it turned out, the same Russian from before and a newer, somehow larger one. Jeremy followed Gavin and the girls down a narrow set of steeply descending stairs, moving in the direction of the throbbing bass located some-where near the molten center of the earth. Once at the bottom of the stairs, they were told to check their coats with a young, blonde-haired, black woman tucked neatly behind a counter of an adjoining alcove, dressed, if her visible upper body were any indi-cation, in nothing whatsoever.

"Ten dollars for the coat check," said the now familiar Russian. "Pay the girl."

"What if we don't want to check our coats?"

"Everybody checks their coats. No exceptions," Gavin was told.

"What about those of us not actually wearing coats?" ventured Jeremy with an expression appropriate to what was, in retrospect, a somewhat hypothetical and therefore entirely inappropriate query.

"Ten dollars," put in the naked coat-check girl from behind, no doubt sensing some sort of ruse in the making here.

"Uh, each?" asked Gavin, patting his pockets absentmindedly, peering down an adjacent hallway filled with pulsing red light.

"Yeah, uh, each," chided the second Russian. "Fifty for five."

"Thanks for the deal."

"Sorry?"

"Nothing. Relax." Gavin looked appraisingly at the girls, one after another, before turning to rest his attention on Jeremy a moment. "You got any cash, Jer? Cash, right?" he said to the Russians. "You don't take credit or debit perchance?"

"Cash," answered the familiar Russian inflexibly.

Jeremy shrugged. "Sorry, man."

Gavin looked to the girls again. "Anyone have anything? Anything at all?"

They all shrugged helplessly, just as Jeremy had done.

"Let me get this straight," said the second Russian incredulous-ly. "You come to an after-hours club and you don't bring any *cash*? What the hell were you thinking?"

It did sound a little silly now that he heard it conjured in words, and Jeremy found himself wondering what, exactly, if anything, he had been hoping to achieve by coming here. In the highly colourful world of the underground, this became a matter of supreme importance just then.

"Dunno," Gavin shrugged. "We all just wanted to dance."

"Yeah, dance," echoed the chorus of girls, together imploring a street-level heaven with their hands.

The Russians rubbed their large stubble-strewn jaws and rolled their wide-set eyes. "All right then, who's going to get the money?" one of them eventually asked.

Jeremy offered up, "Well, if there's a bank machine nearby . . ." Left there to float in the air, the words managed to take on a surprisingly optimistic tone, and the one Russian leaned forward hopefully.

"How the hell should we know?" snapped the second a moment later, bringing them all crashing down.

"Well I guess we'll have to go find one," Gavin put in.

"I guess," said the first Russian. "Which one of you is going to go then?"

"Well can't we all go?"

"No, just one. The others stay here."

Gavin looked steadily at Jeremy from beneath those corrected brows of his, managing to convey much or even all of what went entirely unspoken here.

"So what do you think, Jer?"

"I don't know, Gavin. After all, this is your show."

Gavin smiled sourly, and turned to the first Russian. "All right, we'll send this guy here," he said and, surprisingly or not, indicated Jeremy with a nod.

"You know where you're going?" asked the first Russian a little later, having conducted Jeremy once more to the top of the stairs.

"How the hell should I know?" he said, but his escort failed to get the joke, or else had no sense of humour. The Russian stood strong, silent and, in a clearly characteristic attitude, rocked himself menacingly from foot to foot, as though bracing for rebellion.

"Your friends will be waiting," he said at length, exchanging with Jeremy a single cool nod before slamming shut the large metal door behind him.

Disorientated, Jeremy initially traveled northeast, but as he neared the old cenotaph where he had so often watched his brother march on Remembrance Days past, he realized that he was heading in a very dangerous direction—skid row lurking on the not so distant horizon—and so reversed his bearing and headed steadily southwest instead. There were few people out on the streets. Few respectable ones, at any rate. For a brief romantic spell, Jeremy considered hiring himself a prostitute, even going so far as to stand forlornly on a corner within earshot of one or two tired looking specimens, but then realized his performance would prove suspect at best, not to mention the question of affordability at present. Eventually he moved on and found himself a bank machine, but of course it was inoperative as a result of a recent rash of vandalism, and so he continued along up the street instead.

Finally he hit upon a machine that was amazingly neither vandalized nor broken, and promptly withdrew one hundred dollars in crisp twenty-dollar denominations—enough to get Gavin and the girls successfully installed in the after-hours club and, more importantly, himself back home again. He considered withdrawing more—that one prostitute had, after all, smiled at him—but then he did not want to overspend his budget any more than he already had that night. And exiting the well-lit bank he saw, floating towards him from the window of the coffee shop directly opposite, his brother's sweating smiling face. Jeremy stopped, grinned, offered up a sort of benediction with his hands, and finally made his way across the street.

"What the fuck happened to you?" he said, dragging back a stool alongside. It was the same thing each brother always uttered after such a performance by the other, although in truth it never grew too tired for either of them.

"I had to go. Sorry, I thought you heard me. Those girls . . ."

"Yeah I know what you mean," Jeremy said. "Still, I can't believe this town even *has* a Russian mafia." He frowned. "You drink too much of that stuff by the way."

"What stuff. This stuff?" Robert elevated his cup for inspection. "It's fuel for all the long hard nights of fish-feed packaging heading my way. I tell you, Jer, I'm gearing up. I'm geared up. I'm like a machine that way."

"No, seriously."

"Yeah like you should talk."

"It's true though, Robby. You drink way too much coffee. Did you know that one cup of percolated coffee contains more than—"

"Hey Jeremy," interrupted his brother. "Shut up."

Jeremy leaned heavily against the countertop and watched his brother a while, watching him with all but outright disdain to better enunciate some forgotten point.

"So how are you feeling, Jer? You were really cut for a time there."

"I was blind."

Robert, still sweating, indicated the corners of his lips, and Jeremy, still annoyed, was obliged to wipe away the pockets of spittle that had recently accumulated there.

"Your friend Gavin's still at that after-hours thing."

"He's not my friend, but thanks."

"Regardless," said Jeremy, "he's still there, and I'm supposed to go back. He's waiting for me to bring back some money for these Russian fuckers you got us mixed up with."

"Ditch him, did you? My, my, you're a chip off the old Jacks block, ain't ya."

Jeremy waited while Robert, exceedingly pleased with himself, finished filling up his cup with smiles. At length he said, "Well I'm supposed to go back. And those girls—"

"Don't worry about the fucking *girls*," Robert cut in. "Christ, the girls'll be just fine. And as for Gavin, well, Gavin can take care of Gavin. Believe me, he does it all the time."

"Hey Robby, you know what? You have a wife. At some point here you might want to acknowledge that fact."

They looked at each other with stunned amazement, and Jeremy, in a spasm of embarrassment and regret, retreated immediately to a position he mistakenly conceived to be far removed from any and all affronts of this nature.

"Yeah, little Stephie," Robert repeated with a soft chuckle, wiping sweat from his forehead with the back of an arm. "You should see her now."

"I bet."

"No, I mean—I mean you should see her when . . ."

"I know exactly what you mean," Jeremy lied.

They sat there together, staring out the window for a time.

Finally Jeremy blurted out, "Well I just don't think we ought to be doing this sort of thing so much anymore. I don't want you to feel you have to, you know, disrespect your wife or anything, just to keep me entertained."

"You don't want me to *what*? Jesus Christ, Jeremy, I dragged you to a whorehouse all of three hours ago. How much more disrespectful can you get? Or tell me, are there degrees to that sort of thing too."

Jeremy studied Robert's damp profile a while, then shook his head. "Well like I said, I really don't think we ought to be doing this sort of thing anymore."

"From what I saw tonight, that's probably a good idea," his brother retorted.

"Not to say you don't, you know—"

Robert interrupted, but just barely. He was gazing over Jeremy's shoulder at the corner of the room where two adjoining walls met the ceiling. In time he returned from wherever it was he had gone—the corner, Jeremy concluded, for lack of a more concrete option—and considered instead the wall of semi-reflective glass before them.

"What? What is it?"

Robert hesitated.

"It's good to have you home, little brother," he answered eventually.

They sat there together, staring out the window, watching a battalion of street-cleaners make their slow painstaking way down the sidewalk. At that exact moment Jeremy realized he was dealing with, or rather trying to help, a man who had never, either physically or emotionally, required any sort of help in his life.

"Hey Jer?" Robert said a little later, still sweating but more subdued than ever. "It's all right, hey. You don't have to worry. We'll have you home in an hour and everything'll be okay."

"Yeah I know, but it's just that . . . well there's something I want to tell you. Something I need to get off my chest." Jeremy worked himself into a position more suitable for late night coffeehouse confessions and continued at length, "I don't know if you remember, but last time I was out you took me to a party. No big soirée or anything, just a bunch of your teacher buddies getting together after work. Anyway, one thing led to another—we were all drinking a fair bit, if you remember—and, well . . ."

"Forget it. I don't want to hear about it," Robert cut in. "Let me please, *please* keep intact the image, however distorted, of my somewhat ill-tempered but otherwise morally upright, misunderstood genius of a brother. Please. I beg you. In fact I im*plore* you. My faith in you is the one unsullied thing I have left in this world, so let me at least keep that, all right?"

Jeremy fell silent, falling into his new routine of studying his brother's distorted reflection in the glass. He was searching for something, some new clue perhaps, that would in some way portend permanent and positive change on Robert's behalf. A long unproductive minute passed.

"You really don't like being married do you, Robby."

"Actually, whether I like or dislike being married is entirely irrelevant at this point."

"What's that supposed to mean?"

"It *means* this anxiety or guilt or whatever it is you're presently experiencing has nothing to do with the current relationship, or lack thereof, between your brother and his wife," Robert said. "It has everything to do with *you*. There is something fundamental missing from your life, Jeremy, and I think we both know what that something is. You've become completely detached from life, pal. You have, though. And it wouldn't be such a bad idea if you simply got laid every once in a while as well."

"But—"

"And what's *more*," continued Robert in this new spirit of truth-telling, still staring out the window as if expecting, at any moment, a series of fascinating phenomena to finally take place there on the asphalt, "and what's more, whatever excess of affection you insist occurred one night between you and my wife has more—everything—to do with the fact that *she* no longer feels any sort of exclusive affection towards *me*. Or devotion, I should say. Believe me, there's an important difference here, Jeremy. And an important lesson, too, by the way."

"That's not true."

"Yes it is. We both know it is. And I think we both know the reasons for it too. And moreover," Robert concluded, "I haven't really given her much reason to devote herself exclusively to me, obviously."

They each took a turn staring out the window, each brother exceedingly aware that the other had little to gain and everything to lose by his remaining here.

"Well I think I know what the problem is," said Jeremy eventually, unable, despite his better judgment, to harness the inherent impulse to heal his relations who seemed determined to live in an atmosphere of constant peril. "And maybe even how we can fix it."

"It can't be fixed, Jer."

"But we could try."

"It cannot be *fixed*," said his brother more firmly, still gazing into the reflection of his own distorted life.

"So what the hell do we do about it then?"

Robert turned on him fully. "But that's the thing, Jeremy. And to be honest, that's the one critical difference between you and me. I would never, *ever* ask you to do anything about it, understand? Now really, do you understand me?"

Angry, Jeremy turned away. "No, you know what, Robert? When it comes to you I've never been able to understand anything."

Posted by Lucy @ 3:15:37 a.m. 4/7/2007   0 COMMENTS

July 12, 1972

Dear Mom & Dad:

Slept for ten hours last night—and sure do feel better this morning. Have you noticed that my room number has changed? It's South 4052 now, facing College Street.

Today has been a good day—Misty, Maria and I polished off fifteen belts each—we're starting to feel it now, and there's still loads of room to improve from here.

So far I seem to be the only one weaving in the big lounge. Everyone else toils away in their rooms, for the most part keeping to themselves. Maria and Misty joined me this afternoon for a wee while though, which made for a nice change. Speaking of change, Lorna and I had a good chat this morning—she's *really* glad to see me, and the feeling is mutual—all things being forgiven in time, as they say. I guess she was finding things fairly quiet the last week or so. She and her roommate Rena are down the end of the hall, near the dining area.

Strangely enough, I'm still enjoying the food. I drink gallons of unsweetened grapefruit juice and chocolate milk—have cut out bread, potatoes and cheese—the latter being rather expensive, not to mention hard on my bowels, and I tend to eat the right substitutes anyway. However, salad, meat, vegetables, eggs, etc are still on the menu, and my weight has dropped down to 125 lbs, where I intend to let it stay—if I'm to be sitting on my backside for the next twelve weeks, I certainly don't want a whole lot of flab settling on my seat and legs. Favourite snack item: Dad's oatmeal cookies, my only sin.

I'm feeling fine, spirits are high, time to sleep now—bye.

July 13, 1972

Quiet day today as I'm feeling the strain of yesterday's work between my shoulder blades. It's like I'm training for the Olympics: my discipline, the handloom dash. Although I do admit I took it easy today—only thirteen belts—I find I can work up to only so fast a rate before my hands start to bleed from the wool anyway. It's like playing the guitar in a way: each time you pick up the instrument you're rusty for the first song or so, until you recapture the rhythm of the thing.

It's been raining all day, and the lawn in the courtyard is almost flooded. Are you still getting pelted up there? I guess that storm you had really messed things up (by the sounds of your letter last week anyway). However, be strong, as it's mid-July, and spring must surely be on the way (wink, wink).

Lots of love, Birdie

P.S. Have you broken your writing hand? Not much news from the outside reaches here.

JULY, 2002

One morning Jeremy met up with his recently acquired agent in order to discuss the sale, or lack of sale, of a second manuscript. Val Henderson lived locally, in the quietly affluent seaside town of White Rock, and borrowing his brother's truck, Jeremy drove out to meet her at White Rock's only remaining independently owned coffee shop, the now defunct Java Stop. Arriving early, he sat and read the local paper at a table near the window, the very table the still missing Sukhvinder Rai had once sat at admiring her recently installed, improperly administered, soon to be infected navel ring. Initially, Sukhvinder thought it made her look a little too much like a slut, or at the very least part of some white rapper's entourage on Much, but then her friend Michelle, secretly pierced and slightly infected herself, immediately assured her that it did not. Still, Sukhvinder hid the ring from her parents for months, until finally, shockingly unveiling it for all and sundry at her eighteenth birthday party with the aid of a midriff-bearing tank top. After the party, her father took her aside and hit her hard in the face, then hit her hard again, after which he apologized profusely, and neither one broached the subject again.

Nothing much seemed to be happening in this little part of the world, or so at least the editorial department of the local newspaper had evidently surmised. The feature story, in conjunction with a large, colour, front-page photograph of the woodland in

question, endeavoured to engage the reader with the various pros
and cons of building a brand new skateboard park therein. Jeremy
was bored enough. Outside, across the way, an Asian convenience
store merchant was busy rearranging his considerable flower stock,
while white upper-middleclass girls, counselled repeatedly in
recent days about becoming just another Sukhvinder Rai, strolled
by on their way down to the beach, or else up to the mall, and of
course the Starbucks there on the corner, the economic linchpin
of it all. Jeremy was still staring out the window of the Java Stop
when Ms. Henderson arrived fifteen minutes late. He had been
getting a little concerned about the time as he had, of course, this
forklift course to attend. Robert had placed a call to his friend
Joan in Human Resources at Moore-Mathers, the fish feed mill
he had worked at sporadically while attending university, and
where he was now, since being forced into stress leave from his
teaching job, with the exception of a little injury time, seemingly
gainfully employed once again. Joan herself promptly contacted
Jeremy with his starting date (Thursday), starting time (six o'clock
in the morning), starting wage (thirteen dollars an hour, cranking
up to fourteen with the successful completion of his forklift training), equipment requirements (steel-toed boots) and an agreement
that he would undergo a full physical and drug test at some future
as yet unspecified date. Out of curiosity, Jeremy asked which drugs
they were concerned about, and Joan said all of them, though for
this mill in particular, located as it was out here in Vancouver, marijuana remained of course the primary offender.

"How's the army treating you?" inquired a voice at one point
prior to Val Henderson's arrival, raising Jeremy from his window-
rooted stupor. He turned to find an old, weathered, grey-haired
Negro addressing him from across the room.

"Sorry?"

"The army, how's it treating you?"

"But I'm not in the army," said Jeremy, almost apologetically.

The old Negro studied Jeremy more closely, his confusion
mounting steadily. "Well aren't you the boy from the paper? The
one who fell out of that plane?"

"Oh, that. No, that's my brother. You're thinking of my brother," Jeremy said too cheerily, pleased to be relieved of the burden of someone else's senility. "And he jumped by the way."

"What's that you say?"

"I said he jumped. He didn't fall. He *jumped* out of the plane."

"Yes, yes," the old Negro said as though, for him, at his age, jumping and falling amounted to virtually the same thing. "When I saw you come in here I thought for sure you were the boy who fell out of that plane."

"Well there you go," said Jeremy, trying to assure with his tone that it was a mistake anyone could make, not just the elderly.

"Well I'll be damned. And here I was going to offer to buy you some banana bread." The old man indicated the empty dish before him. "Y'ever tried the banana bread here? Delicious. Absolutely delicious." He paused reflectively, returning his attention to the dish as though it posed a small but intriguing problem in itself. "So tell me, how is he?" he asked eventually.

"My brother? Oh he's okay. Improving rapidly, as they say. Miracle he's alive though hey," Jeremy added quickly, so as not to seem any less impressed by the incident than the old man was. Which he was not, by the way.

The old Negro thought hard about that, mumbling through withered lips, "It is that . . . It is that," or else something similar to that, following up in good time with a more spirited, "Well you give him my best, okay? You tell him to get right back at it."

"Will do," Jeremy said, turning to stare once again out the window, trying to seem captivated by everything that was there and nothing that was not, hoping to convey in just this way that he too was worthy of a slice of banana bread from an African American admirer, if and when one or both were made available.

"Jeremy Jacks!" cried a voice at last that could only have belonged to Val Henderson, Literary Agent. Jeremy turned to find sailing towards him a robust lady of about sixty, her dealing hand decisively outstretched, before she obviously reconsidered and reached up for something suggestive of a hug instead. Disengaging himself, Jeremy offered to buy her a coffee, but she would not hear of it and thus sailed on up to the counter herself, eventually returning with a ridiculously large green tea in a partially recycled paper cup.

"Jeremy Jacks," she said again, this time, however, much less breathlessly, instead lifting up and weighing each syllable separately, lest, in her initial sweep, she had somehow missed some hidden opportunity well worth flogging in some way. "So we finally meet face to face. Well I must say, what a surprise it is having you all the way out here on the left coast. How long are you planning on staying?"

"The summer anyway."

"Have you ever been out this way before?" she smiled provocatively, blinking repeatedly, betraying the fact her thoughts were somewhere else entirely.

"I was born here. I grew up here."

"You were? That's right, you *were*." She shook her head despondently. "My, what an airhead I am. Old age maybe. Alzheimer's undoubtedly. Well sorry I'm a little late," she said, and again shook her head, this time checking the region of her arm where, were she to wear one, her watch surely would have been. "I had to go to the dentist's and, well, you know how *that* can be." She smiled again, just as vividly, and Jeremy smiled too, trying to show by the degree and complexity of his smile that he knew just how ridiculously tardy a dentist's office could be, even though, as a self-published writer, it was of course one of the compensations of his station that it had literally been years since he had last been treated to so much as a proper cleaning. A piece of information, he was sure, plainly visible from her present position.

"Working on anything new I should know about?" she asked eventually.

"Not really. Nothing important anyway."

"Oh it's all important, Jeremy. *All* of it. Now what we need is a really good leap forward from that first book of yours."

"Well that's what I thought we were here to discuss today."

"Yes, that. I've been meaning to speak with you about that." She paused to gather her thoughts, pursing her lips contemplatively. "No one's biting, Jeremy. Not a one unfortunately. And to be honest, I can sort of see why. What we need is something maybe a little more . . . oh I don't know . . . manageable. Something a little less . . ."

"Misogynous?"

"Well, yes, to be quite frank."

"Well it's not misogynous. At least not like the first one was. There's a design to it, believe me, and——"

Val raised a single finger to interrupt. " 'Woman bearing the scars of man's excesses,' was the phrase you used in your query letter, if I remember correctly."

"Yes. Exactly."

"I see," she said, though he could see that she did not.

"No, you clearly don't," he said tidily.

She regarded him intently. And finally: "Well it's simply too ghastly, Jeremy. And graphic. And publishers don't want ghastly and graphic, not since the Nine-Eleven tragedy. Tell me," she said, "did you ever read that book I sent you? That one by Ferguson Henry?"

"Ferguson Henry . . . Oh that one, yes, I did."

"And what did you think?"

"Well I thought it was okay."

She studied him intently again. "Just *okay*?"

"Believe me, that's a ringing endorsement from me these days. I mean it's pretty damned difficult to find anything even remotely——"

"I just got off the phone with him incidentally," she cut in. "Ferguson, I mean. Got to tell him the glorious news that we just sold the Finnish rights to his last book. Yes, exactly, the Finns—sells like gangbusters all over the world except for here at home for some reason. . . . People here just don't get it, do they. Don't get his humour. His *style*." She sighed. "Anyway, paid for my son's braces—the Finns, I mean, not his humour—well indirectly, I guess. . . . Regardless, you know what I mean. Of course it's not really my son who needed braces—he's my godson—the real parents, well, that's a different story altogether. Speaking of stories, have you read his latest?"

"Whose?"

"Ferguson's?"

"Ferguson," Jeremy said. "My how that name does come up."

"*Be Positive*? Yes, just the letter 'B' with a little addition sign beside it. Clever, though, don't you think? Incidentally, that's his blood type. B Positive. Tell me, what type are you?"

"Me? A Negative, I'd think."

"Ha! Funny! See, that's what I'm talking about. Humour. Wit. *Comedy*. Black, yes, but comedy nonetheless. And incidentally, you should find out your blood type too, and then you should read this book. I tell you it's a real laugh. A lark. Turns his keen cutting wit on the entire self-help genre," she quite obviously quoted straight from the back of Ferguson's keen cutting book itself. "God, he's a riot!" she laughed at the ceiling. "People here just don't get what a riot he is. Check it out." She opened her bag and extracted, what else, but a copy of *B+*, the cover of which featured a man in suit and tie sporting, in lieu of a head, a bloody looking exclamation mark. "Yeah, terrible cover," she admitted with a sad cluck.

Jeremy turned the book over and read, right up near the top, 'With his enormous gift for satire, [Henry] turns his keen cutting wit and shrewd ironic eye on the entire Self-Help genre.' "What's the cover supposed to mean?" he asked, returning the book, eager to revisit his own misfortunes as a writer, topped up already on Ferguson's latest international triumph albeit curiously domestic debacle.

"Lord knows," she said, closely examining the spine of the book before absentmindedly flipping through. Eventually she placed it aside. "So you're not working on anything new?"

"Nothing literary, no."

"Well what are you waiting for? Get cracking! Ferguson here," she declared, tapping *B+* with a blackberry fingernail, "has a rule that you should always be one book ahead. You know, that you should always have one in the can when you have one out there in circulation."

They talked some more about literature in general, and Ferguson Henry in particular, until Jeremy explained that he should probably be going as he didn't want to be late for forklift school. He need not have worried. Recently installed in an old commercial building in Whalley, Greater Vancouver's unofficial second skid row, located just up the road from Royal Heights but even further down King George Highway than Queen Elizabeth Secondary (where, prior to his suspension, Robert had taught physical education to slothful obese teenagers displaying little or no interest in all but the original physical activity), the school, or what passed for the forklift school, was simply not conducive to punctuality in any way. 'Rent-a-wreck alley,' the immediate, vaguely delineated vicinity was referred to by those in the know, where, on this fine morning, with the summer sun out and the distant blue mountains sharply defined against a brighter blue sky, Jeremy was treated to an obscure run of third class, twenty-dollar hookers and their hazy, heroin-addicted associates, each of which, as Jeremy passed, measured him with a shrewd ironic eye worthy perhaps of even the talented and prolific, yet domestically misunderstood, Ferguson Henry himself.

POSTED BY LUCY @ 5:05:19 P.M. 4/8/2007   2 COMMENTS

Friday, July 14, 1972

Dear Mom & Dad:

Received your short letter today (from Tues night). I'm sorry there's been no word on the vinyl yet—that always seems to happen when you want something ordered in a hurry, I find. But I'm sure you two know all about that after almost thirty years in business, right? I've been sort of wondering too . . . I haven't heard from my roommate Tracey yet, or for that matter, Ruth. The latter is supposed to be leaving for Edmonton on the 19th I think, but I'm not exactly sure.

I know what you mean about the "no Sunday night phone call," but it's nice to get back into letter writing—one has more time to think of what to say, and it's so much more economical—let's hope I keep it up when I come out anyway.

The address is 4052 South now—I think I mentioned that in my last letter—so keep those letters coming! I'd appreciate if you could pay my medical premium, and I shall reimburse you in October—would that be okay? I still don't think I have to pay any more than $16.^{50}, but we shall know for certain when I finally get my income tax squared away. I think it has something to do with taxable income, whether one is responsible for the whole shot or not. . . . Speaking of (non)taxable income, if I keep weaving at my present rate (and I'm sure I can crank it up a little yet) I shall have made about $4000 tax-free by the end of the experiment. That'll be nice, eh?

Received a Valentine from Doug in Vietnam today, five months late admittedly, but it lifted my spirits anyway.

(outside)	*(inside)*
Valentine,	Then,
Let's have a mad,	after a few months,
gay love affair!	we'll get together and compare notes.

Quite a propos, n'est-ce pas? Anyway, it looks as though he'll be shipped home some time next week, if not sooner, if his February prognosis here turns out to be accurate at all. Not a moment too soon either, as far as I'm concerned. He's witnessed some awful things over there—one need only turn on the nightly news to get a feel for what they're going through—and I hope the transition back to our western brand of lifestyle doesn't prove too difficult, as it seems to have been for some of his mates south of the border.

There were rumours that we were going to start smoking tonight, but nothing materialized, so either the other side is the experimental and we're the control, or they just want to study us for another week or so. It's funny, but now that we're into the weaving on such a grand scale, we're not really looking forward to the grass, because that which they call "government approved" (that which is grown for experimental purposes and the like) is *very* potent—not harmful, mind you, but not like you'd normally buy on the street either—so I suppose it isn't really a "normal" situation at all. Actually, one of the things they're looking to research here is whether the THC (the "drug" of the hemp plant) can be detected in the blood or urine—sort of like a breathalyser for alcohol—so that if it ever gets legalized (word is, that could happen as early as next year, depending on the outcome of our little experiment here) the amount of "stoned-ness" could be tested. I suppose that would be necessary for control of sale and use, just like alcohol. It's quite strange to think of myself as a human guinea pig . . . but just think of what I'll be able to tell my grand-kids, eh?

Saturday July 15/72

Got up at six this morning, got off a good one, and all in all enjoyed a very good day of weaving ever since. Tracey *finally* sent along a letter, along with my driver's licence, telephone bill (for me to figure out who owes what) and the new Elégance magazine, which was a nice surprise.

Taking more time in my day to read, play guitar, write, etc now that the belt production is under control. It's quite a relaxed situation really, and I hope to begin sketching again at some point. My new magazine should prove inspirational on that front.

I've been thinking I would like to see G & J again soon. . . . We'll see how things turn out in October. That much travelling, right after being in complete isolation for so long, might prove a bit taxing to say the least, let alone where they'll be at by that point. I might as well tell you they're not getting on so well, but that's all I really know. Ginny won't tell me much else. They've spent a couple of days apart, trying to sort things out, so we'll have to wait and see, I suppose. I sure feel sorry for that J Jr. though. These sorts of things are terribly difficult on children—this we know. Anyway, cross your fingers.

Lots of love, B

P.S. I shall remind Tracey of the vinyl when I write, okay?

JULY, 2002

"So how's that brother of yours doing?" Jon asked softly, slowly, approaching his quarry warily, as though any sudden movement might cause it to jump, throw the hook, and bolt away entirely. As a gesture of fatherhood, this approach had always appealed to Jeremy.

"Robby? Ask him yourself," he went ahead and answered anyway. He did not feel much like talking, other than to himself that is, but thinking such conduct might be perceived as rude, further immersed himself in his section of the morning paper instead.

Meanwhile, Jon had managed to process this response in his usual admirable way—that is, by taking little or no notice of what was said. And so, as a substitute for conversation, he returned to his own section of the newspaper, and then a little later on a new one, this one as yet unmolested by his progeny. Finally, serious and haggard, he said as though to the paper, "I sure wish I knew what the hell was going on with that kid."

Jeremy stepped grudgingly into the breach. "You do, do you," he sighed. "Well we've been wondering the same thing about you, hey."

"Sorry?" said Jon, glancing up, eager to be engaged. His expression extended a temperate glow, its draught adjusted to exactly the right range.

"You heard me," said Jeremy, speaking with the calm authority of a son who believes, however erroneously, that he is long past the point of growing older and wiser in the ways of the world than his father. "Or wait, maybe you didn't. Maybe you ought to have your hearing aides in."

Jeremy looked up, as casually as possible, to see if his father had taken this as hard as intended. Slowly, Jon placed his paper flat on the table. His expression never changed quickly. In fact, it seemed to Jeremy a considerable undertaking to rearrange those sunstained cheeks and stiff grey eyebrows into anything not resembling a conventional, if somewhat satirical, seaman's scowl.

"What's on your mind, son." Saying this, Jon allowed his flat blue eyes to gravitate to the window and out over the great gulf of ravine beyond. His mind, ever in search of the farther shore, showed its intensity in slow-running currents and eddies across his brow. Despite his best efforts not to, Jon held a grudging, long-lasting respect, bordering on jealousy, for the residents of that other country there. The reason was as simple as it was painful: when he had first applied for a mortgage some forty-odd years before, his annual fishing income had failed to qualify him for those slightly more desirable (if for no other reason than they were slightly more expensive) homes being built on the southern side of the gully. Failed to qualify him by fifty dollars a month, that is. And so it was that, in the years that followed, now and again and seemingly at random, he took great joy in tipping the scales a little, mostly by way of cutting down various old-growth trees that had, as seedlings, experienced the great misfortune of alighting in areas that would one day be subject to Jon Jacks' continuously shifting property lines. In the wake of this activity, the protests raised by the neighbours were all the expected ones—destruction of beauty, of shade, of habitat—even the issue of the embankment's ever-increasing destabilization was brought up from time to time. A chainsaw, if nothing else, remains to this day a great leveller in the ongoing struggle between the classes, I find.

"Tell me, what's on your mind?"

"Oh," said Jeremy, "I've just been wondering when it is you plan on acting your age, that's all."

A briny smile washed up on his father's face, revealing, behind it, that veritable levee of preposterously white teeth. "Come again?" he said, blowing and wiping his nose in a mechanical back-and-forth fashion. Jeremy winced. Since his return out west, he found himself increasingly agitated with the workings of his father's body, in particular the increasing amounts of time the old man spent defiling the one washroom with a shower, and the increasingly dreadful state he subsequently left that washroom in, not to mention the increasingly painful-sounding grunts and groans he was apt to emit therein, the unwitting witness of which Jeremy frequently found himself via the house's simple, but surprisingly effective, network of air ducts and heat vents.

"Bob File says any more fuck-ups and you're going to wind up in jail. Tell me, does the prospect of extended incarceration bother you, Dad? Because that's sure as hell where you're headed here." He had been meaning to broach the subject for quite some time, but due to his continuous shirking of domestic responsibilities, yet another in a long list of inherited characteristics, the appropriate moment had simply not presented itself till now.

"Not in the slightest," said his father. "Not for a worthy cause anyway."

"Oh and what worthy cause is that, Dad? The right to pay one's parking fee to a real, live, honest-to-goodness person, to hell with advances in efficiency and technology? Christ, let it go. You're retired. Let someone else fight the good pay-parking fight now."

Jon looked at him, leadenly, his good humour lashed down. Then, gradually, he began to smile, shook himself from stem to stern, and heaved up out of his chair with a creaking groan.

"Perhaps one day, preferably one in the not too distant future so that, God willing, he'll still be around to witness the blessed point of departure, you will begin to appreciate what little effect your relentless sarcasm has on your father. And—"

"But—"

"And I'll tell you this, Jeremy," Jon continued. "The fact I happened to get pinned with it doesn't necessarily mean I'm guilty of having committed the crime."

In his character of resident critic, Jeremy brought his hands together with one resounding clap. "My, how Kafkaesque," he spat. "Ever the incurable romantic, eh? Well I wouldn't know anything about that."

Jon blinked steadily. "No you wouldn't, would you," he said. "But I'm thinking your brother might."

Now I do not wish to come across as a liar, or as any more of a liar than I admittedly already am, but when one strives to be entertaining, or at the very least engagingly droll, one does feel the need to stretch the truth from time to time. For instance, I have not to this point been completely honest in my portrayal of Jon Jacks, not as honest as I possibly could have been, and probably should have been, had certain extenuating circumstances already come to light, and am therefore running the risk of painting an overly fragile impression of not only Jon himself, but by extension the entire clan de Jacks. Hence, it should probably be noted that, the ebb and flow of the present philosophical conversation aside, at this very early stage of the experiment Jon could not have been more pleased with either his situation or himself. Not only were his two sons back home, living under one roof, but both were about to be engaged in blue collar labour for which he had long held the utmost respect. He may have spent over half his life at work on the ocean, but Jon Jacks was salt of the earth through and through. Not that he decried an education—after all, he had wept openly at each of his son's respective university graduations—but simply that, in his experience, an honest day's labour was often the only strain of labour that warranted an honest day's wage in this world.

Which brings us, by way of segue, back to the subject of forklift school. Forklift school was by no means difficult. At least the theory portion of it was not. All told, Jeremy and two other suckers spent some four hours in the classroom watching videos, staring at overheads, enduring mandatory smoke breaks, and listening intermittently to what one would have to presume was intended, with no real evidence to the contrary, as the lecture, prior to writing a conspicuously simple, seemingly fail-proof twenty question quiz, before proceeding out to the yard to try their hand at the actual contraption itself. This practical portion of the course lasted all of twenty minutes. One assumes the instructor only wanted to get out of that part of town before dark, a sentiment shared, to be sure, by all three undergraduates themselves. For his part, Jeremy had only to demonstrate that he could indeed negotiate an obstacle course of five widely-spaced pylons in both forward and reverse, followed by the careful restacking of two wooden pallets (there was supposed to be more pallets, in fact a whole stack of pallets, but they had unfortunately been stolen a few weeks before) to fulfill this practical requirement, before he was handed his laminated card verifying that he was indeed certified to operate a Class-5 SDCB/IC truck, whatever the heck that was.

The following day, in keeping with the theme, the brothers ventured down the ravine to assess the site where Robert's daughter's tree fort was to be located. Robert had finally, grudgingly, gotten onboard with the idea, if for no other reason than, knowing his brother was involved, he wanted to see the project through to its completion. And so, after painstakingly clearing and roping a path to the site, the base of the multi-trunked maple some twenty meters down the embankment, employing an assortment of cedar and spruce en route as intermittent stations of support, they cleared the area of brush and all the rotting residual debris from their last aborted experiment of this sort. Jon chose not to make the initial expedition down, but by no means was he less involved in the affair. With customary Jacks protocol, he stood atop the jetty overhanging the ravine and shouted down suggestions to the general vicinity of his sons. Some of these suggestions they eventually accepted, while others they promptly discarded, with the remaining few being bandied about between the brothers under the incessant drone of their father's subsequent instructional bombardments.

It appeared, according to the initial crude sketches Jon and Jeremy had made, that they would need to dig at least two meters into the steep bank of the ravine and therein construct a retaining wall of considerable strength. Not only would this cleared and buttressed space provide a suitably level stage for work, but it would also afford the necessary depth in order to make the project worthwhile in the first place. Twenty meters or so below the site, running left to right, east to west, along the floor of the ravine, the stream meandered its way around boulders and under logs on its way to draining into the distant Fraser River. They did not go down to the base of the ravine. They did not want to go there. And anyway, there would be plenty of time to go down to the stream at the base of the ravine later on in the summer.

Sun, July 16/72

Dear Mom & Dad:

Very long, tiring, but for the most part satisfying day. Seem to be over the whole sore back and stuffed bowels thing anyway. Still, I ordered some liniment and a natural laxative from Stan (the shopping man) for tomorrow—

HE: Liniment? What's liniment?

ME: You know, ointment. Cream. *Salve.*

HE: Like a balm, you mean?

ME: Yes, like a balm. Not a smelly one though. Make sure it doesn't smell, Stan.

—as the Olympic theme grinds into yet another gear. To wit: we've decided, if we're going to be sitting on our backsides for the next twelve weeks, that we're definitely going to have a leg exercise class in the mornings. When we do get out, we'll of course have obstacles like stairs and subways to contend with, and nothing makes your legs more rubbery than not actually using the damned things.

We have great giggles at the thought of looking like a group of slightly paraplegic, very pudding-complexioned idiots with "weaver's disease" (a back and forth, up and down motion of the hands that continues even in sleep) when we come out. All kidding aside, we'll have a few "new" challenges to cope with, mainly in the way of crowds, telephones, and (gasp!) washing one's own dishes.

Monday, July 17/72

News flash! At lunchtime today, conceptual gymnast Dr. Congreves vaulted into the fishbowl to announce in his carefully modulated voice that, as of that very moment, we could purchase marijuana cigarettes at $.50 each, and that we'd also be required to smoke some later on in the day. This news was met with a variety of reactions, including trepidation and outright fear, but in the end nine of ten had slowly but surely made their way up to the nursing station to receive their first dose of "medication," as it were. You guessed it: Birdie stayed behind on the couch and kept weaving, partly because she was hung up on her belt production for the day, and partly, I suppose, because of that trusty Cormack reserve shining through yet again. I figured I'd sit and watch the others, and wait until the mandatory 8:15 group smoke to try it for myself.

This means we're starting off as the experimental side. Rumour has it that very mild joints can be purchased on the other side, but that they don't *have* to smoke yet. Presumably this will change around from side to side as the experiment progresses.

At 8:15 PM came the gathering of the clan in the big lounge, complete with two nurses, one attendant, and much pulse-taking. We finished two joints by about 9:45, at which point everyone got a little hungry, and out came the oranges and bananas, toast and jam, after which I readied myself for bed, and fell asleep by 10:30 precisely. I sure couldn't weave, I'll tell you that.

July 18, 1972

Up at six this morning, took a good crap, and wove thirteen belts with comparative ease after that. I felt no hangover (one never does with marijuana) but some of the girls just slept and slept and slept! But then they also stayed up until 3 or 4 AM following the session, some weaving (with varying degrees of success) and some just watching cable TV.

The evening smoke starts at 8:15 PM, but everyone must be assembled at 8:00 for pulses. Also, bring whatever you want for the next hour and a half because you can't leave the lounge area at all. Tonight I shall shower and get ready for bed first, so that I can just crawl into bed afterwards and get up early in the morning. Our schedules are certainly going to change, I can see that already.

July 19, 1972

Up at 5 today, and out weaving by 5:30 AM. No hangover effects— I feel fine!—and the craps are coming along rather consistently as well—knock on wood for that. A total of seventeen belts today, followed by our goodnight smoke at 8:15, then off to bed by 10.

July 20, 1972

Up at 4 AM, which is the earliest I'm going to get up—ever! Thought I was over the whole aching back syndrome, but I'm actually pretty stiff this morning. No early morning "movement," that's my problem. Anyway, finished weaving at 7:30 this evening, made the usual bedtime preparations, then picked up a letter from Tracey at the nursing station. Also the new Vogue magazine.

Our group is getting along quite nicely now as we get to know one another a little better. I forgot to mention one other bombshell that hit us last week. On Saturday evening, Maria and Misty, having made the move with me the previous Tuesday, were switched back to Ward B in exchange for Evie and Barbara, part of my original group. Well there went my two weaving companions, so I certainly had mixed feelings about that. Evie is such a cheerful, bubbly girl, and everyone loves her, but Barbara, on the other hand, never stops talking. Such a tedious way to spend one's day, listening to her! Would you believe I now wear earplugs?

Big belt number for the day, eighteen—that's $45.^{00}—so you can appreciate that my bank account is flourishing nicely. Weaver's disease took a turn for the worse though.

Friday, July 21, 1972

Up at 4:30 this morning, received your letters from July 16th and 18th—I'm glad the whole vinyl thing has finally been squared away—also Ginny's from the 16th. Nice to get mail, even if G's was a little depressing. Evidently (and you didn't hear this from me) she's thinking of getting out of D.M.A.W. for a while. Nothing permanent, mind you, she just feels as though she needs a break, even if just a little one. Those old Sierra Club friends of J's, as wonderful and energetic and forward-thinking as they obviously are, can be very demanding at times—I saw that much when I was out west a month ago. Sometimes I think my sister is raising two boys, not just one, and believe me that J Jr.'s a handful all on his own. Anyway, I'd tell you to contact her and inquire for yourself, but then Jonathan might overhear or something, and there'd be hell to pay for sure.

On a lighter note, I wove ten belts this morning before quitting at eleven o'clock. I'm going to take some time this afternoon to write—my first day off!

Saturday, July 22, 1972

Going to write Ginny, Doug, Tracey, Michael Beauchemin (Montreal Theatre Michael—you remember him—double-jointed dude that went on that ridiculous "hunger strike for peace" that one time) and a host of others either tonight or tomorrow, after I finish this letter to you.

Finally tracked down my OHSIP notice, and I'm filing for assistance for '72, based on total projected taxable earnings for the year. My A.R.F. money is strictly under the table, or over the counter, as it were, so with the new basic $1500 tax allowance I'm sure I qualify, as my '72 earnings—at least those earnings the government will be aware of—will only be from January through June.

Your Peterborough purchases sound great. I'm so glad you got brown—I'm sure it looks fabulous. I'm planning a bit of a wardrobe overhaul myself when I get out of the fishbowl, that's for sure. By the way, is there anything in Peterborough in the way of suits to look at? I think Dad would really like some of the knits—they're *extremely* comfortable, keep their shape well and, in most cases, are available at the same price as the worsteds. Think about it anyway, okay?

I presume the gift show is high on your list of things to do today. Don't go all hog-wild in Hogtown now. Take it easy. I don't want you folks getting all prosperous on me while I'm not around to reap the harvest.

July 23, 1972

Between the two wards there are a total of six different shifts of staff (three per day per side), and since they change wards every two weeks, I've of course met them all in their travels. They're all very cooperative and nice to us, and do their best to put up with our various shenanigans. Apparently this is the best experiment yet—the atmosphere and social activity is 100% better than the previous one—something to be said for girls, I guess. I must say, we do get along amazingly well, although I wouldn't have believed it myself, at first.

July 24, 1972

Nothing new to report. Bowels are great. Enclosed are a couple of belt samples to give you an idea of what I'm up to in this god-forsaken place.

Love, Birdie

Cuckoo's Nest
The Combine
Monday, July 24/72

Dear Ginny:

'What is that feeling when you're driving away from people and they recede on the plain till you see their specks dispersing? It's the too-huge world vaulting us, and it's good-by. But we lean forward to the next crazy venture beneath the skies.'

~ Kerouac

HAPPY 16TH ANNIVERSARY! (Well, in six days anyway). I thought a little Jack K might be just the thing to start your next crazy year off the right way. Sorry I can't "vault" back out to pick out the new yacht, but as you've always been so fond of telling your little sister, "we must have our priorities now, mustn't we?"

We've gone through 101 changes since my last letter of July 10th—where shall I begin? Tuesday, lunchtime, the always preoccupied Dr. Congreves announced that five of us would be switching with five from the other side. What the fuck?! Nonetheless, Misty, Maria, Connie, Anne and I were to be moved and installed in Ward A by 3:30 that afternoon. What followed was a great drunken farewell party, replete with silent tears of sadness and spoken promises of lifelong friendships never to be broken yada yada yada as we moved through the magic portal to Ward A—or, in other words, ten women trying desperately, yet ineffectively, to say goodbye to one another. But what a *difference*. Although the two wards are physically identical, all likeness ends there. It seems cold, sombre—no spirit, you know? Which is rather ironic, as they had these two neat Wicca chicks roaming about in here. Too bad they had to leave just when I arrived, huh? What an evil trio we'd have made! Anyway, we new arrivals revamped the atmosphere soon enough, and I must say, I'm glad to be back in cahoots with the lovely Lorna again. Things are quite patched up between the two of us, but I was sure wondering for a while there, no question.

On Saturday, July 15th, ol' Congreves announced yet another switch: Misty and Maria back to Ward B, and Evie and Barbara over to Ward A. The former were my two weaving and slumber party compadres, and of the latter two, Barbara, for whatever reason—maybe it's the shoes—reminds me of several tough young hard-ons I messed around with in high school. Alas, we Bobcaygeon Cormacks will survive anything, I guess.

On Monday, July 17th, nodding and mumbling to himself as though Dr. Myles (I've just found out it's spelled with a 'y' and not an 'i') had installed a one-way radio inside his head, Congreves came to speak with us at lunchtime. "Ladies," he said, clearing his throat, "you will be happy to know that, as of noon today, at your own discretion, you will be allowed to purchase cigarettes containing marijuana at fifty cents each from the nursing station. Please bear in mind, though, that you will be *required* to smoke this evening." Of course this was met by great howls and shouts of glee, as nine of ten went parading up to the desk to slap down their money expectantly.

You guessed it: Lorna stayed behind on the couch and continued weaving. Partly because she was, in her words, hung up on her "belt production" for the day (now how lame is *that*) and also, of course, that trusty Truscott reserve shining through yet again. She figured she'd sit and observe the others, and wait until the mandatory 8:15 group smoke to try it for herself—or so at least she told me through a thick grey cloud of my own leafy exhaust. By the way, ARF weed is known high and wide as the most potent smoke on the planet, so you can see why I literally burned holes in the floor trying to be the first in line.

Ah yes, the group smoke . . . Is there nothing pot can't do? At 8:15 PM precisely, with the gathering of the clan in the big lounge, complete with one attendant, two nurses, and one Stan the Shopping Man (that's a one-two-one, for those of you scoring at home), general bedlam and much pulse-taking ensued. Two *massive* joints were literally reduced to ashes by about 9:45, followed, naturally, by an acute attack of the hungries in which all sorts of goodies were consumed, from roast beef sandwiches to Dad's Cookies to chocolate bars to beer—ah, the sacrifices we all must make for science—before I decreed that Stan should wheelbarrow race me to bed, where I would fall asleep instantly, snoring profusely, my head propped high atop his oddly comfortable hunchback. Needless to say, my routine and schedule have now changed dramatically. I get up at 4 AM, take a shit, start weaving at 4:30 or so, then work straight through till 7:30 in the evening, take a shower, throw on my nightgown, and make my way into the lounge for the smoky warp of the evening toke at 8:15 precisely. The two joints, each about the size of a lipstick tube and packed tighter than hell, are *very potent*. Did that underscore hit home? Good. We're even afforded roach clips by the excellent staff so that we can smoke them right down to the bitter end! The mind *boggles*. It's such reverse psychology—the fact that you *have* to smoke, that you *must* smoke—it's a plot, I'm sure. Or perhaps we've all been selected for "the cure." Whatever the case, when we finally do get out, I'll probably never touch grass again. Yeah, sure.

Unlike letter and/or journal writing, essentially standardized and dignified mediums, a marijuana stone will vary with different people, different crops of grass, and different situations. One typically experiences a lightness of the head, slight dizziness, coordination problems, as well as changes in hearing, vision and balance. These changes may include extremely acute and overdeveloped senses, or conversely, senses that feel dull and narrowed, depending on each experience. Oftentimes you'll laugh at anything, till the muscles in your cheeks literally ache. You may also be feeling blue before you start, and finish up feeling more so by the end.

I suppose one of the most noticeable changes is in your perception of time, which seems to stop dead. You can sit and watch a feature-length film of memories and incidents flash through your brain, and then look at the clock and find that, in actuality, only a minute or two has elapsed. In this way, then, a grass stone is very much like dreaming while awake.

These and other reactions vary according to the intensity of the grass, and of course the amount you smoke. Let me put it this way: the ARF joint is equivalent to about four of the kind you'd normally smoke in Vancouver, so I've never been anywhere even *close* to this stoned before. Fuck me!

Still, my belt production continues steadily. I'm up to twenty per day, but it's a long hard struggle, to say the least. In keeping with the theme, though, time passes very quickly. (The doors of perception are wide open, baby!) Up at 4 AM, weave till 7:30 PM, smoke from 8:15 to 9:30 or so, then more or less straight to bed, do not pass GO, but remember to collect your 200 bucks anyway!

The new orange chesterfield you bought sounds absolutely *wonderful*. I can hardly wait to see it. And where are you going to put it? Under the big front window, I take it? Now, as for the backyard "dropping into the ravine," as you say, I wouldn't worry too much about that—that house of yours will still be standing long after you and I have reached our final resting places in this world. Besides, a little erosion is nothing to worry about—gravity will take its toll—believe me, I can see the initial effects of it in the mirror already, and I'm only twenty-two years old!

I'm glad you're willing to work through this trying time with J. He really needs you, what with everything that's happening now with the Committee, not to mention that son of yours. I mean where would sons be without their mothers, Ginny? Men need their women. They need the balance, the equilibrium, otherwise they all end up like some horrible Hemingway caricature, despising all womankind, or else abusing us in some weird way (but then Hem's mother, when he was a child, did dress him up like a

girl . . . but I digress). Anyway, I've enclosed two little reject samples to give you some idea of how I'm making my millions—
apart from stepping through the looking glass, that is.

Would you believe I'm not bored yet? Write soon though, if
you don't mind, as all Mom and Dad can seem to come up with
are questions and comments about vinyl—yikes. Plus it sure is
nice getting news from the Shire, so keep those cards and letters
rolling, okay?

Love, Birdie

July, 2002

Sitting in his brother's old bedroom (having been rather opti-
mistically referred to in the interim as the 'reading room'), amid
the collection of books he had long ago cut his literary teeth on,
one of which, *1984* by George Orwell, Sukhvinder Rai had once
successfully plagiarized a book report on, Jeremy contemplated
the cultivation of some sort of radical facial hair design.

"Hey fag," interrupted his brother. "What's going on?"

"I was just trying to hook up this old computer here to the
internet."

"Can't. Tried. No modem. And no modem, no porn unfortunately."

"Oh," said Jeremy, disappointed for not having recognized as
much himself already. And so he returned to the heady subject of
his beard for a time.

"How about all these old books, huh?" Robert said, gazing
about abstractly, touching one volume then another with the
abraded toe of his slipper. Suddenly he frowned, and the toe of his
footwear in turn flopped down. "Say, I was at Chapters the other
day and they didn't even have your book. Check this out though."
He rummaged through the considerable paraphernalia atop the
desk, eventually emerging with a small scrap of paper that read
'Donald Jack' and 'Lisa Jackson' in his distinctive chaotic script.
"Yours should've been right between these two hacks hey, but
when I asked, they said they'd never heard of it. Said they could

maybe order it for me if I wanted, so I of course told them to go fuck themselves. Yeah, I did," he insisted. "Quite rightly, too, I might add. Here they got this Donald guy pumping out volume six of God knows what pap, and this Lisa chick punching out her own brand of murder mystery crap, and they don't even have the decency to carry one of their own? I mean really, how fucked up is that?"

"Pretty fucked up," Jeremy granted, not bothering to explain how that particular chain of bookstores did not actually carry his book in stock.

"Anyway, how was work last night?" his brother asked, mimicking, for no discernable reason, a long graceful golf stroke to nowhere, the very idea of which seemed absurd to Jeremy, for to his knowledge Robert had quite rightly never golfed a stroke in his life.

"Fine. Fun. Actually, tons of fun. Still, the initial romantic sheen's begun to wear off, so now it's just packaging fish feed unfortunately."

"Seriously though."

"Seriously? It stinks, Robby—like fish. The whole place stinks like fish. I actually don't know how anybody can stand it."

"Yeah ain't it grand? But you know, besides that," Robert said.

"Well I do find I'm spitting a lot. And swearing. Actually I can't believe how much I spit and swear there. And you know what else I can't believe? That they actually require a fucking *drug* test to work there."

"Yeah, well, you don't worry about that. I can set you up to pass that. So what'd you do then, Japan or Bulk?"

"Bulk," Jeremy said. "All night."

"Bulk, hey. That's all right."

"Not really. Had to change screens twice."

"Ouch. Well who'd you work with then?" Robert asked.

"Uh . . . Evan. And James. And some other dude I can't quite remember his name."

"What'd he look like?"

"To be honest, like a Mexican Meat Loaf. Minus the—"

"That'd be Ben," Robert reasoned. "Definitely Ben. Watch out, though, that Evan's a woman. James is all right, but watch out for that Evan—total, complete woman. American too incidentally—don't know if anyone's mentioned that yet. Got this guy Marcello fired just for showing up stoned at work."

"The woman," Jeremy scowled facetiously. "What a woman Evan is."

"I'm serious," Robert said. "Guy's a jerk. James, though, he's all right."

"James, good; Evan, woman—got it," Jeremy said. "And Ben?"

"Ben's a blast. Though he does have that annoying habit of manicuring himself with an Exacto knife."

"I noticed that."

"Sort of disturbing how short he gets them, hey. Right down to the quick where they start to bleed and crap."

"Well I didn't notice *that*."

"Calls it a Muslim pilot's licence, hey. The knife."

"That's funny."

"Yeah, that's all right. . . . Anyway, get to ride the forklift at all?"

"Not once. Got to ride the supervisor a little though."

"Ah it's always like that for new guys," Robert said, chalking up his brother's long night of non-forklifting, and hence his long night of heavy lifting, bagging and tying, to some sort of fishy conscript status. "So hey, you coming out to help or what? Dad says he's coming down today. Or wait, are you quitting already."

"Tell me, Robert," said Jeremy, ignoring both question and criticism, posing some of his own instead. "Have you ever wondered what it might be like to belong to a family that becomes gradually more established one generation to the next?"

"What do you mean."

"I mean why are you even *at* this place. It's disgusting."

"What, the mill? Ballast, I guess. . . . Plus I needed the extra cash. You know, to buy some things."

"*Ah*. Like Dad's hearing aides," Jeremy said. "Though you realize of course he never actually wears them."

"Almost never," his brother corrected.

"That's because he doesn't listen, Robby. He can *hear*, he just doesn't *listen*. There's a difference."

"Yeah about four thousand dollars worth," Robert admitted. "So hey, you coming down the ravine or what."

"Later, yeah. But I have to go see Jonathan first."

Robert blinked once, but before he could formulate a reasonable protest, Jeremy had already made his way past.

Once dressed, Jeremy fixed himself some breakfast before asking to borrow his brother's truck. At the last minute Robert decided to come along, although neither brother mentioned where it was they were going to their father of course.

The nondescript suburban house stood halfway down a nondescript suburban street out near the Trans Canada Highway on the outskirts of Langley, from Royal Heights about a half hour's drive due east. Owned and operated by the non-profit Community Living Society, it was indeed a fine house, and big, and had recently undergone, in addition to a spanking new paint job, a complete window and roof replacement, and I always considered it far too lavish a residence for one measly occupant to knock around in. The reason our one measly occupant lived here in this fine old house and not, say, in a brand new prison was due to the fact that he had long ago convinced the powers that be that he was, in a word, insane. Following a lengthy period of imprisonment, under just such false pretences he had for several years inhabited the mental hospital on the other side of the Fraser River, but ever since the government closed the hospital and shifted the majority of its patients into community care, had quite happily made his home alone out here. Well not alone. Not entirely anyway. There were, of course, the four aides assigned to his case, two of which were always working at any given time of day, one of which came out to meet the brothers that morning when they pulled up into the driveway.

"He ain't here," reported the large muscular aide, transferring a greenish-yellow banana to his armpit in order to firmly shake each brother's hand in turn. "He's out on his route."

"His route?"

"His paper route," smiled the aide who, due to various acquired characteristics of his station, reminded Jeremy of his old friend Bob File in a handful of ways.

"Really? That's allowed?" Robert asked.

"Oh sure. Don't worry, though, there's always at least one of us out with him. He never gets out of sight for long."

"Not for long, huh. Well now that's reassuring. And when's he going to be back?" Jeremy went on.

The aide, whose name was Mark, tapped his watch meditatively with the heel of his unpeeled, unripe banana. "Oh not for a while yet. But come on, we'll see if we can't catch him. A man like J.J.'s never too hard to find."

Mark returned inside the house to trade banana for keys, then locked the door and accompanied the brothers out to the end of the driveway where, turning right and walking a fair distance east in the bright midmorning sunshine, he pointed out all the nice, quiet, suburban homes whose altogether nice, quiet, suburban inhabitants had absolutely no idea there was this veritable monster living there.

Eventually Robert asked, "Does he ever, you know, give you any trouble?"

Mark shrugged, "Oh no, nothing unusual. I mean don't get me wrong, he's extremely dishonest and incredibly manipulative—and nuts, the man is definitely nuts—but we have him on the maximum medication allowable under provincial law so no, he's not pulling anything over on anyone here. Most of the time he just sits in his chair. And when he is out and about, we have him on a pretty short leash, you can be sure. We call it the Three Question Rule. Yeah," he said, suddenly interested in what he was saying, "whenever he's around a female—for instance, if we've taken him into the office for some reason, or maybe taken him out to the Red Lobster for dinner—he always gets excited and tends to ask a whole shitload of questions, so we've instituted what we call our Three Question Rule. Typically it's 'How are you?', 'What's your name?', 'What are you doing?' and stuff like that. Nothing too extraordinary, understand. But then every once in a while he gets a little too wound up, a little too aggressive, and before you know it he's scaring the shit out of some poor girl, trying to get her to reveal something personal about herself, some private detail, that he can take home with him to his chair. And he tries to touch them, hey. Any female, any girl, he's forever trying to touch them. And so of course that's where the boys and I come into the picture."

"And you're always with him?"

"Always at least one of us, sure. Except . . ." Mark started to laugh, struggled to stifle it with a fierce toothy grin, then started to laugh uncontrollably once again.

"What? What's so funny?"

"Oh it's just this one time." Attempting to wave the image off, Mark continued leaking fits of laughter just the same. "When we first got him his paper route," he said. "One of the new guys managed to lose him somewhere, and as you can imagine all hell broke loose—police are out, dogs are out, office is in an absolute panic, I swear. I mean no offence, but that man's a full-on sexual predator, and not someone you want out there alone on the streets somewhere.

"So anyway," Mark continued, "we eventually find him right where we thought we'd find him, down by the schoolyard there." He pointed down the side street to a small, flat, fortress-like elementary school tucked in amid a stand of second-growth firs.

"What was he doing?" Jeremy winced.

"Oh just sitting there, at the bus stop, watching the kids play—they were outside on their recess, hey—but really, all things considered, he was extremely well-behaved."

"Not, you know . . ." Robert made the familiar motion with his hand.

"No, no, nothing like that. Not that time. But you're right, that's something he definitely likes to do. Definitely a big part of his Master Plan. His turn-ons are carbon copies of his fears, see, and, well, if you'll pardon the expression, 'jacks' is how we refer to the practice around here. Take this one time." Here Mark began to chuckle again, quietly, under his breath, and Jeremy was about to ask what the hell he was laughing at now, but before he could, Mark went ahead and volunteered the information.

"A few months back we tried to introduce this female aide, Sarah, because some brainiac at the office thought it'd do him a world of good to have at least *some* semblance of a female around. So here it is, hey, her first day, and she shows up at the house in her little red rusted-out Corolla, and we run her through the usual accounting drill. Everything in the house, see, anything sharp that could possibly be used as a weapon, must be constantly accounted for. No exceptions. Every knife, every fork, *everything* stays inside the house. *Nothing* gets outside the house. But then he's really sneaky, see, so we have to be extra vigilant on that front.

"So we decide to play this little joke. You know, a little initiation to the tribe. So here we've got Sarah—lovely girl, but an absolute head of lettuce, understand—standing at the sink with her back to him, counting forks or something—something that's already been done that day like a dozen times—and, well, he's already exhausted his three-question limit, so he's just sitting there at the table watching her from behind. And then of course he pulls it out, and swear to God, starts flogging it to beat the band. And by the time she turns around and catches him doing his thing, he's already jacked his wad all over the back of her slacks. Man, we just about died." Mark laughed long and hard, bent over at the waist, hands on knees, until finally recovering enough to continue on for his audience's doubtful benefit. "But that wasn't even the best part. No, the *best* part, by *far*, was watching her fill out her incident report afterwards, knowing full well that everyone gets a copy—*every*one, from the Ministry on down."

Mark waited, eagerly anticipating another raucous round of laughter at our hapless pervert's expense, but then nothing of the sort appeared to be forthcoming from his guests. Quickly he censured himself, adjusted his considerable rigging, and then continued on with a cool resumption of competence. "So as you can imagine, the 'introduce the estrogen' experiment kind of came to a screaming halt right there. It's better that we keep the ladies completely out of the equation, see, otherwise he just gets too carried away. Speak of the devil," he said, and together they turned to find, stack of *Langley Times* in hand, the eldest embattled brother, Jonathan Jacks.

POSTED BY LUCY @ 8:26:14 P.M. 4/10/2007   7 COMMENTS

Afraid of Heights

Dear Mom & Dad:

Received your Sunday letter today . . . I guess you're in Toronto right now. It's like the funny feeling Tracey experienced when she dropped her letter off at the ARF main desk: so near, yet so far.

So Edith Lowden's engaged, eh? And you thought *I* was crazy. Who's the (un)lucky guy? When are they to be married, and more importantly, who's her dressmaker? You know what? I wouldn't touch that one with a ten-foot pole, no matter what they paid.

Very happy, satisfying day today. Started early, hit the big twenty in belt production, and in doing so realized my timing is now down to two belts per hour, so I'm definitely well on my way. Stopped at 7 tonight, and having just now emerged from a hot shower with my weaver's disease slowly winding down, I'm getting ready to read for an hour or so. Feeling a bit weary though, as I've been up since 4, and weaving steadily since 5.

We watch "All in the Family" too! Quite a program, isn't it? Apparently it's G & J's favourite too. Speaking of Ginny, I talked to her tonight, and she and her hubby seem to be sailing along quite well, all things considered. She has a party lined up for all those Sierra Club folks (not sure what for, no doubt some new victory on the "ecology" front though) she introduced me to when I was out, so she'll be busier than she wants to be, I'm sure. Actually, she sounded quite cheerful, in her own despondent way. Time will tell, as they say. She went on to say that J Jr. is all agog at the books I had you send out their way. I hope he doesn't mind all my scribbling in the margins and such, and gets some good use out of them.

Wednesday, July 26, 1972

Letter arrived from Doug today—he's home safe and sound from Vietnam, and he and some old high school friends will be fishing up in Wawa this next week. He's changed a lot—that is, according to Doug himself—though no real surprise there, I guess. The atrocities (my word) he witnessed over there have left him (in his words) scarred for the remainder of his days. On a brighter note, the weather up in Wawa is supposed to be good—overcast skies and not too hot, so perfect for fishing by the sounds of it—still I'm sure glad I won't be up there with that lot. Actually (and ironically) a part of me is hoping the fall comes early, because even with the automatic temperature control in here it's still a bit chilly. Too chilly in fact, at times.

Our little group is growing closer by the day. Mealtimes are a treat: we barter and trade with each other, and it gets pretty competitive at times, especially between Barbar(ell)a and me. A couple of the girls are very health-food orientated, so I have all sorts of new meals and snacks to try. One favourite of mine is crunchy granola—a mixture of rolled oats, grains, nuts, raisins and dried honey—which makes for a nice snack or breakfast cereal. Add some bran, pour a little milk on it, slice a banana or whatever, and voila: Liquid Plumber, ARF style.

When I first transferred over to this ward, only Lorna and her roommate were bothering to weave more than one or two belts a day. Now everyone, with varying degrees of exertion and success, is trying to catch up to ol' pistol-packin' Cormack, by far the fastest weaver on Ward A. It feels good to know I may have helped boost the morale around here, and it looks more like a workroom now than it ever did before.

Thursday, July 27, 1972

I guess you're back in Bobcaygeon now. I hope you enjoyed the gift show in Toronto, sold a whole bunch of stuff, and found some nice things to buy as well.

Ah, Bobcaygeon . . . yes, I've been remembering Bobcaygeon today. . . . Remembering a little girl in the Minthorn house

picking holes in the plaster because it felt so agreeably pulverizable, like rolled oats in a way.... And playing with the presently
engaged (and in my mind, thoroughly un-engaging) Edith
Lowden in the summer kitchen, and how we were both way too
big for the baby carriage already. Myron and his sister, they had an
electric train next door, didn't they? Their dad they called
"Spider" and their mom they referred to as "Bee"—funny names
when you're so small and they're so big—relatively, I mean. I recall
I once walked all the way up to town to see Aunt Zelda, back
when Uncle Perce was still in the hospital with TB.... And cousin
Sophie, why she was just little, even littler than me! When you're
young, see, you enjoy foraging in behind Aunt Zelda's night table
and playing with her Vaseline—it's smooth and gooey, and makes
shiny marks on the walls when you finger-paint with it. Now it
may not have helped me get over the mumps any quicker, but it
sure was fun, wasn't it? Ginny ate a worm once, and she also built
little fires around the back of the house. But that must've been
long before I came into the world, so I must be remembering
someone else telling me the story at some point, despite the fact
that I can picture it in my mind clearly enough.

I remember when you packed all our dishes and the old oil burner and even my toys into Dad's brand new blue Chevrolet, and
drove us to the new house way out on Perfectus Point. "My Dad
built that house," I used to tell anyone who'd listen, "and my Mom
helped!" When we first moved in, as I recall, you could see from
one end of the house clear to the other. We didn't have any walls
inside at first, just pretend walls marked out with tape on the floor,
and there was a little hole in my bedroom floor I used to poke my
finger into, and drop dead bugs and curls of dust and even my sister's bobby pins into, and just like that they'd disappear. My first but
by no means last encounter with the "rabbit hole," as it were.

I remember climbing in onto the Lazy Susan once, and getting
so scared that I wouldn't be able to get back out that I never dared
do it again. And my sister, she used to hide things on me ... just
so that I wouldn't hide them on her first apparently! Thus we
have the only permanently preserved collection of belts (various

colours, and probably Mom's) in Bobcaygeon, sealed where else but in under the bathtub of course. And so it comes as no surprise, perhaps, that I'm presently stuck in here making what? Karma is a harsh taskmaster, is she not?

When my sister went away to school, I used to play with Edith in the sand pile outside my parents' bedroom, and use Mom's old kitchen spoons as shovels. And when I went away to school I became a dancing star in grade one. That is, for one brief moment one afternoon I was allowed to model my dancing costume for Mrs. Crowe and all the kids in class. I made it out of curtains and things from Mom & Dad's store, as I recall. Boy, it was a beauty! Though I really wasn't supposed to try it on.

Do you remember how I used to come into the shop and try on all the jewellery when I thought you weren't looking? All those diamonds, they made me feel like a princess. . . . Of course I feel like a princess now too, albeit for entirely different reasons. ("Locked in a tower" springs to mind.) Anyway, remember when you caught me trying on something or other in the store, and how I was so afraid of getting in trouble that I faked falling down— quite the clever ruse, I tell you—managing in the process to *truly* hurt myself, leaving me quite certain that part of my brain had fallen out on the floor? Or how about that other time, when I cut my head open on that old auto wreck out back of Pogue's Garage and, well, I thought I'd gone and bought the farm right there for sure. I also caught my finger (thumb?) in Mom's washing machine once—an episode that's left me terrified of wringers ever since— but I don't remember which digit got squished, do you? However, I do remember my hair catching fire, and Ginny throwing the pink bedspread over my head to put it out, clever girl that *she* was. And now, how many years later, and she's still my big sister—older and wiser and so much more engaged with the world than I—but with any luck I'll someday grow up to be just as wise and engaged as she is, with a husband as wild and wonderful as J is—at least I'll try!

Other than Edith Lowden though (after little Peter Pogue passed away, sixteen years ago this week by the way) I really don't remember too many kids my age when I was young. . . . I guess I played by myself a lot, I don't know. . . . But to be honest, I'm glad I learned to play by myself, and to entertain myself, as these are the skills that serve me so faithfully hour after hour here in the fishbowl. But then I did have trees, and rocks, and the lake when I was a kid, not to mention minnows, frogs, flowers, grass, leaves, mosquitoes, gravel, sand, sunshine and a raft! My God, I had a *raft!* And of course two wonderful parents who let me cut up old curtains to make ballerina costumes, and doll clothes, and then my clothes, and then other peoples' clothes, and here I am (weaving belts, yes, but) on my way to designing costumes and clothes, not for dolls anymore, but for real actors in enormous theatre shows. I guess that's where the child's fantasy becomes the adult's reality, and I'm very glad it has of course.

These are the kinds of things I think about while I'm weaving. It all seems odd now, and far away, as though it happened to someone else entirely, and I just happened to read about it one day. Is it all too sentimental? Perhaps. To be sure, country living does have its downside, and yet I've had so many good experiences in my short life, and there are so many more to look forward to, so you see it really doesn't matter where you are—in the country or in the city, indoors or out—it's your memories and your expectations that keep you alive, entertained and enthusiastic about life. Especially if they're good memories, like I have. Thank you so much for that.

Love, Birdie

AUGUST, 2002

The foundation was set, anchored deep into the recently levelled, retaining wall-buttressed embankment with four enormous concrete piers. Jeremy was fairly sure they were overbuilding, but then he was also fairly sure he did not care. If the intention was to make it permanent, then why not make it as permanent as possible? This was his thinking on the fort anyway, even though, as a graduate of the Jacks school of construction, permanency had never really been his forte.

Not surprisingly, the project was growing in both size and scope, metamorphosing into something that, for a three-and-a-half year-old, was of course entirely inappropriate. No longer were they content to build a mere tree fort, but instead a genuine liveable cabin capable of boasting most if not all of the modern conveniences available. These included, but were not necessarily limited to, running hot and cold water, electricity, a stove and, naturally, a working chemical toilet. The layout of the floor, too, had grown, blooming to a fifteen-foot square, with another three feet of sheltered veranda supplementing both the eastern and southern perimeters. These dimensions, while admittedly ambitious, still allowed for a modest gap of two feet between the rear, or north, wall and the corresponding retaining wall for easy workspace access. Such access was necessary as, due to the severe space constraints afforded by the steep bank of ravine in back and the enormous outcropping of maples out front, the cabin was slowly taking on the character, if not yet the characteristics, of a two-storey tower of vaguely biblical proportions. And knowing hours of sunlight would be in relatively short supply this deep in the earth, and shorter still with the surfeit of trees fashioning an effective canopy overhead, they were determined to build the tower as high as possible in order to take full advantage of those limited hours available.

One afternoon, following a long but productive morning of lag-bolting the first floor frame together and installing twelve-inch joists at standard sixteen-inch centres, the brothers watched their father, with heartbreaking seriousness, slowly stiff-leg his way to the floor of the ravine. Moving out amid the cluster of trunks, Jeremy checked his father's progress from the vantage point of one enormous moss-covered branch. A few feet farther out from where he stood, as if still constricting the chunky fractured fabric of bark, he noticed the telltale scar of what must have been, at one time, a thick weight-bearing rope of sorts. He had no memory of any such device. Meanwhile, having reached the uneven floor of the ravine, Jon took to one knee, not without difficulty, in the sand alongside the stream, and cupped a double

handful of water to his mouth, repeating the feat several times
before reaching around and washing his neck to further hydrate
himself.

"Dad, I really doubt that river's too clean," Robert warned, suddenly appearing behind Jeremy on the branch. Together they
looked down through the deep, green, over-foliaged ravine
toward their father's position on the bank. The stream looked
slightly different than it had the previous day, just as, the previous
day, it looked slightly different than it had the day before that.
This was not unusual, the brothers knew, as they recalled the more
nomadic nature of the stream of their youth. Occasionally, deep
reflective pools emerged, assuming the look of seemingly permanent fixtures before evaporating, often without a trace, by the following afternoon. Only the hardest promontories of pure stone
seemed capable of anything resembling actual permanence,
around and over which the stream continued its ongoing, gur-
gling struggle towards the Source. It was, I have often thought (all
too romantically no doubt), as though the stream were determined to explore each and every path available for transit over
any given stretch of landscape. However, incapable as I am of
moving about without constraint, and hence unable to spend as
much time in its vicinity as I would in fact like, perhaps I tend to
ascribe the stream a great deal more weight, metaphorical and so
forth, than it would otherwise warrant. (Am I being a little too
Birdie-like in my musings here perhaps? A certain Jacks has suggested as much. Call it the avian flu if you must—and I know you
must.) I shall let you, dear reader, be the judge of that.

"It's clean."

"You might think so, but I doubt with all that sediment—"

"I said it's clean," Jon repeated, rapidly growing irritated.
"Christ, you boys don't realize how good you've got it." That said,
he nodded his head slowly up and down as if to communicate to
an unseen audience the utter injustice of the world—a world in
which two younger versions of himself could have nothing better to do than climb out the length of a maple branch and call
into question their father's good sense while he, the father, long

past climbing out branches maple or otherwise, with nothing more to look forward to in this life than a decent drink of cool water from his own meandering stretch of stream, was expected to stand idly by and take that sort of crap.

Jeremy looked at Robert, and Robert shrugged. "The man's thirsty," laughed the latter at once.

"Now I suppose we've got to go down and rescue the old bastard."

"I heard that, Jeremy," his father shot back. "Christ Almighty, I might be old, but I'm not an invalid." He levered himself up to a standing position and looked around as if seeing it all for the first time. "Come down here a minute," he said at length, and together Jeremy and Robert made their way down.

"What is it?" Robert asked upon their eventual arrival.

"Nothing. Just wanted you both to come down here, that's all. You know," Jon began, his voice suffering a sudden decibel dive, "when you boys were young, you used to come down here almost every day."

"I remember," Jeremy said. And suddenly, despite all best efforts to the contrary, he found himself mired in a strange fellow feeling with his father, a feeling only one of them had wanted but which neither of them had expected, and which Jeremy now had to shake off with difficulty, but shake it off he did.

"For hours at a time too," Jon continued, nakedly reminiscing amid a small patch of sunlight. He had an unusual way of standing, unusual on land at least, what with his feet splayed wide apart and his center of gravity pushed down about his bowed knees. Even the carry of his shoulders was somehow suggestive of a rocking boat underway.

"Used to concern me at times, you boys being so far out of earshot, spending so much time down here alone. . . . But then the more you did it, well, the more I got used to it and, anyway, boys need time to go off on their own.

"Look at this," Jon said, quiet and almost embarrassed, as he seldom spoke so much or for so long on any given subject. He pointed to a nearby stump, old and rotting but enormous, and the horizontal notch in its trunk perhaps six feet above the base. Beneath and through its complex network of roots the stream presently made its way, although within a day its path would no doubt have changed, and changed severely. "Know what those things are called?" he asked, idly fingering the notch.

"Isn't that where loggers used to insert their springboards?" Robert said as his brother pivoted away. A major beneficiary of his family's longstanding contempt for authority, Jeremy had never been all that comfortable with this vaguely instructional side of his father, though probably more for the fact that it so rarely went on display.

"Way back when they used handsaws?" Robert continued, inconceivably as far as his brother was concerned anyway.

"Two-man crosscut saws," his father corrected, pinching his nose and sniffing in the direction of Jeremy's turned head. "Know what it's called, Jeremy, that notch there?"

Jeremy turned around grudgingly, and dredged up an apathetic shrug for good measure.

"Know what they used to call that, back when I was your age?"

Jeremy shrugged again, smiling fondly, if facetiously, at the idea of these dear dead days.

"Yeah, me neither," said Jon, at which point he and Robert shared a quiet chuckle together. With nothing to offer, and not really wanting to partake in this latest round of Jacks family nostalgia and fun, Jeremy tipped his chin at the cabin and said, as though to himself, but loud enough for all to hear:

"Of course we'll have trouble with the neighbours at some point."

"How do you mean?" Robert said.

"It's not to code," Jon explained, having already grasped the insinuation, forever at close moorings with anything so much as resembling an un-neighbourly notion. "You can't build outside the code."

"What *code*."

"City code. One structure per lot—*that's* the code. Course the goddamned East Indians'll put about thirty people in one house

if you let them, but you and I can't build something like this without the entire municipality coming down on our heads."

Somewhere a dog barked. A black squirrel bounded out along a
nearby branch. And Robert filled his lungs with air as Jeremy
withdrew into silence, their respective and customary responses to
their father's occasionally racially laced rants.

"But it's a *tree* fort. Who would possibly care about a tree fort?"
Robert asked.

"You'd be surprised," answered his father, adding, after a short
pause, "I always thought we might build an extra floor on the
house. You know, so that you and Linda and little Stephie could
maybe move back in at some point. That condo of yours doesn't
have a yard, and kids need yards," he stated, as though explaining
a simple fact to the uninitiated, or hard-hearted, or both.

"You already have too much house though."

"Yes . . . too much house," Jon said, and Jeremy could tell that
he had lost his train of thought again, a relatively new develop-
ment in his father's steadily accelerating disintegration. A frown
ran in a slanting direction between Jon's eyebrows and halfway up
his forehead on familiar, well-worn lines. Confused, he rubbed
his forehead, leaving behind as testament a thin rusty streak of
blood.

"Dad, you're bleeding," Robert said.

"What's that?"

"You're bleeding," repeated both brothers together, and Jeremy,
staring fixedly, indicated the hand at fault.

Jon frowned down at the cut on his finger, squeezing out as
penance a single droplet of blood. "And it would be private," he
said, finally able to finish the thought.

No one spoke for a time, each man doing his best to be captivated with what little existed of the cabin halfway up the ravine.
Finally Robert said, full of resentment, "Fuck the code."

"Yeah fuck the code," echoed Jeremy.

"And fuck the neighbours too," Jon said. Never a regular prac-
titioner of crude language, in times of crisis he had always stood
convinced of its more tonic qualities, and when circumstances led

either of his sons to take the lead, he was known to follow suit and even up the ante occasionally.

Eventually the trio made their way upstream, picking a path over slippery fallen logs and moss-covered boulders with plodding determination, before thinking better of it and hiking back down the length of the ravine instead. The warm moist air stood thick with pollen, and tiny translucent insects zigzagged drunkenly in the sour canted light, but as the Jackses laboured down along the streambed with sawdust powdering the branches of even the smallest trees they were afforded, back through a few half-fallen firs, a fine view of the cabin's spacious first floor projecting like an open drawer from halfway up the embankment. For a while the stream was much as it had been, narrow and relatively deep, but suddenly it jumped its conventional barriers and spread itself thin across a wide grey gravel bed. Here and there, large scabs of soil had ripped away from the ravine's steep banks, revealing, there beneath, dripping grey striations of clay and the like. Together Robert and Jeremy helped their father negotiate the gnarled remains of a freshly fallen pine, its trunk and branches twisting back and forth and around themselves, strangling themselves, and then the trio were out on the wide flat expanse of gravel beyond. The ravine turned slightly left in the shade, then hard right, continued straight for a time, and finally they were free of it altogether, immersed at once in a wide warm sea of sunlight. The gap opened wide, the banks of the ravine sloped down to meet the base, and the once natural stream joined a man-made culvert running under the recently repaved River Road just ahead. In the distance, arranged side by side along the Fraser River's heavily industrialized waterfront, stood the large grey nondescript buildings of no decipherable motif, and the gravel path, that path the ravine had more or less become by this point, ended as a parking lot at this place. A transport truck thundered up behind them. Forced almost to a stop, the driver honked his horn repeatedly in order to be heard above the tumultuous din of the waterfront. And just off to the left, in direct contrast to all this activity, lay the stagnant, oil-stained waters of Annieville Slough, filled seemingly to capacity with idle fishing boats of various size, design, and intent.

Once at the slough, they crossed a rickety wooden bridge in the direction of the grey, weather-beaten remains of salmon cannery at its end. Here in the shadow of some other industry, apart from the bare expanse of floor itself, there was in truth not all that much cannery remaining. Stripped of everything but weeds and grass, and the occasional wind-loosened board, the cannery stood a great naked memorial to the silent slough on one side and the industrial furore of the Fraser on the other. The sun glinted off the still surface of the slough, revealing random patches of rainbow-patterned oil, while down below in the shadows, through the gaps between the boards, there could be vaguely discerned, upon an unjustly exposed shelf of mud, a broken oar, a pair of bleeding car batteries, several empty jugs of bleach, and the ribs of whatever else had been discarded here over how many previous generations of usage. Irregular collections of dark and decomposing driftwood lay piled up at intervals, the vast majority of which had escaped the log boom and subsequent sawmill only to end up captive here. Weeds grew high around the neighbouring sheds and broken-down, abandoned shacks. Plastic door shrouds shifted in the wind. And Jon turned around to face his sons, a pale red crescent of dried blood still visible on his forehead. Jeremy refused to meet his eyes, but Robert nodded back in sad comprehension. And in back of the cannery were fishing boats, and everywhere they looked there were more fishing boats, and ahead the river stretched out wide toward the utter vastness, and apparent emptiness, of the once bountiful Pacific Ocean.

POSTED BY LUCY @ 4:20:01 P.M. 4/20/2007   2 COMMENTS

Friday, July 28, 1972

Dear Mom & Dad:

Approaching the end of our fourth week now. . . . Remember when I used to say TGIF? The Ryerson newspaper used to headline each Friday's edition with that. It doesn't apply here though, as we run a very tight ship, seven days a week. Regardless, only ten more weeks to go. . . . Won't be long now, I keep telling myself.

I know I've said this before, but I'm fairly certain I've (finally) gotten over the whole "sore back and plugged bum" thing now. The newest physical challenge is trying to remember not to keep my hands in hot water for too long—when I'm having a bath, say—as of course the water softens the calluses I've spent so much time developing lately. As an added bonus, because I use this one side of my left index finger for pushing and separating the threads on the loom, all this grunt labour really benefits barring on the guitar—I can literally play hard all afternoon.

If you have the Simpson Sears catalogue handy, Mom, you may have noticed an outfit on page 10, a russet brown pantsuit with long knitted auburn vest. That would look awfully smart for the fall, with plums, rusts, oranges and yellows, or even golds and bronzes in earrings & bracelet as accessories. What do you think? Why don't you give it a try, if you like it? It would look *really* smart on you, in my opinion.

Saturday, July 29, 1972

Did my twenty today, with time off at lunch to read the Star (weekend edition) cover to cover—not as straightforward an activity as you'd think, not when you're saddled with a bad case of weaver's disease. (Thus the poor penmanship—sorry.) My, but the world does move on, doesn't it? Have you been following this whole Watergate fiasco? Three of the men are native-born Cubans apparently, and another is said to have trained Cuban exiles for guerrilla activity after the 1961 Bay of Pigs invasion. Scary. Still, a fish rots from the head down, as they say.

Unlike Washington, the atmosphere around here seems to be gradually improving as time goes on. Ward A is a much more cohesive unit now than we were immediately following the transfer of populations. Why that is, exactly, I really can't say. For a while it was the "us" and "the other girls" kind of talk, because of a whole new set of introductions we were forced to contend with, whereas now we're beginning to think of ourselves as a collective, a group—*the* group—and in a fishbowl like this that is definitely the healthiest attitude to have, rather than an atmosphere of feminine cliques of twos and threes forever shifting allegiances and gossiping behind each others' backs. Barbarella, though, for whatever reason, seems determined to remain something of an outcast. So much the better, methinks.

★   ★   ★

Sixteen years ago today, in the Bobcaygeon Trinity United Church of all places, G & J were married amid thunderstorms aplenty, a hectic round of photographs at the residence of the bride, and, as I recall, a real hullabaloo courtesy of the groom's parents concerning the fact their youngest son was about to link his life forever to a (gasp!) sixteen year-old neophyte. The fact the bride-to-be had finished high school a full three years early seemed entirely irrelevant; all they saw was an eight-month pregnant adolescent, an impending bastard, and a family's everlasting embarrassment. Among a bevy of others (whose names, to protect the innocent, shall not be repeated here) I still had a massive crush on J, and was less than thrilled to be escorted down the aisle by that irascible friend of his, Robert Hunter. Funny, the things you tend to remember more than a decade and a half after the fact. What was the name of the man who played the organ at Pine Ridge Lodge? Phil? Did I not play a tune or two that day as well? Seems to me I might have.

I enclosed a homemade anniversary card in my letter to Ginny posted on the 24th. I didn't really want Stan the Shopping Man picking one out for me, as I'm sure (I hope) our tastes would differ somewhat in that regard.

Today has been somewhat exhausting. Stopped at twenty belts, but still felt rather weary by the time seven o'clock rolled around (my hands, despite my best efforts to quell them, are "weaving" the air even now, echoes of a long hard shift at the loom), everyone else, with the exception or Lorna and I, having slept in till noon—we two weaving warriors arising at 4 AM as usual. From midnight tonight till noon tomorrow we're fasting again, with urine & blood samples, EKG & EEG to be taken sometime in between. I think I'll sleep in till eight or so, because I can't weave on an empty stomach for very long, this I know.

Sunday, July 30, 1972

An envelope from Tracey arrived today with a letter from Ruth enclosed, along with a rundown of the latest happenings at 37 Pleasant Blvd. If she could get a flight out on time, Ruth should have finally left for Edmonton yesterday for three weeks. She's been having second thoughts about moving out there—the Interthink company she's been working for is paying her very well, and she enjoys the atmosphere, so she may just stay on with them a while. I figured she couldn't just up and move without at least *some* shilly-shallying, and I was right: exactly ten days' worth.

News flash! Tracey has taken in a boarder! She put up an ad on the bulletin board at the local A & P, and some peach-fuzzed eighteen year-old named Cory, a mathematics and chemistry whiz at U of T, answered the call almost immediately. Apparently his parents live just over on Balmoral Ave, but he wanted to live on his own (but still have someone fetch his dinner, etc) until the end of summer, or possibly even longer. She says he's very considerate when he's there, and no bother at all, so I'm sure there's nothing to worry about. Be that as it may, I have endeavoured to enclose a few "landlady's tips for schoolboys" in my return letter. Having lived with G & J, even if for just two weeks, certainly gave me a few insights into the pros and cons of contemporary domesticity.

Taking the afternoon off to write letters and go through my Elégance magazine for ideas. Mail time is really quite an occasion around here, and when you consider that we females supposedly spend a third of our lives on the telephone, this solitary link to the outside world is rather exciting, to be sure.

Monday, July 31, 1972

Received a letter from G today—just a short one—she's contacted UBC for information regarding enrolment in a Bachelor of Science degree (on a part-time basis it would take six

years apparently). She's hopeful of course, though characteristically not of much, and is thus never far from disappointment,
seemingly her position of choice in life. Me, I really hope she does
get in, as it would be wonderful for her to dust off that great big
brain of hers, not to mention valuable insurance in the event that
(God forbid) something should happen to J out there on the high
seas. He leads such a perilous existence, that man, and one has to
maintain at least one eye on the future, doesn't one? Especially
with a teenaged boy around. Have you seen any photographs of
him lately? What *eyes!* That J Jr. sure is an interesting one.

Ah yes, thank you for writing. Just kidding, I know you've both
been busy this last week or so, but it sure was nice to see that letter on the counter this morning.

Remote control, eh? I guess I can expect to see a monitor and
stereo (or quadraphonic!) speakers installed in my bedroom when
I come home. Now Father, all you need is an automatic peanut
butter-bologna-dill pickle sandwich vending machine installed in
that wee space between the fireplace and stereo, and you'll be all
set. Mom still makes the coffee though—trust me, it's terrible
from a machine—speaking as a Ryerson refectory veteran, I know
this all too well unfortunately.

And slip-covers no less! Great, I won't even recognize my own
house when I get home. Now how about some new drapes, say,
medium chocolate brown, beige walls (*no* rose tones), some new
pictures with small but definite fire-orange touches, then take the
top off the coffee table, do a ceramic mosaic (like Sophie had
done to Aunt Zelda's vestibule floor, if you recall) in blue-greens,
taupes and rusts, et voila: living room extraordinaire. I'll even do
the coffee table for you, if you like. It's actually fairly easy, not to
mention effective and decorative in its own right, and quite a
sturdy finish when done correctly.

Now about OHSIP. Don't worry, I filled out the application for
assistance (one of the alternatives to sending in the money, it said)
and mailed it in. So I shall be hearing from them presently.

Life insurance—thank you! This is for three months then, I take
it? Write and explain the entire policy, please—I really have

forgotten my Grade 10 classes with Mrs. Young—in fact, I can't even recall if it was in Economics class or what.

Honestly, getting up at 4 AM is no real hardship—my brother-in-law taught me that—as I've elevated my weaving to such a state now that in the early afternoon I can afford to take a nap and still be in bed and asleep by 9:30 PM precisely. Don't forget that my only energy expenditure is weaving—no sewing, no gardening, no stairs, no walks to the post office, nothing. I really am very well rested—no bags under the eyes—and contrary to this impression you seem to be under, no one is *making* me do anything, all right? I actually have everyone here bug-eyed with my discipline and strong will—can you believe it? I sure can't.

Love, Birdie

P.S. Next letter, my eagerly awaited, highly anticipated fashion forecast for the fall!

AUGUST, 2002

To be honest, if you did not know to look for it, you might not even know it was there. And yet it was plainly visible, rising up a massive tower of concrete and steel from the heavily industrialized north bank of the Fraser River. Just one division of an enormous, and enormously profitable, multinational, the headquarters of which were located somewhere in Scandinavia, Moore-Mathers ran twenty-four hours a day, seven days a week, pumping out dark, brown, cylindrical fish feed pellets of various sizes and compositions to so-called fish farms up and down the west coast of North America and around the Pacific Rim. And yet the fact that it was somewhat politically incorrect to be associated with aquaculture at this particular point in time did not deter the Jacks boys in the least. Although, having long considered himself something of a sleeper-agent activist, Jeremy did take some time to rationalize his pulling down a regular paycheque there—ten minutes, at least.

Located in the long shadow of the Knight Street Bridge, actually just west of it, Moore-Mathers was a colossal complexity of extruders, elevators, silos, catwalks, boilers, bins, belts, lifts, motors and other mechanical contrivances, each with its own specific noise that together formed a fusillade of such continuous thunder that, if not for the spongy orange earplugs each employee was enthusiastically supplied, many an ear would have been rendered useless long before Jeremy's debut in this bluest of blue-collar environments. Of course the only thing worse than the noise was the stench, which fluctuated between awful and dreadful depending on the season and the specific ingredients with which the given product was being prepared.

Finishing up their shift one evening, Jeremy and Robert made their way back out to North Delta and, as a treat for a hard day of sweaty, dirty, gruelling physical labour, the local pub at Royal Heights. Long referred to as the Royal, and in the interim, the King's Head, it was now dubbed officially Doolin's Irish Pub, not through any legitimate connection with the Irish, mind you, but simply as a clever marketing ploy adopted by the recently installed, suddenly liquor-enthralled, Punjabi ownership group. It was here the brothers had toiled briefly upon completing their university degrees, spelling each other off as doorman or bartender depending on the mood each happened to be in on any given shift. Incidentally, it was also where Sukhvinder Rai, missing now for almost a month, had only recently gotten into the habit of commissioning from promising looking patrons the bootlegging of wine coolers in convenient two-litre bottles, paid for with wages earned mostly as a hostess at her father's local run-of-the-mill restaurant. Fortified with one of these magnums, preferably, though not necessarily, in a flavour known vaguely as Glacierberry, Miss Rai performed oral sex at weekend parties on one or more of her recently graduated Caucasian classmates.

Predictably, the brothers took their seats at the bar. Jeremy ordered a Crown and Coke for himself and, for Robert, an iced tea as usual. They both ordered the Doolin's Duellin' Curried Vegetables and Rice™ for dinner, one of few viable options on an already limited menu, as both brothers had given up the benefits of animal protein years before, Robert as an ongoing experiment in health and animal welfare, and Jeremy as an ongoing experiment in pissing off his father of course. To no one's surprise, except, of course, Jon Jacks, fish had been the first item to go, followed by red meat and lastly, poultry. Pork had never made the list to begin with, as Jon himself had decreed early on that any animal willing to fornicate in its own excrement was not an animal he was willing to put in his mouth. Such logic was readily accepted by his sons. Still, their collective refusal to receive the fruits of his labour—that which he made his living by, and in turn fed, clothed, and sheltered their bodies by—had, for the longest time, proved a real source of irritation for the easily irritated head of the family. Not that mealtime in the Jacks household had ever been all that inspiring an event. In fact, meals had always existed as a triumph of function over form, a simple matter of caloric necessity rather than one of taste or, heaven forbid, enjoyment. Beyond salt and pepper, spices were frowned upon to say the least, and it was generally considered a severe oversight in protocol if the ingredients had not been boiled or fried into submission by the time they made it in sight of someone's plate.

The bartender, a fat black man named Harris, served each brother his curried vegetables and rice—as it turns out, an altogether benign affair, but a welcome departure nonetheless from the vegetarian's typical pub-food refuge, the wholly humdrum veggie burger. In the meantime, Robert and Jeremy took note of the various familiar faces around the pub beginning to take notice of them. How many of these patrons they had managed to toss out of this very establishment during their brief tenure it was impossible to know for sure, but suffice to say, that evening anyway, there were a few heated stares being levelled their way.

"Where's ol' Captain Video been hiding?" the bartender Harris asked Jeremy prior to the arrival of curry, taking advantage of a rare break from the waitresses' seemingly never-ending drink requests to acknowledge his own largely neglected guests. In his free time away from Doolin's, Harris could typically be found volunteering his services at one of several local self-styled 'ranches,' small, seemingly plain country residences that managed to maintain their 'ranch' status simply by selling one another the occasional llama, all for the explicit purpose of deflecting unwanted attention—and tax—from their true commercial pursuit and passion, the booming pay-as-you-go orgy industry for decent self-respecting swingers in the Surrey/Delta/Langley area. That has nothing to do with the story. However, regarding Jon Jacks, the recent whereabouts of whom he presently found himself inquiring, Harris finished what he had to say by saying what it was he really wanted to say: "He ain't been spending any money in here. Actually, he ain't been spending any *time* in here—in years in fact."

"He's sober," Robert said, anticipating with his tone an abrupt end to the conversation. "He's been sober a long time."

"Yes, apparently he's channelling his energies into spirits of a different sort now," added Jeremy as sarcastically as possible, not a note of which could have possibly been missed by those within so much as hailing distance of the bar.

"Actually I heard that," said Harris, wiping down the surface of the bar. As well as being terribly overweight, Harris was also exceptionally tall, but despite all that still managed to maintain a general air of friendliness in that characteristic gay man's manner.

"What'd you hear?" Robert asked, leaning forward portentously against the bar.

"Well nothing definitive," said Harris, bending over to ream some gunk from the tread of his shoe, reeling equally under the weight of his abundant back fat and Robert's leaden stare. "But I did hear he was in trouble with the police."

"Excuse me?"

"Well that's what I heard," shrugged Harris, bending over once more. It seemed to Jeremy that Harris was doing a great deal of bending over right now.

"And hey, how about you stick to hearing, Harris, instead of flapping those big fucking lips of yours. Hey Jer, remember that guy there?" Robert asked upon Harris's immediate and rather hasty departure, pointing out a short moustached fellow currently holding court over near the dartboards.

"Yeah I remember him," said Jeremy, pushing aside an ashtray. Unlike many municipalities, including South Delta, North Delta refused to enforce its anti-smoking bylaws, much to Jeremy's dismay. "Phil. Fearless Phil. Paramedic or something, if I remember correctly."

"Remember that night we had to kick him and Dad out though?"

"Yeah, that was a definite low point."

"That was your first night, wasn't it?"

"And my worst, too, as I recall."

Presently their curry arrived. Both brothers ate steadily, neither talking much of the time, and near the end of the meal a voice caught their attention out of the general hum of conversation, and together they turned to find an Indo-Canadian man of about their age saying, "So, what, we got both you bastards back in town now?"

"Sorry?" said Robert when he realized the man was most definitely speaking to them.

"What, you don't remember me? Come on, how can you not remember me. We played ball together when we were kids." The man held the palm of his hand at a right angle to his thigh to illustrate just how small a ballplayer he might have been.

"Sorry," Jeremy shrugged, exchanging quick glances with his brother.

"Come on, you remember," said the man, addressing Robert exclusively. "You used to pick on me."

"I'm sorry," said Robert readily. "I really don't remember. I don't remember anything before grade seven actually."

"Well you—"

"And if I did pick on you," Robert continued, "I apologize. Although, to be honest, I do kind of find it hard to believe. I mean, I got picked on a lot myself, and I doubt I would have picked on anyone else in those days."

"Still, you did."

"Well like I said, I'm sorry. Believe me, it wouldn't have been anything personal."

"No, it was because I was a *brother*," insisted the man, at which point he introduced himself as Jeevan something-or-other, a name Robert was quick to insist he had never heard before in his life. The brothers looked at the brother. The brother looked at the brothers. Unbeknownst to even Jeevan himself, he had once briefly and unsuccessfully hit on Sukhvinder Rai at a local gymnasium whilst supposedly celebrating, in his own desultory way, the Khalsa Panth. Finally he very softly said, as though rapidly, sadly losing faith in the process, "Come on, you remember me."

"I don't. Sorry."

"Well then you must remember Leslie." Jeevan pivoted sideways to reveal the table where Robert's estranged first wife sat cheerfully. Robert nodded and Leslie laughed, and a moment later she was over at the bar, her long thin arm draped about the waist of Jeevan's jeans, her long thin fingers busily seeking contact with the waistband of whatever it was he wore as underwear.

"Well if it isn't the twin towers," she smirked at last.

"Hello, Leslie. Who's this guy you're with?" Robert asked.

"This? Why this is Jeevan," she said, and let go his waist. "Jeevan here takes good care of me. Don't you, Jeevan."

"What's that?" Jeevan asked, returning her winning smile, albeit only in theory, for all this time he was staring at Robert as though there were something a little bizarre about him, perhaps an extra appendage of some sort, or an eye where it was not supposed to be. Jeremy ordered another Crown and Coke off Harris, and then requested the bill at the bartender's earliest convenience.

"I'm sure he does," Robert said to his ex-wife. "But that other guy, I mean. At your table there." And together Leslie and Jeevan turned to acknowledge the one remaining individual at their table, an impeccably dressed middle-aged man smiling and waving back from behind a thick blue cloud of smoke and an impressive collection of recently emptied glassware. Robert reluctantly returned the favour.

"That's Calvin Cassidy," said Leslie smugly. "Come on, Robert, even *you* must recognize Calvin Cassidy. He played that lawyer Richard Rock on *Law and Order* in case you don't remember."

"That's where I know him from," said Robert, saluting Calvin Cassidy half-heartedly. In answer, Cassidy stood, bowed elegantly, and invited the world to his table.

"Pleasure to meet you," he said with the faint remains of enigmatic accent he had carefully constructed for himself since alighting this far north of the border. At long length he switched his cigarette to the opposite hand and reluctantly retook his seat, without once losing any of the staged elegance of his gestures or, for that matter, his character. Meanwhile, having paid the bill at the bar, Jeremy helped his brother hunt out the one or two remaining chairs available. It was a good excuse not to look at Cassidy who, in Jeremy's opinion, sported that high-cheekboned, thin-lipped, overly ruddy alcoholic's head, born of that conventionally oversized actor's head, which in one or two vague and unpleasant ways reminded him of his father's unfortunately.

"Something to drink?" Cassidy asked Robert.

"No thank you."

"Robert here doesn't share our limited notion of entertainment," Leslie explained in a way entirely peculiar to herself—that is, in a pleasant conversational tone utterly devoid of malice yet at the same time chockfull of scorn. "Read about you in the paper," she went on to Robert directly once everyone was more or less established around the table. "No real surprise there, I suppose."

"Yeah, well, you know the army," Robert shrugged. "Clusterfuck as usual."

"Oh I wasn't talking about that. I was talking about that little fiasco at the school."

"Oh *that*," he said, and shifted about uncomfortably.

Leslie paused long enough to calculate the return of inquisitive expressions, and sufficiently satisfied with the number, turned to Cassidy. "My ex-husband here beat up the principal at his school."

"Vice-principal," Jeremy corrected, all but avoiding Leslie's eyes, susceptible as always to the dubious allure of his brother's wives.

"*Vice*-principal, yes. You got me on a technicality, Jeremy. But right in front of his students no less."

Cassidy, who not six weeks before had bootlegged successfully for Sukhvinder Rai, earning himself in the process her best ready-made smile, choked, coughed and sprayed what little gin was left to him onto the laden air. Then, throwing back his oversized head, he laughed loud and hard as was originally intended, and Jeremy found himself further disgusted at the sight of all those mercury-filled molars unjustly exposed.

"But all is not lost," Leslie continued, casting Jeremy an ostensibly affectionate look. "His brother here has written a very bad book. Haven't you, Jeremy. A book that skewers not only me personally, but by extension all women everywhere." She smiled wanly, her eyes wrinkling up at the corners. "Tell me, Jeremy, does the very presence of women in the world exist as an affliction to your sense of propriety? Or is it just me."

"Just you."

"But you hardly even know me."

"No, but I know your place."

"Oh *please*," she snorted, glancing away. "Find some bigger fish to fry."

"But why should I, really, when it takes all my time coming up with new and inventive ways to keep insulting you?"

And they smiled plainly at each other a while.

"So what are you working on now?" asked Calvin Cassidy in his oddly impressive way of speaking, odd in that it was impressive, impressive in that was still considered speaking, while lighting a fresh cigarette seemingly for no particular reason.

Jeremy looked at him, wondering whether or not he should reply. In his experience, people often asked that sort of question when they really had no desire to hear the answer. "Actually, I'm packing fish feed," he said.

"Excuse me?" said Leslie, pressing in against the table.

"I said I'm packing fish feed. At the mill. You know, the one down on the river there. Oh you'll like this, Leslie. You'll appreciate this sort of thing for sure. We pack feed, drive forklifts, and at the end of the workweek, if we've just worked a graveyard, some of the guys get together under the Knight Street Bridge to bitch, complain and get in the occasional punch-up with one another. It's a real hoot, believe me, and just your sort of thing, I swear."

"That's enough, Jer."

"And what, pray tell, do you do on your days off," Cassidy inquired, no doubt eager to hear how well his conspicuous instrument carried in such a dialogue-driven atmosphere.

Robert looked at him steadily. "Well then we come here."

"And so you're working there *too*," Leslie said. "Congratulations. My, but it's nice to see the Jacks boys finally reaching their enormous potential."

Jeremy smiled at her, disliking her more out of habit than anything. Though he had long considered Leslie at the very least visually appealing, particularly when crying hysterically, her consistently bitter and angry face, together with her consistently bitter and angry disposition, had always been just a little too much for him to tolerate on any sort of regular basis.

It should probably be noted that, throughout this entire exchange, Jeevan had sat silently, staring rigorously at Robert's profile. Robert seemed not to have noticed this concentration of attention, though Jeremy certainly had.

Leslie reached across the table to cover Robert's hand with her own. "So how's Linda and . . ."

"Stephanie."

"Yes, little Stephanie. How are they? Good?"

"Fine," Robert said, trying but failing to extract his hand from hers without drawing anyone's attention to the operation. "Yeah, they're fine," he added after a time.

"I heard they were. I also heard they were taking something of a sabbatical from you," she said, releasing her grip at last. If nothing else, it must have been terribly exciting for her to have an audience like this, Jeremy later recalled during his regularly scheduled review of the day's events, when superior witticisms he might have uttered, could have uttered, in reality should have uttered, were he anything even remotely resembling his fictional characters, seemed to come to him unbidden, all of a sudden, and amazingly complete.

"Sabbatical, yes," Robert said, dropping his head and sighing down into his chest. "That's a typically overstated way of putting it, sure. Is there something you'd like to say to me?" he asked at once, turning his attention Jeevan's way.

"Nope, not me," said Jeevan, taking a brief break from his vigil in order to survey the table in general. "I still can't believe you don't remember me."

"Oh don't be annoyed," Leslie said with a flush of pleasure. "Robert here doesn't remember anything. It's the basis of his character, this not remembering. A defence mechanism of some sort. Why, he probably doesn't even remember why he and I broke up."

"Well I do remember *that*," Robert laughed, an admission Leslie seemed to accept as flattery reflecting herself.

"You see, Robert here told me he didn't want children," she continued curtly for the benefit of no one in particular, probably Cassidy. "Can you believe it? He didn't want children, and he didn't think that I should want them either. But then I find out he's sleeping with my best friend, and more, that he's knocked her up. Tell me, Robert, how did you come to the decision that sticking your cock in my friends would prove beneficial to our marriage? Was it something that came to you in a vision? Or was it simply something you were powerless against. Yes, that's it. That must be it. You were powerless against Linda's *charms*. It was the name, really. The alliteration. Just watch, he'll be moving on to the M's before long.

"Oh you'll like this one," she went on, briefly addressing Cassidy on her right before returning to Robert her full unbridled attention. "You'll appreciate this little nugget for sure. In fact, it might just make a suitable screenplay at some point. Perhaps Jeremy here—that is, if he could ever steer his way clear of the burgeoning fish feed business—might choose to set pen to paper. You see, Robert here convinced me that we shouldn't have children, and I was so convinced that I went ahead and had a tubal litigation—sorry, that's *ligation*—litigation being Calvin here's area of expertise of course."

Cassidy smiled, elevating his unsmoked Camel jauntily.

"Anyway," said Leslie, "I did it as a gift. You know, as a gift to my husband, conventional gal that I am. Offering up my corporeal self as testament to our eternal love and all that jazz. But then Robert, well, he must have had second thoughts as, lo and behold, he planted his seed in the aforementioned best friend. And now he and Linda have this beautiful little child while I, well, while I get to hang out in pubs with you two gentlemen."

"Lower your voice, dear," Cassidy warned her, appearing all too glad, however, to have added something—anything—to the existing conversational equation to have any real subduing effect on her.

"But wait, there's more," she continued on at steadily increasing volume regardless of who could hear. "Apparently our Linda has now in fact *left* Robert, taking with her their three-year-old daughter. Isn't that ironic? Isn't it though? You ought to put that in one of your books, Jeremy. Yes, I think something literary might just come of it, given the appropriate care."

Here she stopped, seemingly too moved by her insights to go on. Meanwhile, Jeremy watched his brother, who now sat sweating, head bowed, eyes registering nothing insofar as Jeremy could tell. He could not believe Robert would just sit here listening to this bitch without defending himself. Finally Robert looked up, looked hard at Leslie, and after a token interval said quite plainly, "Enough."

"Enough what, Robert? What are you talking about?"

Jeremy could stand it no longer. "You bitch," he said, this time out loud.

And with that Jeevan stood up and, standing there alongside the table, his fists clenched into tight brown balls, asked Robert to step outside.

"Sit down," Robert told him. "Quit being such a dick. You're going to get yourself in trouble."

"Wonderful!" Cassidy shouted, leaning way back in his chair, apparently for no other reason than to admire the scene from there.

Robert sat, staring at the table. Eventually he said, seemingly to no one in particular, but obvious to everyone present this brand new adversary here, "Trust me when I tell you you're in way over your head here."

Jeremy looked fixedly at Leslie sitting chin lifted, proud and defiant on the other side of the table. "You're a real bitch you know that?" he found himself saying, and felt so good saying it that he promptly said it again.

"Now hold on a minute," Cassidy shot back, thrusting forward in his chair. "I suggest you take that back."

"Fuck off," Jeremy told him, managing to look him squarely in the eye. Jeremy did not like looking people in the eye, especially those people he did not respect, as he was afraid they would know exactly what he was thinking, as he knew you could and as they often did. This practice, often repeated, had long ago earned him the label of shy. And now, seeing all this in Jeremy's eyes, and knowing exactly what it meant, Cassidy dismissed him with an abrupt wave of his cigarette.

"Don't you talk that way to Calvin," said Leslie, standing and threatening Jeremy in her own entirely unthreatening way.

"Shut up," Cassidy told her, grabbing Leslie by the arm and forcing her bodily back into her chair. Leslie looked hard at him, opened her mouth as if to speak, wrestled in her mind with some elaborate speech, and finally enunciated in a fragile, unlikely way:

"*He's hurting me!*"

"Take your fucking mitts off her," said Jeevan, switching targets grudgingly.

"Why? She obviously deserves it," Jeremy put in.

Jeevan looked hard at Jeremy, and at long last observed, "She doesn't deserve anything that has you motherless pricks mixed up in it."

And at that Robert stood from his chair and, having already suggested, in his own quietly suggestive way, what it was he was about to do, took Jeevan up on his invitation to accompany him outdoors, as it were. In one swift burst of movement, he grabbed Jeevan by the throat and dragged him up to the front door of the pub, where, reminiscent of his days as a bouncer at this very bar, he wasted not a moment in employing his stunned and severely overmatched adversary's head as a provisional battering ram of sorts. Once outside, he naturally made quick work of the balance of his opponent, and, without further ado, returned his formidable strength and workmanlike focus to the task of pounding poor Jeevan's head repeatedly against the blacktop. Here and there Jeremy caught a glimpse of the latter's rapidly distorting face, wide-eyed now with that unique expression he had seen in similar situations so many times before. It was a rule of confrontation, one which Robert faithfully maintained, that there be invoked in the eyes of every combatant he faced both fear *and* fury, mixed in a primal blend. It came when that first fist landed, that was when the understanding first set in—he is winning, so I must be losing—a perpetually oscillating understanding that has existed in one fight or another, in one opponent or the other, ever since there were faces to be pushed in. A rustle of steps and curses. Harsh breathing through clenched teeth. Fingers curling instinctively into fists seeking the sudden intimacy of rupture of someone else's skin.

Jeremy watched all this from the half-open door, and watching, failed to stop Leslie as she made her way by. After Leslie came Calvin Cassidy, creeping forth commando-style, and Jeremy saw, not without reservations, where it was his duty lay. And so, heaving what was for him a premium sigh, he stepped out of the relative peace and quiet of the pub and into the blossoming parking lot fray.

Absorbed as he was in the business of thumping Jeevan's head against the asphalt, Robert did not realize Leslie was in the immediate vicinity until she was essentially riding rodeo atop his bucking back. Cassidy grabbed Leslie, whereupon Jeremy grabbed Cassidy, and proceeded to punch the actor, with all the strength that he could muster, in the back of his outsized, oddly resilient skull. This went on for several seconds, probably far longer than it ought to have, really. Finally, though, four of the owners' seven sons arrived, and more or less brought an end to the bloody battle in

Doolin's parking lot. A voice shouted out that the police were on their way, and so, having been separated from their respective opponents, the two Jacks boys ran off to Robert's truck, secure in the fact that, if nothing else, they were covered in the blood of someone else entirely.

POSTED BY LUCY @ 11:45:12 P.M. 4/21/2007   4 COMMENTS

AUGUST, 2002

Bob File, four days into his mandatory weeklong stress leave at the time of the fight at Royal Heights, but sporting his familiar uniform and a legitimate looking firearm regardless, overheard the call on his police scanner at home. He was eating takeout from Boston Pizza when the call came over the radio (having taken complete and arguably illegitimate advantage of the discount that franchise provides officers of the law), and so, refusing to take leave of his pesto chicken pasta, justifiably took his time in taking action, so to speak. It was during this delay, between the broadcasting of the complaint and the arrival of the constables both on-duty and otherwise, that Paul, Sukhvinder Rai's boyfriend at the time of her disappearance, sped past the pub in his friend's father's now month-old Lexus. When Bob finally did enter Doolin's, quietly, by way of the kitchen, and approximately a quarter-hour after the on-duty officers had come and gone through the front door, most of the principals involved had already fled the scene. But a few key particulars gleaned from a few key witnesses revealed all the information necessary to make the next step in this altogether private investigation a relatively promising, if not entirely profitable one.

Minutes later, having parked his Honda Civic out of sight up the street, Bob made his way slowly up the Jacks' driveway on foot.

"Hello, Robert," he said when Robert opened the door halfway, standing there in nothing but his jeans and a dried-up drop or two of Jeevan's blood.

"Hello, Robert. I didn't start it."

"Never said you did," Bob said.

He asked to have a look at Robert's driver's licence.

"To serve and collect, eh Bob?" said Robert, fishing around for his wallet. Once he found it, in his back right jeans pocket, he opened it up and extracted his licence. "So, what, Bob File the only cop that works in this town?"

"No, no, we've got a few more," said Bob, studying the licence in the dying evening light. "Don't you think you maybe ought to be keeping a lower profile these days?"

"Like I said, I didn't start it."

"Certainly exercised an excess of justice in finishing it though," Bob said. He frowned. "Robby, this licence is expired."

"Still, it's perfectly all right. You see? It's got my picture, my birth date, my height and weight, and no driving restrictions to speak of—so it's a perfectly serviceable licence."

"But it's expired."

"So? It shouldn't have."

"Oh *I* see," said Bob, returning Robert's licence. "Well if you wish to change the law concerning the life of a driver's licence, Robby, or even lodge a complaint, you should probably write your Member of Parliament."

"But I'm lodging my complaint with you, Bob. You're enforcing the law, therefore you're an agent *of* the law, and consequently I'm lodging my complaint with *you*. Now if you'd like to make something personal out of this, or if you feel you ought to make more of a statement on the issue but don't necessarily want to fill out all that ridiculous paperwork, why don't you take off that silly badge of yours, put down that silly gun, and we'll ramp this thing up right here, right now. How 'bout it, Bob. You in or what."

His voice was gentle, almost mechanical, as if he did not attach much meaning to what was said. Bob looked at Robert standing perfectly still before him, pale-skinned and muscular and at about the same height, and finally, reluctantly, shook his head in the negative. "Christ, Robby, we've known each other way too long to be fucking around like this."

Just then Jeremy appeared atop the stairs. "Evening, officer. I thought you were on vacation this week."

"Hey, Jer. Your dad around?"

"But he wasn't there," Robert interjected, shifting a few inches closer to Bob for the fun of it, if nothing else.

"Oh I don't care about any of that," said Bob, poking absent-mindedly at his chest and upper arm. "Though I must admit the frequency of these little feuds of yours does seem to be on the increase these days. Talked to Linda lately?"

"No, I haven't actually."

"Talked to your ex though."

"Matter of fact, I talked to her tonight. Talked to Calvin Cassidy too, if you're interested in that sort of thing. You know who Calvin Cassidy is, Bob? He's that actor who used to be on that *Law and Order* show."

"Yeah I know who he is. We get complaints about that prick all the time."

"Really. Well then maybe you can see that I was justified in whatever you think transpired tonight."

"I thought you said you didn't start it though."

"He didn't; Calvin Cassidy did," Jeremy put in, having since moved to the bottom of the stairs and alongside.

"Calvin Cassidy," Bob sighed. "You'd be surprised how much I deal with that asshole." He looked at Jeremy, then at Robert, then back to Jeremy. "How long you say you're in town for?"

"What are you going to do, Bob? Save us from ourselves?" Robert laughed.

"No, you're both well beyond my reach. So, again, you two did-n't start it?"

"Nope."

"But we sure did finish it," Jeremy said, in his mind a little too proudly perhaps.

"Oh I realize that," Bob said, forcing a laugh. "Tell me, though, who's this Jeevan character."

Robert smiled at Bob. He smiled at Bob in a way no one else would have dared smile at Bob, not condescendingly or confus-edly but bemusedly, as though Bob were an ally somehow led adrift, whose company would always be appreciated if and when he finally made his way back to the side of the just and the good. "My, but you're all business this evening aren't you, File?"

"Hey Robby, this is my job, okay? *My job.* Now quit fucking around and tell me who this Jeevan is."

"Dunno. Some Indo-Canadian dude. Local, or so he maintained at least. Apparently I used to pick on him a little when we were kids. But then of course I don't remember anything like that. Maybe he's got me mixed up with ol' Bob the Bully, huh? Or maybe I just don't remember the guy. I mean hey, I hardly remember anything before I was twelve or thirteen years old."

"And did you pick on him tonight?"

"As a matter of fact, he was picking on me. Actually—"

At that moment, however, the distraught voice of Jon Jacks erupted from somewhere around the back of the house. Bob followed the brothers through the foyer, out through the garage and into the backyard where they found Jon down on his knees between pool and pond.

"They're all dead."

"Dad, what happened?" Robert asked.

"They're all dead," Jon repeated, holding up evidence of recent atrocities committed here in the yard. In his hands lay the remnants of what had previously been a large and impressive Koi, reduced now to a single loosened eye in a mutilated head with an ugly exposed skeleton constituting all that remained of the body. Here and there throughout the backyard, with scales stripped and strewn reflecting the amber light of this otherwise gentle summer night, lay the ruptured remains of at least a dozen other inhabitants of the pond where they had been dragged to, where they had been ripped into, and where they had died.

"What happened? How did this happen? Dad, who did this?" Jeremy asked.

"Must've been the raccoons," Bob decided, speaking directly to the severed fish head on his right before turning to the ravine where, invisible from here, the partially constructed cabin resided.

Tuesday, August 1, 1972

Dear Mom & Dad:

Greetings and salutations from the fishbowl, or as we now refer to it in these truly blue-collar parts, "the Factory"—à la Warhol. Everyone here is fine, though admittedly starting to go a little crazy from all the marijuana. To wit, Doreen is running around soliciting patrons to visit her exhibition of pretty clean underwear in the laundry room; Shelley is kneeling about three inches from the stereo, grooving to Beethoven's Ninth Symphony op 125, her toenails painted with not one but two coats of Elmer's glue, meticulous thing that she is, understand; Rena and Lorna are playing a long, drawn-out game of "Hermit" behind the sofa, in which—oh forget it, it would take far too much ink to explain; here comes Debbie, staggering back from the nursing station with yet another bottle of Pepsi (Give your teeth a fighting chance, girl!), braying like an ass all the way; Connie is sitting cross-legged by the window reading A.A. Milne's Winnie the Pooh, her literary pursuits curtailed somewhat by an unfortunate and always debilitating attack of weaver's disease; Anne and Barbarella are still sleeping, having stayed up until 4:15 AM to watch the complete and uncut version of War & Peace on television (they decided it was time to crash when they heard *my* alarm go off), Barb guaranteed to be incapable of operating the loom today anyway as, last night, during toke time, she went ahead and picked all her weaving calluses off; oh and here comes Evie, running down the hall (runs everywhere: super energy)—wait, she's almost here—Hello there, kiddo. She's come to join me in the "big house," she says, as she's determined to weave today as usual, this despite the fact that weaving for Evie seems all but synonymous with dashing about like a darned fool. And each one, to a (wo)man, is absolutely *amazed* that I am the sister-in-law and niece of two of these so-called "peaceniks" they keep hearing about on television. Isn't it wonderful? And I haven't even mentioned my more famous namesake! I feel like some sort of celebrity, and I haven't really done anything yet.

And what, pray tell, did you two do today, hmm?

Another nasty summer storm rolling in across the city—sure glad
I'm not out in that. In keeping with the theme, though, I've had
an absolutely awful day of weaving, but since it's my first one I
really don't mind that much at all. One must expect such days
once in a while, mustn't one? Nothing drastic, mind you, just little annoying interruptions all the time, i.e. the blood lady, the
cleaning lady, the EEG lady—all *ladies*. Ugh! It's like I'm on a ship,
beleaguered by the various indifferent and unrelenting forces of
Mother Nature. Not their fault though. Not entirely anyway. And
yet, in dire need of a good strong dose of masculinity, no matter
what the source, I had Stan the Shopping Man read Connie's
Winnie the Pooh book to me over dinner, cover to cover—

HE: Pooh sure is dumb.

ME: Pooh's a bear, Stan. He just is.

HE: Yeah, but he sure doesn't know much, does he.

ME: Like what liniment is, you mean?

—which was decidedly nice, dare I say therapeutic, despite the
fact he managed to read it with all the warmth, sensitivity and
style of a recently hired, soon to be fired, funeral home employee.

A great sigh of relief rippled its way across the country today.
Ginny finally received a phone call from J, who, as I'm sure she's
told you, has been gallivanting around in Mexico this past week.
(Actually, it was the previous week, but bear with me; the lag in
mail-time confuses me.) What he's doing down there I haven't the
faintest idea—she wasn't entirely clear—all I do know is that late
one night he loaded up the Camino and took off, prepared to
drive non-stop all the way. Anyway, he's fine apparently, albeit
extremely exhausted, as was she, if for no other reason than she
hadn't heard from him over the course of the entire week, and
was justifiably upset ever since getting wind of some terrible run-
in between some Canadian "tourists" and the Mexican federal
police. She's all (cold, competent) smiles now though. Everything
is fine (as it gets) on the good ship Virginia.

Shelley played all her classical records today—a real treat to be
sure. Naturally, the music sent all the rock freaks screaming off to

their rooms, but she and I enjoy it immensely, and weaved our way through what was, apart from Beethoven, an aggravating and overly hectic afternoon.

Oh I almost forgot! Did you hear Dr. Myles on the news yesterday? Additionally, in today's paper, there should be something pertaining to the LeDain Commission on Drugs, and the work that Dr. Myles and his trusty manservant Congreves are carrying out here at the Factory. Apparently there's something in the New York Times too, on the subject of the American government's growing concern regarding our little experiment, and its possible ramifications for our country's future drug policies. Well, if nothing else, I'm sure Mr. Lennon in New York would be keen to be let in on our findings here. Evidently they want to extradite him from the States on some marijuana charge dating back to '68. How lame is that. Got to love that good ol' USA, eh?

Thursday, August 3

Now, as promised, my fashion forecast for the fall of '72.

F—is for Figure: clearly defined, basically slender but slightly wide-shouldered, waistline shaped in, with or without belt.

A—a swing to Asia: Chinese dresses, Mao tunics, Ming princess accessories and oriental-influenced jewellery all the way.

S—Skin. As in none. Except evening wear with halter necklines, décolletage, deep plunge backs and circle cut-outs.

H—Hips and how to help them: you're a woman, so show that figure, baby!

I—from the Italian designers: back to femininity with frills galore.

O—Oriental prints featuring colours like imperial yellow (chrome), lacquer red, vibrant green, and plum, plum, plum!

N—the Nautical look in hats, sailor pantsuits, middy collars on dresses, anchor buttons, chevrons and stripes, red, white & blue.

Length—about the knee or just below the knee.

Sportive—relaxed, ageless, naturally casual.

　　　　—blazers, shirtdresses, vests, and pants!

　　　　—vibrant prints with oriental or nautical colouring.

Plum—lots of it, in shoes, bags, gloves and hats.
You heard it here first, people.

Love, Birdie

P.S. Approaching $1000 mark in earnings, and just getting start-
ed, baby. Alive and well and living at 33 Russell, so don't fret so
much, okay?

AUGUST, 2002

The dayshift at Moore-Mathers started early, just shy of six-thirty,
but the nightshift, especially the final nightshift, ended long after
that. It seemed the workweek was just not complete until you had
made your way under the Knight Street Bridge for some early
morning binge drinking, chronic pot smoking and wide-ranging,
if frequently narrow-minded, pondering of life. Jeremy enjoyed
these gatherings, if for no other reason than seeing his brother hold
court in such new and, in a manner of speaking, exotic
environments.

That night's shift had proved particularly exhausting, what with
both orders having been churned out on what was known as the
Japan line. This meant filling, flattening and stacking 9.5 kilogram
bags of feed for hours at a time. The feed itself was six-millimetre,
which was a little more difficult to manipulate than, say, some of
the larger varieties. The bags were stacked on skids, eight bags per
layer and ten layers high, at which point the entire stack was
wrapped in plastic, then cardboard, then plastic again, labelled
appropriately and abundantly and finally sent on its way, one
would presume, to Japan. Because he was new, though, Jeremy
only ever got to stack the bags. He, for whom the very principle
of 'stacking' remained something entirely abhorrent, enjoyed a
long night of brute labour from beginning to end. For this reason,
then, unlike many of the mill's more veteran members, Jeremy had
no objections to spending part or even all of any given shift on the
Bulk line (at one thousand kilograms of feed per bag, and often as
many as five hundred bags ordered at a time) where the vast
majority of work was accomplished by the attendant forklift, and

all he need do was lay down a pallet, open a bag, set it up on the
forks and yank on a lever, then stand back and watch the moist
brown pellets rain down in—an orchestration of movement
administered by that sixth sense which only awakens once the
other five are sound asleep.

As I said, though, at the end of this particular shift on the Japan
line, the last of four in a row, approaching six-thirty in the morning, the Jacks brothers met up with the rest of the crew under the
Knight Street Bridge for the customary wind-down. This curious
exercise never ceased to amaze either of them, especially Jeremy,
for whom the early morning cocktail had always existed, quite
rightly, as something of a sub-urban, or suburban, myth. Out came
the bottles of liquor and the cases of beer, some from coolers
stashed in trunks overnight and others from the company's own
off-limits refrigerators; out, too, came the marijuana, literally by
the bag, sewn into cigarettes the size of middle fingers thrust up
in defiance of yonder mist-enshrouded feed plant. Under the
bridge the men sat in a circle on the grass, or, if the grass were still
too damp with dew, stood with backs against cars, watching the
sun wash up over an inner city horizon, tipping back bottles and
sucking back joints. Everyone, with the notable exception of the
brothers Jacks, took part in both bottle *and* pot—Robert,
naturally, avoiding alcohol completely, and Jeremy holding steady
to his diet of Crown and Coke for now. His drug test, as he had
yet to hear anything new on the subject, was still waiting out
there somewhere in the uncertain future. And while advised
repeatedly, via an assortment of seemingly reliable and well-
informed sources, of the existence of a mysterious and magical
'potion' (available for purchase apparently at any of several local
marijuana-endorsing establishments, the most controversial and
lucrative of which, the Amsterdam Café, had once sold
Sukhvinder Rai some sterile, long disposed of starter seeds) that,
according to lore, enabled the imbiber to pass almost any drug test
known to man, no matter what type or intensity of toxicity he
happened to be enjoying at the time, Jeremy had also heard far
too many horror stories of this so-called potion inducing a most

dreadful and debilitating diarrhea, therefore he decided to steer clear of weed as a rule until the test had been legitimately resolved one way or the other. No one seemed to mind. Everyone seemed to understand. These were true blue-collar men, and their livelihoods depended exclusively on Moore-Mathers income, and anyone who took a chance at sabotaging his own sole means of employment was a true-blue fool in their eyes, no question.

Finally there were only three men remaining under the bridge, the Jacks brothers and an often amusing, easily agitated, somewhat monkeyfied little fellow named Giovanni. Gio, as he was known by all but his mother, had been cursed with an unnaturally high-pitched voice and legs far too short for his torso, and supplementary to these shortcomings were a propensity for heated argument without anything resembling the slightest provocation and, of course, a passion for reciprocating the ideas of others as if they were his very own.

"Know what *really* gets me though?" he said at one point, a query relevant to nothing insofar as his audience could tell. "The price of fish has almost doubled since this time last year. *Doubled*. So that obviously means they're making a profit, no?"

"Not necessarily," said Robert, exhaling a great plume of smoke into the hollow morning air. "Don't forget, last year the price hit a six-year low."

"Still," trilled Gio, accepting the joint, eagerly anticipating its effects with his narrow hips floating out in a graceful and circular, entirely unconscious motion. "Still, holding back our raises to next quarter, that's just not right. Not good for business either, am I right? Am I not though? Of course I am. You've got to keep the workers happy. You've got to. Of course it's these fucking environmentalists who keep screwing it up for the rest of us," he went on with vigour out of all proportion to his stature. "Fuckers like this David Suzuki Foundation. Call themselves a charity, see, but make no mistake, they're a commercial industry just like we are here. And I tell you what," he squeaked, having since drawn heavily on the joint, and so speaking now without expelling his breath, "I tell you what, you take away those bastards' funding and

I bet they all just disappear. Gone. It's all about the cash, boys—am I right?—and Suzuki, well, Mr. Suzuki can go right ahead and kiss my hairy Italian *ass*."

This last image seemed to sum up the entire matter, which Jeremy's mind now presented, much to his chagrin, as something of a fleshy interlocking structure with working hydraulic parts. Robert, too, seemed to consider the image carefully. At last he said, "Well have you ever considered the possibility that Mr. Suzuki might just have a valid point?"

"Point?" said Gio, finally expelling his smoke. "What point? The man's fucking with my livelihood—my *livelihood*, Robby—tell me, what am I supposed to do with that?"

Robert agreed that such a practice was intolerable. "However," he added, "just so you know, the fish farms we supply helped destroy our father's livelihood as well."

"But I didn't have anything to do with that," blinked Gio emphatically, one brother to the other, while proclaiming with studied dignity his absolute innocence with regard to such tragedy—a matter of shrugged shoulders and imploring hands principally.

"Not personally maybe, but your employer did. Moore-Mathers did. This plant," Robert contended, gesturing over his shoulder at the mill, "supplies the feed for over eighty percent of the fish farms on the West Coast. *Eighty percent*," he said. "That's a lot."

Gio blinked again, on the theory that it looked good on him, then shrugged and shook his head in bewilderment. "My God, man, whose side are you on?"

"Actually, I'm trying to figure that out myself," Robert admitted with a grin.

His point he felt made, Gio eventually made his way home to his wife. He was a little sad when he finally had to say goodbye, but his sadness was tempered with the knowledge that he would be back again amongst the mill and its men in less than four days' time.

Gio's departure left Jeremy and Robert alone on the small patch of grass in the shadow of the bridge. It was quiet here despite the mass of traffic roaring past all of fifteen meters overhead, and even the attendant shrieks of the industrious gulls registered only as distant, vague complaints. In time Robert nodded off, sinking easily beneath the day's rising wave of heat, and later, lying prone on the grass, his face in the sun, he awoke to the sound of his own stifled snoring mistakenly ascribed to a backfiring engine some distance off. Groggily, he arose to a sitting position, before thinking better of it and settling back onto his elbows in a more relaxed arrangement of limbs. "What the fuck happened to you?" he asked, yawning and blinking against the bleached glare of the sun.

"You fell asleep," answered his brother.

"Did you sleep, Jer? A man like you really ought to get more sleep. Them there's the facts, Jacks—it's important, not only for maintaining optimum health, but—"

"Maybe a little," Jeremy broke in.

"Wow," said Robert, mystified. "Wow, now that's some killer weed. Good to know my guardian angel's always here watching over me. Know where I got it though?" he asked, sitting up again. "Got it from Leslie."

"*Your* Leslie?"

"That very Leslie," Robert grinned. Stiff from sleeping on the ground, he stretched and rubbed his eyes, and afterwards sat and waved listlessly at a routinely orbiting fly.

Meanwhile, Jeremy considered his feet, trying by strenuous mental effort to ward off what was coming regardless of what he did. "Please don't tell me you went and saw her."

With a cat-quick stroke, Robert squashed the fly that had just that second alighted on his knee. "Of course I went and saw her. How else was I going to sleep with her? Went and slept with her last Thursday night, I did."

"Thursday? But aren't you supposed to be at the army on Thursdays?"

"Sure I'm supposed to be at the army. But you know what? I took that night off. Now don't worry, little brother, the nation's still safe. The flickering lamp of democracy's not quite gone out."

"But why?"

"Why? What do you mean, *why*? What else was I supposed to do? Ignore my first wife's blatant cries for help? Exactly what sort of wedding vows do you think I uttered that fateful night, huh?"

"She wasn't angry about the other night at the pub then?" Jeremy continued, indulging in a little conventional anger himself over the frustratingly transitory quality of relationships in general, with women in particular, his brother's wives especially.

"Leslie? Angry? Why would she be angry? Leslie always felt disappointed and unappreciated if I didn't find a way to get in *some* sort of fight over her."

"Especially in bars."

"Es*pec*ially in bars," Robert echoed right back. "Gets better though," he eventually went on.

"What gets better?"

"The story. Or more precisely, the story of the weed. Oh you'll like this one," he said, shoring up excitedly. "You'll appreciate this bit of irony for sure. Leslie got it, see, from young Mrs. File. Yep, this stuff here's Bob's wife's cancer weed," he grinned, turning all too triumphantly and tellingly in the direction of the river.

"Jody's got cancer? *Now?*" Jeremy exclaimed in bald-faced disbelief, as though the presence of the disease itself were secondary to the fact that even now she might be the object of Robert's relentless affections.

Robert shook his head. "Had it though. Had it in the head if I'm not mistaken."

"A brain tumour? Really?"

"Really. But then who doesn't have a little brain tumour now and then. No, she's nothing special, believe me. Although . . ." He considered something briefly, frowned at the thought, then concluded, "Although Bob thinks she is, no question."

"Jesus," said Jeremy, frowning himself. "So what then, it's in remission?"

"It's officially in remission, my friend." Finding a roach worthy of ignition, Robert set about the task of relighting it without any of the necessary implements, clearly a difficult proposition. "Remission: a temporary lessening," he recited under his breath, still holding aloft the sadly unlit roach, still seeking a modicum of cooperation from the mysterious world of spontaneous combustion. "Well anyway," he said, perking up again, "as you can imagine, Jody's pretty keen on having kids. Christ, she even talks about *us* having kids. That is, when she's not doing yoga and 'journaling' and shit like that."

"So why's she giving away her cancer weed then."

"Simple. Bob doesn't like it in the house now that she's finished her chemo. Makes sense too, 'cause this stuff knocks you on your *ass*. This is certified government-grown, grade A cancer weed, Jer. Too strong for the likes of you. No, after your drug test we'll start you on some of the B weed stuff. Nothing too intense, understand—just enough to get you where it is you need to go—like back on track with Dad perhaps. Might be just the ticket needed there. Then again," he reflected, examining his unlit roach up close, "Dad doesn't particularly need any more on his plate. Being, as he is, after much bigger fish right now."

"What bigger fish."

"Well lately, hey, he really hasn't been feeling all that well."

"How do you mean?"

"Well Dad thinks he might've suffered a little stroke a few months back, and—"

"A *stroke*? Are you *serious*? Why the fuck am I just hearing about this now?"

"Take it easy. Because, as it turns out, it wasn't a stroke. Least that's what the doctors said. Of course they don't know what the hell it was if it *wasn't* a stroke—maybe the onset of Parkinson's, though I doubt it. . . . No, as far as I'm concerned, all symptoms point to an Ischemic, or at the very least a T.I.A. in the cerebellum, though naturally I have no way of proving it either way."

For a moment Robert considered the river running past, dappled now with sunlight, before placing his roach reluctantly aside and ripping from his provisional bed handful after handful of thick green grass.

"Anyway," he resumed eventually, "one night Dad fell and smacked his head on his way to the toilet, managing, in the process, to completely soil himself. So picture this: old bugger drags himself to the telephone at the end of the hall and dials not nine-one-one, not me, but Bob fucking *File* of all people. Yeah, exactly. Of all the people he could call, including his own very capable, highly trained, impeccably credentialed son, he calls your old buddy *Bob*. Christ knows what for," he said, and shook his head at the downright complexity of fathers relative to sons.

"Now where was I . . . Oh yes, Constable Bob, he rushes on over in the middle of the night, no questions asked, and helps Dad clean himself up—getting him into the shower, putting in a load of laundry and whatnot—salvaging the old man at least a *few* shreds of dignity, and believe me, Dad won't forget that. Or maybe he will, depending on what all's happening in that decrepit old head of his. . . . At any rate," Robert said, "as you can plainly see, I'm fully within my rights taking liberties with Bob's bald-headed wife. Not to mention the fact I've always found any suggestion of a lack of self-esteem incredibly sexually enticing."

Now it was Jeremy's turn to shake his head, utterly mystified. "I can't believe I'm just hearing about this now. You are—the *both* of you are—quite unfathomable to me."

"Yeah, well, I thought if I told you, you might not make it out here, hey."

"Why the hell would you think that?"

Robert shrugged. He aggressively massaged his eyes with his palms. Then at long length he said, "Well I know how much Dad annoys you, so . . ."

"*So?*"

"So cut me some slack, all right? I mean what'd I do: I decided to sit on his condition a while. You know, until I had something concrete to tell you. And so a few days went by, and then a few more went by, and it all just seemed to fade away after a while. . . . And besides, I did call you eventually, remember."

"Yeah because Dad was locked up for taking apart his successor at the hospital."

"Yeah, I do feel kind of bad about that," Robert said, slowly shaking his head in that telltale Jacks manner. "Anyway, it was all happening about the same time: Dad's falling in the hall . . . my, what, falling from grace at school . . . even my falling out of that fucking plane. And hey, here you are, right?"

"Here I am," said Jeremy, gazing over at the mill. "You know what the worst part is about working here though?" he asked after a time.

"The fish smell?"

"No, the absence of it. Here I am not, what, two hundred feet away, and I can't so much as get a *hint* of it. I'm become completely acclimated to it. And I find that fact completely fucking depressing."

"A more positive man would say that's a blessing."

"Yeah, well, a more blessed man wouldn't work here in the first place, I'm guessing."

Together they sat, gazing out at the river running past, and at the log boom sentenced for the neighbouring sawmill languishing over near the opposite bank. Robert made one last-ditch, labour-intensive effort to locate a lighter—turning out his pockets and ransacking both knapsacks in the hope that, in the interim, some miracle had take place there, but none had—before flicking, with fine accuracy, his roach into the nearby bush, and as a result forgetting about it entirely. "You know what, Jer? You smell a lot like fish," he said, and reached over to cuff his brother on the back of the head.

"Ah this literary life," Jeremy said.

POSTED BY LUCY @ 6:25:09 P.M. 4/23/2007   3 COMMENTS

Friday, August 4, 1972

Dear Mom & Dad:

Slept in till six o'clock this morning in preparation for my first early morning excursion outside. Lorna and I dressed in shorts and T's, but brought along pants and sweatshirts just in case it wasn't quite as warm as we expected it to be, then ventured up to the front desk to pay our nickel and, in turn, pick up the nurse and male attendant assigned to accompany us on our first little foray back into the world of the (supposedly) weed-free.

It was sunny outside, but cool, and dawn was slow in coming, yet even at six in the morning there are interesting things to see and smell on College Street. Peter, our male attendant (and resident armament), suggested we walk westward, toward Bathurst. We did just that, and passed several bakeries pulling the first of the day's goods from the ovens. The smell was, in a word, heavenly. It's been so long! Every store window we passed was a surprise, and something of a small wonder and adventure in itself. We laughed a lot, mostly at ourselves, and our reactions to the things we witnessed as we walked. The four of us helped push a car to the station that was out of gas—the driver was pleased, but somewhat bewildered too, I think, at our auspicious appearance on the street just in his time of need.

We returned at six-thirty warm, happy, and glad to be home. That was fun, but not something I'm going to take advantage of all that much, as I'm fairly well-conditioned to the fishbowl now, and don't want to start missing the outside world too much. It's a strange sensation, though, living this way. Both captive and complicit in your own captivity, in a way.

Didn't weave a whole lot the rest of the day—just ten belts—but spent much of the time reading the paper from cover to cover, looking at all the used pianos for sale—absolutely my first purchase when I get out—and catching up on all the good new shows I've been missing. No matter, I'll catch them on the reruns, I suppose.

The marijuana dosage has been much heavier this past week, so unfortunately "high" tide takes that much longer to subside. Thus I shall be sleeping from 9:30 PM until 6 AM for a while, to see if that doesn't leave me a little cheerier and spunkier in the daylight hours. Don't misunderstand me, I'm feeling good—great actually—but a little draggy (druggy?) if you know what I mean. Everyone else feels about the same, only they're sleeping even more than I am.

Saturday, August 5, 1972

A nice bright, beautiful sunny day in Toronto again. Got up at six and weaved (wove?) my standard twenty, so I feel better about that anyway. Ginny feels a bit better now too apparently. Jonathan is back from Mexico and looking, in her words, "wild as hell," so she isn't worrying about him *quite* so much—Mexican authorities being notorious for throwing people in jail for hair even slightly longer than business executive style, let alone J's lengthy locks. Evidently his car has seen better days though.

In my spare time, whenever my weaver's disease subsides enough to allow it, I'm working hard at improving my sketching—or at least getting it back to where it was a few months back. When you're not a natural at drawing, I find you must really keep it up, practicing constantly to maintain the talent, or else it simply drops off. In contrast, I've gotten my guitar as good as it's ever been, so all I need now are some new songs—these old ones are absolutely killing me.

I'm really overjoyed at the thought of owning my own piano. In fact, if you happen to hear of any good deals up your way, let me know, OK? Of course a baby grand is slightly too extravagant for my meagre budget, not to mention my crappy little apartment, but I think one of those little low console kind might fit in quite nicely—how about you?

Must write Ginny today; her letter arrived Wednesday, but I haven't had a chance to answer yet. By the way, have you gotten any of that film developed yet? If I remember correctly, there should be a few of J and J Jr. on it, along with the rest of the crew of my favourite fishing dinghy, the Phyllis Cormack. The ones of Jr. will be particularly good, I think, though I suppose I could've taken more. . . . That young man is just such a handful though! And the way he looks at you sometimes . . . well, you just have to wonder what he's thinking, that's all. Another shot, I recall, shows the front part of the house—my room was the upstairs window on the far right there, above the garage. The rest are of various species of flora and fauna G planted in the backyard while I was out, but darn if I can remember any of their names now. . . . One's a rhodo, that much I know . . . At least that's the flower Jr. has tucked behind his ear in that one shot. And there's one of me on his "secret swing" in the ravine, if I remember correctly. Oh yes, and a few of Mr. Jacks and his car, or his truck, or whatever the heck you want to call it. He looks good though, doesn't he? Alas (sigh), all the good ones are married. But then maybe it's their being married that makes them good ones, right?

Sunday, August 6, 1972

Tracey's envelope arrived this morning with plenty of goodies enclosed. She's going great guns moonlighting for Interthink (market research, interviewing)—that's Ruth's company—plus her own catering thing as well. She sent along a phone bill for $159 (I almost croaked!), only $63 of which is mine though, and $53 of that is from the previous month (my cheque didn't get through before the billing date, I suppose), the rest being the responsibility of Ruth and Lorna—Mike's collect calls from Kansas, Phoenix, etc. I've sent a cheque to Tracey for my part, and Lorna is sending her a money order from her ARF savings account.

Property insurance—yes. You'll be relieved to know that Tracey has arranged some for me, at *my* request. The policy is already in effect, and costs approximately $25/year. It is a tenant's package policy, covering all personal effects, in my apartment or out on the street (if, say, my purse were stolen)—anywhere in the world actually. It protects me against liability should anyone fall down my stairs, fall in the bathtub, or if the bathtub should overflow and fall into the apartment downstairs—even if the house itself should somehow fall down, I'm covered from stem to stern with this baby. Hence, I feel it's worth it. I've sent a money order, along with the signed policy, to Frank J. Casey, Insurance Agency Limited, on Yonge Street.

Love, Birdie

P.S. My long lost T4 slip from the Children's Festival finally arrived as well.

Sunday, August 6, 1972

Dear Ginny:

'The extensions of man's consciousness . . . could conceivably usher the millennium, but it also holds the potential for realizing the Anti-Christ.'

~ Marshall McLuhan

Ah yes, day #38 here in shmecker's heaven, where we continue to adjust to new feelings and developments as they appear on the pot-hazed horizon. Speaking of new developments, Mom and Dad recently took out a life insurance policy for (on) me—can you imagine?

We've been smoking hard now for three weeks, but some time during the second week the dosage was increased considerably, resulting in very tired little potheads suddenly requiring a great deal extra sleep. I sleep now from 9:30 PM till 6 AM, then weave like gangbusters till about 7 or 7:30 PM, at which point I sketch, play guitar, write letters, play practical jokes on Stan, etc before mandatory toke time arrives like a fucking freight train at 8:15. The smoking hasn't actually cut down on my rate of weaving by any discernible degree. However, adjusting to my own moods, as well as the ongoing and, in some cases, mounting psychoses of the other inmates has certainly taken its toll. Not surprisingly, I'm getting a little backed up because of it.

(Ironically, I really only started weaving at maximum speed this past week or so, and now have my first $1000 socked away. My first purchase, after student loans, etc are cleared up, is going to be another trip to England—I can hardly wait!)

Every Sunday, Tracey delivers a big brown envelope to the main desk in the lobby, with her weekly report of comings and goings at 37 Pleasant Blvd, plus any mail that's arrived for me. She put up an ad on the bulletin board at the local A & P, and as a result of said ad, managed to rope herself a boarder, a.k.a. Cory, an eighteen year-old chemistry whiz at U of T, who, not surprisingly, she's taken to humping habitually. This little boy-toy of Tracey's will be staying with her (or under her, whatever the case may be) until the end of September apparently, so that takes care of the rent anyway, and it won't cost me a penny—not that it should of course, as she's the one now getting it regularly. Ruth, Lorna and Mike split June's rent and hydro, so that left me with enough in the bank to cover everything else until my parole in October.

I'm really delighted with the thought of a bachelor's degree, Ginny. In fact I think it's wonderful. For obvious reasons your education got derailed way too early, especially after having shown so much potential at so young an age. Lately, I've been giving more thought to what and where I'd like to study too—they're starting the fourth year of my course at Ryerson this fall, so I'll unfortunately miss that with my commitments here, but if I were to return in, say, the fall of '73 (how far away *that* seems) I could get my degree, and perhaps even teach there, either in the Fashion course or in the Theatre Arts program—we shall see. Actually, with any luck it'll be the latter, when I have a little bit more experience behind me. I'm really looking forward to this next trip to England though. . . . The fucking Brits don't know what they're in for with me.

Aunt Birdie wants to know when she's coming back out too! Not till next year though, I'm afraid, and it will depend on Stratford, at any rate. My chances are excellent, though nothing official as yet. If I do get work there (June thru August approx) then I could be out your way at the end of August, or perhaps early September '73—if I don't go back to Ryerson, that is. Barring an outright return to school, I hope to be available for le Théâtre Nationale du Montréal and the Nat'l Arts Centre, Ottawa in late September, so I'd have about three weeks at the end of next summer, if that works for you folks okay. Oh I know this is all more than a year away, but unfortunately I'm all booked up already.

8:15 pm—Toke Time

This experiment is the most incredible experience I shall ever encounter, bar none. I am in awe. We have ten distinct personalities here, continuously changing direction and scope, running the gamut of emotions, reactions, sensations, philosophies and thoughts. We've taken an initially unnatural situation and made it natural—this is our home, and we each, in our own way, have settled down to more or less accept what is, in effect, a hazy approximation of reality. Psychologically speaking, the environment is, believe it or not, an extremely healthy one. For once in our life we feel no inhibitions, either with the staff or with each other, and hence there is a kind of freedom to work out any potential personality conflicts, problems, dilemmas or whatever that happen to arise. You can drop all the "games people play" if you want to—there's simply no need for them here. Gradually we are becoming more honest and open, not only with each other, but with ourselves too—how we think and feel, what we want to say and do—evolving, as the experiment progresses, into something of a freeform group therapy project as much as any government-regulated, data-related drug test.

Physically, though, it may be a slightly different story, at least for me. And this has nothing to do with weaver's disease. Interestingly, though my notoriously finicky bowels have so far more or less toed the line, and despite the fact that all the other inmates have been busy aligning their respective cycles with varying degrees of success, for whatever reason I've not had my period since the experiment began. Now I know what you're thinking—that I've been jumping all over one or more doctors of vaguely swarthy persuasion—but trust me when I tell you that's simply not the case. Not yet anyway. If you must know—and I know you *must* know—it might, repeat *might* have happened when I first returned from Vancouver six weeks ago. It doesn't matter who. And anyway, let's not jump to any conclusions, Ginny, as it might simply be this overly isolated, heavily hormoned, exceedingly fertile albeit alien environment I'm presently locked up in. I've certainly heard of that sort of thing. Anyway, don't worry; I'll get to the bottom of this mystery of omission as soon as humanly possible, believe me.

Now what's all this about J drinking? I never knew him to take a drink—at least not while I was around to see it. Be careful with that though, sister. Men of that temperament and alcohol simply

don't mix in a very appealing way. They didn't mix so well in
Dad's case either—but then I suppose you're the last one who
needs reminding of that nasty bit of family nostalgia, eh? Anyway,
must close for now. Shelley's about to crank up yet another of her
brutal Beethoven records—all she'll listen to are the classics, she
says, because (I say) she's a snob and a bitch and so much older
than the rest of us—sending the rest of us "ingrates" literally
scrambling, ears covered, for the exits.

Love, Birdie

AUGUST, 2002

Finishing off their second, and final, nightshift of the week,
Robert and Jeremy met up with the rest of the crew under the
bridge for the usual post-shift festivities. I probably need not
mention that the shifts were twelve hours long, two days followed
by two nights, with a full four days off to recuperate before the
next block of four began. Afterwards, the brothers went home to
steal a couple of hours sleep before framing in the second-floor
walls of the cabin, the project's next scheduled assignment on
what Jeremy quietly felt was becoming an insurmountable list of
obligations. By the end of the day all four walls were in place,
though for the most part incomplete, and the narrow staircase
ascending to the second floor, started the week before, had been
installed on the cabin's west side, under which the toilet was projected to be located should their ambition ever take them that far.
Jon had by now stumbled upon an old Federal wood-burning
stove, and to retain its yield the walls were to be stuffed with
thick pink R19 insulation. The two floors had already been likewise insulated, and covered in half-inch tongue and groove plywood sub-flooring, while battened plywood skirting sealed the
cabin's otherwise open base not only for aesthetic purposes, but
to prohibit any potential draughts seeking to infiltrate from that
direction. Six double-glazed windows had been purchased, three
for each floor, with the largest two intended to face the maples
and the stream and whatever else went on in the ravine below.

There had been some talk of taking the tower up further, to a third floor with the option for an open fourth, but in the end they decided against it as two floors would undoubtedly be enough, especially as the cabin was intended for just one little girl's enjoyment—or so at least they told each other whenever the subject came up.

That night, Jeremy took up the recently reinstated Bob File on his offer of a ride-along. They met up at the Delta police station at six o'clock, at which point Jeremy suddenly realized, not without some distress, that Bob had lost a great deal of weight over the previous six weeks, especially through the arms, shoulders, and chest. Naturally he did not mention this, knowing as he did far more of what was actually going on in Bob's personal life than even Bob himself did. Bob offered Jeremy a walk-through tour of the facilities, and afterwards walked him through a waiver, the gist of which safeguarded the department against any and all legal action should Jeremy be somehow injured or killed while out and about 'on the job,' as it were.

Next, Jeremy sat in on the officers' pre-shift briefing, wherein the moustachioed Indo-Canadian sergeant, in a quiet unassuming voice—the same quiet unassuming voice with which he had once spoken to Sukhvinder Rai when she had been briefly interested in pursuing a career in the police force—ran through a long, impossible to remember list of ongoing cases and suspects-at-large each officer ought to be familiar with. Not surprisingly, one of these cases was that of Sukhvinder Rai herself, still ongoing, still unsolved, though none of the six officers in attendance, including, remarkably or not, the moustachioed Indo-Canadian sergeant, seemed all that interested at this point. At the conclusion of the meeting Jeremy made a point of saying, "And remember, let's be careful out there," but then none of the six officers in attendance seemed to find that allusion all that funny or interesting either.

An hour later found the pair cruising around Delta on a quiet summer night, contemplating where it was they ought to have dinner on their gradually approaching break, the excitement of punching up licence plates on the onboard computer to see what infractions arose, for Jeremy at least, having more or less run its course. Undecided as they were, Bob emailed their query to another officer, a stocky and excitable Greek named Nick, and as always Nick suggested Boston Pizza so as to best employ that restaurant's unwritten, yet entirely expected, police officer's discount. This dogged allegiance to Boston Pizza was rather amusing, Bob insisted, as it was a fact well known and much discussed on the force that Nick's father had recently passed away and that he, Nick, had come into a great deal of money on account of it.

"Nick's cheap," Bob pointed out quite needlessly, if somewhat hypocritically, once the final decision had been reached. They were drifting along Scott Road at the time, punching up licence plate numbers, and in turn driver's licence numbers, without probable cause and for absolutely no justifiable reason. Jeremy was amazed at the remarkable lists of criminal convictions that arose for what would otherwise seem altogether unremarkable citizens. 'Unlawful confinement' was one such charge he found particularly amusing, especially considering the perpetrator appeared to be an elderly Asian man driving a decade-old Plymouth station wagon.

"You'd be surprised," said Bob. "Or maybe you wouldn't, I don't know. . . . Hey, want to key in your dad? I bet you get an absolute catalogue of convictions there."

"Thanks, but I'd rather not."

Bob asked if Jeremy's father was still upset about his fish getting mauled.

"Oh," Jeremy sighed, "he's pretty much put the ordeal behind him, I think. Turns out he only lost about a dozen, but he's gone ahead and installed this kind of steel grate over the pond anyway, so that ought to curtail their pursuits a bit. Raccoons, hey. Vicious buggers. Ripped the stomach out of my cat when I was a kid. By the way, I heard what you did for him. The night he fell and you came over and helped him, I mean."

Bob shrugged, staring straight ahead through the windshield. "Yeah, well, I probably should've called an ambulance or taken him in or something—in fact, I absolutely *should* have called an ambulance or taken him in—but of course, if I had, your dad would've killed me."

"And sorry to hear about Jody by the way." Jeremy said this quickly, floating over the name 'Jody' as swiftly as possible lest he betray anything inappropriate by dawdling unnecessarily. "You know," he mused, "it never ceases to amaze me the progress of other peoples' lives."

"I'd hardly call cancer progress, Jer."

"Sorry—rate of change, I mean. It's like nothing out of the ordinary ever really happens to me, while other peoples' lives—yours included—just seem so full of, you know, *ev*erything."

Neither Bob nor Jeremy spoke for a time, content as they were to stare out the windshield and watch the black of the asphalt vanish into the bright white hood of the car. "Ah well, she's pretty much put the whole thing behind her," Bob said finally, poking hard at his chest. "Through the worst of it, I mean. Say, don't you find it sort of weird your father never got married again? Or even had himself a girlfriend?"

Jeremy pushed back an advancing cuticle. "Not really, to be honest. No, I think he was pretty much finished with women after our mother left him. And really, who can blame him."

"Still, you'd think he would've at least hooked up here and there."

"Actually, he did. Now that I think about it, he used to bring home the occasional woman—from the pub, I'm sure. I remember this one chick, kind of beat-up looking—real prize—getting into a wrestling match with my father over a case of fucking beer. I'm serious. Here they are in the kitchen, struggling back and forth, this case of Extra Old Stock a tug-of-war between them, when all of a sudden Dad lets go and the case hits her square in the forehead and knocks her backwards onto the floor."

Bob laughed.

"Not funny. Concussion. Hospital. Worse, it all takes place in front of Robby and me."

"Well that's unfortunate."

"Unfortunate nothing—fucking tragic's what it is. Know what the judge told them? 'You two are pathetic.' That's good."

"Yeah that's pretty good," Bob admitted. "Check this out though." He pointed across the nearly vacant Royal Heights parking lot to where a single white police cruiser stood all too solemnly parked, its bright white hood gathering in all it possibly could of the gradually dissolving daylight. Bob turned into the lot and up alongside the cruiser, in which they found another officer currently on duty, this one a short, dark-haired woman named Caroline quietly dozing off with her head resting awkwardly against the steering wheel.

"Hey pig. Catching up on a little sleep, are we?"

"Hey pig," said Caroline, evidently unconcerned with the fact that she had just been caught, quite literally, on the nod. "Anything happening?" she asked.

"No, pretty slow," Bob told her. "This is my friend, Jeremy. He's a writer, and he's going to do a story on this."

"What's 'this'?"

"This ride-along."

"Should make for a hell of an interesting read," chuckled Caroline crazily.

"Yes, should be pretty exciting," Bob agreed with a smile.

Finally, with nothing more to say to Caroline, and Caroline still chuckling crazily, Bob and Jeremy were once again on their way. But not before Bob gave her a good ribbing for sleeping the entire first third of her shift away.

"Caroline used to be married to another cop," Bob explained as they exited the parking lot, ever the eager storyteller, always ready with an appropriate anecdote to further illustrate his escalating contempt for his job in particular and the world in general. "Guy named Tony. Now Tony was a great old guy. Only thing is, see, Tony was maybe a bit unstable, and more so when he had to go on injury leave for a while." He hesitated. "Maybe I shouldn't be telling you this."

"Maybe," said Jeremy, not really caring one way or the other just yet.

Bob considered, then shrugged, already far too committed to the narrative to possibly back out. "So anyway, this one day Tony and Caroline are at home, you know, just messing about the house, when all of a sudden he remembers he's got to go to court for this case that's already been delayed like five times to this point. Assumes, quite rightly, that he'll be gone all day. But the thing is, as luck would have it, he gets to court and the defence lawyer hasn't even bothered to show up, and the case gets pushed back yet again. So Tony, having happily clocked his half-day's pay, heads on home to spend the rest of his suddenly free day with his wife. And what does he find? Why, Caroline, in bed with Nick, riding—"

"Cheap Nick?"

"That's right—riding the son of a bitch bareback and screaming to beat the band."

"Damn," Jeremy said. "How'd Tony take it?"

"Not very well, I'm afraid. Unstable as he was, not two days later ol' Tone shot himself in the head. You probably heard about it in the news a while back."

"So how'd Caroline deal with that?"

"As well as can be expected, I guess. I mean she and Nick, they stayed together for another few weeks, maybe a month, but then Nick inherited all that money and, well, that was that."

"Wow," Jeremy said. "Good story. Tell me, though, have you slept with her?"

Bob regarded him uneasily. "Caroline?" he said. "Why do you ask?"

"Don't know. Thought I detected something there on our widow's part. Something of an underlying resentment perhaps."

"No, no, I haven't slept with her. Not that she hasn't put forth the offer. And on several occasions, too, I might add. . . . No, I tell you what, Jer, it may be all the rage with my fellow officers, but having an affair just seems like a real hassle. I'm not completely *against* the idea, mind you, but it just doesn't seem quite worth the hassle. Not to mention the fact you're fucking over some poor bastard who, chances are, hasn't so much as wished upon you a moment's grief in his life."

Jeremy shuffled about in his seat. "So, what, is Caroline joining us for dinner?"

"Are you kidding? With Nick there? No, it's definitely one or the other—him or her—which makes for some fairly comfortable situations around the office, you can be sure. Speaking of which, how's it going for you?"

"Work? Work's good. Though they sure do smoke a lot of pot there."

"On shift?"

"No, afterwards."

Bob laughed. "You know I can't even remember the last time I arrested someone for possession? It's literally been years. . . . Yeah, *years* I bet."

"Good on you, we'll make a decent criminal of you yet. Hey, this is where my dad used to send me for cigarettes."

Together they stared at Ben's Market on the corner, a small white square of a store from another era entirely.

"I remember," Bob said.

Driving to the bottom of Ninety-Sixth Avenue, less than two blocks away from the Jacks house, Bob and Jeremy turned left where the road ended at Fisherman's Trail. Down the tree-lined trail they could just make out the heavily industrialized Fraser River waterfront, and beyond it, though neither man was willing to talk about it, the red and gold-tinged clouds queued up one after another towards yet another model West Coast sunset.

"Not much fishing going on down there these days."

"Not much, no. Though of course the Indians take whatever they need."

"They would," Jeremy said, though it must not be supposed that he meant anything malicious by this.

They drove on, up past Jeremy's street and around and down towards their old school, the sadly outdated, pathetically handicap-integrated Annieville Elementary (which, incidentally, the author himself attended back in the sixties, back when it was a real school, taking home the highly esteemed Academic Award in grades four, five and seven, grade six being merely an anomaly, the

unfortunate result of a minor accounting error really, and hence
hardly worth mentioning here—but bear with me) squatting dark
and sullen against the mealy evening sky, its interior lights all gone
out, the exteriors as yet to spring to life. The adjacent park, too,
grew steadily darker, with the attendant playground and baseball
diamond retreating into shadow even as they passed.

Down they went, down River Road, past all the houses where
the air first begins to feel damp, where the brisker evening wind
first begins to rise up off the flats. Arriving riverside, they stood
leaning against a wooden guardrail looking up towards the massive concrete Alex Fraser Bridge. Below them the water ran
smooth and dark, making no sound as it passed. A car pulled into
the lot, and inside were a young boy and girl, limbs already enthusiastically interlocked. But then, not surprisingly, having made
note of their welcoming committee, they were on their way once
again in a hurry, but not in too much of a hurry, lest they somehow appeared overly suspicious in departure.

"We probably just foiled their plans for a pleasant sunset screw."

"Of course we did," Jeremy grinned. "Then again, when I think
of the things *I* used to do to girls. . . . By the way, what's the statute
of limitations for that sort of thing?"

"There isn't one."

"Lucky for me. I mean hey, I should probably be put away on
poor technique alone."

"They did suffer a great deal under us, didn't they?"

As planned, Bob and Jeremy went for dinner at Boston Pizza on
Scott Road, where they were joined by Nick just outside the front
door. The restaurant was crowded with young men and women,
many of them Indo-Canadian, most of whom possessed at least a
working knowledge of the sad and still unresolved story of
Sukhvinder Rai, some with considerably more than that, and the
three men had to stand and wait for a table and, in the meantime,
find something interesting to say to fill the gaps. In passing, one of
the wait staff, a young, flirtatious, recently implanted but otherwise
commonplace blonde who, back when she first applied for the
hostess job, despite the fact she possessed no experience

whatsoever, managed to secure the position over the experienced Sukhvinder Rai anyway, apologized for making them wait so long. Boston Pizza had recently become very popular with the East Indians, she said, as the dishes were relatively inexpensive and of course they were open late. Hindus were nocturnal and notoriously cheap, she added by way of explanation, and for whatever reason, probably because she had such enormous breasts, none of them bothered to censure her in this. Still, the sense of relief and eagerness with which she sought to serve the white guests—guests like Nick and Bob and Jeremy—embarrassed each of them in his own way, especially in comparison to how tersely she treated anyone suggesting so much as a hint of Indo-Canadian ancestry.

Finally they secured a table, and promptly ordered, as their break time was rapidly ticking away. It didn't really matter if they exceeded their allotted time, Nick explained, but generally they tried to hold to it as much as possible anyway. After a while it began to amuse Jeremy how cordial the entire staff was acting— and it was most definitely acting—all because Bob and Nick were in uniform apparently.

"Doesn't get us a table any quicker though, does it," Nick observed with a laugh.

Both Nick and Bob ordered chicken burgers and chocolate shakes, the latter of which they both purported to be well below average in both texture and taste, while Jeremy enjoyed a decent meal of vegetarian fajitas. After coffee they asked for the bill, chalked up not two but three police discounts, flirted some with the bigoted, big-breasted waitress, then left.

"I never asked," Nick said to Jeremy outside. "You thinking of joining up?"

"Wouldn't dream of it."

"He's a writer," Bob explained. "He's going to write a story on our night out together."

"Not much of a night," Nick said, and retreated with a wave to his cruiser.

They drove back down Scott Road. The sky was dark now, and clear, and all the lights of the restaurants and shops were on, despite the fact that many of them were closed, awaiting the miracle of provisional reincarnation under Indo-Canadian ownership.

"Quiet night."

"Yeah, sorry about that." Bob said this as though it were somehow his fault there was not more crime in the world, which was to some extent accurate, I suppose.

They drove by On the Roxx, a nasty looking nightclub on the Surrey side of Scott Road.

"We don't go in there," Bob said. "Hell's Angels bar."

"What, it's like their local?"

"Well occasionally, sure, but my point is they own it. Mostly Indo-Canadians drink there though."

"Angels and Indians," Jeremy said. "That must make for an interesting mix."

"Oh, quite. Like I said, though, we don't go in there. Fortunately it's on the Slurrey side of the fence, so it's the RCMP's problem, not ours. Grow-op capital of North America now, hey. Surrey, I mean. Or 'City of Parks' as they now refer to it in the official literature. Yeah, exactly. Part of some bright new multimillion-dollar marketing campaign.

"But yeah," Bob continued, "grow-op capital of North America. Quite the target-rich environment, too, I must say. Some streets as many as half a dozen grows per single block. But what can we do? Laws have no teeth. Raid them today, they're sentenced to house arrest and back in the game by tomorrow afternoon."

They doubled back—Bob wanted to run a plate, but the computer turned up nothing enticing—and passed the Sikh Temple, an enormous, brightly lit concrete structure also situated, surprisingly or not, on the Surrey side of the border.

"A year or so ago there was this huge riot, hey—two factions fighting over tables or some such thing—and they were attacking each other with swords. *Swords*," Bob repeated. "Can you believe it? Several people stabbed and cut. One killed. Then, a few weeks later, in a completely unrelated incident, a bunch of white kids wander up and beat the Indo-Canadian security guard to death. Said in court that it wasn't premeditated or anything, that it wasn't racially motivated or anything, but that they just sort of felt like it.

"Christ, it's getting lovely around these parts," Bob said. "Not like when you and I were kids. Remember how, late at night, we used to walk up and down Scott Road here on our way to Seven-Eleven or some such place? Yeah, well, I wouldn't walk it at night now by myself, and I'm a *cop* for Christ's sake. Young girls abducted from the fucking Dairy Queen," he sneered. "No kidding, this whole area here's a powder keg. Oh well," he sighed. "Too much change too fast, I guess."

"I guess," Jeremy said.

They drove through the McDonald's drive-thru in quest of a sundae for Bob. And it was here in the queue that Jeremy recalled, along with his brother and father, getting kicked out of this very restaurant.

"That's hilarious," Bob said. "Your dad's one hilarious old man."

"Oh you think so, do you? You think he's hilarious? Well let's just see how hilarious you think this is," Jeremy said. "I remember we were like ten or eleven, and Dad had just gotten back from a couple of months out on the water. Dad was always going out for long stretches like that—he was never around or he was always around—and Robby and I were pretty much forced to raise ourselves half the time."

"I remember," Bob said.

"Anyway, we'd just had dinner, the three of us here at McDonald's, and my brother's tying up his shoe, the heel of which he has resting on the very edge of his seat, when all of a sudden this pimply little busboy comes out of nowhere and demands my brother remove his shoe from the chair. Yeah, exactly. Pretty stupid. Well anyway, Robby says he will remove it, just as soon as he's finished tying it, but *no*, that's not quite good enough for our little employee-of-the-month here. So they start to argue, he and my brother, until my father—Mr. Hilarious—who happened to be off in the washroom at the time, comes strolling on back to the table. Well naturally he wants to know what the hell the problem is here. So now, getting a good look at our father, the pimply little busboy scurries off to get the manager. Long story short: manager and Dad get into an argument, manager kicks us out, and so we wait outside in my father's car for no less than *five* hours for the manager to finish up.

"It was late, I remember, around midnight maybe, and Robby and I'd been sleeping for quite a while when the manager finally came walking out. Well there goes Dad, bolting out of the car and . . ." Jeremy shook his head at the memory of it. "Well listen, you have no idea what he's capable of, all right?"

"Jesus," Bob said.

"My brother and I, we just waited in the car. Watched it all happen right outside the window. Actually, now that I think about it, we were parked right over there." Jeremy indicated the exact spot. "For whatever reason, though, Robby's blocked all that out."

"Jesus," Bob repeated. "Jesus Christ, that would do it. But did your dad ever, you know, hit you guys?" he managed to very delicately inquire.

"No, never. Not once. Like I said, though, he used to go off fishing for weeks or even months at a time, and whenever he got back it always took him a little while to, what, 'readjust to his environment.'" Jeremy paused, then added almost as an afterthought, "They used to rub cocaine on their gums to keep awake out on the water, hey. I was told this as a point of fact when I was a child. My father told me *he did cocaine*," he said. "Good Christ."

"It's a wonder you made it out as healthy as you did."

"Yeah, well, there are those who would definitely dispute that."

Finally, having received the sundae, they parked facing the Sikh Temple so that Bob could eat comfortably without having to watch the road. In the meantime, two tall, lean, hollow-chested skateboarders glided on past, bound for the drive-thru and what was to be a long, drawn-out argument with the staff. As a species, skateboarders annoyed Jeremy. As a rule, they always had.

"I tell you Robby and I went to see Jonathan the other day?"

"Jonathan? Who's Jonathan?"

"Our older brother," Jeremy said.

Abruptly Bob ceased inhaling his ice cream, looked up, looked over at Jeremy, and said, "You and Robby. Have a brother. That I don't know about."

"Sure we do. Punch up the name sometime—talk about your catalogue of convictions—the vast majority of them quite nasty too. Of course he's a good sixteen years older than Robby and I, but still the high watermark for Jacks family dysfunction, let me tell you."

"What, he's like adopted or something?"

"Nope, full-on part of the family Jonathan is. Sort of a cross between Rainman and Hannibal Lecter if you want to get a good visual of him."

Bob shook his head. "I never knew this. How come I never knew this? I should have known this. So, what, it's like some big secret, this so-called 'brother' of yours?"

"Yes, I suppose he is. Turns out he molested his first victim when he was all of fourteen years old, and—"

"*What?*"

"—and went on to molest three more girls," Jeremy continued, "three more they know about anyway, by the time he began grade twelve. So then they put him away for good after that. Said he was a quote-unquote predator, and I believe he probably was—is—to this very day in fact. Anyway, that's why you never knew about him, because, except for maybe the first few months after we were born, we never really lived with him. Now why my parents waited sixteen years to have Robby and me is a question I've never really had answered to my liking."

POSTED BY LUCY @ 11:30:21 A.M. 4/24/2007   8 COMMENTS

Monday, Aug 7, 1972

Dear Mom & Dad:

Received your Friday letter this morning, and I figured you must have been pretty weary when you wrote it. Did you realize that you hadn't finished it, or even signed it? That's quite all right, though, as it gave me quite a chuckle, especially considering I'm the one in the drug experiment.

We heard we made the news last week, but unfortunately no one had sent Stan out for either the Star or the Globe on that particular day, so we missed it. Could you please enclose the Star piece in your next letter? I'll send it back of course—we're just curious, that's all. Maybe we're making history, you know? Actually we are, in a way. And poor Myles and Congreves, you can bet those two are suffering a fair amount of abuse because of it. Apparently the switchboard's literally been flooded with calls ever since the piece appeared in the paper. Now I know what you're thinking: your son-in-law and now this. . . . Never thought I'd be this sort of celebrity, eh?

Had a good day today, and you were right: I do need the extra sleep, especially under these particular, and increasingly peculiar, circumstances. My weaver's disease seems to have finally abated at least.

Tuesday, Aug 8, 1972

New Vogue and Bazaar issues arrived this afternoon, so I've taken a couple hours off to do some reading and sketching. Lots of fun things in the fall Paris and Rome collections—pants everywhere, lots of plum, and a great oriental influence in prints and style lines, just as I thought. Now that my school days are over *temporarily*, I think it's about time I started dressing in a slightly more stylish or "dignified" manner, don't you think? What's that you say? Oh come now, loads of surprises ahead yet, Mother! Who knows, I may even come home with short hair. . . . No promises, however.

I guess Dad has the chair almost finished—I'll bet it looks great. Such talent in that man. I don't suppose he'd care to try his hand at the early Depression set at 37 Pleasant? If I could, believe me, I'd pitch the lot, but unfortunately it won't fit through the doors—I've tried, but the legs always get stuck. I swear that house was built around half the junk that's in there.

Ah yes, Seigmiller and company. I'll bet you were surprised to see Dennis, no? Has he changed at all? Probably not. That's an

Englishman for you though. That detached and baronial air of superiority they habitually affect can get a little tiring, I know. Do say hi to him for me though.

Ta for now. Love, B

AUGUST, 2002

One evening, with his brother away for a few days on a scheduled military exercise, and his father passed out for a few hours on the old orange sofa that, for personal reasons, he would soon learn to despise, Jeremy went up to Doolin's to meet Linda, Robert's second and, technically speaking, still active wife. She was not there when he arrived, so he sat down at a table near the window and ordered a Crown and Coke from the waitress and waited for Linda to show up. In the meantime the waitress returned and said they were out of Crown Royal, so would he like another rye instead? Canadian Club? Nope, out of that too, she said. Make it a Wiser's then, he said. It was not very good rye, he knew, but he hoped the Coke would help it. Linda did not turn up, so he used the payphone in the hall to call her at the house where she and her daughter were currently holed up at. Linda answered, and apologized for having had to cancel at the last minute—it unfortunately could not be helped—and trusted he had gotten the message she had left. What message, he said, and she explained how she had left a message with Harris at the bar. Good old Harris, he said. Linda apologized again, and asked if he was free the following day, Wednesday, and he said that he was, so they agreed to meet at the park sometime after two. Finally he hung up the phone and returned to his table, but not before stopping by the bar to see Harris.

"Hey, Jer. Sorry about the Crown Royal."

"That's okay. Any messages?"

"Yeah. One. Get a cell phone."

"Any messages, Harris?"

"Linda called and said she can't make it. Want the number she left?"

"Thanks, I got it."

"And Jer?" said Harris, beckoning him back to the bar. "Your brother coming in tonight?"

"No, he's not. Why?"

"Well the owners decided to bar him, hey. For a month. Can you tell him that?"

"Sure I'll tell him. Can't say it'll do much good though. And just for interest's sake, did they give any reason for barring him?"

"That fight the other night."

"But he didn't start it."

Harris shrugged. "Like I said, it's only for a month or so."

By this time, some of the regulars at the bar were beginning to position themselves for a quick infiltration into the conversation, so Jeremy excused himself to his table where his rye and Coke waited. And where Calvin Cassidy awaited.

"Surprised!" he said in a way Jeremy would soon realize was entirely peculiar to Cassidy himself, halfway between a question and a declaration, while offering Jeremy a seat at Jeremy's own table. "I saw you sitting here and, well, assumed you wouldn't mind."

Jeremy shrugged and sat down, albeit on the extreme opposite side, a position as far removed from his would-be host's as possible to still be considered, technically, to be sharing the same table.

"We are all of us such damned fools," Cassidy began, adjusting the lay of his jacket collar against the soft spongy flesh of his neck. "All of us . . ." he added with a long comprehensive sigh indicative, in its essence, of an idea already entirely forgotten, for there remained for Cassidy the more practical matter of finding a viable collaborator with whom to get pissed drunk. "What I am trying to say is this: I apologize. Yes, I do. I apologize. Because unfortunately for me, Jeremy, being delivered into the hands of more powerful and violent men seems to be a hallmark of mine.

"Actually," he continued on in this disagreeably quixotic tone, so much fugitive flotsam from safer harbours of conversation he had known, "I've been meaning to speak with you ever since that night I ran into you—or was it you who ran into me?—about that nasty little piece of—"

"Look, I don't want to discuss my brother's ex-wife," interrupted Jeremy flatly.

"Oh I didn't intend to. She's a hell of an interesting lady but, you see, I too am writing a book—an autobiography—one I intend to publish online, so in truth I'd much rather discuss you at this point—that is, if you don't mind. What I mean to say is, I very much doubt whether you're strong enough to undertake this position you have at present."

"What position is that?" Jeremy asked, slowly leaning back.

"A diplomat by instinct, eh? Well I think you know what I mean." Cassidy smiled his deeply artificial, yet somehow deeply affecting smile, the smile of one conditioned, through repetition, to think of only pleasant things, while butting out, with considerable aplomb, his most recent in a lifelong series of Camel cigarettes. He picked up his glass, and over the rim of it very jauntily said, "Here's to Alcoholic's Anonymous and all the irreparable damage it's caused." And then, having taken a good long drink of gin and tonic, managing in the process to all but finish it, added, " 'Thou shall not slap thy common-law wife,' said Janet," whatever the heck that meant and whoever the hell Janet was, before turning his glass upside down so that the ice remained inside and in place, melting there against the tabletop, on its way to becoming a first-class mess for the waitress to eventually clean up.

"Now I can see by your face that I'm not making a great deal of sense," Cassidy said. "And for that, too, I must apologize. I'm afraid, as has become habit of late, that the juniper has taken its accustomed hold, causing me to lose my keen edge, while stirring up all sorts of debris into an already disorganized mind, rendering the vast majority of it inappropriately occupied the vast majority of the time. Something you, too, seem to suffer from occasionally, I might add."

"Sorry?"

"Leslie lent me your book," Cassidy immediately clarified. "And some of the things you attempted appear, on the face of it at least, to be quite uneconomical, and consequently rather a waste of time. For example, your more descriptive passages.

They're so . . . well, descriptive. Which is to say, repetitive. And any craftsman of merit ought to achieve his goal via the most efficient means possible, don't you think?"

Jeremy said nothing, sipping routinely at his Wiser's and Coke instead.

"Anyway I won't talk a lot of rot, unless of course you're up to it. Just remember: the downbeats are as important as the notes. Tempo and intonation come first." Cassidy sighed and changed the subject, having just now realized perhaps that the one and only topic in any way fit for discussion he had foolishly, recklessly compromised well beyond redemption. He gazed routinely about the bar, skimming over each of its various inhabitants, as though together they constituted little more than a new and unusual vista to be enjoyed. "My but I do love this country," he declared, mellowing his voice persuasively. "This country was nice enough to take me under its protective wing after all my problems down south."

"What sort of problems?" Jeremy asked, frustratingly and in spite of himself.

"Oh all sorts," said Cassidy, waving off each consecutive problem as it arose. "The trick, naturally, is to keep moving. A moving target is that much more difficult to hit of course. Fine lady?" he said, catching the attention of the passing waitress. "Another round, if you please? Don't tell Janet though. Step four's a real bitch." He turned to Jeremy. "What is that you're drinking, sir?"

"She knows."

"I know," confirmed the waitress with a watery, impatient smile.

"Well since the two of you are in such cahoots, perhaps you might let me in on a little secret." Cassidy beckoned both Jeremy and the waitress closer, and upon their arrival in close lit himself a fresh cigarette for potency. "The secret of why, in all honesty, the two of you can't be together. You know, so that I might film you. In an artistic sense," he hastened to add as each member of his audience recoiled in horror.

"Go fuck yourself," said the waitress, stepping away from the table in a huff.

Cassidy laughed, started to cough, cursed repeatedly both the Canadian cold germ and its resultant phlegm, then turned to examine the waitress' departing legs with diagnostic appraisal, scrutinizing her through a provisional director's lens of thumbs and forefingers.

"Apparently," he said, "she didn't appreciate our offer."

"Apparently not, no."

"Love is a game of inches," Cassidy observed, shooing all memory of the waitress away. "And like I said, I do love this country. The people are so . . . unsophisticated. Blasted cold germs always get the better of me though. Tell me, what do you think of Stockwell Day?"

"The politician? Well to be honest, I don't. Not anymore."

"Well I like him. Always have. Reminds me of my dear friend Janet in a way. Seventy-eighth and first woman Attorney General of the United States, by the way." Cassidy leaned forward from the waist, as if to divulge a secret of some significance. "Did you know that in nineteen-seventy-eight, as a mere state attorney, she was responsible for an office of nine hundred and forty employees, an annual budget upwards of thirty million, and a yearly docket of one hundred and twenty thousand cases? No, probably not," he said, leaning back again. "I mean really, why would you. It would be ridiculous. It *is* ridiculous. But not, I repeat, *not* if you are an object of her seemingly unlimited affection as I, Calvin Alvin Cassidy seem to have become in recent years. Coincidence? I think not. And there is nothing I detest more than when the weak and addled-minded bandy *that* word about with such flippancy," he snorted in disgust.

"Now am I making too much of this? Perhaps I am. But then perhaps I am also onto something of incredible international importance, such as the enslavement of men by a brutal, stinking, abortion-savvy sorority of socialist-empowered women seeking poetry from pop stars, and that is the reason she wants me tarred and feathered. And *that*, Jeremy, is why I have adopted Canada as my country of residence. That and its people. You are all such wonderful people," he said, leaning forward from the waist to teasingly slap Jeremy across the face.

Jeremy smacked Cassidy twice, the first in retaliation, the second for instigation, and left. On his way past the bar he paid the waitress, then made his way out to the nearly vacant Royal Heights parking lot, on the far side of which his father's blue 1970 propane-converted El Camino stood parked, out front of the fruit and vegetable place no less, and then home, eventually, to rest. The next day, as suggested, he met Linda at Annieville Park. She was there when he arrived, just after two in the afternoon, watching her daughter at play on the swings from a nearby picnic bench. Her dark hair was longer than Jeremy remembered, and seeing her sitting there, alone, in her overalls, out of the harsh glare of the sunlight, he wondered why his brother had ever cast his eye at any other girl in the world.

"Maybe, like your father, he's just not meant to be with a woman," she said. "Not one woman, at any rate."

"What do you mean?"

Linda waved him off. "Look, I know Robby's been with other women. Or has. And believe me when I tell you I could almost forgive him for that. But that's not the worst part. No, the worst part, by far, is the way he ignores his daughter. He *ignores* her, Jeremy. And there's simply no forgiving that."

They sat watching Stephanie at play on the swing. Alone, at three and a half, and therefore too short to reach the ground, she was unable to enjoy the more conventional application of the apparatus, but still managed to have some fun despite her shortcomings, or so at last Jeremy gathered.

"Isn't she pretty now?" Linda asked, and Jeremy answered, in all seriousness:

"I think she's the most beautiful thing I've ever seen in my life."

That sat there together, silent for a time.

"We've been building her a tree fort," Jeremy eventually began. "Down in the ravine. Robby, me and Dad. You should see it, Linda, it's amazing. All the amenities a girl could ask for."

Linda smiled at the thought. "I heard you were taking shifts at the mill," she said. "You're not writing anymore then, I take it?"

"Not right now, no. I did publish the one book though," he added, wincing as he said it, as it felt too much like bragging, and bragging was the last thing he wanted to be caught doing, present secret meeting of in-laws included.

"Yes, I read the copy you sent me," Linda said. "Tell me, what did she do to you?"

"Who?"

"Whoever it was that ruined you."

"I don't understand."

"Let me put it this way," she said. "Have you ever even been in a relationship with a woman, Jeremy? A *real* relationship?"

"Well, back in university—"

"Back in university you were all of twenty-one years old," she said. "You're what, almost thirty now. And I don't mean relationships that are explicitly of a sexual nature either. I mean real relationships. Of trust. And intimacy. Have you ever had a relationship like that, Jeremy? Do you even want one? Are you even *capable* of one?" She dropped her gaze to the ground. "These are the things I think about when I think about my brother-in-law. And, too, when I think about the woman who so damaged you somehow."

They sat silently another moment, watching Stephanie worm her way through the seat of the swing. Ever adept at evading the importunate, Jeremy reconciled himself to remaining silent a good deal longer if need be.

"Stephie, come here. I want you to meet someone."

"No," snapped Stephanie emphatically, dragging the back of a hand awkwardly across her eyes.

"Stephanie, come here," Linda repeated, more forcefully this time. Grudgingly, her daughter made her way over, but not before offering the swing one last look of longing for good measure.

"Well hello there, Stephanie," Jeremy smiled upon her roundabout arrival at the table.

"Daddy, did you eat my candy?" Stephanie asked, shielding her eyes against the sun. Jeremy started, and Stephanie's hands came away from his forehead. "Daddy, did you eat my candy?" she repeated, hands on hips this time.

"Not Daddy," Linda corrected. "*Uncle*."

"Yes," said Jeremy formally, nervously, and with enough embarrassment for all. "And while I do admit to a certain profound resemblance around the eyes and perhaps even the ears, further than that I feel your accusations here are completely unwarranted, and therefore I ask you—in fact I implore you—to please desist at once."

Evidently the only way Stephanie could process such a tedious stream of dialogue was to place her hands squarely over her eyes and hop three times across the earth on one foot—hopping forward once, followed by two backward hops in quick succession—before falling gleefully into her mother's arms.

"Stephanie, this is your *Uncle* Jeremy. Do you remember your Uncle Jeremy? No, probably not. You were too young when you saw him that other time."

"Watch this," said Stephanie, freeing herself from her mother's grasp to leap as high as humanly possible—about two inches, give or take.

"My, but that's quite a leap. You're an excellent leaper, no question," Jeremy said. "You know, I've been known to be a bit of a leaper myself on occasion. Back in the day at least."

"Look," she said, working an object free of her pocket.

"Look at what? What is it?" Jeremy asked as she held out her hand to reveal, amid the expected collection of purple-pink lint, a single marble of considerable calibre. "And a green one at that," he said, rolling it around her palm with a finger. "My my, but it has been a while. Years, I bet. I must say, your immeasurable capacity for the marvellous floors me yet again, Stephanie. Hey, you know what?" he went on in a manner peculiar, but not necessarily limited, to a man conversing with the marble-carrying, purple pants-wearing, three and a half year-old daughter of his chronically absent brother. "I've got something neat to show you too. You see this? Well you know what I call this? I call this the perfect flower pot."

Stephanie took a single quick step back, but not nearly quick enough, for suddenly, unbelievably, she was once again caught up in the intricate web of her mother's arms. She neither struggled nor cried. Instead, allowing herself to be held captive without actually submitting to it—she refused to be complicit in such an obvious act of abuse—she saw before her on the picnic table a smooth, grey, vaguely foot-shaped stone about the size of, say, one of those brand new yellow rubber boots at home she was quietly looking forward to growing into. Into the top of the stone had been drilled a single hole, a perfect cylinder measuring exactly one inch in diameter, and into this cylinder had been placed a solitary daffodil. Now it is true that in the bottom of the cylinder there stood about an inch of water and even a sprinkling of soil, but Stephanie could not see any of this from her vantage point, therefore it mattered little. All she could see was the single green-stemmed, yellow-blossomed flower, standing all of six inches tall and staring, it would seem, directly at her.

"So what do you think?" Jeremy said. "Is this not the perfect flower pot? My father—your grandfather—purchased it not two days ago from a local nursery, and now it stands here, on this table, ready and eager for our mutual enjoyment. And it's yours by the way."

Stephanie stared at the flower, and in turn, the flower pot for as long—or in reality, as little—as she evidently felt was necessary to bring a hasty end to such an arduous ordeal. Eventually, though, having lost all interest in the gift, and in truth, having forgotten completely what it was she was supposed to be doing with it, she began to take stock of all her various appendages until, finally, having carefully named each one in sight, she squirmed, then squirmed again, before quietly begging her release when all manner of squirming proved futile.

"Fine. Go," Linda told her, spanking her lightly on the backside, an act of parenthood still considered permissible in those post-politically correct times. Together they watched her stomp off towards the swings, a militant demonstration that in due course devolved into a protracted series of peaceful, if asymmetrical, somersaults across the grass.

Eventually Jeremy said, "Do you think you'll ever go back to him? I mean, do you think that's even possible?"

Linda studied her brother-in-law intently, a brief trembling of lips implying an inner hesitation. "But Jeremy, Robert left me."

"Pardon?"

"He left me. Your brother left *me*."

"I don't . . . I don't understand."

"It's pretty straightforward," she said, and looked away.

They sat there, at the picnic table, watching Robert's daughter set herself up in the swing. Eventually Jeremy said, "He'll come back to you, Linda. I know he will."

"Maybe. Maybe he will. But that won't alter the fact he went away any."

POSTED BY LUCY @ 10:40:16 P.M. 4/25/2007   19 COMMENTS

Wednesday, Aug 9, 1972

Dear Mom & Dad:

Another slow, lazy, constipated day today. Worked till lunchtime, then took the afternoon off to sketch and research fashions etc, but midway through I lay down for a nap, and that was that till the supper bell went off.

Received your letter today, along with a brief dispatch from Robert Hunter. Nice to see some mail! Robert, at your son-in-law's suggestion, has bought a piece of property where the new airport site's to be located (Uxbridge), so he's putting his house in Bridgenorth up for sale right away. Eventually he's going to be building on this new lot in order to increase the value, or that's the plan anyway. It's quite close to one of his father's homes apparently, so, in the meantime, one or two of his deadbeat brothers will be staying there, living out of a trailer, while Robert heads back out to Vancouver to sail the high seas with his good friends J, Uncle John and Patrick Moore.

News flash! We may have smoked our last night! Pure rumour though—we shall see tonight. Yesterday we had a mood test (It was exactly three weeks to the day since we started smoking—is that right? No, I guess it isn't—oh well.) and they took more pulses last night, inserting a fifteen minute break between the 1st and 2nd joints, but most curious of all was the fact the other side smoked for the first time (mandatory) last night. It would be quite funny if we did actually switch over now, as both Lorna and I decided this morning that we weren't going to inhale anymore. After all, one of the things they're trying to prove is that marijuana is non-addictive, right? That's how we justify it anyhow. So the decision is up to us, as patients (guinea pigs) to react to the whole situation with as much conviction or spontaneity as our personalities allow. We shall see what happens two hours from now. (As I write this we've just finished supper.)

Guess what? I just got a letter from Jonathan's older brother Jeremy, currently visiting friends in Edmonton, and what a treat it was to read. He writes with such wonderfully sardonic humour, that man, and he's *very* interested in the experiment naturally. So of course I'm going to write back with all the gory details as soon as possible.

*   *   *

11pm. Well, can't be right all the time. Still smoking, but I didn't inhale tonight, so I barely felt any effects, and stayed up till 10:30 weaving like a madman. There were some good movies on tonight, but I decided I'd rather get some sleep. I'm getting back into yoga again—I do my exercises the moment I wake up—feels great!

Actually today is Saturday (missed a day—oops!) but I can't remember anything of grave importance happening yesterday, other than a good, quality, tremendously satisfying crap while reading a piece in the editorial section of the Globe, a response by the assistant director of ARF to the accusation that appeared a week ago, concerning the experiment and its possible political ramifications. Oh yes, and your letter of August 8th arrived too—thank you!

Saturday, Aug 12, 1972

Up early as per usual, but managed very little weaving after lunchtime . . . A head full of ideas and no place to go—what a predicament she's got herself in, this Birdie girl. Tracey's weekly letter arrived a day early—twenty-one pages in all—a minute-by-minute account of the past week or so. She sent along my T4 from Ottawa, via Audrey, plus plenty of wishes for a happy day. Ruth and Kelly (a co-worker at Interthink) have taken an apartment at Bloor and Bedford Rd, so I guess that settles that anyway. Cory, our young boarder, was off to a dance on Friday night . . . Tracey said she felt like a mother, making sure his tie was straight before she'd let him out the door. I got a good chuckle over that.

Sun, Aug 13, 1972

Hello there. Well into week #7 here and, I might add, feeling just fine. Today was a "how to decorate your apartment on a pot experiment budget" kind of day. Whatever keeps one's mind occupied while weaving, eh?

Do you need help with your income tax? Not trying to be flippant, but I figured mine out last night, and I only owe $38.⁴⁰ to Mr. Trudeau's lovely government—a nice shock, I must say. I think I can write a cheque, and then transfer sufficient funds from my savings here over to the bank, so I should be all right. Should get them off my back for filing late though, right?

We've been following the radio and newspaper reports quite a lot lately, and it seems the LeDain Commission's Report might just become something of an election issue before it's all said and done. Very interesting!

J Jr. will be sixteen years old next Sunday, so I made a card to send out his way. I'll wait till October to send a gift out, as it's a bit awkward to manage presently.

Monday, Aug 14, 1972

Power failure for half an hour early this morning . . . Aren't emergency generators the greatest? Our room lights go off of course, but the hall lights and clocks remain running, so we weren't left completely in the dark.

124 pounds this morning, and fit as a fiddle too. We've started running quite a lot, whenever we move from one place to another, down the hall etc à la Evie, in order to keep the bowels moving—I'm not the only one cursed with a pernickety system forever on the verge of industrial collapse, it seems. It's really quite funny seeing people bounding about all over the place. . . . Reminds me of the Olympics in a way. Speaking of which, those should be cranking up in another month or so, shouldn't they? In Munich or some such place? God I love the Games, especially the camaraderie and respect shown between otherwise rival nations. Inspiring stuff, regardless of the actual competition taking place.

Speaking of athletics, poor Stan the Shopping Man is kept running ragged trucking supplies back to the Factory. Tons of writing paper, new records (when the stereo is constantly playing, you get tired of the same old tunes), leotards from Malabar's (the most frequently seen outfits on the ward, and the most comfortable too, especially for wrestling, of which I seem to be the only true-blue aficionado around here), all sorts of exotic health foods (I'm glad I'm not into that bag; it costs more than ordinary food!) and heaven knows what else. Still, I've managed to keep my spending to a minimum, though I'm eating very well. My sole purchase, aside from my daily supplies and the occasional laxative, has been writing gear and one record, Ray Charles. Oh yes, and that insurance policy for the flat.

We're still smoking (so is the other side now apparently, blowing the whole "control group" theory all to hell), but I've made a compromise with myself: I inhale only on the two nights preceding the Mon & Thurs blood and urine tests. That way I won't mess up their data, and I'll be a little wider awake in the daytime hours. Forget about it: it just doesn't work. Can you imagine polishing off a 26 oz bottle of vodka in one hour every night? Well, the effects are somewhat similar, only nothing happens physically (accumulation-wise) other than sleeping a heck of a lot more of course. We won't be smoking right through, though, so don't worry about that. I'm sure we'll be off it shortly.

Tues, Aug 15, 1972

Received your Aug 13th letter today—sounds like you had exciting times on the Point this weekend. I must drop a wee note to Audrey to thank her for sending along my T4 . . . Only you have to tell me what you told her I was doing, OK? Was it "working for the government" like we decided initially? Let me know. After all, we must keep our stories straight now, mustn't we?

Also a card from my double-jointed friend Michael (Beauchemin, from Mont.Theatre) currently down in Barbados of all places—my God but it must be hard hunger-striking down there—in which, for artistic purposes, he's requested that I spell his name "Mikel" now (which I won't of course, as he forgets that I used to tie flies and watch Canadiens' games with his old man), and another letter from J's brother Jeremy too—he's thinking of quitting his job at Canadian Magazine to start up a monthly of his own. I must press for details on that. Anyway, he's getting quite a kick out of knowing one of the "infamous 20" stirring up so much dust in the news. Being involved in a news publication himself, he would hear a lot more than simply what gets printed, I'm sure. Maybe he and Robert H should partner up in that venture.

Thanks for sending down the news clippings—I'm returning them to be put in your scrapbook.

Wed, Aug 16, 1972

You'll be interested to know that I've spent most of the day fulfilling my duties regarding correspondence, making greeting cards, and removing a year's worth of skin from the bottoms of my feet. Never a dull moment around here. Write soon!

Aug 16, 1972

Dear Ginny:

'Go placidly amid the noise and haste, and remember what peace there may be in silence . . .' ~ Max Ehrmann

How goes the battle? As well as can be expected, I guess? Here, generally speaking, spirits are "high," but I seem to be going through a lot of ups and downs these days, resulting from a variety of factors:

1) Being cooped up like a chicken.

2) Beautiful weather outside (and too many ugly women inside).

3) Grass makes me tired and groggy (dosage heavier still).

4) All sorts of great films, rock concerts, etc going on "out there."

5) Friends, lovers, enemies sadly missed, not forgotten.

6) General discouragement of some of the other inmates regarding belt-making.

7) So many great things to eat, and a great big fat scale to tell the tale.

8) A persistently tight-fisted gastrointestinal tract.

9) Barbarella. Need I say more?

10) I'm pregnant. Yup, it's official. Got Stan the Shopping Man to hump me down to the maternity ward the other night for tests, and there it is. Fuck. I don't know what to do, Ginny. I'm at a complete loss at this point. Here we are in the seventh week, almost halfway through a fucking *marijuana* experiment, and I find out I'm two months pregnant for Christ's sake. I don't know how you ever went through with it. I mean if it were up to me, or people like me, the entire human race would very rapidly reach extinction. Anyway, before I make a decision as to what I'm going to do, I've decided to cut down on the smoking as I don't want to harm the, uh, baby. Ugh! That sounds so *wrong* now that it pertains to me. It does to you too, doesn't it?

On the bright side (or rather, the slightly less bleak of two very bleak, growing progressively bleaker by the day sides), I'm feeling fine. Back into yoga seriously now, hovering around 119 pounds (though *that's* sure to change) and generally fit as a fiddle, whatever the hell that means, even if literally full of crap. I'm taking more time to read & write, sketch etc, as it's very hard to just sit and weave all day. Got a good letter from Tracey too, which brightened up my day considerably. To no one's surprise, least of all hers, she and her boarder are altogether inseparable these days. A real smitten kitten, that's for sure. Actually, if you ask me, she seems to be growing a little manic about the whole thing. For instance, the other night he's getting ready to take off for some dance, and there's Tracey helping him get ready to go, fixing his tie etc, and all of a sudden she starts to cry! Can you believe it? She sure couldn't, I'll tell you that. So there he is, Cory, scrambling to get out the door, and Tracey, hysterical, literally begging him not to go! Of course they ended up ripping each other's clothes off and going at it right there on the vestibule floor. Geez, and I'm the one who gets knocked up. Birdie the breeder. Go figure.

In other news, there has been quite a flap in the media of late concerning the ARF experiment in particular, the Foundation in general, and the LeDain Commission's Report on Drugs. I'm afraid we've become something of an election issue. I can just picture telling my (at this rate) seventeen kids about the "Battle of the Belts" back in ol' '72. A suffragette? Hardly. But it's amusing to think about too.

How's summer out there in the Shire? I take it your husband's back from his latest adventure? Actually, probably not, now that I think about it. Thank God he's got that endless supply of salmon to harass between pitched battles with the Establishment. Actually, it's kind of a weird stance when you think about it, fighting on behalf of the very habitat from which you seek to extract a living through slaughter . . . But alas, we all have to eat. Sustainability, I suppose, is what's important. Tell me, what does Jonathan think?

Speaking of J, I've received not one, but *two* (!) letters from his brother Jeremy in the last five days. What's that all about, I wonder? I mean I like the older men, but come on, how much older can you get! Anyway, when was the last time those two so much as spoke, do you know? Their father's funeral? They are indeed as different as two brothers can be—Jeremy just so outgoing and affable, while J remains remote and meditative, but in a good way obviously—and yet they definitely share those one or two idiosyncrasies woven intrinsically, it would seem, into the Jacks family tapestry.

How's J Jr? I'll bet he's having some fun up at summer camp, eh? Wish him an early happy birthday for me, will you? He's an interesting young man, that's for sure. And getting so *tall*! He must be getting right up there in the rarefied air of his father by now. Hey, maybe you could ship him out east in October to help his old, pregnant, obese Auntie Birdie carry her bags home. That should be a sight, no? Fuck that. (As you can see, I'm still kind of in shock at this point.)

I hope everything is going okay for you.

                                          Love, Birdie (the Breeder)

AUGUST, 2002

Jon Jacks moored a twenty-four foot Pro-Line sport fisher, the recently rechristened *Jacks Be Nimble*, at the marina in Point Roberts, Washington, just across the border from South Delta, or as it is now known, Tsawwassen, and occasionally he still went out on the water for a day or two, oftentimes, surprisingly or not, to catch salmon. Fishing, that is, fishing for a living, had never really interfered with or diminished his love for the simple act of dropping a line and seeing what it was he could find. In fact, the one had always seemed completely unrelated to the other, or so at least they had in his mind. In commercial fishing, which was something he endured, he was forever in pursuit of a commodity in ever diminishing supply, while in sport fishing, which was something he enjoyed, he was in search of long periods of relaxation interrupted, or not, by only the occasional tug at his line. To him, the two activities had always seemed as dissimilar as, say, Koi and salmon, and now, approaching seventy, and more than fifteen years removed from the industry, he was able to fish as much or as little as he wanted to on any given day. And so it came as no surprise, least of all to his sons, that he asked them to accompany him out on the water one ominous August day.

Succumbing, as always, to their collective instinct for ordeal, and intrigued at the prospect of spending a few quiet hours not buried in the confines of the ravine but out on the open water, both Robert and Jeremy agreed to go, though neither one wanted to actually fish per se, or so the story goes. Jon, of course, brought along all the obligatory gear and tackle, although, even at the time of casting off from the dock, he was still undecided as to whether he was actually going to make use of it or not. And besides, much to his chagrin, neither one of these two sons had amounted to all that much of a fisherman.

The night before they were to head out, there occurred a tremendous storm. Before dark the wind grew strong, the sky churned threateningly, and after a short while there was much lightning and thunder, followed by an enormous downpour. The wind piled up waves at the mouth of the Fraser, where they waited for the returns of the deluge to carry them away. By sunrise the storm had passed, and the Point Roberts marina, swept clean by the wind, lay all but deserted in its wake. Occasionally a car or truck pulled up, evidently thought better of heading out, and left. And so it was not without serious reservations that Robert and Jeremy shipped out on the *Jacks Be Nimble* that day.

Once clear of the marina, Jon pressed down on the throttle, opening up the massive Mercury outboard. Eventually they came to rest at a spot long considered fruitful for fishing, where Jeremy could see, in the distance, sporting a frothing white wake for a tail, the ferry departing for Vancouver Island and superior daytrip destinations. Here Jon switched over to the small outboard, and on a whim, together with Robert, hooked, weighted and baited two lines, running them off with the downriggers to disparate depths, before turning their collective concentration to waiting patiently and silently for something more interesting to appear on the horizon. For his part, Jeremy quietly wished he was someplace else, anyplace else, secure on that sturdy looking ferry perhaps, rather than at the so-called mercy of the elements out here on the *Jacks Be Nimble* floating prison. The grey clouds bulged. The wind gathered strength. Eventually it began to rain. There was a good chop, and it was unseasonably cold, and Jeremy lasted all of two minutes before starting to feel nauseous and disappearing into the small forward cabin. He lay there on the cabin's short abrasive carpet reading *Offshore* by Penelope Fitzgerald, a good story about a houseboat community on the Thames in which a woman named Nenna kept waiting for her husband to return, while the husband kept waiting for Nenna to leave the barge life behind, and they were both still waiting when Robert put his head in through the door and asked, "What the fuck are you doing?"

"What the fuck does it look like I'm doing?" answered Jeremy, equally annoyed, armed at all points against any manner of reproach.

"Well why can't you do it out here?"

"Because it's windy, and dark, and freezing, and I don't feel like talking anymore."

"You haven't said a word all morning."

"Well I haven't had a word to say. And besides," added Jeremy smugly, "it's long been considered something of a virtue not to talk unnecessarily at sea."

Robert shook his head slowly. "Look, why'd you even come if you weren't intending to take part."

"Believe me, I've been asking myself that same question ever since we woke up."

Again Robert shook his head, refusing to hide his dissatisfaction, as Jeremy reached up and grabbed him by the face, pushed him bodily back through the entranceway, and out. He returned to his book, reading slowly through a slight throbbing headache attributed incorrectly to the slight throbbing reverberation of the outboard, but a page later the chapter came to an end, and lacking both the energy and the conviction to start the next one, he dog-eared the page and reluctantly emerged on deck once again. Bundled up against the cold, he took his customary seat in the stern, and sat there staring at the grassy outcropping of land passing to starboard at a distance he estimated at roughly two hundred meters—which might as well have been two hundred kilometres for all the good it did him. Meanwhile, the wind continued to scratch the skin off the waves and tumble it into foam, leaving the ocean's face raw and pockmarked with rain.

"Well this is fun."

"Nice attitude," Robert said.

"What's that?" asked their father, not hearing.

"I said nice atti—Christ, Dad, where the hell are your hearing aides?"

"I'm not bringing those damned things out here on the water. *Get real.*"

"Yeah, *get real*," said Jeremy, happy to share in this air of general irritation.

"Well then what the hell'd I buy them for if you weren't ever going to wear them?"

"Believe me, I've been asking myself the same question," Jon said, echoing the sentiment of his other son earlier.

"I saw Linda the other day," Jeremy put in, pointing his nose into the wind, feeling this was as good a time as any to drop the proverbial anchor on this particular conversation.

Robert looked at him, eyes narrowing, ears folding back threateningly against his head. "What for?"

"Yes, what for?" echoed their father.

"What do you mean *what for*? Can't a guy go see his sister-in-law and niece without having some sort of ulterior motive?"

"Stephie was there? Where?"

"At the park," Jeremy told his brother.

Robert almost laughed. "At the park," he said, more to himself than to anyone else. Together he and Jeremy stared down at the water, as though by doing so they hoped to turn it into something else.

"Yeah so anyway," Jeremy resumed, "I went and saw Linda and Stephanie, and we had ourselves a little chat."

"Oh yeah," said Robert, drawn back from a muse the wind-stippled water had momentarily fostered.

"So there we were, Linda and I, having our little chat at the park—quite a charming scene actually: there were trees and everything—when she told me that it was you who left."

"What?"

"Just a sec, Dad," Jeremy said. "Well being the good brother I am, I of course corrected her, telling her how distraught you were ever since she left you. But no, she was quite adamant on the subject, Robby. She was quite adamant that in fact it was *you* who left *her.*"

"*What?*" said Jon again.

Robert did not respond, but continued to gaze out over the water instead. Jeremy looked at him, then at their father, then turned to Robert again.

"Why would you do that, huh? Why would you just up and leave your daughter like that?"

Still Robert said nothing, and both his brother and their father fell silent. Jeremy bundled his coat more tightly around himself and studied the transitory shoreline again. And so it was that, imprisoned on his father's boat, staring longingly at the passing beach, praying that nothing really interesting would happen so that he might soon return to the comforts of dry land, or at the very least below decks, he all of a sudden saw the port line jump free of its downrigger and his father jump to life again.

"Reel in that other line!" Jon barked, taking hold of the active rod and dragging the line out and away from the stern. While Robert leapt to the wheel to steer, Jeremy snapped the second line free of its downrigger and hastened to work the reel.

"Keep it out to the side," Jon told him. "Keep it clear."

"Aye, aye, Captain. Like this?"

"Out to the *side*, I said! *Away* from mine."

Jeremy reeled in the line as fast as possible, and for a time he thought he had it, until suddenly, frustratingly, his hook rode part way up his father's line.

"Christ!" Jon snapped. "Keep it *clear*, I said." The old blue veins, summoned by the strain, bulged reproachfully against the skin of his thin rucked neck.

"I tried to," Jeremy very calmly said. He could not recall, in recent memory anyway, having seen his father so animated, and so he instinctively attempted to remain as calm as possible, a tactic he had often employed in the past in order to get the old man more agitated still.

"Never mind," said Jon, relaxing back into character, having managed to sniff out the scheme before blowing a gasket of any importance. "Now you'll have to cut it," he went on pleasantly, smiling benevolently, as though teaching a lesson to the very young or the very retarded—an Annieville graduate, at any rate—with an eagerness that far exceeded the necessities of civility in its falseness.

"Cut it?"

"Cut it!" his father shouted, unable, despite himself, to control the impulse to berate one son in front of the other. Jeremy looked at him in amazement, struck by the fact that not many people in recent years had told him what to do. In fact, not since he had been a child in his father's house had he readily accepted the authority of another. And so it was not without a mix of resentment, amusement, and even a complex sense of appreciation and pride that he now said plainly, the slightest of smiles astir on his lips:

"But with what shall I cut it, dear Liza, dear Liza?"

Jon regarded him evenly, straining enormously under the weight of whatever grade of submarine had attached itself to the business end of his line. "With the *pliers*," he said with far too calm a calmness.

"These ones?" said Robert, holding a pair aloft.

"Those ones," his father grunted.

Unhappy at the prospect of actually having to touch the tackle, Jeremy nevertheless proceeded as requested. Placing his rod aside, he gathered in the remaining fishing line until the hook had slid its way up to him along the unbelievably taut cable of his father's line.

"There," said Jon, flexing backward against the pressure of the line. Pursing his lips, he continued to expel his breath in short sharp bursts, and Jeremy quietly prayed that he not suffer some form of visitation, transition or stroke before all was said and done.

"Here?"

"Yes, there. Now cut it. . . . No, *cut* it! Christ, Robert get back here."

"No I got it." Jeremy grabbed hold of the hook and brought the pliers into play. A three-pronged device of surprising sharpness, the hook lodged itself repeatedly in the skin of his fingers, then his thumb, so that it took much longer than anticipated to actually cut the line in question. In the meantime, Jon Jacks grew increasingly exasperated with his son.

"For the love of—"

"Got it!" Jeremy triumphantly held up the hook with part of it, a very sharp and painful part of it, still lodged in the flesh of his thumb.

Now the real battle began. At different times and with varying intensities, Robert and Jeremy offered to take over for their father, but naturally Jon would have none of it. He continued to play the fish, aggressively reeling it in, grudgingly letting it out, sometimes gaining line, oftentimes losing line, until it plunged into the water at a sharp angle just beyond the stern.

"Christ, this bastard must be thirty pounds."

And suddenly they saw it, breaking the surface not ten feet from the boat, its silver and rainbowed scales reflecting beautifully what limited light there was before driving down again and out of sight. It certainly was a very big fish, Jeremy remembered thinking right after the seal came and took it from them.

Jon was standing with one foot on the seat in the stern, the rod shaped an impossible quivering horseshoe in his hands, the fish tiring not two meters from the boat when the head of the seal arose beside it, blinked affectionately, and took it with one enormous chomp. And if Jeremy thought his father was animated before, he was all but enraged after that.

Jon fought the seal for all of a second before the line itself snapped. In disgust, he turned and threw the rod into the bottom of the boat where it landed with a resounding clatter, as some-where below the dark surface of the water the seal made off with his catch. Watching his father stomp and curse about the back of the boat, and seeing as there was really nothing more to be done at this point, Jeremy retired once again to the relative sanctuary of the forward cabin, where eventually he fell asleep on the car-peted floor, not waking again until almost noon, the unusual res-onance of his father's barrel-chested laughter finally bringing him to.

In his multiple layers of coats and sweaters, he found himself incredibly hot, and when he opened the hatch he was surprised to find the sky had actually cleared somewhat. Gone, too, was the wind, along with the chop, leaving behind a pleasant summer day on the water just off Point Roberts proper. Stepping out of the cabin, Jeremy stretched and yawned, not really because he need-ed to stretch and yawn, mind you, but because he felt it the appro-priate seafaring thing to do at this time.

"What the fuck happened to you?"

"Gimme one of those," said Jeremy, accepting a small flattened sandwich from his brother. "How long was I out?"

"Oh about three hours or so," Robert told him.

Jeremy noted immediately that both lines were in fact back out.

"Anything happen? I miss anything?" he asked, flopping down into the captain's chair. With his father and brother taking up both seats in the stern, the so-called captain's chair was the only remaining spot available.

"Not really," Robert answered. "Thought we had something a little while back, but it was nothing. Those guys over there got something though." He indicated another boat about fifty meters to port. Counting that one, then, there were more than a dozen boats out on the water now.

"I'll find the fish," Jon pledged, his anger towards the thieving seal having more or less run its course. "Don't you worry about that."

"I know you will," said Robert inconceivably, restoring Jeremy's need of a swift and sweeping mutiny at some point.

Together they sat eating their sandwiches, Jon slowly masticating a chicken and cheese, his sons powering through cheese and vegetarian salami.

"How's that stuff taste anyway?" asked Jon after a time.

"This stuff? It's okay. Pepperoni's better though, hey. What do you think, Jer? You like the pepperoni better?"

"I like them both. Why, Dad, want to try?"

"Yeah, Dad, want to try?" Robert offered his father his sandwich. Jon took the sad little sandwich in hand, took one small bite, and thoughtfully chewed it for about ten seconds.

"Not bad," he said at length, returning the half-eaten sandwich.

Taken aback, Robert looked at Jeremy. "You hear that? He said he liked it."

"No," their father corrected, "I said not bad."

At this moment, then, precluding any sort of permanent dietary conversion on the part of the captain, the port line struck, launching the crew to life once again. And a few labour-intensive minutes later, with Jon instructing him meticulously in the proper deployment of the net, Jeremy managed to lift into the back of the boat a slippery, thrashing, for all intents and purposes prehistoric thing.

"Got to be what, twenty, twenty-two pounds," said Jon, sweating and breathing heavily. "Not bad, eh?" he smiled at his sons, revealing twin rows of unbearably bright white teeth. "Your old man, if it were up to him, would put food like this on your table every day."

"Lucky for them," Robert said.

"It's darker than I thought it would be," Jeremy said. "Don't you think it's dark, Robby?"

"Yeah it is actually. It is dark. And what's with all the *blood*," Robert said, mesmerized by the flipping and thrashing of the oxygen-starved salmon.

"Fish bleed. They're alive so they bleed," Jon responded at once. And so, having stated the obvious, and following protocol, he took hold of a short metal bar and proceeded to club the fish to death in the back of the boat.

The brothers stood watching. "I can't believe how much blood there is," Robert said. "I mean there's a lot of blood, isn't there? I didn't think there'd be *that* much blood. *Red* blood."

"There is a lot of blood," his father admitted. Hauling it up by the gore-slathered gills, poking his fingers up through its sad gaping mouth, Jon slapped Jeremy playfully on the shoulder with the salmon. "You like that?" he snorted.

"Quit it," Jeremy said. "I said quit it, Dad. I mean it."

"What's the matter? Afraid of a little fish?" his father smiled, slapping him on the shoulder again. Dignity demanded that Jeremy ignore this absurd assault on his person, or, at most, endure it with a sort of good-natured grin. Unfortunately, his nature betrayed him, and his grin failed him, coming off as little more than an awkward exposure of gnashed teeth. The sound of cheering arose from a nearby boat, and Jon turned and waved, displaying for an appreciative audience the size and beauty of his catch, before returning to the task of assailing his son with it.

"Quit it, Dad."

"Yeah, quit it, Dad," Robert said. Throughout this short uncomfortable exchange he had been staring at the bottom of the boat, the vast majority of which lay literally awash in red. "Was there this much blood when we were kids? I don't remember there being this much blood. *Red* blood."

"No there's definitely a lot more blood in fish these days," said his father flatly, slowly shaking his head.

At long last, but not before admonishing him with a few more good whacks, Jon ceased hitting Jeremy on the shoulder with the catch. He proceeded to clean it instead, tossing the guts over the side of the boat where some seagulls, having since gathered, dove into this expected treasure with relish. Finally Jon packed the salmon on ice in the cooler, rinsed and scrubbed the boat of blood, reset the lines and ran them out, then retook his seat in the stern, triumphant.

"There's more where that came from," he pledged.

"Excellent. Super," Jeremy said, feeling for a moment as though he might puke, but fortunately the feeling passed before it

materialized in tangible form, taking, as it had, the path of least
resistance.

By this time, not surprisingly, the brothers had seen enough.
Having never expected to actually catch anything, they had certainly never expected all this. The death throes. The blood. The
stench. The utterly ridiculous humiliation of being physically
assaulted with a fish. Again Jeremy looked longingly at the passing shoreline, at the tufts of long green grass bent flat by the wind
and the smooth grey waves breaking slow, white and methodical
against the sand.

They came around to take another pass through the same lucky
stretch of water. And it was not long after they were trolling again
that the starboard line struck heavily.

While Robert jumped to the wheel and started up the Mercury,
Jeremy leapt to the free rod on the gunwale and reeled the line in
expertly. In the meantime, their father continued his tug-of-war
with this his newest unseen adversary.

It appeared, to Jeremy, that there must have been a true leviathan
on the other end of that line. The strain he saw his father's body
endure, not to mention rod and line, must have been just shy of
the breaking point, if not actually exceeding it by some small
measure at times. Every time Jon seemed to gather in a few precious inches of line, out it went spinning by the yard again.
Incredibly, to Jeremy, his father seemed to be losing the battle
with the fish, and so he, Jon, instructed Robert to turn the boat
and chase it down.

Robert did as instructed, though Jeremy could see plainly that
he did not feel all that right about it. Both brothers had given
their father strict guidelines with regard to what they were
willing and unwilling to do insofar as any fishing were concerned, and now, with Jeremy having netted the last one and
Robert quickly closing the gap with this one, they both felt
their father was taking advantage of their overt good
sportsmanship.

"Speed up," Jon insisted, and Robert pressed the throttle down,
but not before offering his brother a look of despair bordering on

utter despondency. Jeremy shrugged helplessly, not knowing what to do.

"Kill it. . . . Kill it now!" Jon bellowed as the *Jacks Be Nimble* drew up over the stretch of water into which the line disappeared, the tip of the rod pointing straight down over the gunwale. Jon pulled hard on the already arched rod, leveraging with his whole body in an attempt to drag up a few scant inches of line, but whatever it was on the other end was having none of that this time. Down it went, straight down for at least thirty meters, before heading straight out to sea again.

"Blast," said Jon, wheezing with exertion.

"What should I do?" Robert asked.

"What do you mean? Follow him out of course."

Robert put the engine in gear and guided the boat gradually in the direction of the line.

"Faster! Come on, faster! There—stop!" Again they were drifting straight overhead. "God-damned thing must weight forty pounds," Jon grunted after a short pause.

Again he leveraged, and again he lost, as the line spun grudgingly off the reel.

"Again!" Jon demanded, and Jeremy could see that he was really beginning to tire this time.

"Dad, maybe we should—"

"What? What should we do? Cut it? No way. I'm not losing any more gear."

And just then the dripping belly of the line surfaced for maybe fifty meters, maybe more, before concluding at the whiskered, wide-eyed face of a slowly bobbing seal.

"Son of a bitch, not again," Jon growled, jerking hard on the rod. "Not again, you son of a bitch!"

"Dad, maybe we should cut the line," Robert suggested.

"*What*? I told you, I'm not losing any more tackle. No way are we cutting this line."

"But Dad, it's a seal. We've hooked a seal."

"And believe me, we're going to take great pleasure in punishing the bastard too."

"But Dad—"

"Enough! Drive the boat!" Jon commanded, struggling mightily to keep the line from snapping.

"Dad," Jeremy said, "cut the god-damned line!"

"And just what, exactly, do you think that's going to accomplish?" his father asked in a voice explosive with outrage. Then he added, with a quickened maliciousness of tone, "We've already hooked him, so it's going to abscess and kill him, never mind whether we actually catch the bastard or not." He reached into his tackle box, extracted a good-sized sinker, and pitched it hard at the smooth disembodied head of the seal, managing to miss his target by a fairly wide margin.

"What do you mean?" said Robert, his voice, despite the commotion, little more than a whisper at this point. "Dad, what do you mean?"

"Mean by what?" said his father almost pleasantly, wrenching the rod with everything he had. "Christ! I'm going to kill you, you son of a bitch!" he roared at the sea.

"What do you mean it'll abscess."

Struggling again for calm, his father explained, "I mean a seal is a warm-blooded animal, very much *un*like a fish. You hook a fish, and you lose him, well the fish will still be all right, as the hook will simply rust and fall out. But a seal . . ." He paused. "Well you call yourself a medic, you figure it out."

"You mean we're going to *kill* it?" Robert asked.

His father shrugged. "It's going to die anyway, once the infection sets in, so I might as well be the one to put it out of its misery."

Jeremy looked at Robert, then at his father, then at the seal. "Dad, cut the line."

"I told you, I'm not losing any more—"

"Dad, cut the god-damned line," said Jeremy.

Jon glared at him a moment, then slowly turned away. "Robert," he said, "take us over there."

"Are you kidding?" Robert laughed harshly. "I'm not taking us anywhere."

"For Christ's sake, do as I say! Now take us closer. And Jeremy, hand me that gaff there."

"You've got to be joking," Jeremy said. The massive outboard coughed once, rumbling irregularly but threateningly.

"Closer, Robert! Can't you see he's spent? Well can't you? Now's our chance, so take us closer. And Jeremy, will you please *hand me that gaff.*"

"Fuck that."

"I'm not going to do it," said Robert, staring straight ahead.

"Robert!"

"Dad, I'm not going to do it," he repeated, eyes welling unexpectedly. "I'm not going to kill that seal."

"Exactly! *I'm* going to kill it, you can be bloody sure of that. Now come on, get me closer."

"Dad, no."

"I'm not going to do it," Robert said. "No way, Dad. I'm not going to let you hurt that seal."

"But it's dead already! Can't you get that through that thick skull of yours? We've hooked it, and it's as good as dead."

"You don't know that."

"*What?*"

"I said you don't know that," Robert said, wiping his eyes with the back of an arm. "Not for sure."

Jon looked at him, aghast. "Fine then," he said, stepping up alongside. "Get out of that chair; *I'll* get us over there."

"I won't let you hurt it," Robert said.

Jon's weakened eyes narrowed in disgust. "Look at you. Look at both of you. Crying over a god-damned *seal.* Can't you see it stole something from me? Well can't you?"

"It doesn't know it stole anything," said Jeremy, whose concern for his brother, whom he had never seen so distraught, had reduced him almost to silence. In a hoarse whisper he went on, "It's just looking for a meal."

"A *free* meal," said his father. "You two don't understand, these seals, they're parasites. Nothing more than parasites. They hang around fishing boats, looking to steal whatever's available."

"So?"

"So basically it's us against them. Now get out of that seat, son, and let me get in there."

Robert stood steadfast. "I won't let you do it."

"Get out of my way."

"No, I won't let you do it. Jeremy, cut the line."

"*Cut the* . . . ? Jeremy," Jon warned in a low brutal voice, "you cut that line, and so help me God . . ."

"What, Dad? What are you going to do? Jeremy, cut the line."

"Don't you dare, Jeremy. Don't. Now Robert," Jon pleaded, speaking slowly and evenly, "this isn't your world. This is my world. And out here certain rules apply."

"I won't do it," Robert continued unwaveringly.

"And these certain rules dictate——"

"Look, I said I won't do it! I won't tell my daughter I killed a fucking *seal*. I can't. Now Jeremy, cut the god-damned line!"

Jeremy just stood there, dumbstruck by both.

"Don't you see, Dad?" Robert gasped. "I don't want to hurt anything. Do you understand that?" he asked Jeremy. "I don't want to hurt anyone. I'm afraid, if I stay, I might end up hurting someone. And I don't want to end up like *him*."

POSTED BY LUCY @ 3:03:57 A.M. 4/26/2007   9 COMMENTS

Falling from Heights

Dear Mom & Dad:

Five months ago today it was St. Patrick's Day (I know I've said this before, but it's absolutely unbelievable how *remote* that all seems now: the ever-accelerating pace of my personal history threatening to consume my memory forever.) and so, in order to get some of that old Irish feeling back, and in lieu of any sort of potato famine re-enactment (never very popular, I find) we pint-hoisters here in the fish tank have declared it a kind of Ward A holiday today. All non-Irish receive an honorary shamrock-shaped membership card, enabling them to drink and hold forth with streams of oaths, as many as they can muster, effective noon till midnight, with all those true green-blooded sufferers free to do the same, only more so naturally, and for a longer length of time—perhaps two days. House rules strictly forbid any sort of bare-knuckled fighting though, so Stan (full-blooded Irish, or so he maintains) and I will have to postpone that much anticipated match until mid October unfortunately.

Took yesterday off to write letters to various friends, but have enjoyed a good weaving day today. Back to the grind, as they say. Received a letter from Ruth—she was down in Chicago for a couple of days on business, and had her wee red Volkswagen stolen and smashed, so I imagine she's going to have a few problems with the insurance settlement. Or so she seemed to think anyway.

Friday, August 18, 1972

Great homemade card from Robert Hunter today, currently flat on his back in hospital with a slipped disc courtesy of some protest he attended last weekend—poor thing. Anyway, they gave as good as they got, he says, as a result of which Jon got to spend another couple of days in jail for striking a police officer, though you didn't hear that from me. Your son-in-law must be racking up quite the criminal record, eh? What a radical! Anyway, Robert said he'd write a full report when he can sit up again (hopefully soon).

Sat. August 19, 1972

Well here we are at day #51, and into the second half of the experiment. Constipated, yet still feeling great—eating wisely and sleeping sensibly, etc—but believe me, looking forward to the end. Still smoking regularly (so much for the theory that we'd be quitting anytime soon) and inhaling when I have to, which is, admittedly, pretty much every day, as I simply feel too guilty not to.

Things are fine here—Lorna and I had a long talk this afternoon, about four hours actually, as it seems she feels I've been ignoring her lately. Naturally I had to convince her otherwise, breaking out such time-honoured tactics as deeply furrowed brows, warm benevolent smiles and, of course, the occasional well-timed tear. We sit weaving so much that we hardly see each other, she feels. Strange, these female creatures.

Sunday, August 20, 1972

Well, today is Jonathan Jacks Jr.'s sixteenth birthday. Remember when he was born? Doesn't really seem all that long ago, does it? I bet it does to him though. After all, he is the self-described "old soul." I wonder what he's doing at this exact moment. Terrorizing some poor girl, no doubt.

Put in a good day's weaving today, and have been thinking, thinking, thinking all day long—call it philosophy-building, whatever—a result of inspirations from a variety of different sources: H.D. Thoreau, Norman Vincent Peale, M. McLuhan,

M. Ehrmann, etc. I'm going to write my thoughts down presently and send them along—a sort of *Desiderata* revisited maybe—
not yet though.

A short letter from Ginny today—J is back from jail and J Jr. is
back from camp, the latter saddled with the mumps apparently—
poor fella. Anyway, G's been rushed off her feet this past week. On
Friday she had a party for 25 "activists"—turned out well—and
has another for 30 coming up she must prepare for, so I guess
that's well underway, or into the planning stages anyway. (Do these
people do anything but party?) She sent along her business card—
standard size, white with black ink (enclosed). That phone number is for the new office on West Fourth in Kitsilano, in the old
War Amp's building, so please make note of it. Use only in case of
emergency though.

A note from Aunt Zelda arrived, via Tracey, thanking me for the
pictures I sent. She's been sick with the flu while Uncle Perce was
off in Ottawa doing God knows what for the government. I must
remember to drop her a line at some point, though I must also
remember not to tell her where I'm at. How clandestine my life
has become, has it not?

Ta for now. Think I feel something vaguely astir downstairs . . .
And if not, then I must go string my loom for yet another belt—
duty calls, as it were.

Love, Birdie

SEPTEMBER, 2002

When the telephone rang the second time, I could tell he actually considered not answering it. Instead he very quickly rolled
up to a sitting position on the sofa, and the movement, or rather
the speed of the movement, brought stiff opposition from the cat
that, until that very moment, had been kneading her way to a
trustful intimacy with his abdomen. Now, standing squarely on
the hardwood floor, she stared up at him in stunned silence,

wondering at the summary treatment of it all. His castaway's costume of long black corduroy shorts, with the front pockets reversed, sported several crudely stitched and overlapping patches, while the ever-attendant sweatshirt, long-sleeved and red, bore on its chest a vintage white maple leaf crest. He had been staring out the large bay window in the direction of the sun when the telephone rang, and it is perhaps for this reason why he blinked so arduously at this time.

"Hello?" he said hopefully into the telephone, settling back into the sofa, dragging one slow hand through his short-cropped, shipwrecked hair. The matching brown stubble of his lower cheeks and chin, combined with his all but complete absence of moustache, always made his beard, or what passed for his beard, resemble a hirsute chinstrap of sorts.

"Oh, hey, it's you," he said dreamily into the phone. "It double-rang so yes I was, I suppose. . . . Sitting here in his chair," he continued in that same faraway tone, turning to glance at me. "Nothing, just sitting here. . . . Oh not bad," he said, dropping his free hand to his crotch. "At least we got the cat back."

He looked down at the cat with genuine affection—and tipped her over with a toe after that.

"Oh nothing really. You know, just trying to fly a little under the radar these days. How'd you happen to hear about it anyway?" he said, stretching out to tip the cat again as, not without some indignation, she moved ever so slightly out of range. "Mark told you? Any idea where that bastard's at?" he asked, sitting up straight, checking and then rechecking his watch to ensure that it was in fact still not working. "*Fuck off.* He knows I'm late for hockey already and . . . All right, tell him to get his ass over here after that." And at that he hung up, adding, for the benefit of no one in particular, though presumably me, "Mark's running a little late."

"I see."

At that moment the doorbell rang, and Derek, in a complete departure from his more subdued telephone routine, leapt up to answer it. Though I could not see who it was from my vantage point of the chair, I could plainly hear Derek discussing something at the door with a stranger.

"Who is it?"

"Guy here says he's your brother," Derek hollered up the stairs. "Looks like he could be your brother anyway."

"Well ask him in," I said, leaning towards the window to see, much to my surprise, what looked to be my father's old El Camino parked there in the driveway.

"Come on in," I heard Derek say, and bounding up the stairs he returned to his post on the sofa, settling in heavily to an angry chorus of springs. A moment later Jeremy's face loomed up beyond the half-wall looking, of course, much older than I remembered.

"Well, well," I said for lack of anything remotely befitting the occasion.

Jeremy stepped slowly into the room, looking at me in a curious way, as though all too aware of just how intently I was looking at him. Suddenly he stopped, and lowered his eyes to his shoes, his sudden silence almost tangible, accompanied as it was by an audible change of breath. "Should I take these off?" he asked, turning first to Derek, then to me, with a genuine graciousness and simple dignity that impressed me.

"If you want," sighed Derek to the ceiling, restoring his earlier impression of a sailor sadly lost at sea.

"Don't bother. Have a seat," I said, indicating the sofa on which Derek currently lay sprawled, trying hard to get into the spirit of the thing. Derek looked at me, his expression an unrealized yawn.

"Well then I guess I'll leave you two to chat," he said, scowling balefully at me before offering a benevolent and obliging smile to Jeremy. "He gives you any trouble, or makes you uncomfortable or anything, just give ol' D-Rock a holler, a'ight?"

"Will do," said Jeremy shyly, and in those two words I sensed all his uncertainty. His soul is too good, too innocent, I remember thinking. He won't know how to handle me.

Once Derek was effectively removed from the equation, Jeremy sat down on the edge of the sofa and cast about for something tangible to focus his fractured attention on. He considered the drawn brown drapes, and then the irregular vertical stripes of the pale brown walls. In time he arrived at the cat, presently sitting old, grey and shabby on the floor, one eye shut tight against the square of sunlight angling in through the window, the other open and alert and observing him speculatively from afar.

"Nice cat," he began, in an effort to break the awkward silence. "Is it yours?"

"No, she belongs to the house. She's something of an inmate here—like me of course."

His attention shifted restlessly about the living room, lingering briefly at the bookcases. "No pictures."

"No, no pictures. They won't allow me any pictures. 'Against the rules,' as they say."

He nodded appreciatively, as though, in his world, such a policy would be deemed not only appropriate, but entirely necessary. "Still, this is a pretty nice place you got here," he remarked with searching earnestness, doing his part for the conversation. "I like all the windows."

"My prison of glass," I said. "Still it's not bad, for taxpayer money. Too clean though. Your brother's keepers, you'll find, insist on keeping the place oppressively clean. I learned to drive on the Path."

"Sorry?"

"That car you arrived in. The Path. El Camino means 'the Path' in Spanish."

He gave this worthless bit of translation trivia the very little due it deserved.

"And how are they treating you here?" he asked.

"Me? Royally. Like a fish in a barrel actually."

He almost laughed as again his eyes made a rapid circuit of the room, radiating, as they travelled, a clear but quiet anxiety. Having expected to be tense, or at the very least uncomfortable, he in fact found himself quite calm, and it was precisely this feeling of calm that disturbed him presently. And so, following a short pause and cursory inspection, he very quickly told me, "Look, if you don't want me here, I'll leave."

"No, no, stay. I want you to stay," I assured him, readjusting, by degrees, the drape of the afghan across my knees. "Tell me, though, where's my other little brother?"

He shifted backwards in his seat, levelling his attention at the cat. "Oh he's busy," he explained. "You know, with work and all."

I nodded slowly, stroking my chin thoughtfully. "Didn't want to come see the big bad monster, huh. Well I understand," I went on. "One Faust in the family's enough, I suppose."

He smiled, refusing to rise to the bait. Actually we both smiled, each of us feeling how strange it was that we should be here together. "We did come out to see you a few weeks ago," he said, "but Robby, well, he didn't want to . . ."

"Disturb me? What exactly did he imagine he'd be disturbing, Jeremy?"

Obviously not a good move on my part, this uttering of the word 'disturb,' as his face immediately drained of any sort of ready engagement and he retreated quickly inward. He sat there for a time, stone-faced, until, rather suddenly, he shrugged, and I watched his curious eyes flicker over and past me. "Well you were out there on your paper route and, to be honest, you did appear rather . . . intense, I guess would be the word."

"It does take a lot out of me."

"I guess."

"Sure."

This was, admittedly, less than poignant talk, and in the meantime the cat washed herself fastidiously with a series of rapid, deft movements of head and tongue, all the while paying stirring tribute to the consoling proximity of Jeremy's churning fingers with a purr trembling just on the verge of coherence somehow. Suddenly, though, she stopped cleaning, arresting her tongue mid-stroke, and instead studied something conspicuous at the base of the sofa before hopping up abruptly to Jeremy's lap, seeking continued affections at the source.

"Stretch out. Make yourself at home," I told him.

"Thanks, I'm okay."

"But Lucy, she wants you to lie down."

"Lucy?"

"The cat."

"Okay," he said, pivoting slowly so as not to disturb Lucy, or so as to disturb her as little as possible, stretching out lengthwise over the sofa, in the process tumbling a pillow backward onto the floor. Lucy, of course, took his reclining as an indication that she was once again welcome wherever, and consequently moved up onto his stomach, seemingly her lounger of choice at this juncture. He gently nudged her down. It was not that Lucy was all that heavy—she was old, and suffered from a hyperactive thyroid, and thus weighed in at a mere seven pounds—but that she managed to concentrate that weight so effectively into such a remarkably concise area.

Then I started to laugh. I laughed and laughed until tears ran down my cheeks, and finally, mercifully, the spell passed.

Jeremy lay there, a silent steadfast audience of one. "You, uh, okay?" he ventured tentatively, measuring his words carefully.

"Fine, yes," I told him, wiping a few errant tears away. "It's just I'm so happy to see you and Lucy together. I've actually *dreamt* about you and Lucy together. Tell me, how's the old homestead? I take it Dad's still there?"

"Still there," he said. "Actually everything's still there. Everything's *exactly* the same as it was as far back as I can remember. All the furniture, everything, exactly the same. . . . For instance, he's got this ridiculously ugly couch in the living room that's apparently some thirty years old—"

"Orange couch?"

"That's right."

"I remember that couch," I said. "In fact I remember the day it got delivered to the house." But I could see he was uncomfortable with any sort of mutually inclusive memory, so I immediately abandoned that scheme, and once again he fell silent. Then, by slowly inching his way up the cushions, and by propping his head uncomfortably, almost masochistically, against the arm of the sofa, he was just able to see out the large bay window in the direction of the school without disturbing the cat excessively.

"Anyway," he went on to the window, "the reason I'm here is, I found these letters crammed behind some books. In your old room. At Dad's. Tell me," he said to the ceiling, "did my—I mean our—mother have a sister? The reason I ask is, well, Dad hey, he won't say much about it. Nothing in fact."

"He is rather appallingly reliable that way," I said, trying to remember. It was difficult to remember. Having been dry-docked for so long, you see.

"When was the last time, you know, Dad came to see you?" he asked, turning to face me.

"Oh a few weeks ago," I told him, "maybe more. He usually comes every second week or so."

"Really? Every second *week*?" he said with barefaced disbelief. The words were coming faster now, spilling out in a patter of excitement and surprising, though not entirely unexpected, intrigue.

"Virtually," I said. "Admittedly not much lately though. Actually the last couple of months I've hardly seen him at all. I read the novel you sent me, Jeremy."

At the sound of his name he looked at me, and when I pointed out his book's position on the shelf he looked away hesitantly.

"Who knew I'd translate so well to the page. It's a very, what, stimulating read," I said.

Having returned his attention more or less to the world outside the window, he chuckled softly to himself, as though I were making a joke of some sort that he was somehow naturally the butt of. I could tell he was trying to think about something else.

"What?"

"Nothing." He waved me off.

"What is it? Tell me, Jeremy."

He examined me momentarily, then shrugged, "Well no offence, but coming from you, I really don't know whether 'stimulating' should be considered a compliment or not."

"I see what you mean," I smiled. "Still we're a lot alike, my would-be biographer and I."

His good humour ceased immediately. "I don't fucking think so," he told me.

Just then there occurred what was, for me, a pleasant, not in the least laboured break in the conversation. In the interim, petting the cat absentmindedly, Jeremy continued to stare his way through the window, in this way escaping the silence now organizing itself almost palpably between us.

"To answer your question," I said, "Mom did have a younger sister. Quite a bit younger, if I remember correctly. Quite an age difference, really. Rather like you and Robert and your incarcerated older brother actually."

He considered that briefly. "What was her name?"

"Birdie? Yes, Birdie. Rather appropriate too, now that I think about it. Flighty like a bird, see. Real flirt. Highly energetic, if you know what I mean. Made you want to squeeze her up into a tight little ball, then squeeze yourself inside all that energy."

That image seemed to at first shock then disappoint him, as his face gradually took on an expression of concerned incomprehension.

"Why so interested in the extended family, Jeremy?"

"Well these letters I found in your room, they're from a Birdie."

"Uh yes, the letters. *My* letters."

"Right," he said, smiling down at, and thoroughly petting the cat, until she tumbled over onto her side contentedly.

"Actually, most of them were originally addressed to the author's parents," he went on eventually.

"That being your grandparents. *Our* grandparents."

"That's right, our grandparents. Why, do you know them?"

"Are you implying you don't?"

"No," he said, eyes flickering to the floor, "I don't." He looked up at me anxiously, as though hoping I might share this particular facet of Jacks family detachment and disloyalty.

"Oh," I winced. "Sorry. And to answer your question, yes, I did meet them, whenever they drove out from Ontario. Though the last of these visits was admittedly a long, long time ago, before you and Robert were even born. Of course they're both dead now. In fact all our grandparents are dead now."

"I see," he said, having obviously suspected as much. He asked what they were like and I told him, beginning with honestly painted portraits of thoroughly nice, thoroughly unexceptional small town Ontario folk, but then something inside me slipped, slipping as it always did, and the honestly painted portraits morphed into voluptuous ones altogether grotesque and untrue, as I slid into a long impressionistic account of how amazing and generous they all were, especially at Christmastime, and naturally at birthdays too. He listened attentively, nodding steadily, his downcast eyes focused on Lucy exclusively.

"And Christmas," I said, nearly wincing at my own wickedness, for in all probability I knew the answer as well as he did. "How was Christmas for you and Robert? Good, I'm guessing?"

He shook his head. "Donations to charities in each of our names," he said. I could see it embarrassed him somewhat to say it, so much so that his voice trailed off at the end of it. "Anyway, getting back to these letters," he continued. "They were written at some government experiment."

"The, what, the LeDain Commission's experiment."

"You've heard of it," he said, almost sitting up, almost toppling the cat from her post.

"Of course I've heard of it."

He paused, and I watched his face change in the light. It was a fine face, with a strong bone structure in the tradition of his father's, and handsome too despite that likeness. Actually it was remarkable how much Jeremy resembled his father, and I of course told him as much. This, too, seemed to unsettle him.

"So when did she leave us?" he asked.

"Mom? Mom, I believe, left in or about the fall. . . . Yes, the fall of seventy-two, though I can't quite remember exactly—"

"Fall of seventy-*two*," he interrupted. "But Robert and I weren't even *born* in the fall of seventy-two."

"Weren't you?"

"No. We weren't."

"Oh," I said, "I suppose that's true. . . ."

He looked at me, then looked away, then gazed down at the cat doubtfully. "Anyway, I brought some of the letters," he said haltingly, as though unsure of the propriety of delivering something written by a woman a generation before into the clutches of a man like me.

"Good. I'm looking forward to reading them again," I said, silently admonishing myself for being so presumptuous. "Say, I hear you have some little ones now," I added quickly so as to smooth over any perceived impropriety.

"No, that's Robert. And he has one—Stephanie."

"*Stephanie*," I heard myself say, all too strangely evidently. And in an effort to conceal yet another conversational blunder, I went on knowingly, "That's right, Robert *does* have the girl. It never ceases to amaze me the information one can glean from the dailies. Say, you should bring her by some time."

He regarded me fixedly. "Not bloody likely," he spat.

I held up my hands in mock surrender, and in turn his face burned red to well above the hairline.

"Robert and I, we're building her a fort," he continued hurriedly, no doubt eager to atone for his own abasement this time.

"In the ravine? Well of course I remember the *ravine*," I told him when he looked at me sceptically. And I did too, this time.

He tried to smile warmly, failed miserably in the attempt, then asked if I remembered the maple about halfway down, and I had to admit I did.

"I think it might've even had a little makeshift rope swing," I said. "In fact I know I did. Tell me, is it still there?"

"Rope swing? Don't think so."

And we sat there staring at each other some more. Good thing, too, as I was about to embark on a long detailed account of things I had no real working knowledge of anymore.

"This Birdie," I finally said, having lost my train of thought for all the other self-propelled lies suddenly underway in my head, "she was a very intelligent girl."

"Fucking renaissance woman," he said.

Trying to settle myself down, I smiled tenderly at the memory of my dear dead something-or-other—I forget what. "Anyway, the letters, may I see them?" I took a chance and asked.

"Sure," he said, and retrieved a bundle from his pocket.

"Tell me, any mention of me?" I ventured as the collection of letters slid its way towards me across the hardwood floor.

"Occasionally, yes. A 'Junior' anyway."

"That's me. And that's right about the time I started getting myself in all that trouble," I told him excitedly. "Still, you and Robert certainly turned out all right."

"Oh sure, we're *real* healthy," he said, shaking his head. "Tell me, is that why . . ." His voice dropped off as he sought a suitably inoffensive phrasing.

"Why what?"

"Why our mother, you know, left us?" he concluded carefully.

"What, because of me? Well I don't really know. But to be honest, I doubt it. No, they didn't get to the root of ol' Junior till long after that."

He considered me in what I could only assume was his calculating way. "So what then, because of some sort of do-gooder phase Dad was going through?"

"God no, not at all. No, Mom was really into that."

"What exactly was it by the way? I mean this whole thing he was involved in."

"You mean to tell me he's never told you?"

"Not really, no," he shrugged, and bowed his head in humiliation and resentment. "Never in fact."

I shook my head. "Same old Jon Jacks. Patron saint of mutes and martyrs."

He nodded appreciatively, and we both stared out the window awhile. He certainly does wear his heart on his sleeve, I clearly remember thinking at the time. Too bad, too, as such bad habits would undoubtedly hold him back in his chosen profession.

"Well why'd he do all that stuff?" he asked.

"Who knows. Just felt the need, I guess."

"Still it must have been pretty major."

"It was at the time, yes."

He smiled to himself as Lucy immediately, but with dignity, assumed her customary sitting position.

"So, what, the old man was out there leading chants at rallies and all that?"

"No, no, nothing like that. His approach was much more— direct, I guess would be the word. I mean once he recognized those tests as a threat to the fisheries, the old man, he went to war after that."

"What tests?"

I looked at him, stunned. "You mean to tell me you have no working knowledge of our family's history? And yet here you have the gall to call yourself a writer? And a Jacks?"

Again that same expression of humiliation and resentment clouded his face, and so I relented long enough to explain how, back in the late sixties and early seventies, the American government had scheduled a series of nuclear tests on Amchitka, one of the Aleutian Islands off the west coast of Alaska, and how Jeremy's father, our father, along with a few selfless and dedicated others— including, of course, our great uncle—had decided to 'bear witness' in that old Quaker sense of the phrase. I explained how they never actually got to Amchitka, and how the Americans still detonated the bomb, but that in the end the voice of reason had been heard, people had listened, and nuclear testing on Amchitka came to an end not long afterward, the very next year in fact.

"So it was a success then."

"It was a success," I said.

"And they went on to do other things?"

"A few," I smiled.

"Like what?"

I smiled again.

"What?"

"You're serious?"

"Sure," he shrugged.

"Greenpeace, Jeremy. They founded Greenpeace."

"Oh," he said. "I didn't know that."

I was, I must admit, altogether astounded by that.

"But like I said, Dad was primarily concerned about the fishing industry," I resumed, explaining how no one knew what detonating a nuclear bomb would do to the salmon runs, let alone anything else in the vicinity. "And anyway, back then people were more apt to act on their impulses, without considering the, um— consequences," I said.

Jeremy shook his head, utterly mystified. "So you're telling me Dad started fucking *Green*peace?" he said at length.

"Well no, not *him* exactly. But some of his more celebrated colleagues certainly did."

"But he was on that fishing boat that went up to Alaska."

"The Phyllis Cormack? Oh, absolutely. In fact he was the one who finally persuaded Uncle John to take her up."

"Excuse me?"

"John Cormack? Captain John Cormack? He was our mother's uncle, and a very close friend of Dad's."

Okay, so 'close' friend was admittedly a bit of a stretch, but Jeremy had no need to know that.

"Was?"

"He's dead now. They're all dead now. In fact—"

"Well I'll be damned," Jeremy smiled, bemused, no doubt baffled, at the mere thought of his father having any friends, let alone his actually asserting any real influence in their lives. "Well I wonder why he quit then."

"Who knows. Maybe it was hard to justify an activist's ideals through a fisherman's eyes, especially when he suddenly had all these mouths to feed at home. Or maybe he thought he'd already failed with one son, and didn't want to fail two more."

"Yeah, maybe. Still you hate to see a man have to compromise himself like that."

"Who's to say he did? I was under the impression that, at least on some level, he was still fighting the good fight."

"Yeah, well, if you count smashing the occasional pay-parking machine he is." He sighed, shrugged, and chucked Lucy gently under the chin. "And here I thought it was just the booze and the bitterness that made him do all those things."

"No, not just. And anyway, he rarely drank when I was a kid."

"Really?"

"Though I do remember him getting into it a little just before I left," I said.

That, too, was a lie. I did not remember anything of the sort, certainly nothing that would have led me to believe that our father had been in any way an alcoholic in the making. In fact, I would have liked to ask Jeremy about that, about growing up the son of an alcoholic, just as, I suspect, he would have liked to ask me what it was like growing up the son of one who was not— but I did not. One could imagine it clearly enough.

"When Virginia went away?" he asked.

"Maybe. It's difficult to remember. I mean I find it difficult to remember. In my mind it all seems to have happened at the same time, see."

"Well I wonder why," he mused, returning to the window.

"Why what?"

"Why she left."

"Who knows. Women are such perplexing creatures."

He turned to look at me. "Oh aren't they," he said with a laugh.

"And hey, if you really want to know, why not just ask her yourself?"

"Sorry?"

"Now unfortunately you've already missed her this week, but she'll be by next week if you're—"

"Ask *who*?"

"Mom. Mother. Mommy. Whatever you're comfortable calling her," I said.

This time he did sit up, sending Lucy tumbling off to the kitchen where Derek could be clearly heard delivering a series of threats into the telephone. "She's *alive*?"

"Of course she's alive. Why wouldn't she be alive? Healthiest I've seen her in years in fact."

August 22, 1972 (Tuesday)

Dear Mom & Dad:

Greetings from your wee chicken. Things are booming here at the abattoir—all are alive, well and kicking.

Had the marvellous Dr. Congreves look into us inmates renting a piano for the remainder of the experiment. With a minimum 2 mo. rental, including moving fees, the total cost will be about $70. Split between two of us (Shelley says she's keen), that comes to $35 each, or half a day's work if we push it. He just has to remember to check with the maintenance department here to confirm that all is clear, and if so, we shall have ourselves a piano, perhaps as early as Friday afternoon.

Wed. Aug 23/72

Your Aug 18th letter arrived today—I was getting worried for a minute there—and no, Ginny has never mentioned anything to me about a Jonathan "outburst" (I take it you mean the Junior circuit) so I wouldn't worry too much about it if I were you. So does this mean you've heard from her lately? That woman is an absolutely lousy correspondent, especially of late. Give her a kick in the rear, will you? She has some opinions I'm interested in.

About that unsigned Aug 9–16 letter, could you please send it back with your next one? I just want to check . . . It seems rather silly, but we're still not sure whether they read our outgoing mail or not. There may have been some information on that last sheet (if there is in fact one missing) that was somehow "classified," but I can't really tell until I see the whole thing again. It seems such a trivial matter, I suppose, but believe me, it's important. Then again, I might just be suffering from some sort of pot-induced paranoia. I wouldn't be surprised.

There are stages in weaving, and then there are *stages*. For the past month I've been able to average about twenty belts a day, getting my hands, arms and back strong enough to increase production even further when I decide I'm ready. As one increases the numbers, or, should I say, cuts down on the time spent per belt, the actual weaving becomes increasingly difficult. Right now I'm over this last hump (but by no means the *last* hump) and able to bank $60/day, or $75 if I push it. By next Wednesday I shall have saved $2000, and by the end of the experiment, even if I were only to maintain my present daily quota of twenty-six belts, I shall have at least $4500! I think that takes care of the student loan nicely, don't you? Actually, I already have that completely covered. The real battle is keeping the skin on my hands tough enough to withstand thousands of yards of wool passing through, without building up so much callous that it cracks in the dry air—a fine balance, to be sure. Now I know I may have missed a few good home-cooked meals, a little privacy, the odd rock concert or good movie, telephone calls and get-togethers with friends, but these things will always be there. This experiment was merely a once-in-a-lifetime opportunity to take a wee break away from it all, to step off the beaten path and live like a hermit a while (admittedly a rather well-watched hermit), but still accomplish something worthwhile. Could I have paid off the loan from tips as a waitress at the Gasworks or Coal Bin? I think not.

We are, in all probability, going to be smoking until September 20th or so. Apparently the other ward only smoked that one night I mentioned to you before. They can purchase joints still, but don't *have* to smoke yet. Optional not obligatory, I guess is what I'm trying to say. Probably one of the most poignant (is that the right word?) indicators of the effects of marijuana can be seen in the area of "motivation." In one sense it is a physical decline—coordination, concentration, etc are temporarily undermined—but in another sense it is entirely psychological—constantly dwelling on how "heavy" the grass is, and using that as an excuse for "feeling too tired" to weave on any given day. Your strength of character, or willpower (or lack thereof) shines through here, no question. Either you persuade yourself that you don't feel like weaving, or you exert some discipline, refocus your remaining energy, and bend forward to the task at hand. To be sure, I've experienced a few off-days myself, but not many. I guess I'm just a very stubborn person (as you've reminded me, repeatedly) but in this case it proves something of a positive quality—Birdie's a permanent fixture in the main lounge from 5:30 AM till 7:30 PM, believe me. Lorna keeps her vigil in one of the small rooms off the lounge, but she's on a completely different schedule than I— she's just going to bed when I get up at 5.

Must close for now. Lunchtime is over and the loom, as they say, looms large.

Love, B

SEPTEMBER, 2002

It was turning out to be a dry hot summer, one of the driest and hottest on record. The upside of this unusually prolonged bout of fine weather were the many days available for continued work on the cabin, as many as were needed really, the downside being that dayshifts at the mill became almost unbearable, surrounded as the men were with all that hardworking, heat-producing machinery. A large fan had been stationed alongside the Japan line so that those of the lowest caste, those required to stack the feed bags, like Jeremy, would not dehydrate too quickly. Still, an hour into the shift his protective glasses were chronically fogging over, the backs of his coveralls were soaked through, and the pores of his skin, having dilated in the heat, were all but oozing thick oily fish stink continuously. The nightshifts were okay; it was the dayshifts that made him wonder just what the hell he was doing here. His brother, though, appeared not to notice the heat. Or so at least it seemed to Jeremy. Then again, Robert typically operated the forklift, and was therefore unlikely to do much in the way of heavy lifting, if any.

Sometimes if, say, for whatever reason one or both extruders were down, Jeremy and the other recent hirelings were banished to the upper floors of the plant, for purposes of cleaning and the like. Up here, of course, the heat proved excruciating. The stench, unbearable. Sweat poured in streams down your back. And crawling in to clean under feed dryers and coolers and other assorted machinery put you in direct contact with all manner of hideous insect life, including one such specimen erroneously referred to by the men as a maggot. In actuality I guess it was some sort of grub. A small, brown, vaguely caterpillar-like creature able to set a large forgotten pile of feed ingredients to crawling with its numbers alone. Squeezing himself in under some massive piece of mechanization, armed with only a vacuum hose, Jeremy found it difficult not to wretch uncontrollably whenever he encountered one or more of these nasty creatures moving across some section of skin mistakenly left exposed. It was enough to make him want to quit right there. But then he needed the money of course, and besides, the real nuisance at the mill was the rampant salmonella.

Down in the shade of the ravine, however, the summer wrote an entirely different story. Now certainly it was hot, and the work itself certainly proved gruelling, but being the sort of labour it was—not exactly of love per se, but more of an affinity by proximity—the brothers seemed not to notice the heat, nor even the long hours they regularly put in. And after working hard in the ravine all day, Jeremy got in the habit of going for a swim. And it was during one of these late afternoon dips in the peanut-shaped pool that he first noticed the crack in its foundation.

"Dad, it looks like you've got a crack here," he announced upon surfacing in the deeper and larger of the two nuts, as it were.

Not listening, Jon laughed to himself, and tossed one more handful of feed through a gap in the pond's protective steel shell. "What's that?" he very absently asked.

"I said—"

"Dad, if you want, we can get you more of that feed," Robert cut in from his position halfway down the shallow end steps, or 'West Egg' as his brother had referred to it in one early aborted attempt at a story he later quite rightly considered far too Fitzgerald-esque for its own good.

"It's got to float though," Jon said, smiling down at the few colourful fish he had left. Jeremy was still not sure whether it pleased or annoyed him that the fruits of his labour could be of possible use to his father, an irony that seemed, at this point of the summer, completely lost on him. "Can't use that sinking stuff. I mean I can *use* it," Jon said, "but it's not as *good* to use it. They prefer this floating stuff."

"No, I think we've got a run of floating coming up. It's four-millimetre though," Robert said. "Don't know if that's too large."

"Four millimetre? What's that in inches?" Jon asked, looking first to Jeremy, then to Robert, then to that standard point somewhere between his two sons where he often found himself by default.

Both brothers shrugged.

"Yes, well, four-millimetre sounds about right," Jon nodded, returning his attention to the suddenly animated inhabitants of the pond.

Replacing his goggles, Jeremy dropped down below the surface of the water to double-check his earlier diagnosis. And sure enough, there it was, the crack, running on a jagged diagonal near the curved plaster bottom of the pool's ravine-side wall.

"Dad, you've got a crack here in the deep end," he announced upon resurfacing. This time Jon heard him clearly, and endeavoured to say something that in the excitement transformed itself into a long hacking cough, ending, after much effort, with his clearing his throat into a clump of nearby shrubs. Finally he blew his nose violently, each side separately, with both sons looking painfully on.

"There's a crack," Jeremy repeated for everyone's benefit, lest something had been lost in translation from lungs to shrubs. Jon pitched and rolled his way from pond to pool and, once there, bent down alongside. He creaked as he settled, with a tortured groan of protesting joints and, if one did not know better, metal on metal.

"Where?"

"Here." Jeremy indicated the location with a toe.

"You sure?"

Jeremy rolled his eyes as Robert swam over and, equipped now with Jeremy's goggles, dove down to register a second opinion.

"Yup, there's a crack all right," he agreed at once.

"Well I'll be damned," muttered their father. "Well then we're going to have to drain the son of a bitch," he added, slapping his thighs and sighing despondently.

"But maybe it's not that deep," Robert ventured. "I mean it's not like we're losing any water."

"Not yet anyway. But either way we're going to have to drain it. Son of a bitch!" Jon said.

"Well how come it's cracking?" Jeremy asked.

"Because it's old, you idiot," Robert answered.

"Yes, it's old, and eventually all old things crack," their father said snidely.

"You know what I mean," Robert shot back.

Jon waved him off, and then explained to both sons how it was a simple by-product of erosion and gravity. "We're losing yard to the ravine. Always have been."

"*No*," Robert said.

"*Yes*," countered Jeremy.

"See that spruce there?" Jon said, indicating the nearest of three trees, around which the brothers had years ago managed to anchor and build the deck overhanging the ravine. "Used to be that spruce there was the edge of the yard. In fact, the lawn used to extend a good three feet *beyond* that spruce, but then every year we lost a little more to the ravine, and a little more, and now this deck here"—he rapped the planking with his knuckles— "thanks in large part to you boys, is nearly all the backyard we've got left."

Jeremy picked over the statement at least twice, trolling careful- ly for the insult he assumed must be hidden in there somewhere.

"Well then why the hell'd you put in a pool if you knew that was going to happen?" Robert demanded.

"Because I was assured the frame of the pool would hold. It's all rebar-reinforced concrete, so by rights it should have."

"Well," said Jeremy, "it's not."

Later that evening, with his brother still serving his one-month sentence, Jeremy made his way up to Doolin's to meet Cassidy, his drinking partner of choice of late. When he arrived, Cassidy was seated in his usual spot in a booth near the window, recounting for an audience of one a long series of fantastic stories you would have to assume were made up on the spot.

"It's about time," Cassidy said, waving Jeremy into the booth alongside a long-haired man of smallish stature and perhaps forty-plus years of age. Jeremy shook the man's hand and, when the waitress arrived, ordered himself a Crown and Coke along with another round for his companions.

"So Calvin here tells me you're a lyricist," said the man, whose name was David, while tapping out a quiet beat against the rim of his glass.

Jeremy cut his eyes to Cassidy. "Well then he lied."

David took this as a joke at his expense and proceeded to get ugly about it. "Listen, do you have any idea who I am?"

"Not at all. Sorry," Jeremy shrugged, pretending not to notice the man's forest of hair plugs, focusing his attention on the stone-faced, suddenly tree-like Cassidy instead.

"I'm Mr. Big. You know, *Mr. Big.*"

"Like I said: sorry."

David tapped out a beat, slow and poignant, on the edge of the table, and began to sing along with it. "Remember?" he asked upon the song's completion.

"I think so . . . maybe."

David sang again, his face contorting unattractively but passionately. "Well?"

"Sure," said Jeremy, feigning acquaintance, growing embarrassed not only with all this singing, but with all the additional attention it was garnering from the other patrons.

David looked stunned. "Man, how can you not remember?"

"Well that's the thing, I think I do."

David shook his head, burping down into his chest. "I can't believe you can't remember."

"I'm sorry. I'm not all that much of a music enthusiast."

"*Enthusiast,*" David said, standing up angrily. "You're not even a real *musician,* I bet."

And then, in a huff, he left.

"And there but for the grace of God go I," sighed Cassidy who, somewhat uncharacteristically, had sat quietly smoking through-out the entire exchange. Leaning back in his chair, he stretched out his two shoeless feet in the direction of the rapidly departing, irate and deeply wounded David.

"Nice socks," Jeremy observed, and Cassidy leaned forward to stab out his cigarette, triggering the two plaid socks to retreat rapidly from view beneath the table.

"That, my friend, is a poet. A *poet*. Now come on, let's get down to business," he said, and slid a shot glass across the table at Jeremy.

"I can't stay long. I have to go meet someone."

Cassidy smiled knowingly. "What, a secret rendezvous?"

"Go fish," Jeremy said, shaking his head. "No, this is family unfortunately."

"To family," Cassidy said, hoisting his own shot, and together they drank them down.

"*Jack*," Jeremy winced, having identified the shot's content by its cruelly sweet aftertaste.

"Only the best for me and mine," said Cassidy with contrived sincerity. "Still, it's a nostalgic throw-back, I suppose. Much of it comes from my memories of childhood and the types of people I had around me at the time—which is to say, blacks—and the help my father retained for household duties and the like. As an ensemble they were remarkably unattractive," he went on in that peculiar expansive way he had, which, as anyone who has taken a drink with him will tell you, was as engaging as it was sad. "But oh how they entertained me. Endless games! And now I see those early days as prophetic of course as the African American has once again reduced himself and his kind to a race of minstrel-like marionettes. Oh you laugh but it's true. I mean what can they possibly hope to accomplish by aligning themselves thus? These are the sorts of questions that I constantly ask myself."

Cassidy turned his head and coughed, as though undergoing a rather painful medical examination of some sort.

"Now, in David's absence, let us speak fondly of music," he continued at length. "In doing so, though, I must first segue back into the subject of family, my father especially. He was a doctor, you see, and he owned one of the best record collections in Detroit, both classical and jazz, and incidentally Casablanca was his

favourite film." His eyes began to close, and then shot open violently, as he floated a languid hand above his own head. " 'The
problems of two people don't amount to a hill of beans in this
crazy, mixed-up world,' " he quoted. "Now that's a line. And a line
of prose, too, by the way—by which I mean poetry—and there
goes a man," he added, raising his glass in salute towards the door
and by extension, Jeremy supposed, the recently departed Mr. Big,
"lucky enough to earn a living with nothing *but* his poetry. And
like him, and Dylan before him, fate has made you the messenger
of nothing less than your entire generation, Jeremy."

At that Cassidy took up another shot and promptly tossed it
back, then thoroughly licked out the glass, all the while repeating
this oddly effective imitation of puppetry above his own cherry
red, oversized head.

"I'm a six-time Scorpio. Don't know if I ever mentioned that."

"No," Jeremy said, "you haven't."

"Well it's true. I thought maybe you'd read about it in the news.
Everything one reads in the news is true, especially when it concerns yours truly. Another?" he said, indicating Jeremy's drink.

Jeremy considered his still full glass. "Sure," he said. "Like I said
though, I can't stay long."

Cassidy flagged down the waitress and, between coughing
attacks, managed to order another round.

"Tell me, have you ever been to Miracle Valley?" he ventured a
little later, without doubt for lack of anything even remotely
interesting to say. "That's where I went to escape the long arm of
Karl Marx, the Liberals, and all the lovely ladies at Revenue
Canada," he grimaced, lighting a fresh Camel, "and admittedly to
get sober for a while. My father, you see, always appreciated sobri-
ety, even though he was stone drunk himself half the time. In fact,
even before I was born, the good doctor was treating his wife—
my mother—like some sort of concubine, forcing her to have at
least two abortions because he wasn't ready to ruin his parties
with any nagging children, and feeding her highballs at night
because for him it would mean a higher probability of violent acts
of sodomy in the morning. A plague on *both* your houses," he

coughed, lurched forward, and slammed down against the table-top what Jeremy observed to be a severely crippled left hand. Twisted and broken though it was, he had somehow never noticed it before. And finally, having managed to recover from his nasty coughing fit, Cassidy took a series of good long drinks to bolster himself, occasionally sucking on his Camel whenever the routine required further reinforcement.

"Now having touched on evil, let us speak of Satan," he said, no longer conversing but broadcasting instead. "By which I mean, of course, socialism. Believe me, there is a plague of such profound evil descending upon us that it can only be comprehended by the Book of Revelations. Speaking of revelations," he said, sucking on his cig-arette in a curious manner, very curious considering how many cigarettes he must have gone through in the course of any given conversation, as though this simple white device were all that con-nected him to the oxygenated world, "how's that brother of yours?"

"Robby? He's all right. Though still barred from this fine estab-lishment."

"And your parents? Tell me all about your parents."

"Well that's sort of what I'm going to find out about tonight."

Cassidy nodded deeply, studying closely the burning end of his Camel. "Families," he sighed profoundly, "are indeed a constant source of mystery for us all."

Two Crowns and two shots later, Jeremy left Doolin's and made his way out to the parking lot and his father's utterly ridiculous vehicle. Not surprisingly, the Royal Heights Shopping Centre appeared nearly empty. Two Indo-Canadian children, their sex indeterminate from this distance, strolled across the large expanse of blacktop hand in hand, passing by the closed front doors of what had been, not so long ago, Jon Jacks' store, *Captain Video*. Meanwhile, across the way, near the enduring Dairy Queen, some teenagers stopped their car atop a speed bump in what amount-ed to a feeble, entirely inaudible attempt at a brake-stand, much to Jeremy's disappointment.

In the El Camino now, he drove quickly along Ninety-Sixth Avenue to King George and past Queen Elizabeth Secondary, his

brother's school, up alongside Surrey Memorial Hospital where
he and Robert were born, and out towards Guildford Mall and
the Trans Canada Highway beyond. Where the road curved to
merge with the highway he saw three cars scattered in the ditch
alongside. Two cars had suffered considerable damage, while the
third, a two month-old Lexus, seemed all right. Jeremy stopped to
see if any assistance was required, but no one seemed too put out
about the accident, though they all spoke with great confidence
and tactical knowledge on the subject of how it had in fact transpired. Other cars pulled up, among them a white RCMP cruiser, so Jeremy returned to his father's car and, checking the time,
accelerated along the shoulder before rejoining the stream of traffic further on. There were trees along both sides of the split highway now, with shorter shrubs in between, and through the line of
trees across the highway he could see, alongside the farmhouses,
horses of an indeterminate breed. They were feeding on the grass
in the meadow, their heads hovering down around their hooves,
and a little further along, out towards the valley and its barricade
of low blue mountains, the farmhouses transformed into industrial storage centres and Jeremy checked the time once more. He
wanted to arrive just shortly after Virginia did, but when he finally did arrive I had to tell him that, unfortunately, his mother had
already been and gone.

"Why? What happened?" he asked, standing forlorn in the middle of my living room.

"She got scared."

"Scared? How do you mean?" he said, looking upset. More than
upset, he looked downright hurt, and in the end I was sorry I had
said it.

"Well she hasn't seen you in thirty years, Jeremy. Not since she,
you know . . ."

"Abandoned us," he said.

A silence arose while we contemplated, from our respective
positions, the perfectly pathetic story of his life. Eventually my
tank-topped custodian Mark came loping in from the kitchen to
offer Jeremy what little was left of his protein shake.

"No thanks," said Jeremy kindly, taking his customary seat on the sofa. Down the hall, I could hear Derek and Tom plunging the toilet. Derek and Tom were always plunging the toilet. It seemed to be an obsession with them. Occasionally such commotion made for an unsettling environment, although, this time, with company, it only seemed to inject some much needed energy into what had suddenly become an overly comatose atmosphere. Meanwhile Jeremy sat, that habitual look of disquiet clouding his face.

"So you told her I was coming," he said as Mark hauled himself down the hall to help the others.

"I did."

"And she got scared."

"She did."

"Maybe this was a bad idea," he said, shaking his head.

"I don't know. What does our father think?"

"*Dad*? Are you crazy? He doesn't know I'm here."

"Why not?"

Again he shook his head, evidently in no mood to explain.

"Obviously, if you have to ask that question, you don't know him very well," he said.

"You're right, I don't," I said.

And with that we sat staring out the window at the slowly setting sun, the twilight sky beyond an optimistic quickening of crimson, pink and gold. Eventually Lucy came stalking in, returning her affections directly to Jeremy's lap, much to my chagrin.

"Who's this?" Jeremy asked, indicating with a nod the stereo in the corner.

"This? This is Warrant. *Cherry Pie* by Warrant, unplugged version. Why, do you like it?"

"I thought it might be Mr. Big," he said. He watched Lucy make slow, tail-raised circles of his thighs. "It's funny, but you remind me of this guy I sometimes see at the pub. Or rather he reminds me of . . . Well I don't know who he reminds me of," he conceded, indulging the cat just once, as though to better express the futility of this particular line of thought. "Do you know Calvin Cassidy?"

"You mean the actor?" I said, smoothing the afghan with the flats of my hands so as to make my own lap appear that much more enticing to the cat—if only to complete the effect, understand. "Only by the characters he's played on TV."

"Well he's very—odd. And annoying. And a terrible drunk. An absolutely terrible drunk. But in a rather entertaining way of course."

"Well thanks, Jeremy. Thanks a lot."

"No, I mean . . . well you know what I mean."

"Actually no, I don't," I told him.

He inhaled heavily through his nose, avoided my gaze, and stared down at the cat a while.

"And why is it, do you suppose, you've sought him out?"

"Pardon?"

"What is it about this Cassidy character that attracts you?" I said. "Other than his ability to assimilate copious amounts of alcohol of course."

He frowned, still focused on Lucy's rhythmic kneading of his lap. "I don't understand."

"Well there must be something about him that intrigues you. Something he provides that members of your own generation— do not. You do have friends your own age don't you, Jeremy? Tell me we're not *that* much alike."

"So much for the Three Question Rule, eh?" he replied, rapidly losing patience with me. As usual, his attention shifted to the window, compelled there more or less by the force of my interrogation. I must scale it back some, I told myself, or else he might throw the hook and escape completely.

"So with Dad and Virginia having us sixteen years after you, I suppose we were some sort of mistake then," he said, his eyes flitting across the room.

"I suppose," I shrugged, though of course I had no idea either way. And together we gazed out the window to where the shadows grew long over the short-cropped lawn, sending any lingering daylight scurrying to the treetops for safety.

"I'm glad you've come to see me, Jeremy. You don't know what it means to me. You *can't* know what it means to me. And to be honest, if I'd known you were this interested in your mother, I would have made something up long ago, believe me."

"Yeah, well, it's only since I found these letters that I've actually been interested in her at all."

"Uh yes, the letters. Tell me, did you bring the rest?"

"Most of them, yes." He looked at me narrowly, weighing something in his mind, as the last of the amber light leapt free of the trees, relinquishing to shadow the remainder of the lawn.

"What?" I said, switching on a lamp. "What is it you would like to say?"

He continued to regard me in that unusual way. Then finally he said, "Well, I—I was just wondering why you, you know, did all those things you did."

I smiled in what I hoped was a Lucy-like way. "Well because, J— Jeremy, according to the doctors, I'm a very sick man apparently."

POSTED BY LUCY @ 12:03:52 P.M. 5/02/2007   51 COMMENTS

Thursday, Aug 24, 1972

Dear Mom & Dad:

And now for something completely different!

We've had a wonderful time around here today, ever since the September issue of Cosmopolitan magazine surfaced mysteriously this morning—complete with male nude centerfold—a take-off on the whole Playboy situation, I'm guessing. Women's Liberation? Not really. We just wanted to hang this month's hunk of flesh in the main lounge where we can chuckle over it at toke time. See if you can guess: a current Hollywood star, very hairy and virile he-man type, reclining on a bearskin rug with his favourite drink and, clenched between his unbelievably white, unbelievably false teeth, the token tough-guy cigar, from which his much publicized image seems all but inseparable of late. Anyway, the reactions of the male attendants have been interesting to say the least, from chuckles to scoffs to Stan the Shopping

Man's red-faced "Geez, Birdbrain, there must be something
wrong with that guy's head!", old scene-stealer that he is. When
the tables are turned the other way, one sees how women really
have been typecast by Hugh Hefner's emporium et al. Personally,
I think it's hilarious, but we have one *very* Women's Lib chick
here—Shelley Cartwright, 33 years old, pretty & petit and a very
successful Canadian artist, but unfortunately very caught up in the
whole "movement" thing—and she of course finds the whole
thing nauseating. Me, I've never felt threatened by "male chauvin-
ism" or by the typecasting of the "typical female," so I find a lot
of her beefs somewhat invalid. Now certainly the statistics on
wage and job opportunities are accurate, but there will always be
people lesser and greater than yourself—and always someone
willing to step on your head when you insist on carrying it so low
to the ground. Mind you, you can't see much with your head in
the clouds either, so there must be a happy medium somewhere,
mustn't there?

Friday, Aug 25, 1972

Received your Sunday letter this morning, which surprised me,
as I usually get it on Tuesday or Wednesday, or even Monday occasionally. Mind you, I'm certainly not complaining, but we've had
this idea lately that maybe they're holding back mail for some reason. . . . Anyway, by the sounds of things you two seem to be sailing along quite well. I haven't written any poetry lately, no, but
why the sudden interest? Was it something I mentioned in my last
letter? A pleasant turn of phrase perhaps? A memorable line?
Speaking of lines, how's the fishing going up there? Are the trout
half as big as I remember?

Everything is fine here: a few rabbit pellets to start the day;
another mood test; the blood lady switching to secondary veins in
order to give the primaries a rest. We still trot out twice weekly
with our contributions of pee in plastic containers, and word has
it we'll be having medicals, EEG, EKG, and chest x-rays again
next week. That really puts a dent in a good weaving day, don't
you think? On a brighter note, the piano I told you about (I did

tell you about the piano, right?) will be arriving Tuesday from
Long & McQuade. We've managed to rent it for just one month,
and they might even let us keep it a few extra days, as the L & M
boys are big fans of the ARF and its weed apparently.

Did you know there's a specific clause in our contracts requir-
ing us to return for 6 and 12 mo. follow-ups to the experiment?
No matter where I am April 8ᵗʰ (and next October 8ᵗʰ) the
Foundation will fund my flight here and back again. Pretty good,
eh? I wonder if they'd still pay if I just happened to be over in
Paris or something. An intriguing thought anyway.

Saturday, Aug 26/72

Tomorrow is Sunday, which means I haven't taken a bona fide
dump in almost a week.

Sunday, Aug 27/72

Today is Sunday, exactly one week since my last executed bowel
movement of any merit. (Now I know for a *fact* you're well aware
I'm in no way a proponent of the non-natural laxative, so would
you kindly stop suggesting that?) Speaking of crap, did you happen to catch *The New Majority* on CBC @ 4:30 today? Ian
McGregor's film on black people in Canada was on (it's a one-
word title, but I can't quite recall it now), and in my opinion it
was rather poorly done. By the way, that went into production
well before Xmas, so you can see just how much of a delay there
is between conception and fruition. As it happens, I got a very
sweet letter from his ex-wife this week—nice to hear from her—
she's pitching a couple of film ideas to ETV as we speak.

Michael Beauchemin (Montreal Theatre Michael) is back from
Barbados and in town visiting his brother Guy (part of the engi-
neering team for some enormous new project for Canadian
National, a tower or something, scheduled to begin construction
downtown in February), and was generous enough to deliver
Black Sabbath's latest album to the main desk, which of course I
was obligated to pay for (I do get my money back at the end
though) as we're not allowed to receive any gifts in here. Black

Sabbath. How lovely. You can imagine my joy when I opened the package and found *that* cheerful cover. Anyway, "Mikel" leaves again on September 8th for London, Paris and Munich, where he'll be catching some of the Olympics—as if he needed a vacation, the reprobate. He says it's for work, but you have to wonder at the timing of it. Double-jointed hunger-striker my ass. He ought to see me at 8:15 each night.

Must close for now.

Love, Birdie

SEPTEMBER, 2002

Jon Jacks suffered his second and by far most debilitating stroke while working on the pool one early afternoon in September. Having drained the pool in order to repair the newfound crack, or more accurately, to significantly improve his position in order to better frown at it, he suddenly lost consciousness and toppled, with the full force of gravity, to land face first in the deep end with a resounding crack, where he proceeded to bleed profusely from the nose, mouth and even eyes as luck would have it. Eventually his mind returned from wherever it was it had momentarily gone, and on his elbows and backside he dragged a bloody red smudge across the pool's unbelievably bright white plaster to the short set of stairs at the shallow end. Once at the stairs he managed, not without some difficulty, to hoist himself up and out, before dragging and sliding his way back around the pool's peanut-shaped circumference to where the cordless phone lay.

Robert and Jeremy were at work at the time, and so did not learn of their father's fall until returning home that evening. As it was, Bob File was parked on the orange couch in the living room when they arrived.

"What the fuck?"

"Take it easy, Robby," Bob said, standing up and poking nervously at his chest. "Your dad let me in. Or what I mean is, I let myself in, with your father's keys. You see, he's had a fall," he said, and proceeded to tell them what he knew, which, he was quick to admit, was not a lot, beyond the fact their father had called him at home after falling flat on his face in the pool, and that he, Bob, had come straight over and, despite Jon's many objections, driven him straight to the hospital.

"Which is where he's at now. At Surrey Memorial. In the maternity ward," Bob almost smiled, just managing to retract it before any real lasting damage was done to either his mission here or himself.

"Why the *maternity* ward?" Jeremy asked.

"That's all they had available, I guess. Anyway, he's doing all right. Or as well as can be expected, I guess. Face looks bad, but I'm sure it looks a hell of a lot worse than it is. They're keeping him overnight for tests," Bob added, checking and then rechecking his watch for emphasis. "And hey, visiting hours end at eight, so if you want to go see him you've only got an hour, at best."

Robert wanted to go, but Jeremy did not, primarily because he was angry their father would inexplicably call Bob again and not his sons, even if they were unavailable at the time of the accident. Truth be told, though, he did not want to see his father fallen. That is, further fallen than he already was. Finally, though, at Robert's repeated requests, he did go, and seeing his father lying there in the bed was harder on him than anticipated, although, it must also be said, his father's actual condition was better than perhaps expected. As well as exhibiting all the standard signs of an embolic Ischemic stroke, including a loss of memory and a diminished capacity to coordinate his movements, Jon, it turned out, also suffered from a minor arrhythmia, or abnormal rhythm of the heart, for which he was scheduled to receive an elective cardioversion, or mild electric shock. This procedure, Robert patiently explained, would temporarily wipe out all electrical activity in the heart, allowing its natural pacemaker, the sinus node, to re-establish a steady regular beat of sorts. It sounded dangerous, he said, but really it was not. Their father would be given a mild sedative or else a general anaesthetic and then, once he was totally relaxed or even asleep, two special gel-covered pads would be positioned on his chest, and when the heart monitor registered the appropriate heart wave, an electric shock would be delivered through the wall of the chest. If the initial low-energy shock did not cause the heart to beat normally again, then more shocks would be delivered at intervals of about one to three minutes until normal heart rhythm was achieved. The procedure was not painful, Jeremy was assured, but it was also not permanent—a robust routine of medications would need to be established immediately. Although the mere suggestion of any sort of shock therapy always came as something of a shock to Jeremy, none of what was now happening to his father surprised him. Not really. What he did find entirely surprising, though, was the fact his brother felt he might need to sneak into the hospital initially.

"What? *Why?*" Jeremy asked when they were as yet parked out in the parkade, yet to enter the maternity ward, yet to see their father's already well-aged but still dignified vessel reduced even further to a toothy, tubed-up, too small husk of flesh in a bed. Retrieving a joint from his pocket, Robert dipped his head in the direction of the nearest pay-parking machine.

"Because I was the one who wrecked those things," he said.

A wave of cold discouragement closed over Jeremy as he cast a quick penetrating glance at his brother. Robert's head was bowed, his mind seemingly absorbed in the ritual of his weed. "What are you talking about."

"I was the one who took the boots to those machines," Robert explained matter-of-factly, pressing in the truck's lighter.

"Fuck off."

"I'm not joking. It was me, not Dad."

"What, and you just let him take the *rap* for it?"

"Hey that was his idea. I mean there were no witnesses—I made sure of that—but Dad, he turned himself in anyway. Thought any sort of criminal record would further jeopardize my teaching position. Not that that's an issue now though," Robert rather sheepishly admitted.

"How do you mean?"

"Well I got this letter from the school board last week, telling me I've been let go."

"What, like permanently?"

"Like permanently," Robert said, curling the words around the thick white cannon now elevating from his lips. He turned his head away, and as an approaching car's headlights caught his face at a certain angle, Jeremy realized in anguish that his brother in fact wanted it that way. The anguish, however, was not for Robert, or even for Robert's career, but for his wife and their daughter, to whom Jeremy now suddenly realized his brother was never going to return.

"Well have you consulted anyone about this? A lawyer for instance? Or a counsellor?"

"No I haven't consulted anyone about this. No lawyers, no counsellors. Believe me when I tell you I'm well beyond the reach of counselling these days."

"Well isn't there some sort of public statement you could make?"

"And what do you expect such a statement to contain?" Robert said. "An appeal for clemency? A plea for mercy? *Get real.*"

"How about an admission of wrongdoing?"

"But I have admitted guilt. I'm guilty of whatever it is they accuse me of doing."

"Yes, well, it seems to me there's a difference between admitting guilt to an accusation and admitting one was wrong."

"But that's the thing, Jeremy: I wasn't wrong. I wasn't wrong at all. And the sooner you understand that, the sooner you can put it all behind you and move on."

They both fell silent until the lighter announced itself ready with an abrupt outward click. Robert held the lighter's red glow up to the joint, sucked repeatedly, and promptly offered his brother a toke. Jeremy declined of course, citing for what seemed like the hundredth time how he had yet to take the drug test at work. Watching Robert smoke in silence, he eventually said, "Why'd you do it?"

Robert shrugged, "Don't really know. Not anymore. Things seemed a lot . . . a lot clearer before somehow. And hey," he said, straightening up in his seat, "they did kill my fish. And Dad gave me those fish—as a gift. And he'd never really given me a gift before."

"No, I mean why'd you wreck those machines."

"Oh *that*," Robert said. "Because they took away Dad's work. They had no right to take away Dad's work. A man still has a right to make a living in this world, Jer, and sometimes he has to fight for it."

"So, what, your little act of retribution was supposed to get him his shitty job back, is that it?"

"No, no, it was more of a message," Robert said, extracting one more quick puff before tapping out, in the ashtray, the sizeable remainder of spliff. "Direct action, it's the best kind," he winked.

"You're unbelievable," Jeremy said, shaking his head. "I can't believe you'd do that."

"Yeah, well, you don't believe in anything," Robert said. "So it really doesn't surprise me that you don't understand."

POSTED BY LUCY @ 10:44:22 P.M. 5/03/2007   16 COMMENTS

Monday, Aug 28/72

Dear Mom & Dad:

Made the big move today, into my room to weave, and oh what a difference a door makes. After fifty-nine days one's tolerance runs a bit low in the fishbowl (or should I call it the birdcage?) listening to acid rock at 10,000 decibels on a mediocre stereo twenty-five hours a day. Today I had my first decent BM in what seems like weeks, and on top of that finished thirty belts, so my point is proven: no distractions + no interruptions = more work accomplished = more pay.

Tuesday, Aug 29/72

Received your Sunday letter this morning, and you know what? I'll just have to admit it: I did forget to sign that letter, so we're even now, and you can have it back.

I'm so sorry the slip covers didn't fit, but perhaps it's for the best. Now if you can find some fabric you really like, and have Pete

Hill do the upholstery, then you'll probably be that much more satisfied in the end.

Received a strange letter from G this morning too—she seems entirely out of sorts about something. However, in keeping with Cormack family tradition, it remains supremely difficult to determine just what that something might be. She seemed rather hysterical (every second word heavily *underlined*) as well as unduly terse with me. Perhaps you could write or call her and find out what's going on? I feel so cut off in here, powerless to help even, and it's as though she's suddenly lost at sea out there. Now maybe I'm blowing it all out of proportion but, well, get in touch with her and see if you can't see what I mean—the woman is drowning, I swear. I too must get busy and write her back, as well as Tracey, Ruth, Michael, Jeremy, Robert Hunter, Doug et al, as they all seem to get well ahead of me.

Today at 3 PM our piano arrived, a lovely apartment-sized console in replica mahogany trim—it sounds so good, and looks good too—now to find some time to actually play the damned thing. This morning I sent good ol' Quasimodo out to pick me up a couple of song books (I also have two Brubeck books in my guitar case) so that I can work on my sight-reading, and have that in hopefully decent shape by the end of the experiment. After ten years' absence I'm more than ready to get back into piano seriously now. What talent I do have, whatever the potential may be, should not, *will not* be allowed to simply lie dormant through sheer laziness and neglect. That, to me, is a sin. As for Stan the Shopping Man, I rewarded his efforts with a brand new Black Sabbath album—his favourite naturally.

It's so strange, only 5½ weeks left to go, but I'm very anxious to get the hell out of here now. At the same time, though, I find myself wishing there were more hours in the day. It's really great having the loom in my room—I open the curtains to let the sun shine in, and since I'm facing south, I benefit from the light most of the day. It's nice to see all that blue sky, even if I can't enjoy it firsthand. Work continues steadily, though the pot's more potent all the time.

Wednesday Aug 30/72

Oh the tangled webs we weave . . .

Thursday Aug 31/72

I'm glad you've been on this Battle of the Bulge with me. Despite my seemingly unrelenting constipation, I've still managed to lose approximately one pound per week, and now weigh exactly 120 lbs, and feel I'm maybe ready to relax on that front a bit. There hasn't been any real struggle involved. Mainly I take care not to go to sleep on a full stomach (yes, I've been battling the marijuana hungries, the principal danger involving grass if you ask me) and to keep plenty of unsweetened grapefruit juice close at hand. Whenever I feel the need to rush out and gorge myself, I simply reach for the juice and voilà, the hungries are gone. Another brilliant discovery: chewing gum makes you hungry! Well, being a two or three pieces per day girl, that's been quite a habit to break, believe me.

Speaking of gums, I've written Dr Meckler for a dental check-up & cleaning for October 9th. . . . If all's OK then we'll *finally* take the impression for my plate. I haven't heard from him yet. Sometime next week, I guess.

Friday, September 1/72

Just having an awful time keeping my mind on work . . . Visions of sewing machines dance in my head. I sit here conjuring up fabrics, colours, textures, trimmings, buttons, styles—my eyes starving for appeasement of my overwhelming creative desires. I just want to "see" everything! Also, I'd really like to produce more than a handful of rabbit pellets on a more consistent basis. I'm starting to wonder if I ever will.

Saturday, Sept 2/72

Do you realize that it's been a year now since I've been home? I must say, things certainly have been exciting over that time, and never a dull moment, to be sure. I think my greatest inspiration, other than *Walden Pond* and, of course, the ongoing exploits of my intrepid brother-in-law, has been *Desiderata*, that wonderful piece of positivism by Ehrmann that, having read it, you just can't help but feel slightly more courageous about life—to do the things you feel you "have to," to see the places you really "want to," to "strive to be happy" and to "keep peace with your soul." Maybe that's what that song *The Happy Wanderer* is all about, no?

Sunday, Sept 3/72

Do you realize that your refrigerator is almost twenty-three years old? We've both been running hard ever since we arrived. . . . I wonder which one of us will quit first.

Great day today—spent an hour or so at the piano entertaining the other inmates—they really enjoy hearing me play, as it's quite a change from the raspy stereo and the few well-worn records we have here. Shelley, the girl with whom I split the cost of the piano, doesn't play much (just her right hand, sporadically, and by ear) but she does have a fine singing voice, even opera (and right on key too) so we're having quite a lot of fun trying different songs, despite the fact she maybe tries a little too hard at times.

Monday, Sept 4/72

Happy Labour Day. And boy do we labour in here. Here we are, halfway through week #10, and still going strong in the mill. Weaving from 4:30 AM till 7:30 PM is going to drive me nuts, though, if I try to keep it up every day. I just don't think the extra $100–200 is worth it, to push myself that hard, so I'm taking today off, so there. Not unlike our city garbage collectors then. I'm sure you've heard they're going on strike down here. It will be interesting, as the garbage piles up, to see who breaks first: the city or the union. My hope is that the city will, as at heart I've always been something of a union girl.

Oh by the way, if that tax guy happens to call again, tell him to stuff it, OK? I'm so tired of these bean-counters hassling me. I mean I've paid them their blood money, so they should just kindly stop hounding me. Wouldn't you agree?

Lots of love, Birdie

With their father lying at anchor in hospital, the chore of feeding the backyard Koi fell to Robert and Jeremy—meaning, of course, Jeremy—Robert's gradually narrowing attention span no longer conducive to such mundane tasking. But then Jeremy did not mind. Surprisingly, he found he rather enjoyed it: scattering the feed through the half clamshell of protective steel; watching the water come to a boil as the Koi rushed to the surface to inhale it. There was one inhabitant in particular he made a point of feeding almost hand to mouth, an enormous whiskered thing with a thick white lesion angling down across its black and orange back. Having managed to survive the raccoon attack, but not without suffering this angry looking memento for its efforts, this fish, for the most part, remained low in the pond, hovering more or less in place, content to await the arrival of any odd feed pellet that happened to make its way down that far in space. More often than not, Jeremy had to so satiate the others that they drifted sluggishly away, this so that he might ensure the gentle giant received its fair share of the take. And after feeding the fish, and occasionally cleaning the filter for the pump, he made a point of sitting with his legs dangling down over the side of the empty cracked pool, studying there in the white rounded bottom the blood-rusted, strangely cerebral brushstroke of his father's recently dragged carcass.

Meanwhile, work at the mill accelerated to a furious pace. In fact, there were more orders to fill than ever, more than was even possible, one would think. As of September 1st, Moore-Mathers' eastern sibling, located in New Brunswick, had ceased production for a scheduled period of six months to facilitate the construction of a newly expanded packaging facility and warehouse, meaning that, in the interim, the West Coast operation would be forced to pick up the slack. The workload almost doubled, and with Japan increasing its own orders for the fall, there was plenty of overtime available for those who wanted it, and to his credit Jeremy wanted it all. In fact, he took all the work he could get (as did Robert for that matter, what with no return to teaching on the foreseeable horizon, and no additional work available with the army as yet), at one stretch working eleven graveyards in a row without a single break. All he did, it seemed, was work and sleep. His only moments of reprieve arriving not in the dark depths of pub or ravine, but on the large and level beach of my sunlit living room sofa, or else the landing outside the lunchroom at work, where he could often be found gazing out at the mist rising off the mill's enormous bio-filter at night, or, in daylight, studying the feeding habits and flight patterns of the resident seagulls against the Knight Street Bridge's flat grey backdrop. Though he watched dutifully from his perch there outside the lunchroom, he never actually witnessed anything resembling a direct hit, and yet, without fail, at the end of each and every dayshift, despite the fact it arrived in the parking lot each and every morning sparkling clean, his father's El Camino left encased in a provisional plaster of bird shit. At night, of course, the damage was negligible; the daytime gulls doing their absolute best to more than make up for any lost production between shifts.

During the odd shutdown of the feed extruders, when there was no feed left to bag, Jeremy took on other assorted chores, the vast majority of which, as I believe I have already endeavoured to explain, proved incredibly exhausting and entirely unpleasant. One such task was the salmonella test, taken repeatedly and at various locations throughout the plant (often as not in the nearly tropical humidity of the fifth and sixth floors), in which feed detritus was scraped into small screw-top containers for what one would assume was ongoing scientific analysis off-site. In the process, Jeremy often managed to sweat so profusely and breathe so profoundly that the stench effectively penetrated his flesh, leaving even his bowel movements tainted with that singular Moore-Mathers scent. His hands blistered. His back ached. Perspiration forever fogged his glasses. And so, in a somewhat futile attempt to neutralize this last but by no means least irritating by-product of physical labour, he angled the arms of his protective eyewear upwards against his head in order to better facilitate their ventilation. But then the particles of feed dust, in cahoots, it would seem, with the ever-present perspiration, sought only to sting his eyes that much faster, a condition that proved especially vexing when he was asked to shovel out 'the pits'—those dark, dank, low-ceilinged, concrete rooms located below ground where, for whatever reason, perhaps even a consistently logical one, massive piles of feed dust tended to accumulate. These enormous mounds of powder, more often that not crawling with a wide assortment of truly vile insect life, emitted a stench that, at this altitude, tended to be indistinguishable from that of human excrement. Still, when all was said and done, the shift from writer of words to packager of fish feed had not proved a difficult one. In fact, and to Jeremy's surprise, barring a few blisters and the token infected cuts on his hands, it had to this point proved an altogether painless one. And in the meantime work on his niece's tree fort suffered, all but grinding to a halt for weeks at a time.

One day, however, with both brothers enjoying a rare day off, they ventured down the ravine in an effort to get something—anything—accomplished. Without their father to assist and direct, though, the task proved difficult, as neither Jeremy nor Robert knew where to take the project next. The roof seemed an obvious place to resume their efforts, what with the walls completely framed in and ready for siding, but as each brother had a different opinion on what style of roof the cabin ought to employ, the absence of that third crucial paternal opinion proved most debilitating now.

"So how's Jonathan?" Robert asked at one point, stretching out across the raw blonde plywood of the unfinished second floor to gaze up through the great mass of maple overhead. Having managed to avoid his fraternal obligations, just as Jeremy had managed to all but avoid the hospital where their father was moored up of late, Robert relied on his brother's discretion exclusively when it came to any and all variations, transformations or translations he need be informed of.

"Well he's still creepy, if that's what you mean," Jeremy said. He leaned back until his clasped hands, supporting his head, touched the floor, and lay there prone alongside his brother for an indefinite amount of time. Down below the familiar buzz of insects, below even his breathing, he could hear, alongside his heartbeat, the rippling rush of the stream.

Suddenly Robert slid up to his elbows. "You hear about the salmon run up the coast? Well it's been decimated, hey. Only something like five percent of the expected run's returning, and of course you know who they're blaming."

"Us?"

"Us. Or rather the sea lice that infest us, hey."

"But how can they be so sure the problem stems from the fish farms? I mean sea lice occur naturally, don't they?"

"Well you know all that Slice topcoat feed we make at work? Slice: *Sea lice.*"

"Oh," said Jeremy. "I guess it does then."

This recognition of Jeremy's seemed of great importance to Robert. "Anyway," he said, "what was the name of that ship Dad went on way back when?"

"The Phyllis Cormack?"

"Yeah, the Phyllis Cormack," echoed Robert thoughtfully, sliding down onto his back again. Jeremy drew a deep breath, gathered himself, then breathed out again and shook his head. He told himself he did not share the same degree of fascination with their father's long aborted activism. In fact, the very notion of their father involved in some sort of protest—any protest— seemed entirely absurd to him.

Together the brothers gazed up toward the pale blue sea of sky, of which the intervening leaves, having bathed already, proceeded to rinse themselves clean for a time. Meanwhile, not far away, what sounded remarkably like thunder, but in reality was an enor- mous load of unceremoniously dumped scrap metal, reminded the brothers of their proximity to the Fraser.

"Does Dad know, you know, that I've been going out to see him?" asked Jeremy after a time. Although it was extremely unlike- ly that anyone could hear him, or would even care had they heard him, he spoke these words in what amounted to a gradually dimin- ishing whisper, so that the last element of the equation, the 'him' of so much implicit meaning, was all but lost in the heated air.

"I haven't said anything."

"Good," said Jeremy, returning to full volume with confidence again. And then: "He used to come down here, hey. Jonathan, I mean. Apparently he had this rope swing or something that hung from that big overhanging branch there."

Rolling onto his side, Robert cast his eye down over the edge of the cabin's unfinished second floor, his expression showing clearly what he thought of that notion.

"Rope swing, huh. How gay is that," he said at last, and aimed a large load of saliva through the closest standard sixteen-inch gap for good measure.

"Actually, I think that's where he used to bring his . . . his victims," Jeremy said.

Robert continued to stare down at the branch. At length he remarked, "You've been seeing him a lot then."

"Once or twice a week," Jeremy admitted. "He's old though, hey. Old enough——"

"What, to be our father?" Robert finished, turning his full attention to the removal of a caterpillar-shaped scab from his elbow.

Jeremy watched the operation with critical interest. It was here their sense of purpose first began to waver, ebb, and change places, I guess. After a while he said, "You know, you're nothing like him, Robby. Neither of us is. We may share some of the same chromosomes and a few vaguely similar features, but other than that we're completely different in my opinion."

Neither brother said much for a time as another in a long series of aircraft roared past, the recently installed second runway at the Vancouver airport having relegated their father's house to the vicinity of a heavily used, oftentimes abused, international exit ramp. Finally Robert said, "Well that's good then. That's good you're going out to see him."

"That's what I thought. But now . . ."

"But now what?"

"Well now I'm not so sure," Jeremy told him.

Dear Mom & Dad:

Only thirty-three days remaining, I can hardly believe it. Good day today, weaving and thinking . . . and thinking . . . and thinking—about garbage, no less. What will happen as it all piles up? Will we, as urbanites, be forced to take the trash *into* our homes instead of out? Or live in constructs of our own excessively disposable lives? I can see it all now: enormous waves of rubbish rising up outside our windows here at the ward. Enormous waves of our own unyielding waste. And thus do I segue effortlessly into the subject of my own crap: what I'd give to take an enormous one right now, that is. I feel as though I've been backed up since June. I may have to give myself another enema if this continues.

Letter arrived from Doug today—he's put off starting school at U of T (Geography, as he eventually wants to be a Social Studies teacher, if you can believe it) and is instead hitchhiking out to Vancouver to see Ginny, and if all goes according to plan, maybe get some work with J and Uncle John—we'll see. The Phyllis Cormack is scheduled to sail from Vancouver again soon, purpose classified, time unlimited, destination as yet unknown. My first reaction was "would I ever like to be on that boat!" but on second thought, I decided it would be much more sensible and just as exciting to meet up with Douglas wherever he happens to be hanging his hat in a couple of months. Of course I'll only know when the time comes, as I may have a lot more on my plate by then. Anyway, Doug seems to be in good spirits, and is steadily readjusting to civilian life. Still, they say that sometimes these things can sneak up on you years after the fact (depression, angst, aggression, et al—"battle fatigue" I think they call it now), which is something he seems to be well aware of, and therefore monitoring on a semi-consistent basis. Still, it's got to be difficult.

All over the news today, not the garbage strike (or not only anyway) but the news of the hostage taking at the Munich Olympics. When I think of my children (hypothetically speaking) growing up in such a sad and violent world, it just makes me want to weep. God willing, they will never have to live through something so horrifying as this. Unfortunately, history seems far too determined to repeat itself. We learn so little about ourselves, one generation to the next.

Here in the birdcage, locked away safely from all that carnage (and garbage) we underwent medical examinations again today. Results: everyone still alive and kicking, though some kicking more than others, I'd say. Personally, I've had a really rotten day, what with my loom facing the television, my eyes glued to the screen, watching the atrocity unfold in Munich. Those poor Israelis. (I mean really, who'd have thought Jews would have any sort of trouble in Germany?) And on top of all that, I seem to have no coordination whatsoever, and am very sluggish and tired (due, no doubt, to the pot and my lack of time "on the pot"), each belt proving a monstrous struggle to complete. Actually, right about now I'd like to smash my loom and toss it out the window, take Congreves hostage, and bust my way out. (I told you it was like the Olympics in here.)

Thursday, September 7/72

Well I've made a decision: I'm no longer going to watch TV. I am so thoroughly disgusted by the acts of violence we human beings seem all too willing to inflict upon one another that I've decided to boycott the medium completely. Dragged my cursed loom back into my room, where I can once again work in relative peace, and lo and behold the weaving is going great guns (pardon the awful pun)—twelve belts done already, and it's only 8:30 AM.

I was wondering if you have any access to Piaget watches? I think the American distribution is handled by Piaget, 1345 Avenue of the Americas, New York, NY 10019, but I don't know if there's a Canadian distributor or not. Could you find out, and maybe have a brochure sent up to the shop? I realize they're *very dear*, but they're fine watches, and I'd like to take a look anyway. Maybe when I'm old and grey (and famous) I'll be able to afford one, eh?

★   ★   ★

Hi again. Just received your letter—thanks for sending along that OHI stuff—it's a cheque (refund) for a whopping eleven bucks, as the tidying-up of the old OHSIP premiums begins in preparation for the new health insurance coverage. I've been assigned to Group G0000, whatever that means. I hope it's the Assistance group, but I won't know for sure until they send me a new premium notice. I'll probably be through with the experiment by then. According to one of the nurses, it'll take two or three more months for the mess to be sorted out, so she told me not to worry about it any.

I'm so glad Aunt Zelda and Uncle Perce came up for the weekend. Was it difficult explaining where I was? I'm sorry for that, and I'm sorry I missed them, but I'll be down to see them shortly after I come home, when I go down to see Liz Allen at Stratford.

It's very funny, you know, but I was wondering the other day if Doug will be growing his beard back now that he's back home and out of the military ... But then I'm sure he looks better without one. I'll have to ask G how he looks these days—thin and wiry, I'm guessing. Speaking of Ginny, I haven't heard anything more from her since that somewhat hysterical piece. I hope everything's okay. Have you heard anything from the Shire? If you have, would you please pass it along? I'm keen to know what's going on in the life of that sister of mine—when something's up she just clams up, if you know what I mean.

Forgot to mention I received your Fancy Medicine clipping. It's so true though, isn't it? I too believe that a great percentage of common ailments are brought about by psychological rather than physical factors. A peaceful, contented frame of mind means so much to the way you feel, look and live. That, to me, is worth so much more than any amount of money or medicine, conventions that, however necessary, tend to greatly complicate life, it seems.

Friday, September 8/72

Woke up this morning with a bit of the sniffles, though I doubt it's anything too serious—just a little worn-down, that's all. On the bright side, I had a good sit, so maybe that ol' Cormack colon is finally coming around a bit. And now that we're into the home stretch here, with only thirty days to go, one of these nights we're going to throw a grand whopper of a party, as Connie has a birthday on Sept 19th, Congreves' is the 20th, Debbie's is the 24th I think, and mine of course is the 30th. That'll be a classic, I tell you. Of course I'll be good though. Would you believe they're placing bets on whether staid, solid Cormack gets drunk with the rest of the rabble? That's another thing I gave up in here—for my diet— beer, alcohol and wine, so the odds are very much in my favour.

Oh, what did Pete Hill have to say about the sofa and chair? Does it sound promising? I expect to see that all finished when I return home, OK? Just kidding!

Did I tell you I got a letter from J Jr? Very—oh how shall I put it—peculiar, I suppose would be the word. Yes, peculiar, to say the least. What a strange brain on that boy! So *graphic*. I'd tell you more about it, but I don't think it would get past the censors.

Saturday, Sept 9/72

Quiet day today—not too many devastating or inspiring things happening in any way—everyone just now realizing that there's only one month left to start making all the bread they assumed they'd have made already. Birdie's top weaver on this side, and apparently the whole experiment, so far. At least I excel at something. Outside, the garbage continues to pile up. . . . The medium is the message, or something like that.

Sunday, Sept 10/72

Just emerged from a luxurious hot shower, slathered in baby oil. Consequently, that's my right forearm print all over the bottom of the page there—oops! Consider it a souvenir.

Tracey's mailbag arrived today with all sorts of goodies enclosed. A letter for Lorna, too, from a first-year buddy of ours, Natasha Mickie, now living in Port Moody, BC. She and her hubby Wilson moved out there two years ago after Wilson unfortunately came down with herpes. (No one's supposed to know this, but it's fairly common knowledge around here.) Does everyone now move out to BC? Is there some sort of vast secret western exodus suddenly underway? Anyway, their second child, a boy, was born on Sept 3rd, herpes free. They named him Nick, if you can believe it. Nicky Mickie. Lord, help me.

Monday, Sept 11/72

Forgot to tell you about Ginny's old friend Sally. Remember Sally Nicholls née Junkin? Lived over by the Locks? Well she's into her last year at UCLA, majoring in Anthropology. She just completed her second summer session, so she'll be graduating in the spring. Then it's on to graduate school, but hopefully not UCLA, which, in her words, is "chockfull of protesters and potheads." Wow, if she could only see Jon and me. Anyway, she and Bernie still want to travel, but sound as if they'll be stuck in Santa Monica for one more year at least. I'd like to get down to see them before they move, though I don't know whether Providence has it in the cards for me.

Tuesday, Sept 12, 1972

Forgot to tell you—OHSIP form came back, and I now have *free* medical coverage through December, poor beleaguered beltmaker that I am. Also for '72, my *taxable* (I can claim travel and living expenses working in theatre) income probably won't exceed $1000, so I should receive assistance for '73, or part of it anyway. We shall see.

Bye for now. Love, B

SEPTEMBER, 2002

With his left foot firmly on the clutch, Jeremy pressed down on the accelerator, raising the forks up to the mouth of the bin, head level approximately. Next, he positioned a brand new wooden pallet squarely in front of the forklift, and then, taking a large white polypropylene bag from the nearby stack, hung it from the raised forks by its four corresponding straps. Finally, he wrapped the bag's plastic liner tightly around the bin's enormous mouth, triggered the fan to fill the bag with air, and once it had more or less assumed its cubic shape, pulled the lever overhead to release the feed into the Bulk container.

Once the bin was empty, and the bag was full, Jeremy returned the lever to its closed position and started up the feed conveyer once more. Just then the telephone at the workbench rang.

"What now?" he said, pressing the receiver firmly to his ear in an effort to hear through his earplug. "Still pretty oily," he frowned in the direction of the bag. "Like soup actually."

At length he hung up the phone, filled three more bags with feed—all of it covered in a greasy brown sludge, all of it, regardless, to be shipped out later as is—wrapped each bag in plastic and labelled it OILY, then drove it out to the yard for the warehousemen to contend with. Upstairs in the lunchroom he found his brother reclining comfortably at the table, the arms of his blue coveralls tied loosely around his waist, his big black boots stretched out under the table as far as possible, already a good forty minutes into his scheduled fifteen minute break.

"What the fuck happened to you?"

"Wondering where I was?" Robert grinned.

"No, not really." Jeremy removed his earplugs, first the one and then the other. "Cory had to shut it down for oil, so it's going to be another hour or so."

"Perfect. Check this out though." Robert slid a newspaper across the table. 'PROTESTERS ATTACK FISH HATCHERY SITE,' the headline read.

> OCEAN FALLS—Natives, environmentalists and commercial fishermen attacked the construction site for an Atlantic salmon hatchery on British Columbia's central coast yesterday.
>
> Likening the introduction of parasites and diseases associated with fish farms to the spread of smallpox centuries ago, Chief Corky Nuximlayc of the Nuxalk First Nation said, "Enough is enough. It's like when the first traders came into the valley, introducing the diseases that killed 90 percent of our people. Now they want to do the same thing to the salmon."

The 60 protesters, arriving by boat from neighbouring communities, tore open a gate and ripped down the wooden forms for newly poured concrete at the Omega fish hatchery in Ocean Falls.

"We don't want the fish hatchery. We don't want the fish farms. We mean it," said Jim Tait, 35, of the Forest Action Network, who has since been arrested for ripping down the form. "Our ultimate goal is to drive all the fish farms off the British Columbia coast."

The 20 fish farms operating in the Broughton Archipelago near Alert Bay are being blamed for destroying the pink salmon runs in the area. Fewer than 150,000 of the more than 3.6 million pink salmon that were expected actually returned this year. A scientific study of the disaster suggests the juvenile salmon were killed by bloodsucking sea lice picked up on the way past the fish farms. Natives raised the alarm even before the fish failed to return, and commercial fishermen were finding young pink salmon covered in the parasites near the fish farms. Last week both groups demanded the shutdown of all the fish farms in the area, to no avail.

The B.C. Salmon Farmers' Association said it would cooperate with a scientific study into the problem, but would not comment on yesterday's protest. Omega officials could not be reached.

"Ouch," said Jeremy presently, not because he was interested—he was not—but because his brother would be pleased if he registered some sort of amazement, bewilderment, or concern at some point.

"Yeah, ouch," said Robert. "And commercial fishermen, too, you see that?"

Too tired to feign any more interest, Jeremy pushed the paper aside just as little Gio came wandering into the lunchroom on his way to the coffee machine, the arms of his coveralls, like Robert's, soon to be tied loosely around his waist—for comfort, he maintained. "Jesus, look at this crap we get saddled with," he complained in his high-pitched voice. Gio was the kind of man for whom coffee had become more vital lubricant than occasional stimulant in recent years. "Over in the office there you should see it—it's like fucking Starbucks—but over here we get stuck with 'tea' and 'coffee.' What a disgrace."

"Talk to Forester," said Ben, Exacto-knifing into submission, with near expert precision, the nail of his left index finger. "He's the prick that got rid of our soups."

Recent cutbacks had become a real sore point for the staff of late, not the least of which was the curtailing of the longstanding Cup-a-soup program the previous week. Whole unions had been founded over far less frustrating developments than this.

"Fucking Forester," Gio spat, having brought his grave consideration to bear on the subject of their manager on one or two previous occasions, to be sure. "Christ. Welcome to Moore-Mathers."

"Moore-Mistakes," remarked the lanky bespectacled Don, who, it should almost certainly be noted, had been knocked cold with a pitching wedge outside his favourite pub, the Marine, not two days before, the most significant symptom of which was not the large weeping gash on his forehead but the festering personal grudge against the job that drove him to drink in the first place.

"Hey, you guys see those cops here this morning?" he said.

"Yeah what'd they want?" Robert asked.

"Nothing, really. Just wanted to talk to Forester, that's all. See if anyone knew anything about that girl they found the other day."

"What girl?"

"What's her name, that East Indian one's been missing all summer."

"Sukhvinder Rai."

"That's right, Sukhvinder Rai. Well they found her, hey, couple of days ago, across the water at the sawmill there, all bloated up under a log boom. Awful scene. Real stink, they say. Pregnant at the time too apparently, which is the real sad part, you ask me."

"What, she was murdered?"

"No, suicide. Or so at least they think anyway. Yeah, according to these cops, she hopped off the Knight Street Bridge."

Ben whistled forlornly. "That's a long way to fall," he said, and turned his considerable attention, along with his knife, to the build-up of crud in the tread of his large brown boots, which, to no one's surprise, least of all his, read 'FUCK' and 'YOU' in black felt marker across the corresponding steel-reinforced toes.

"So, what, she drowned herself?" Jeremy pursued while watching Ben carefully, hoping he might flick his boot crud just a little bit closer so that he, Jeremy, might relieve the boredom of his long day by forcing him to flick it someplace else.

Don unzipped his coveralls, revealing everything anyone might wish to know about his bellybutton. "Nope. Cause of death was falling from heights."

"Number one cause of workplace accidents," Ben said sagely, quietly torturing his sole.

"Well she's swimming with the fishes now," Gio threw in for a laugh.

Robert told him to shut his mouth.

"Excuse me?"

"Shut your fucking mouth," Robert said, levelling a look at Gio. Then, pushing himself away from the table, he stood up and walked outside.

"What?" said Gio, gazing about at the sudden sea change of faces. "What'd I say?"

"He taught her," Jeremy explained. "Sukhvinder Rai. Robert taught her. Year before last apparently."

No one spoke for a time. Not until Robert himself returned, snatched the newspaper from Don's hands, carefully cut out the fish farm article with his knife, and tacked it up on the bulletin board behind them. Standing there, he read it again from beginning to end.

"Commercial fishermen," he said at last, with what sounded to Jeremy an awful lot like disgust.

POSTED BY LUCY @ 7:23:02 A.M. 5/05/2007   17 COMMENTS

Wed, Sept 13/72

Dear Mom:

This is, for obvious reasons, a very difficult letter for me to write. In fact, until I started it, I wasn't sure that I was going to write it at all, and even when I finish it, I have no idea if I'll actually send it off. Anyway, here goes . . . So Ginny has told you I'm pregnant. Well I'm not sure what to say about that. Perhaps if my sister would spend a little more time working on her own life (read: *marriage*) she wouldn't feel the need to delve so deeply into mine. Why she felt the need to broadcast what is, in reality, the by-product of one good night out west, I cannot begin to understand, especially in light of the timing with which her own child came into the world, prize that *he* is. Forgive me, that was out of line. I would ask her myself of course, and have, but in her provincial squeamishness she no longer answers my letters, again for reasons I cannot even hope to comprehend.

I'm not feeling too happy tonight. I suppose it's just time to start taking my own advice. But still, I can't help thinking about what you say G said the other night—not the actual words, but the whole psychological meaning behind them, I guess. On the one hand, I could ignore it—we both know that if she were any more narrow-minded in these matters her ears would be touching—however, I still find it very depressing. But then who is *she* to lecture *me* on morality. I happen to have a very strong belief in what I'm trying to do—not just here in the experiment, but in my life in general—and it is a very long difficult struggle, as it always will be, I'm sure. This pregnancy is just one more hurdle to jump. Sorry to make it sound so banal, or commonplace, but that's just how I feel about it: one more obstacle to overcome in order to get on with my life. And you can stop asking me to quit the experiment and come home—it's not going to happen, not when I'm this close to finishing—and besides, I've already made up my mind to have an abortion (how cruelly paradoxical *this* is) as soon as I leave this hospital. There. I said it. I'm sorry if that's not what you want to hear, and if you somehow think less of me because of it—if you think Dad cannot handle it; if he would somehow be "embarrassed" by it—but it's my life, and it's my body, and I'm just not ready to give it up like that. Not without a fight, at any rate. You see, I want to be my own person: to set my own goals, and to try to achieve those goals as best I can. Now perhaps I've never said it out loud, or in so many words, but I am very proud of you, of *both* of you, for starting out with so very little, and building a solid life for yourselves, by yourselves, dictated only by your own beliefs and ideals. Of course you had to "work within the system" as you put it, which, perhaps I need not remind you, is only the particular environment you chose as the staging ground for your particular experiment (i.e. your lives in Bobcaygeon). My point is, you did it *on your own*, and you didn't give up hope. It would be so very easy for me to quit the experiment, come home, then go out and get a "steady job" once the "child" arrives—you and I both know there are countless nothing jobs out there I could perform, nine to five, five days a week, bringing home that oh so respectable paycheque, and growing bored and old, watching my life go down the drain—but I can't bring myself to do that. It would be a betrayal of my integrity to give in. And, for me at least, at this point in time, that is just what going through with this pregnancy would mean, as oddly ironic as that may seem. Now, when I finally do settle down and have children, you can be damned sure that it will be on *my own terms*. I shall be a person with much valuable experience to impart. And I shall also be a few years older than I am right now, you can be sure of that as well. The talents I have within me need time to develop, to expand and envelop the many points of creativity now open to me. I have so much to learn. I have only just begun. Do you see?

Take care. I love you. Birdie

Thursday, Sept 14/72

I was going to send that off this morning, then decided to keep it here and not distress you any more than you obviously already are. But today is another day, a new day, and in retrospect that's how I was feeling at the time, so I've decided I should be honest with us all and enclose it as part of my diary, and send it off as part of this next bundle. I must remember these letters are just that, my experiment *diary*, and not just some moan-and-groan outlet about life. In other words, the target audience is and must remain as much (or more . . . probably more) inside as out. It's funny, though, because once you empty yourself out like that, you feel better. Now if only I could convince my bowels to heed such honest, hard-won advice.

Friday, Sept 15/72

Beautiful September day today—feeling good despite everything (a little tired maybe, but at least the morning sickness, what little I've experienced, has passed) and so, as soon as the garbage strike ends (if in fact it ever *does* end) I'm going to treat myself to another early morning walk outside. Such a bargain you could find nowhere else—just five cents.

Your letter arrived today. Believe me, I understand your "shock" and your "concern," but I've decided I'm not going to let it bring me down—no way. Also, a letter from Doug out in Vancouver with G & J, where you'd think they'd be celebrating a very special anniversary (the P.C. having set sail exactly one year ago today) but of course that's simply not the case. Now I will not go into detail here, as it will no doubt upset us both, but suffice to say that Ginny is officially out of her head—the woman is hysterical—so if you need a target for your shock and your concern, Mom, perhaps it should be out west. And if she thinks I'd ever do anything to sabotage her marriage, she's crazy. I have too much respect for all parties involved to ever so much as contemplate such a thing. I told you the woman is foundering.

On a brighter note, I've started my "coming out" program today: Scholl's sandals, AM/FM radio in the morning, newspaper tomorrow—over the last week I shall change my sleeping times by one hour per night, till I'm back to a 7 AM rising.

We haven't been told officially as yet, but we *should* stop smoking by the 20th or the 23rd of September, two weeks before the end. In the last week, the doors between the two wards will be opened, allowing us to readjust to having more people around, and on the last weekend there'll be a staff-subject party, perhaps at one of the nurse's apartments (of course we'll return here at night), and we may be allowed a phone call or two in the meantime. This gradual approach to reorientation is apparently somewhat necessary, in order to prevent us from suffering any sort of "culture shock" on October 8th. After all, they wouldn't want any of us to end up in that building just south of here, would they? I always wondered why they built ARF so close to the Clarke Institute.

Saturday, Sept 16/72

Into week #12, twenty-two days to go, and we're all a bunch of raving maniacal lunatics to get out. Literally climbing the walls, beating down doors etc, all of which proves futile of course, as another enormous joint gets placed down before us.

This morning has been set aside for letter writing, the last I'm going to do till I get out—except for this journal of course. By the way, have you been watching any of this hockey series? Buncha bums or what.

Sunday, Sept 17/72

Good weaving day today—till 4 PM anyway, when Evie came tearing in to invite me to my birthday party (actually for Connie, Debbie and me), then in saunters who else but Barbarella, propelling out before her an enormous C.C. on the rocks, compliments of birthday boy Congreves surprisingly. Good old rye whiskey, that most quintessential of Canadian drinks. Anyway, from then till five I proceeded to "pretty myself"—clothes, make-up, hair down (the girls hate it up, but it keeps the wool dust out, I find), the works, then wolfed down supper before moving into the lounge—candlelit, incense burning, with four wee glowing chocolate birthday cakes along with gifts wrapped in newspaper for us lucky recipients. Mumm's Dry Champagne, in magnums no less, and Cold Duck wine—if I have to live with this organism inside me for another three weeks, you can be damned sure it's going to be pickled in liquor the vast majority of the time—also a case of '24 compliments of Maria and some others on the other side. We gorged ourselves, sparked up a birthday joint around 7:15, followed by our regular smoke at 8:15, which led to my vomiting profusely around 9. I'm afraid I disappointed any who were waiting to see me get really bombed though (Congreves seemed strangely keen on the idea), as I crashed, literally, in my wee trundle at 10 o'clock precisely. I haven't had a birthday party like that in years. Really fun, for a change. Does all this candour surprise you, Mother? I'm sorry if my attitude/actions disappoint you in any way.

Monday, Sept 18

Ah yes, the hangover. By sleeping in till 8 o'clock, however, I managed to escape its clutches for the most part—feel great actually—but must weave hard today to make up for lost time. Three weeks yesterday . . .

Love, Birdie

SEPTEMBER, 2002

Calvin Cassidy's laugh, that is, his genuine unguarded non-actor's laugh, was, I am told, difficult to listen to at the best of times. Broken down into its concrete components, it proved little more than a stratified series of nasal blasts superimposed upon a tedious collection of tracheal contractions. That sounds like a lot, but really it is not. And anyway, what made it wholly intolerable this time, Jeremy had to admit, was having his brother present to actually witness the awful event.

Jeremy glanced at Robert as Cassidy's head flipped back off its jaw, releasing that brutal racket to all four corners of the bar. First Robert winced, then shook his head in wonder, in doing so bestowing upon his brother's drinking partner what was obvious to all an extremely low appraisal. "Come on, Jer," he muttered. "Let's get out of here."

Immediately Cassidy checked his rising tide of gaiety, and his head resettled slowly onto its large shelf of jaw. "Don't *leave*," he pleaded. "Why would you leave? We're just about to order dinner. I hear the curry here is exceptional, Jeremy," he added confidentially. "Really gets the pipes moving too."

Unfortunately for all those present, one of Cassidy's more distasteful conversational routines of late consisted of a running (Birdie-like?) commentary concerning the sorry state of his bowels. Robert looked at him with lidded eyes, disgusted. "Not at these prices, pal. Come on, Jer," he repeated, standing up.

"But I just got here," Jeremy protested, feeling a vast and flowing loyalty for all things liquor-related, and none for those that were not. "And besides," he added, "we'll miss the meat draw. I've got eight tickets, see? One for each drink. Imagine, Robby, we could win a lamb shank. A lamb *shank!* Wouldn't father be pleased."

His brother regarded him soberly. "No, *I* just got here. *You've* been here all day. And hey, why the hell are you even sitting with this piss-tank anyway?"

"Perhaps I should leave," Cassidy suggested, elevating from his chair unsteadily, looking, for him, unusually solemn and stone-faced, as though finally reconciled to being misunderstood by the world in general.

For a long moment, Jeremy could not recall what it is a drinker does when his drinking buddy is threatening to leave the table, and he felt in no mood to overburden his brain by trying to. But after a time it came back unbidden—one orders another round.

"Another round!" he signalled to the slowly revolving ceiling fan. "Waitress," he said, casting about for any sign of one, finding a likely looking candidate cowering over by the bar, "may we please get another round over here? And don't forget those meat draw tickets! I really want to win those enormous pork sausages you spoke so highly of earlier."

Suddenly, as though to prove some dubious point, Cassidy assumed alongside the table a most unusual and convoluted stance. With his right hand held palm down, flat and level to his waistline, he extended his mangled left hand partially out before him at an angle and position somehow suggestive of a teapot's spout, all the while keeping middle and index fingers pressed firmly to their corresponding thumb and flexing the entire derelict assembly downwards in the direction of his forearm. This delicate and unorthodox position of hand and arm, if nothing else, rendered the immediate and lasting impression of a gimped-handed dandy about to perform the required stoop-and-scoop at the local dog park. And yet, as if this were somehow not scene-stealing enough in itself, Cassidy forged ahead to the coup de grâce of the entire seemingly impromptu, but in reality, highly orchestrated martial arts manoeuvre. Slowly drawing up his left knee, so that the plane of his thigh pulled level with his waist, leaving his shoeless foot hovering in a painful looking arch near his right calf, he blurted a quick "Crane guard" at the blank expanse of wall before him, managing to hold the ridiculous pose until his expertise was adequately acknowledged and, more importantly, any and all thoughts of Jeremy's departure were eclipsed, forgotten, and with any luck, abandoned entirely.

"Keep it up!" exclaimed Jeremy as Cassidy began to lose balance, listing dangerously to the left. "Come on now, keep it up! Wow," he nodded solemnly. "Wow, now that is just fabulous. Absolutely *fab*ulous." At which point Cassidy reluctantly allowed the entire arrangement to disintegrate beneath him.

"Not bad, eh?"

"Not bad at all," Jeremy agreed, having just now decided to consider himself on holiday, actually believing in the idea wholeheartedly, for he had forgotten for some time the need for personal happiness, a spell fated to last only a few seconds unfortunately.

Robert watched impassively as Cassidy slowly retook his seat, then returned his attention to his brother. "Come on, let's go home," he urged, taking Jeremy firmly by the upper arm, thereby ruining the spirit of relaxation the latter had so effortlessly fallen into.

"No. No way," said Jeremy, resisting.

"You're drunk."

"I *am* drunk. You *are* perceptive. Waitress! Another double Crown over here. And tickets! Bring those damned green tickets. I've got a brother hankering for some lamb shank here."

Soon the waitress arrived with the round, smiling vibrantly as she transferred drink after drink, along with the much sought-after meat draw tickets, onto the table.

"Lovely. Absolutely lovely," said Jeremy, drawing her aside to continue in an urgent, almost tragic undertone, "Listen, though, could you do me a favour?" He beckoned the waitress closer, but then pushed her abruptly away, holding up before her a single green meat draw ticket as some sort of proof of bad behaviour. Robert smiled at her consolingly.

"Okay, Jer, that's enough," he said, taking his brother firmly by the arm once more.

"Here on a peacekeeping mission, Robby? That it?"

"Something like that, yeah."

"Careful with trying to do the right thing, brother: we Jacks haven't had much practice with that sort of thing. Our father's back home," Jeremy told Cassidy, some of the booze-induced flush having drained from his face. "Yeah, he's back home, on blood-thinners and, if you can believe it, an altered, more 'veg-etable-based' diet. How's that for . . . well it's absurd, isn't it? Sure it is. And Robby and I, well, naturally we get a real kick out of it. Don't we though, Robby? Don't we get a real kick out of it? Oh guess what, Calvin! You know who I saw again last night?"

"Your older brother," answered Cassidy matter-of-factly, taking up his Camels and someone else's lighter.

"Our older brother, that's right."

Robert shook his head. "You *told* him? What the fuck for?"

" 'He said, looking stern and irritated.' Because I needed some-one to bounce things off," Jeremy said, "that's what for. Someone who doesn't want to plant his fist in your face any time you hit a little too close to home." He yanked his arm free of his brother's gradually slackening grip. "Anyway," he continued more or less Cassidy's way, "he's a pretty good guy. Jonathan, I mean. A little, what, creepy perhaps, but a good listener if nothing else. I mean he *listens* when he does anything at all, which is rare considering the fact he seems to be paralyzed from the waist down. Swear to God, I've never even seen him get out of his chair. Well hardly ever, save for his paper route this one time. . . . Still, he's a good guy to have around. His turn-ons are carbon copies of his fears, they say, and he's definitely been known to turn it up from time to time. Jonathan 'jacks,' if you'll pardon the pun."

"I can't believe you're telling him this," Robert mumbled, slowly sitting down.

"Believe it," Cassidy said, for reasons known only to him, looking, in Jeremy's opinion, entirely too smug for his own wellbeing. Because, however great the risk of physical confrontation, he knew from experience that it was this particular soldier's duty to render it even greater.

Robert levelled a look at Cassidy and said, in that characteristically unadorned Robert way, "Wipe that look off your face or I'll do it for you, okay?" thereby proving his brother's prognosis accurate on this occasion.

Just then, having watched the scene unfold from the very good vantage point of the bar, Harris appeared alongside the table, looking both frightened and irritable.

"Oh look here," said Jeremy to the others. "Our saviour hath arrived."

"Everything all right here?" Harris asked, his voice clearly threatening to break, an embarrassing enough situation in itself, let alone if it actually did.

"I'm not barred anymore," Robert reminded him quickly.

"No, but you're on probation."

"Yes," said Cassidy impetuously, "you *are* on probation, remember."

Robert smiled. "And hey, if it means I get to lay even one more decent beating on you, I'll never step foot in here again, okay?"

"Take it easy," Harris said. "Relax."

"I am relaxed."

"You sure don't look it."

"I'm telling you *I'm relaxed*," insisted Robert menacingly.

"Go home, Robby," Jeremy frowned down at the table. "Just go home. Go see Leslie. Or better yet, go see your *wife*. Yeah, go see Linda," he said to Robert directly, inserting ticket after ticket into his brother's shirt pocket. "And hey, while you're at it, say hi to Stephanie for me. Say hi from good ol' Uncle Jer, the mean ol' meat draw winner here. No doubt she'd like to hear from me. And you know what? She'd probably like to hear from you too."

Just as Robert leaned forward as if to hit him, Harris grabbed Robert by the shoulders and, to his surprise and everyone else's, stood him bodily up and out of his chair. Robert wrenched free violently, and by the time Jeremy opened his eyes, expecting to see bloodshed, seemed to have disappeared entirely.

"He's barred," Harris said, his voice shaking treacherously. "Your brother, Jer, I'm going to have to bar him—permanently."

"Good luck," said Jeremy as he queued up for inspection, along the edge of the table, the handful of meat draw tickets remaining.

POSTED BY LUCY @ 10:29:11 P.M. 5/06/2007   13 COMMENTS

Monday, Sept 18/72

Dear Mom:

A quiet tension and excitement in the air—we're almost there— less than three weeks to go till Freedom Day. I had fun tonight rereading all of your letters, and even the few condescending ones I received from Lady Virginia along the way. I must say, it bothers me that my "condition" has placed this rift between my sister and me. Now I know you don't want to tell Dad, and, well, with the benefit of perspective I "enjoy" in here, I think that, for now at least, that might not be a bad idea. At least until I get out of here and into a place where I can explain things better. Or perhaps he never need know—I leave that up to you and your good judg- ment. Sometimes I wonder what would have happened had Dad answered the phone when Ginny called with the news of his youngest angel's demise. But I have to think she would've at least had the good sense to ask for you. Wishful thinking perhaps?

Anyway, everyone here is working quite diligently now, even the TV-watching loafers. A few bemoan the fact they didn't weave more, earlier in the experiment, but that's life, no? The pot is more than three times as strong as when we first started smoking two months ago, so you can imagine where our heads are at right now. We'll feel a little different when the smoke is finally cut off—for one, we won't be so bloody exhausted all the time.

But then what's the hurry? The garbage strike is into its four-teenth day, and the trash piles up in the city parks. A cloud of sewer stench hangs over the entire city, overwhelming even our own rank haze here at ARF. A field day for the game dogs & cats out there anyway, not to mention all other manner of disease-carrying vermin—like rats. I'll say one thing: with two weeks worth of garbage from the homes of two million inhabitants piling up, I can see a nice bout of Black Plague breaking out in the Big Smoke before long. At least we can be thankful we're in a germ-free environment here in the ol' fishbowl, big(ger) smoke or not.

Sorry this is such a bummer of a letter—I really do feel quite all right—just don't feel like writing at the moment, know what I mean? Tension runs high, paranoia runs deep—we're all as goofy as nanny goats, and super-stoned of course. Actually, we're all being exploited by yet another *Government Conspiracy*.

Tuesday, Sept 19/72

Received your Sunday letter today—thank you—but I cannot believe that *you* of all people are quoting *me* Catcher in the Rye. I am right, aren't I? I had no idea you'd read that book, Mother! How you continue to surprise me. Anyway, it was his teacher, Mr. What's-his-name, was it not, who said all that business about HC's "special kind" of falling? If it's G's book you're reading, well then I marked that section myself (the rampant green penmanship giving that away, obviously). But the thing is, you're wrong, Mom—I'm not falling. I'm not falling at all. Now certainly I have some causes I consider noble, and therefore worthy of "dying for" (your words, not mine) but that doesn't mean I'm going to stop living my own life—on the contrary, this is my point. Please, *please* understand!

Anyway, along with your letter, another homemade card from Doug. He really sounds as though he's dying to see me—it has been a long time—curious then his insistence on travelling out west, but then it has always been rather difficult to explain the motivations of that man.

By the way, sorry about yesterday's entry—bad mood, that's all—after weaving all day I returned to my room in low spirits, and for whatever reason—pick one—I couldn't for the life of me shake it off. There are times when I feel my strength to be all but limitless . . . when I can bear Dad and Ginny and all their small-town insecurities on my back, and that entire town of yours too if need be. But there are other times when a veil of weariness descends upon me, and I long to be borne away to a new life in some distant land, where I never have to so much as hear the name "Bobcaygeon" again. Please bear with me, for I am a Cormack, and we Cormacks, as you have so eloquently remind-ed me, refuse to fall gracefully.

Thankfully the piano has proven a wonderful distraction, not only to my own predicament, but to the daily grind of weaving, and I've actually seen an improvement in my ability since its arrival here on the ward. Now fortunately or not, it's going back the end of next week (Sept 29th) as I could sit and play all day. One thing's for sure, I now know I have enough skill and style (to be developed more yet of course) to allow me to make some money at it, to "play for pay" as it were. In fact, I'd maybe like to join the Toronto local of the musician's union, and then semi-support myself that way, in between cutting & designing jobs. It's a thought anyway.

The CIBC letter was just a reminder that the deferral on my student loan has expired, and asking if I could continue payments soon. I've sent a payment off to them for September—will walk in very proudly on October 9th and pay the balance in cash (that's what we get the day we leave: a bundle of 50s & 100s)—it will certainly be a great feeling to have that paid off.

(What am I doing, they're apt to ask? Why, I'm in Toronto, working very hard paying off my student loans and making clothing for people—ah, the truth, what could be simpler? I needn't say any more than that, I'm sure.)

The next nineteen days are going to be an incredible mental and physical strain. Believe me, it's not going to be easy, and I don't want to be thinking or worrying about *anything* during that time. I'll answer all your questions when I come home, but please, not just now, OK? But I will say this: concerning the "father" (how I hate using that term when the "child" will never see the light of day), no, he does not know. Not yet. And in truth, he probably never will. To be honest, I just don't see what good would come of it, as he already has quite a full plate as it is. Besides, it's my body and my decision and as I told you before, I've already decided to terminate the pregnancy.

Now about the smoking. In *any* experiment, the data collected is only valid if it can be compared to *control* data—even in high school chem-lab we did this. It's not a matter of being unfair or anything—rest easy, they're not "picking on" me—it's just the way you run an experiment: always two or more groups, one of which is the designated "control" group, and as luck would have it we're not it.

★ ★ ★

News flash! Stan the Shopping Man, my personal scratching post, partner-in-crime, and regular wrestling opponent (and occasional tag team partner, whenever circumstances warrant) here in the ward, has talked to a doctor friend of his, and I'm tentatively scheduled for the 10th of October (Quasimodo's connected—who knew?) somewhere here in the hospital. Don't worry, these are fully qualified medical professionals we're talking about here, as well as a fully qualified and sanitized environment to be sure. (Thank you, Mr Trudeau!) I've checked the calendar, and as of Wednesday, October 25th you will have one bona fide, qualified, non-expectant young woman ready and willing to work her way back up the Cormack corporate ladder. Even if the Queen of England wanted a new wardrobe, she wouldn't catch me cutting before I've had a good two weeks rest. What am I going to do when I get out of jail, you ask? Lots of plans . . . but let me surprise you. Do I ever do anything but?

I must say, Mother, it feels very odd for me to be talking to you about all this. As opposed to say, Tracey or Lorna, I mean. Here I've always felt compelled, for whatever reason, to censor my exchanges with you, but now I feel as though I can tell you anything. And so, in that regard, I can't help but feel this pregnancy has been something of a blessing. Thank you so much for being so understanding. I suppose that deep down I knew you would be, having gone through all this yourself that one time.

Must close for now, as I want this to reach Bobcaygeon before the weekend rolls around. I'm sorry if my letters aren't quite as regular as they were in July—I'm trying, believe me.

Love, Birdie

SEPTEMBER, 2002

He turned away from the window. His eyes were a curious shape, showing a more than natural amount of the whites. "Just missed her, huh?"

"Just missed her," I said, sitting here in my chair, held captive by his wholly un-Jacks-like stare. "Said to say hi though. 'Say hello from Virginia'—that's what she said."

"Oh I bet she did," he said. He moved over onto the sofa, stretched out lengthwise, and clasped his hands across his chest. Then, abruptly, he withdrew an envelope from his pocket and slid it spinning across the floor towards me.

"Have you told Robert about her?" I asked.

"Virginia? No, I haven't told him. . . . Oh and I've been meaning to ask you. This Doug guy Birdie's always going on about, you ever meet him?"

"Who?"

"Doug? He's in the letters. He's—"

"Oh, *Doug*," I said. "Vietnam Doug. Sure, I met him."

"And he and Birdie, they were an item or something?"

"No, not really." I bent down to pick up the envelope from where it had come to rest under my chair. "No, as far as I remember, I wrote most of that stuff she thought she was receiving from Doug when he came out west that September."

Jeremy looked at me, amused. "*Why?*"

I shrugged. "Such is my nature."

"What, to lie?"

"We Jacks boys, we're natural storytellers," I smiled.

I watched him while he lay there, staring vacantly at the ceiling, as Derek, masticating an enormous Snickers, wandered his way in from the kitchen. Seeing everything was to his liking—if it can truly be said that Derek actually 'liked' anything—he in due course wandered out again. Upon his departure, Jeremy said, "Well something must have happened to keep her away all this time. Did you . . ."

"Did I what?"

"Did you, you know, do something to her?"

I smiled. "You're a sick man, little brother. A very sick man."

"Well then what happened?"

"Who knows. All I remember is our little Birdie flying east for the experiment, then afterwards flying west, by which point Virginia had flown the coop for good—and then I went away shortly after that."

"Yeah that much I got," he said.

One of our characteristic uncomfortable silences washed its way into the room just then, and afraid he might leave if, for whatever reason, it failed to wash back out again, I said, "So they found her, hey. That Sukhvinder Rai."

"Apparently."

"And how's your brother holding up with all that?"

"Oh," Jeremy sighed, "Robby'll be fine just as long as he has someone to throw punches at him the rest of his life."

"What does that mean?"

"Nothing," he said, waving me off. "To be honest, I haven't seen much of him lately. Not in the last few days at least."

"How so?" I asked, leaning forward from the waist, careful, lest I appear too eager, to check my progress midway. Suddenly he bolted up to a sitting position, and glanced rapidly about the room.

"What? What is it?"

"The cat. Where's the cat?" he asked.

"Lucy? Unfortunately little Lucy's been taken away," I told him, sighing and shaking my head in a melancholy way.

"Really? How come?"

"Well, actually, she's been put down, hey."

"What? *Why?*" he persisted, his forehead furrowing just like his father's in a younger day.

"Well unfortunately she attacked the neighbour's dog," I said. "And, well, you can guess where it went from there."

"Lucy did? Really?"

"Sure she did. Absolutely."

Resigned by now to almost anything, he rotated back into his prone position on the sofa, feet dangling limply over the armrest.

"Anyway," I continued, "you were saying you haven't seen much of Robert lately."

"Well he's moved out of the house and back into his condo. But then I do see him at work occasionally."

"So what's the problem?"

"Other than the fact he wants to kill me, you mean?"

"Why do you say that?"

"Just a hunch. But then I probably deserve it," he admitted.

"My my, but you two certainly are from different stock than I."

He considered me momentarily. "What's that supposed to mean."

"Just that you're so much more violent than your incarcerated older brother," I explained.

He continued to consider me in a curious way as Lucy, her mast held high, sailed her way into the room en route to the sofa.

"You really are a god-damned snake," he told me.

POSTED BY LUCY @ 4:13:56 A.M. 5/07/2007   32 COMMENTS

September, 2002

Later that day, Jeremy came across his father sitting old, worn and fragile amongst the books in his brother's room. Outside the window, the yellowing leaves of the nearest trees, comporting themselves in factual support of the rapidly approaching fall, augured a cool September evening.

"Rather odd, isn't it, that we don't have a copy of your book in here," Jon observed, floundering through something by George Santayana. Assuming he knew where this was going, and not really ready for it to go there, Jeremy said nothing, and at length his father went on, "These books here were given to you boys—as a gift as I remember."

"A gift for Jonathan anyway," corrected Jeremy with a minimum of energy.

"Yes, Jonathan," said his father, negotiating that name, his own name, about as well as he handled his Santayana. Nevertheless, he remained a staid and stoic figure in Jeremy's eyes, despite all the lost weight resulting from his most recent health crisis.

"From Virginia's sister," Jeremy continued cautiously, noticing, for the first time, the tiny plastic handle of a hearing aide protruding from his father's right ear. "Birdie. Birdie Cormack."

Jon hesitated a moment, then nodded, "That's right." They shared a quiet look of defiance a moment as Jon, his head yawing unsteadily, returned to the book now vibrating dangerously in his treacherous and vacillating hands.

"So," said Jeremy. "About that."

His father nodded awkwardly, self-consciously, all in all a rather grotesque movement to behold. He closed the book's cover and, with those same embarrassing trembling hands, slowly and painstakingly worked the book back into place on the shelf. Then, unjustifiably exposed, their mission more or less complete, both hands retreated to that safe harbour between his knees, where they gripped each other fiercely in an effort to quell their unfortunate condition. "I suppose," he began, "you're wondering why I never told you and your brother about her. And about a lot of things."

"Yes I was," Jeremy said. "Actually, we both were."

"Well to be honest, it doesn't make much sense. Not now at least. But at the time," Jon sighed, then coughed, "at the time I suppose I was trying to protect you."

"Like with our mother."

"Well, yes," his father said, finishing off his cough by dragging up into an awaiting tissue whatever it was had been impeding his lungs of late. Finally, good and empty, he secreted away into a pocket somewhere the entire balled-up wad of wretchedness.

"And the Phyllis Cormack? How come you never told us about that?"

"That old herring boat?" Jon smiled, lowering his head in what was, for him, in his present state, a look of bashful embarrassment. "Again, by the time you were old enough to understand, it wouldn't have made much sense. It seemed so far—removed," he said, "even then. And now, well now it's just . . ." His voice grew faint as again he lowered his head in embarrassment. Eventually he looked up. "The hardest thing to do in this life, the *very* hardest thing, is to actually live according to your convictions. You know that don't you, Jeremy."

"I'm trying hard to," Jeremy said.

Jon studied him a while, his head bobbing gently but uncontrollably atop an unseen swell. "You know, you remind me a lot of her. Both you and your brother do."

"The boat or the woman?"

"Pardon?"

"The boat or the woman," Jeremy pursued.

"Both," admitted his father with a laugh.

Jeremy pretended to gaze out the window a moment, something in the breeze-bandied leaves of the adjacent trees having presumably caught his interest. At long length he said, "Yeah, well, this Phyllis or Birdie or whatever her name is, I found her old letters."

Jon shook his head, shaking it beyond even its own broad spectrum of oscillation, recalling something funny in the process.

"And while I haven't actually talked to her personally," Jeremy continued quickly, still staring out the window at nothing in particular, careful not to get caught up in any sort of emerging emotion here, "I have talked to Jonathan about her."

His father looked at him vacantly, and eventually looked away, bobbling spastically all the way. "Figured as much," he said.

"I hear you've gone to see him a few times yourself," Jeremy said, having managed to drag himself back from his bogus jaunt outside the glass.

His father shook his head violently, amplifying the movement to an almost childlike magnitude so as to make certain none of the sentiment was lost on his son.

"What?"

"He's lying."

"What do you mean?"

"I mean that, right or wrong, I haven't seen that boy since they put him away for good," Jon said.

POSTED BY LUCY @ 11:16:34 P.M. 5/07/2007   51 COMMENTS

Wednesday, Sept 20/72

Dear Mom:

There comes a point when I wonder what I ought to be telling you . . . We're still here, we're still plugging away, and October 8th draws closer every day. Our routine varies so little. I really do feel silly, you know, trying to come up with something new and interesting to say. I trust you understand that in some intrinsic way.

Thursday, Sept 21/72

Another card from Doug today—he's such a dear, and his wee cards are so funny, and homemade too. His perception is very acute—he seems to know exactly how I'm feeling, and what would cheer me up the most, as he knows what it feels like to be locked away from the world and, at the same time, forever under a microscope—fishbowl syndrome, in other words. I get the feeling he's trying to tell me something. . . . I wonder, though, if he'd be this interested if he were aware of my unfortunate "condition."

(Hopefully G isn't planning on talking out of turn again any time soon.) It's funny, but here in the ward even my pregnancy seems remote in a way. Disconnected. Detached. Almost as if it were somehow happening outside of me instead of inside—outside even the looking glass walls of the ARF bell jar perhaps. Maybe by talking about it I've somehow dispelled it—as artists say the very act of talking about something mysterious or magical somehow takes the magic out of it. Regardless, I've decided not to dwell on it anymore. Believe me, it's easy enough. Throughout most of the day I manage to place it completely out of mind— it's only when I write you that it tends to sneak up on me from time to time.

Nothing new on the G & J front, at least on my end. And there's another subject for my personal trash heap by the way. I have my own strike going on in here, in cahoots with my union brethren outside, although, admittedly, it does tend to pile up on me from time to time. Stinks, too, I might add.

A letter arrived today from Jeremy Jacks—damn well about time too, I must say. Wants me to collaborate on an article for Canadian Magazine regarding this so-called "Grass Jail" I'm in. It would be worth $300 to me, he says, but I'm afraid that's an impossibility. No nom de plume—my name would go on it, for veracity and all that, but wouldn't the crap hit the fan if I did? Don't worry, I'd never do that to you (or me, for that matter) and besides, blowing the proverbial lid off Bobcaygeon might have unforeseen repercussions down the line, and not necessarily favourable ones at that. What's more, I've signed a contract with ARF, and I don't think I can afford to be sued by either the foundation or the federal government just yet. There goes my first chance to become a famous author though, no question.

Speaking of Ottawa, did you happen to catch last weekend's Star? That piece on the Nixons and the Trudeaus at the National Arts Centre opera back in April? Absolutely hilarious! Makes me wonder how anything at all gets accomplished by this wacky government of ours.

I'm taking utmost care to make my writing legible. It's 4 AM, I've been up for twenty minutes pretty much pissing napalm out my ass, and my hands are a little stiff from gripping the toilet seat so hard. When it rains it pours, I guess. Still, one must be thankful for small miracles, mustn't one?

This is the beginning of week #13, and I don't know where the time has gone. Things are pretty strange now, due to a combination of factors—I shall try to explain. Primarily, for three months, we've been more or less removed from the world at large and all the little things that add up to, and make a difference in, one's day. You know, people, cars, birds, rain, streetcars, billboards, more people, grocery stores—you name it—not to mention the multiple mediums of the McLuhan Age. We've been removed from all this, set apart if you will, and although we really haven't lost touch completely (due to mail, TV, magazines, radio, etc) there has definitely been a reduction in the frequency and quantity of mediums in which we regularly participate. Now, as we near the end, and prepare to immerse ourselves in all those mediums again, there is a great deal of impatience and expectation to begin. We are, in other words, "speeding up" again.

Secondly, we've been smoking now for over nine weeks. There is no cumulative effect from marijuana, but the dosage, as you know, has been gradually increasing all along—approaching 4x now what it was when we started on July 17th—so we find we're a little befuddled from time to time, especially in our subject-staff relations. Oh but I could write a volume on the acute effects of marijuana on speech! A general awkwardness, coupled with a disconcerting temporal shift, compounded by the fact the staff don't bat an eyelash at your mispronunciations or mistaken behaviour, so that you aren't quite sure, at the time, whether it's really happening or simply a figment of your pot-fogged imagination. However, when you *know* that such mistakes are commonplace, and you *know* the staff is deliberately ignoring them, then it becomes endurable, and you aren't really troubled by any acute paranoia or anything. This is all temporary of course, but still very confusing, especially if you don't keep in mind that it will cease to be this way when we finally stop smoking "the medium."

I know my letters have been a little strange this last couple of weeks—not as orderly as the July/Augusts, not as necessarily "coherent," and not as regular. Part of this is due to the weaving—remember, I was only managing 5 to 10 belts/day back in July, and now, these last three weeks, I've been ramping production up to 30 to 40/day, forcing myself to work every possible minute so that, in the end, the letter writing suffers, or I forget a day or two, or else I wait a day then write an account of the last two or three days all at once from memory—as I'm clearly doing now. And part of it is due, of course, to the pregnancy. The fact that each day is an exact replica of its predecessor certainly doesn't help either. Be that as it may, I'm sure that much of what I've written you in the past few weeks has been: 1) grammatically weak; 2) extremely messy; 3) rather incoherent; 4) boring (perhaps, but then what's important isn't always what's "interesting"); and 5) obviously, to a certain degree, upsetting and unsettling for you. It doesn't matter though. The important thing to remember is to keep the lines of communication open.

Another thing. I wonder how much of this experiment you can really understand. You see, much of what has become familiar to us—that is, those of us here in the fishbowl—is still quite foreign to you, generation gap aside. I just wish I'd written much more of what I was feeling day to day instead of sparing you any worry, as I realize now how gravely significant all this could be, not only on the drug front, but in furthering our understanding of the human condition. Still, we've never really spoken like this before, so I suppose, in that way, it has been at least somewhat beneficial. And hopefully I'll be able to recall some or even all of my feelings later on—I know you'll have plenty of questions to ask that might jar loose some facts—and hopefully I've learned something here that could benefit others somewhere down the line.

Have I lost you completely, Mother? I hope not. Though Dad, I suppose, remains something of a write-off.

Saturday, Sept 23/72

Would you believe I got *another* card from Doug yesterday? What a wordsmith! Makes me mightily suspicious of that boy's intentions—Ha! Also a wee note from Tracey: she thinks this garbage strike is simply "outrageous." Well of course she does. Glad I'm in here—can't smell a thing! Did you happen to catch that game yesterday? Devastating.

Sunday, Sept 24/72

I really want to buy a new bed when I get out of here, a really *big* bed. You don't mind that blatant a hint, do you? Tired of little skinny ones. . . . Would like a king if possible, also full box springs. Perhaps you could get Dad to offer suggestions as to the best type to buy—construction, etc—as you both know so much more about it than I.

About two weeks ago, Liz Allen called 37 Pleasant from Stratford and left a message with Tracey that Jack Hutt, the General Production Manager, wanted to offer me a job for next season, and that I should contact her as soon as possible. I sent her a telegram (she knows I'm here) saying I'd be out October 8th, and ever since then I've been in a fluster, wondering what was going to happen. On Friday I had Tracey call Liz to find out what the hell was going on—apparently I just have to wait till Jack Hutt gets in touch with me. Well I may go bonkers waiting for *that* to happen. Perhaps now you can appreciate why my last letter was so "touchy" re future work plans. I wanted to be able to surprise you, I guess, and now, well, now we'll just have to wait and see together.

Must get this into the mail.

Love, Birdie

SEPTEMBER, 2002

The night of the bomb threat, Jeremy was not actually scheduled to work, but managed to get called in anyway. A packager had gone home sick, he was informed by the shift supervisor, Dave, and with a full slate of feed orders needing to be filled on both the Bulk and Japan lines, a full slate of five packagers was required to deal with it. Grudgingly, Jeremy agreed to come in, despite the fact that he had just begun writing again. Nothing monumental, mind you, but rather a short story, a conversation really, between a man, his daughter-in-law, and the daughter-in-law's somewhat exasperating friend. It was to be titled 'Keeping Up the Crane Guard,' this much he knew already, in reference to the unseen crane or heron that had tried, so far unsuccessfully, to eat the man's prized Koi, and the man's ongoing struggle to prevent it from doing so, as well as one particular position or 'guard' the daughter-in-law had recently learned in martial arts class, which she was now working up the nerve to demonstrate for her lunch companion. The dialogue was coming readily enough, with the daughter-in-law and her friend talking easily over a mid-afternoon bottle of wine, and they were still talking when the call came for Jeremy to come into work, preferably by nine. Putting together a quick meal for his late night 'lunch' break, as well as a handful of snacks for the long difficult hours after that, he bid his father goodbye and took the El Camino to work.

At this dark hour the streets were relatively free of traffic, and twenty minutes later he was cruising over the Knight Street Bridge in the direction of the feed mill on the opposite side of the Fraser. It was always strange for Jeremy to see the mill at night, aglow in floodlights, knowing that inside the work continued steadily. The surrounding industries, too, maintained their production throughout the night, including the sawmill directly opposite Moore-Mathers where the bodies of Sukhvinder Rai and her unborn child, one body secretly sheathed inside the other, each a disgrace to the other, had been found bloated and purple under a log boom alongside the riverbank. Jeremy wondered if, the night she jumped, the floodlit mill was the last thing Sukhvinder saw in this life. And he wondered if it were actually the impact with the river that killed her, as reported, or if it were something else entirely. Something before perhaps. Or something after. Something more than simply a falling from heights.

When he arrived at the mill, however, it appeared as though the entire crew were milling about outside, fists thrust deep in pockets of dirty blue coveralls, laughing giddily and making jokes amongst themselves.

"What's going on?" Jeremy asked, pulling up alongside a crowd of packagers and warehousemen farting around under the floodlights. "Extruders down or something?"

"El *Camino*," Clayton said, admiring the vehicle. "Nope, bomb threat. Came in about ten minutes ago."

"*Bomb* threat," Jeremy said. "Really? Then why are you standing so close?"

Clayton shrugged. "No one told us not to, I guess."

Someone asked Jeremy why he was coming in so late, and he told them he'd been called in.

"Oh, for your brother?"

"Robby was working tonight? But why, it's not his shift."

"He got called in too," someone else said. "But then he had to go home—sick."

"I see," said Jeremy, though of course he did not. "Shouldn't someone call the cops or the fire department or something?"

"On their way apparently," Clayton said, employing the toe of his boot to thoroughly pulverize a spent cigarette.

Uncertain of what to do, or even where to go, Jeremy parked alongside the other vehicles in the lot, including, he noted, his brother's pickup.

"Where's Robby?" he asked Dave, currently in crisis high atop a one-ton bag of feed.

"He left," said Dave distractedly, furiously punching buttons on his cell phone. He held the phone higher—not high enough, it turned out, as the signal evaded him once more. "Christ!" he said.

"But his truck's still here."

"What's that?" Dave asked, not listening. "Hey guys! We should probably all fall back a ways," he told the crew, the majority of which, obviously feeling the entire situation to be nothing more than a hoax, managed to ignore him completely.

"I said his truck's still here," Jeremy said.

Dave frowned down from his feedbag perch, and sighed. He was a man who seldom spoke to anyone. His supervision, though committed, was a singularly silent one. However, on those rare occasions when he did speak, he hated not to be able to make himself heard, even when, as was usual, it was himself he was rebuking. "Fuck, I have no idea where your brother is, Jer. He said he was sick, so I sent him home, and that's why I called you in. Now does anyone here happen to know Forester's home number?" he asked the others, but to no avail. "Anyone? Christ Almighty, why can't I get this fucking thing to work!"

Leaving Dave to his cell phone, Jeremy made a quick tour around the perimeter of the plant. He asked a wandering warehouseman, Tony, if he had seen Robert, and Tony told him he had, but not in the last hour or so. And so, cautiously, Jeremy made his way inside the plant, presently empty and unexpectedly devoid of noise.

He inspected the abandoned packaging floor, but his brother was not there. His investigation of the lunch and change rooms proved likewise Robert-less, but suddenly, from a floor or two above, he heard what sounded like a toppled steel drum somewhere. He followed the sound to the brightly lit extruder room on the second floor, where he came upon his brother busily transferring forklift propane tanks into the control room from the service elevator.

"What the hell?" Jeremy said, his voice disproportionately loud in the uncommonly quiet room.

Robert's face jerked up a shimmering mask of sweat. "Jer?" he said, standing up to assume his full height under the lights. "Jeremy, that you?" he blinked, raising a hand to shield his eyes from the glare. "What the hell are you doing here?"

"I got called in—for you. What the hell are *you* doing here?"

Robert, though, would not say. He just stood there shielding his eyes against the lights instead.

"Robby, what are you doing?"

"Leave, Jeremy. Just leave."

"What's going on?"

Robert hesitated, but only a moment, before heaving another tank out of the service elevator and into the control room.

"Jesus Christ, what the fuck is going on here," Jeremy pursued, a languid comprehension settling in.

Abruptly his brother wheeled around, smiling plainly at close range. "You're a smart guy. What the fuck do you think is going on here?"

Jeremy blinked. "I—I have no idea."

"Well let me assure you it's exactly what it looks like," Robert said.

Jeremy frowned down at the four closely arranged tanks, and then up at his brother's closely arranged features. At length he said, "You're going to blow up the control room."

"I'm going to blow up the control room."

"But *why?*"

Robert shrugged. "Commercial fishermen," he said matter-of-factly, showing his brother his back.

Well, thought Jeremy.

"Well I'm not going to let you do it," he said at last.

"Excuse me?" Robert laughed, amused, it would seem, at the mere prospect of his brother's intervention.

"I'm not going to let you do it."

Robert blew him off with a curt wave of his hand. "Leave, Jer. Just leave. You're not supposed to be here."

Jeremy took hold of a tank and carried it out of the control room.

"What do you think you're doing?" asked Robert upon his return.

"I'm not going to let you do it," Jeremy told him, reaching for another tank, this one rigged with some sort of presumably military detonating device. Robert grabbed him by the wrist.

"Fuck off. I mean it. I told you to leave."

"I'm not going to let you do it."

"Look, I told you to leave!"

"No way, Robby. I'm not going to let you do this."

Robert took two steps back, his body coiled and lowering. Then, abruptly, he sprang forward and hit Jeremy square in the chest, driving him backwards over a chair and onto the floor.

Jeremy scrambled to his feet as Robert's fist flashed out a second time, catching him in the face, and Jeremy felt his nose burst as again he fell backwards onto the floor. He rose slowly to his feet. Dazed in the suddenly liquid air, he smiled stupidly for reasons he could not quite fathom, as though unable to believe anything could be so simple as getting your head punched in.

"Leave, Jeremy," commanded Robert quietly, almost bashfully, in a way oddly reminiscent of his daughter actually. "Just leave. This doesn't concern you here."

"Of course it concerns me—you're my brother," Jeremy said, feeling the impact of his head against the desk behind him before he realized his brother's fist had flashed out and caught him yet again. Suddenly Robert was standing astride Jeremy's waist, his face, though hovering closely overhead, cast into black silhouette by a blazing backdrop of light. His terrible fist retracted steadily, preparing to strike.

"I'm not going to let you do it," Jeremy spat, feeling the left side of his face fall away, split in a jagged line from the corner of his lip to his rearmost molars, making for a ridiculous and most hideous grin. He held up his hands in a limp bouquet before him, but Robert's fist quite easily penetrated these fragile defensive offerings, sending a single jet of blood looping out onto the linoleum. Finally he stopped hitting him, and Jeremy relaxed. It was funny. The halo of ceiling lights encircling Robert's head had dwindled to a slender ring of radiance, pitching and rolling upon a rising tide of darkness. He reached out in an effort to retrieve the ring, but it was gone—he watched it dwindle to a remote speck on the horizon before losing sight of it amongst the great sea of stars beyond. Then, all at once, he was fast asleep in a heap on the floor, a sleep over which the appalling state of his face, torn asunder by his brother's knuckles, presided with the violent verisimilitude of nightmare.

POSTED BY LUCY @ 4:26:07 A.M. 5/08/2007   64 COMMENTS

SEPTEMBER, 2002

Jeremy awoke with a start a few moments later, sprawled flat on his back in the middle of what appeared to be, inexplicably, the Moore-Mathers control room. Eventually his mind cleared, and he began to reflect on his position. He remembered falling, and the floor coming up to catch him, which brought back the sensation of the moment just prior to the fall, of successfully catching his brother's fist with his face on several occasions. He looked around. The three remaining propane tanks stood together at his feet, the detonating device having evidently been removed from the scene. The floor of the control room lay literally awash in red. He could not believe how much blood there was. He was, at that moment, quite transfixed by it. He wondered where his brother was.

A wave of nausea splashed over him as the magnitude of the situation brought him reeling in. And so, rising slowly to his feet, pressing his dangling jowl more or less into place, Jeremy examined the propane tanks more closely as the floor heaved and settled beneath him. To his relief, it appeared as though the project had indeed been abandoned in place, just as he himself had been. He took hold of two of the tanks, one in each hand and, lip-loose, staggered his way out to the extruder room service elevator as a fresh wave of nausea crashed over him. Managing to ride the wave out, he doubled back for the last tank and, crowding it in with the others, sent the elevator down to the first floor where, he hoped, their presence would prove less conspicuous and therefore unworthy of consideration. Finally, face in hand, pain flowering out not from his cheek but from a place seemingly deep inside his brain, he made his way across the brilliantly lit extruder floor, employing for stability the enormous horizontal cylinders of the extruders themselves, first the one and then the other, and out the far door. Down the first set of stairs he lurched, cautious lest he miss one, and along the hall in the direction of the lunchroom telephone.

Hardly fifteen minutes later, Bob File found him standing alone outside the rarely used rear gate, the mill itself now surrounded by the expected crews of firemen and police, each faction wholly absorbed in the workplace ritual of daring the other to tell them what to do.

"Where to? Hospital?"

"No no, he won't be at the hospital," Jeremy said, gingerly holding his face in place, each painful pulse of his heart pulling at his cheek with ever-increasing intensity.

"I meant for you, Jer. You're hurt—bad."

"No, take me home first and we'll see if he's there."

When they finally arrived at the bottom of Royal Heights, Jon Jacks was leaning on his walker in the middle of his front lawn dressed in nothing but his sad and sagging jeans. Like his teeth, the pale drawn skin of his withered chest and arms shone almost transcendentally in the Honda's headlights, and reality having lost its accustomed hold, Jeremy suffered the immediate and unfortunate impression of seeing inside his father's ribcage. Having been alerted by Bob, Jon had been impatiently awaiting their arrival ever since, and waved them to a stop in the driveway.

"He's gone down the ravine," he informed them through the open window of the Civic, offering Bob a flashlight with an eager, trembling hand.

Together the trio made their way around the side of the house, past the silent grate-covered pond, around the still empty pool glowing Jon-like in the moonlight, and over to the railing of the deck overhanging the ravine. Below them stretched an impenetrable darkness. They heard nothing but the distant sound of the stream.

Jon said, "I heard the chainsaw a few minutes ago, but it's been quiet this last little while." He was leaning on his walker, his eyes leaking continuously with worry and excitement, one hand reaching up to wipe them, then the other.

"He's still down there then," Jeremy said without knowing how much he said, wincing at the throbbing pain of his still bleeding and cruelly extended smile.

"He's still down there."

Jeremy asked for the flashlight.

"Here, I'll help you," Bob offered.

"No, stay here," Jeremy told him, and opened the gate that led to the first descending stair. It was the ravine's most elusive hour, when darkness concealed darkness, and from one moment to the next the shadows declared themselves as stalking nocturnal predators or as angry thwarted brothers. Still, knowing the way well, and despite his injuries and sudden exhaustion, it did not take Jeremy long to reach the cabin halfway down. When he did arrive, however, he was greeted only by the cabin's ghostly broken remains: revealed there in the flashlight's effusive but erratic eye, an entire summer's work rendered all but wasted. Boards of various dimensions, some still stitched to others at odd aggressive angles, the remainder reduced to crudely severed scraps, lay here and there in a confused and chaotic heap, offsetting the few scattered a short distance off. And somewhere beyond all this destruction, Jeremy heard what he presumed to be his brother's muffled voice.

"That you, Robby?"

Eventually Jeremy perceived, through the amorphous trunks of the maple trees, Robert sitting astride the one great branch extending out over the stream. Drawing his knees up under his elbows, Robert leaned forward to explore with his fingers the thick cracked bark of the branch.

"What the fuck happened to you?" Jeremy said, but his brother did not laugh as intended.

"She fell," he said instead, so softly in fact that Jeremy could hardly hear him, all the while staring straight ahead. Shifting forward onto his hands and knees, fingers sinking deeper into the moss, Robert inched his way a little further out into the darkness. "And I was with her, hey. I was with her when she fell all that way."

"Who?" said Jeremy, too tired now to be surprised by anything. "Who were you with? Sukhvinder Rai?"

Robert shot him a defiant look. "How'd you know about that." Jeremy shrugged. "Just a hunch."

"Well, yeah, I was with her," his brother admitted. "Once. Before I got suspended. But I was actually talking about Corporal Sidhu," he said, stretching out to touch that strip of bark ahead.

Official Residence, Phil Esposito Booster Club
33 Russell St
Monday, Sept 25/72

Dear Mom:

Received your Friday letter today, and I feel bad for dumping so much crap on you last week—or was it the week before? Time has no meaning in here. Regardless, I'm sorry if I upset you. Maybe we'll all be crazy by the time October 8th finally gets here.

I've really been frustrated these last few days. Trying to weave forty or so belts at one stretch is just too taxing—the ambition's there, but the energy isn't, not anymore. All I want to do, it seems, is eat and sleep (and crap, if it happens to be in the cards for me). No surprise there, I suppose, not with this incredibly heavy weed of late. I'm changing my schedule tonight to see if I can't weave 8, sleep 4, weave 8, sleep 4—sounds crazy, but I think it might help. Speaking of eating, I can't *wait* till October 10th to get this demanding little parasite out of me. Sorry, I said I wasn't going to talk about that anymore, didn't I? Oops. Still no visible signs I'm playing the part of unwilling host anyway. Thank God for that.

British Columbia in November—sounds about right, doesn't it? And really, why not? I mean Doug is out there, not to mention G & J, so if this whole Stratford thing falls through I might just end up out there. Lord knows my sister and I could profit from the time together.

About that upholstery fabric—you don't have to pay that much, you know, if you'd just kindly remember that your youngest daughter has a few "ins" in the textile business. I *know* you can get a better deal than that! Pete suffers from the same economic delusions as other merchants who operate: 1) a one-man show; 2) outside the city centres; and 3) with a fund of pre-packaged ideas no longer relevant to the world of modern business. I should think that $5–$10 is feasible—that is, if you know what you want, how much you want, etc. By the way, what are his labour charges? Or was he including that in the cost/yard? I doubt it.

Tuesday, September 26/72

EXTRA! EXTRA! READ ALL ABOUT IT!

ARF WEAVERS ON STRIKE

TORONTO—Informed sources in the city report that early Tuesday afternoon the ARF Smoker's & Weavers Union (local 4052) met with union and management officials in an effort to negotiate a new contract. The weavers have apparently refused to smoke any more of the "killer weed" medication which has kept them under heavy sedation since mid July. Major complaints fall into the "lowered performance" category: reduced weaving ability, reduced hours of alertness, worsening mood, streaking of peripheral vision (seeing things that just aren't there, baby . . . no, really) and last but not least, acute paranoia precipitated by not one, not two, but *three* bomb threats in the last forty-eight hours.

The research centre, located at 33 Russell Street, was finally evacuated late last evening, with the notable exception of the two experimental wards. In lieu of an out-and-out evacuation, the experiment's subjects were instead roused from sleep by nurses on duty (all very stoned of course . . . the subjects, I mean, not the nurses) and requested to huddle together against the emergency doors at the southwest corner of the ward for more than two hours while police, fire and bomb squads combed the entire building, searching for a device supposedly set to go off at midnight. Obviously, since our intrepid reporter (who, incidentally, happened to be present at the scene throughout the entire fiasco) has written this newsflash, nothing was found in the building and, more importantly, nothing exploded. However, the culmination of these events has led to the unanimous decision of the ten *very* freaked-out patients refusing any more of the hallucinatory medication. Thus has everything more or less returned to normal here in the fishbowl—minus the marijuana inhalation.

See, I told you nothing ever happens around here.

Really, though, the tension has been absolutely electrifying, hitting us all at varying intensities and frequencies. One by one we'd all gradually begun to express our desire to stop the smoke anyway, and the bomb threat was simply the last straw in a whole haystack of grievances. Hell, we thought they were hitting us with fire drills! No explanation to make us think differently either, not until the third and (so far) final threat had come and gone. I only hope the garbage strike ends as peacefully as ours has done.

Wednesday, Sept 27/72

Changed onto my new schedule now that we've stopped smoking, and I'm happy to report that it's going to work out well. However, in an attempt to cram twenty working days into the ten days remaining, be prepared that I may be a little inconsistent in my journal/letter writing. We still have to gather in the lounge at 8:15 for pulses, though, so I'm using this time to get some writing done.

Next week, October 1–8, will be one of absolute chaos, what with the doors between the two wards being opened, EEG, EKG, X-ray, physicals, multiple urine & blood samples, fasting, written reports, tests, interviews with psychiatrists and Lord only knows what else. And Dr. Myles wanted us to smoke till October 1st? Ha! What a joke. I now know how Eve must have felt after she plucked that apple—it seemed like a good idea at the time, no?

Actually, things are settling down quite nicely now, so you can forget that crap I wrote in the paragraph before last about trying to "cram twenty working days into the ten days remaining." Not gonna happen. No way. Instead, I'm just going to do what I can, and not be too anxious about anything, as I just found out, just this minute in fact, that the guy who made all the bread ($5700) in the previous experiment was on the *non-smoking* side. And here I was feeling frustrated because I wasn't anywhere even close to that. I've made about $4000 so far, and will have made about $4300 by the end, I imagine. Take off about $350 for expenses and there you have it—the end, le fin, finito! I've also been told that I've been amazing the staff the entire time—like a piece of data that just didn't fit—as the most that's ever been made in the past three experiments, on the smoking side, is about $2500, give or take.

So what else have I accomplished? I'm not quite sure.
Regardless, the end is near.

Love, Birdie

"You're a liar. You lied about everything," he said, rolling over into
the back of the sofa and further away from me. He was wearing
a pair of severely dilapidated plaid slippers, the profound significance of which, due to our family's profound dissonance,
remained completely lost on me.

"No, not everything."

"But Dad's never come to see you. He told me that himself.
And for that matter neither has Virginia, I bet."

"No, neither of them has. I only wanted you to come see me,"
I readily capitulated in a way that had recently become a habit
and it was a mistake, no doubt, to allow capitulation to become a
habit, but that did not prove I was any less of a Jacks.

"Actually, she's dead. Virginia's dead," Jeremy just now realized
for the second time in his life, and when I did not contradict him
he shook his head sadly—I could see him shaking it—raising his
free arm to further shield his face from me, from the late
September light streaming in through the window, from everything. It hurt him to speak, especially with all those stitches in his
face, extending straight back in a cruel jagged line a good inch
and a half from the corner of his lips. The surgeon, it seemed, had
made a real botch of it.

Finally he said, all but straight into the sofa, "Well I've got to get
going then."

"So soon? But you just got here."

He shrugged. "I've got to get going."

"Lucy's going to miss our visits."

"Yeah, well, I'm going to miss our visits too. Mine and Lucy's,"
he said, hammering home the connotation as intended. And
rotating his head, though just barely, he glanced about perfuncto-
rily, as though the cat might just make an appearance yet.

"Heard anything from your brother?" I asked as he spun fully around, pivoting up to place his slippered feet on the floor. The last week had made a sharp difference in the weather—in the air of late there was a distinct feeling of the fall—and at that very moment the branches outside the window began to release their burdens to the ground.

"No, nothing yet."

"Not camped out in his apartment or something?"

"Nope."

"I wonder where he could have gotten to then."

"Who knows," Jeremy shrugged, looking at the floor, his footwear, in fact anywhere but my place here in the chair. Suddenly, though, he turned to face me directly, bestowing upon me a critical appraisal that seemed to be incubating within it an insult somewhere. "And like you give a fuck," he said.

POSTED BY LUCY @ 8:48:43 A.M. 5/09/2007   53 COMMENTS

> *Women's Christian Temperance Union*
> *U.S.S.R. Defamation League, ARF*
> *Thursday, Sept 28/72*

Dear Mom:

I am in love with Paul Henderson. The world must know my love for that man. Amazing. We were on pins and needles in here the entire game. Speaking of early birthday presents, I received your package today—thank you very much—I opened it immediately, and they let me try it on (I love it, really) but I can't have it until the end of the experiment unfortunately. No gifts allowed—I thought I told you that already.

After the frenzy of the game, weaving was of course an impossibility, so luckily we had psychological tests to do all evening (paid, of course) after which we must have watched at least four movies back to back, leaving me permanently cross-eyed and pledging never to watch TV again in my life. In other news, there's a report the garbage strike might, repeat *might* be over tomorrow—what a relief! I don't think the city can take much more abuse of that (or to its) nature.

Friday, September 29/72

Beautiful day today, 80 and clear, so I made my first excursion out into the courtyard, my second (third?) time outside in 92 days. Bare feet, green grass, sunshine—I can't believe I've missed the entire summer! We played catch, threw Frisbees back and forth, lolled in the grass—all in all a very relaxing, reinvigorating day. Not too much garbage around, despite the fact the strike goes doggedly on. Of course the hospital takes care of its own in that regard. Enjoyed a nice dump myself, later on.

Saturday, Sept 30/72

Happy Birthday, Birdie! Slept in till 10 this morning, then ate an enormous breakfast, went for a long satisfying sit on the throne, read the paper, and started weaving at noon. We watched an absolutely great movie on TV tonight—James Stewart, Lee Remmick and Ben Gazarra in "Anatomy of a Murder" made, I think, twenty or so years ago. Still, it was very well cast, extremely well written, and most entertaining. Also *very* long (3 hrs), so finally got to bed about 3 AM.

October 1/72, Sunday

Out to the courtyard again this morning, though only for a ½ hour or so. Still, it was good to get Birdie out of her birdcage, even if it was a little chilly out, and not as nice as the other day.

Did you happen to catch the Boston/New York game today? Very close there at the end, and quite exciting. I think Boston is the better team, and deserves to take the whole enchilada, even though N.Y. put up a good fight.

Tracey's letter just arrived—birthday wishes for her long lost roommate. We're really looking forward to October 8th! Her business(es) is (are) leaping along like a house on fire (nice imagery, Birdie, really)—maybe I'll work for her—Ha! Her boarder, Cory, has started moving out, which has left her a little bummed unfortunately.

Monday, October 2/72

I do believe we've got this thing licked. I'll bet you wondered if October would ever get here—I sure did!

Have had a long, lovely, relaxing day today, as my body continues to process its food smoothly and efficiently—an auspicious change from the last several weeks of severe constipation. Forget that work/sleep schedule I mentioned last time—just too much going on in here.

Up at 5 AM today, wove slowly and steadily right through till midnight, alternating between my room and my old haunt, the main lounge, to watch television. Makes the time pass quickly anyway.

Had our second last blood tests this morning—just Thursday's remaining and then that part is finished—along with our physical examination with Dr. Devegny. His first comment when I walked into the examination room was, "And how is our expectant mother doing?" And the sly little smile that accompanied this remark made me want to punch his lights out—but I held back, naturally.

Tuesday, Oct 3, 1972

Slept in till six this morning, then spent an hour or so painting a wee card to send out to Doug in Vancouver, acknowledging all the cards he's sent me over the last few weeks, dear man that he is.

Despite my suddenly well-behaved bowels, I seem to have picked up a pound or two in the last few days—it's happening—bringing me back up to 122. No matter, it'll all be nipped in the bud in a week.

They finally came to take the piano away yesterday—I didn't see it go but I sure missed it last night. I'd forgotten they were coming, and when I went to sit down and play I was confronted by nothing but a blank wall! Embarrassingly enough I started to cry, which I found even more depressing, which in turn made me cry even more. Must be my hormones all out of whack. Sanity: nice while it lasted.

Wed, Oct 4/72

We've seen a few changes since yesterday. Dr. Congreves, our young clueless corporal, rallied us to the main lounge for a chat after pulses last night to inform us, amid a chorus of impatient groans, catcalls and screeches, that the doors between the two wards would be opened at 9:45 PM precisely. His only request was that we try to sleep in our own beds so as not to confuse the staff—besides that we'd have the run of the place. As well, we can now talk to the staff, and they can react candidly to us. Congreves went on to answer a few of our questions (but certainly not all of our questions), endeavouring to explain what would likely come to pass over the next few days. Despite his many mumbling bumbling ways, and being forever driven to distraction, he really is rather attractive in his own awkward way. To be sure, more than a few of the ladies around here have crushes on him. But it remains virtually impossible to carry on anything even remotely resembling intimate conversation without his nodding repeatedly to himself at some point and staring off into space for the duration. The man's world turns on an entirely independent axis, believe me. "Mad" scientist through and through evidently. Anyway, all hell broke loose when that final barrier into another world was at long last brought down, and in poured all the ladies from the other side, most of them very drunk, extremely noisy and tremendously excited. They had been told first, more than an hour before, and were anxiously awaiting our release while we went about our meeting with Special Agent Congreves, ARF.

Chaos reigned for the remainder of the night—pizza arrived for everyone around 1 AM—some of the girls went out to the courtyard, some for an early morning walk, and some crawled into corners hither and thither at various hours of the morning in an attempt to reassemble themselves. Me, I went to bed about 3 AM, and fell asleep to the chatter of two wandering witches camped outside my door. Don't know what time they left. . . . They were gone when I got up this morning though.

After breakfast this morning I went for my final EEG at 9 o'clock. At 11:30 I had my first interview with Dr Boothroyd (shrink) which lasted about an hour, then chatted with Maria and Shirley all afternoon. I've done about ten belts today, and by the looks of things the weaving is pretty much over with—too many wandering witches to deal with. We're allowed to submit belts for marking up till noon, Sunday, but what's another few hundred bucks? It's like fighting a losing battle now, believe me.

I am to have my debriefing session with Alan (Congreves) tonight at nine till eleven—should prove interesting. I have a lot of questions to ask, as, I suppose, does he. There was some concern about my current "condition"—about the state of health of the foetus (spelling?) and all that—but as I have assured the doctors that I became this way *before* the experiment and not *during*, and that I am committed to terminating the pregnancy just as soon as I get out of here, they are more or less comfortable with the situation. All their bases are covered, as they say. Still, it's strange how much this subject comes up, isn't it? Especially when I promised myself I wouldn't discuss it any further. Alas, it's always there in the back of my mind, waiting to be reborn: my fall from grace.

Don't know whether I've told you or not, but there are only 18 of us left. On September 17th, with only three weeks to go, Misty, from the other (no smoke) ward, went home. According to the rules, she could only take ¼ of her savings, so after working so hard for so long she walks away from a good 1800 bucks. Needless to say, we were all quite shocked, but I found out last night from Maria that she (Misty) had begun to withdraw so severely of late that she was really starting to scare them all. It just wasn't a healthy situation for her—she wasn't strong enough—and she was extremely homesick for her husband, Chuck.

On September 25th, Shelley Cartwright (artist, 33 years old) from our ward left quietly the night of the final bomb threat. She just had a lot of personal problems that, because of the age gap, she felt she couldn't communicate to us. She also felt she wasn't accomplishing anything in here, other than being very coldly "used" by the medical "Establishment." A staunch Women's Liberationist, she just couldn't stand the thought of smoking even one more joint—it was a matter of principle—and she refused to back down and "sell out." (As it happens, of course, we stopped smoking that very night, so she *really* lost out.) Pick your battles, that's what I say. And when you do pick your battles, make sure they're worth fighting, for God's sake. I mean my Lord, if these two only knew the crap I've been trudging through these last few weeks.

★   ★   ★

It's 11:30 PM and I've just emerged from my taped debriefing session with the lovely, beautiful, somehow utterly charming Dr. Alan Congreves. A rather pleasant session considering, very relaxed and interesting, especially talking to someone you've had your eye on for over three months now but haven't really said "Boo" to in weeks. I've written down some points that came up in conversation, but I'll wait until we get together to explain, as it will make much more sense once we've had a chance to discuss the experiment, and put the whole thing into some sort of context. Really must go to bed now—it's 2:30 AM—and I'm very tired from all this late night debriefing.

Tomorrow marks the one-year anniversary of the launch of the LeDain Commission's marijuana experiments. For the staff, most of whom have worked them all, it's going to be a little nostalgic at our party on Saturday night. At the end of this experiment, they all go back to being ordinary run-of-the-mill nurses, doctors and attendants at various hospitals, their mission complete. I know exactly how they feel—it's the same melancholy sensation that sets in on opening night, when the curtains part, the actors finally take the stage, and the weary crew behind the scenes see the end of their long, hard-fought battle drawing to a close.

Take care and God Bless. Love, Birdie

SEPTEMBER, 2002

"Saw that crane again this morning. Way up high in that maple tree there."

Grudgingly Jeremy stood up, looked up over the lip of the pool in the direction his father indicated, and then dropped back down into position once more. The thick morning fog wafting up out of the ravine made it difficult to see even so far as the railing at the edge of the overhanging deck, let alone the maple way out there beyond it, the branches of which had already lost their vast majority of leaves, leaving them thin and vulnerable and, at this height, vaguely skeletal, like the diminished pilings of some ancient rotting jetty.

"Finish that story you've been working on?" Jon inquired from his provisional seat on the second-to-bottom step of the sundeck stairs. With both hands trembling and unsteady, he brought his coffee cup slowly and painstakingly to his lips, managing to get in a fairly impressive slurp regardless of what were now, in his implicit thoughts and explicit suggestions, obnoxiously unfaithful and loose-hinged appendages.

"Sure did," Jeremy said. "First draft anyway."

"So what happens now?"

"Happens?"

"What's the next step?"

"Well I have to work at the mill tonight, if that's what you mean," Jeremy said. "And hey, make sure I'm up by noon tomorrow, okay? I have my long-awaited drug test at two apparently."

Jon watched as Jeremy, down on his haunches, sanded the recently filled-in crack in the pool, just as Jon himself had instructed him to do. A small prop plane buzzed past overhead, bound for the airport, or perhaps the small southern terminal of the airport, that much further isolated from the rest. "So then you're going to stay on there a while," Jon said, absorbed in the path of the plane against the rutted, grey, low-slung sky.

"I suppose. Why?"

"Well I was thinking that maybe you'd be heading back east soon, that's all."

Jeremy turned to consider his father briefly, then rotated slowly back to the wall.

"Take your pill?"

"Yes."

"And your exercises? You did your exercises?"

"I did my exercises," Jon said.

Jeremy suddenly felt bad, as though he were nagging his father unnecessarily, and so turned his attention to his own two hands cut, scraped and sore from work the night before. "What happened with Virginia's sister?" he took a chance and asked, looking now past his hands, as though profoundly interested in this smoothed-over rift in the wall.

His father hesitated.

"Jonathan told you."

"Yes," Jeremy said, not really knowing what his father was referring to.

"Your mother . . ." Jon began, catching himself, "Virginia, she left when she found out her sister was pregnant."

"And you were the father."

"And I was the father."

"And she was in love with you?" Jeremy ventured, putting aside the sanding block and pivoting about on his haunches.

"Birdie?" Jon hesitated again, pursing his lips. "I suppose she thought she was," he managed to say in a voice hoarse and on the verge of breaking.

"And did you love her?"

"I never really considered it an option, I guess."

Somewhere a dog barked, and presently a child's voice called out to subdue it.

"So then how did Virginia know you were the father?" Jeremy continued.

"I told her. I told her when her sister was still back east at that— that . . ."

"Experiment," Jeremy finished.

"Yes, that experiment," his father repeated. "Then afterwards, when she returned out west and she was pregnant—"

"Pregnant? *After* the experiment? But I thought she had an abortion right after the experiment."

"No, she didn't have an abortion. Why would you think she had an abortion?"

"Well she said she was going to in those letters I found."

"Well, as you're here to attest to, my son, she obviously did not," Jon said.

Jeremy felt his entire head flare up red as what felt like a wave washed over him.

"N-no . . ." he said, slowly regaining his conversational sea legs. "No, obviously she didn't."

Again the wave washed over him, and he had to raise his head up out of the pool to keep from drowning in it.

Eventually, having thoroughly explored his still painful stitches with his tongue, in this way extinguishing, for the moment at least, the overwhelming impulse to cry out loud, he said, "So Jonathan, he's our . . ."

"Your, what, half-brother, I guess."

Jeremy breathed a small sigh of relief. At length he picked up the sanding block and returned to the crack in the foundation.

"So then, what, this Birdie just dumped us in your lap and left?" he went on in the direction of the wall, pitched aslant in rough waters though he already was.

Jon hesitated routinely again before answering. "In a manner of speaking, yes," he said. "Yes, I guess you could say that. Though she didn't originally plan on being gone so long, I don't think. Least that's what she had me convinced of. As I recall, she was on her way to spend a season in . . ."

"Stratford."

"Stratford, yes."

"But she never came back."

"No she never did," Jon said. "Took up with some doctor for a time, then moved back to Bobcaygeon on her own, I guess." He gazed out over the gulf of the ravine. "You know, it's not good to be *too* independent, Jeremy. You have to learn that. I *had* to learn that. When all people want is an opportunity to love you, it's a shame to leave them empty-handed."

Jeremy pivoted around again, this time taking a seat leaning back against the curved wall of the pool. "So you raised us yourself," he said, continuing the course of his own thoughts.

His father nodded.

"As a fisherman."

"For a time, yes."

"Aw Dad, you should have told us," Jeremy said, staring down at the collection of leaves and pine needles swimming in a puddle between his shoes.

"I should have, yes."

"I mean Robby and I, we should have known who our mother was. Who our *real* mother was."

"One of the many great mistakes of my life," his father admitted.

That sat there on their respective seats, silent for a time.

"I suppose," Jon eventually went on, "at the time, rather than admitting my own part in the . . . situation, I found it easier just to say it was, well, as I said it was. As I've always maintained it was. And how you've always thought it was."

"Until now."

"Until now," Jon said. "I mean I'd already lost one son. And a wife. And even your own true mother, at least in some respect."

"So then you kept fishing *because* of us, not in spite of us."

Jon laughed. "Believe me, it was an easy enough choice if it meant keeping Thing One and Thing Two around. And besides," he continued on, "I've always been happiest when I've been working. Work—*all* work—is not a curse, son, it's a gift. A holy gift. Some people grow to understand that. Other people can never understand it. Me, I didn't really understand it when I was young. But believe me," he said, indicating his still large but largely unreliable hands, "I certainly understand it now."

Jeremy gazed down at his own scarred hands, turning them over for inspection. "Aw Dad," he began, feeling his jaw begin to

tremble, the words wavering well beyond his grasp, "I should . . .
I should have—"

"Look, I don't want a lecture, Jeremy. Not now. Not from you."

"I wasn't going to lecture you, Dad. I was just . . . I was just
going to say—"

"I should have respected you more," his father said.

POSTED BY LUCY @ 12:58:41 A.M. 5/10/2007   44 COMMENTS

Thursday, Oct 5/72

Dear Mom:

'You can always count on a murderer for a fancy prose style.'

~ Nabokov

Have had a good, fun day today here at ARF—very relaxing and
most enjoyable. Being free to wander about and visit with staff &
patients on both wards makes such a difference to one's mindset.
It's going to seem like a very big world when I come out though.

Weaving seems to have completely fallen off pretty much for all
of us—I think I managed a whopping ten today myself, moving
in smooth unhurried serenity from one belt to the next. I've been
eating quite a bit, too, so I've put on another pound or two, which
is something I'll need to address before Doug gets a look at me
out west. Otherwise I feel fine, both mentally and physically, but
I'll only know for sure when I get out there and see that telltale
look in his eyes.

Friday, Oct 6/72

Finally resumed my normal "outside" hours—late to bed and
early to rise—so I guess I'm just about acclimatized. Starting this
morning we have telephone privileges, apparently limited to ten
minutes per call. But eighteen of us on one telephone (the staff
dials) still means one heck of a line-up of course. I mean have you
seen chicks talk on the telephone? Quite an experiment in human
behaviour in itself.

Called Tracey at the flat this afternoon, and she informed me
that everything was fine, more or less. Cory moved out for good

last night—they had a big fight—but in the final analysis she's glad her little "experiment" is over, as she's looking forward to getting back to "normal" again herself.

Also called Ginny, but unfortunately she wasn't home. I suppose you know she's moved out, poor thing. I did talk to Jonathan, though, and he seemed very relieved to hear from me. It felt funny after such a long time—quite fascinating, really, that sensation of hearing a voice, especially *his* voice, coming out of a black box on the wall. . . . Anyway, I mentioned my condition and he seemed very—oh how shall I put it—intrigued. I also mentioned my plans for October 10th, and he seemed a little mystified that I would even consider such a thing. Despite what my sister may or may not think, he really is a genuinely gentle and caring man. It will be good to see him, I think, however many scarlet letters I may be sporting by that time.

Saturday, Oct 7/72

Tonight we had our final farewell party, a beautiful catered extravaganza attended by all patients, staff and doctors, and of course the one and only Stan the Shopping Man, whom we girls presented with a special commemorative belt, replete with ceremonial fringes and the names of all twenty ladies woven into its considerable circumference. Poor Stan, he started to cry he was so touched—

HE: Aw, Birdie, it's beautiful. It's the most beautiful thing I've ever seen.

ME: No, Stan, you're beautiful. You're a beautiful, loving man.

HE: [Trying on belt] Look, it even fits!

ME: Said Pooh, sniffling a little, a by-product of the stinky liniment perhaps.

—which of course made the rest of us well up like mad. The buffet was served at 7 o'clock from long tables set up in the south ward. Free wine & spirits, carnations for each of us, and the greatest food—especially after the bland, salt-free hospital diet we've grudgingly become accustomed to over the previous 3–plus months. Needless to say, it was a real treat, and most enjoyable.

However, I didn't partake of any alcohol. I simply didn't feel like it somehow.

The remainder of the evening was spent in dancing, conversation, ping-pong and general merry-making, with the staff finally getting a chance to talk to each of us personally. It felt good to hear them open up with the truth, even if some of it stung a little.

I finally went to bed about 3 AM—some of the others were still up at sunrise though, each and every one nursing a hangover, I'm guessing.

Sunday, Oct 8/72

Graduation day. Spent today doing all my laundry, every stitch of clothing I had. Rented a terry housecoat to wear till my clothes dried—with the dry air in here it takes an amazingly brief period of time—the only real blessing of a desert climate, I find.

Tomorrow we face the world . . . with the garbage strike about to enter its sixth week—I can hardly wait! Lorna, Maria and I stayed up late to watch Elia Kazan's "East of Eden" with James Dean and Julie Harris. It's been years since I saw it last, and so I really enjoyed it—I had forgotten so much.

It was really great talking to you today, Mom—I mean that. Sorry about the tears though—hearing your voice just set everything loose—I guess I just have so much on my mind right now. Good Christ, I wish I could see into the future and know what kind of mother I'd make. Would I be a good one? Would he/she be a good person? What would they act like? Look like? Laugh like? Smell like? And what, pray tell, would they think twenty-thirty-forty years from now of one Phyllis "Birdie" Cormack? These are the sorts of questions I find I'm constantly asking myself. These and so many others. Regardless, we've run a good race, haven't we? Haven't we, Mother?

Love, Birdie

October, 2002

The crane spread its wings, hopped once, hovered effortlessly above the railing a moment, then slid down and out of view into the ravine. Meanwhile, having shaken a handful of feed from the container, and sprinkled the pellets through the protective steel shell, Jeremy watched the water come to a boil as one fish after another arced to the surface to inhale it. The one Koi, however, the black and orange battle-scarred behemoth, drifted about as always below. Just then Jeremy heard the screen door open, and several seconds later his father appeared atop the sundeck stairs.

"What time's your flight?"

"Eight o'clock."

"So you arrive at Pearson about, what, four in the morning local time then."

"About that," Jeremy said, smelling his hand. It smelled like work.

Moored awkwardly to the railing, Jon considered something briefly. "And what time are you going over to say goodbye to your niece?"

"In about an hour."

"There's a letter for you here. From Bobcaygeon. Doesn't say who it's from, but the writing looks familiar."

Jeremy caught the letter as it fell from his father's outstretched hand, studying it a moment before placing it in his pocket for now.

"You know," said Jon, gazing out over pond and pool into the great gulf of ravine beyond, "there's a lake right there in the backyard. Literally right outside the back door."

Jeremy hesitated a moment, wondering which yard exactly his father was referring to.

"That's right, you've been there," he said at length.

"Yes, I've been there. A long time ago now. I met your mother . . ." Jon stumbled, then with great effort righted himself, maintaining his trembling concentration as though he held it in his hands: "I met your mother up there. She used to fish up there, as a little girl. Actually, you ought to see the size of the trout they pull out of that Sturgeon Lake," he mused, shaking his head with strained precision. "But then I guess you aren't too interested in that sort of thing."

"Oh on the contrary," Jeremy said.

Jon indicated that he wished to be downstairs now, and so, replacing the cap on the feed container and wiping himself clean on his jeans, Jeremy bounded upstairs to lend the expected hand. Remnants of maple leaves skidded easily underfoot as father and son negotiated the steps one at a time, Jon's grip on Jeremy's wrist increasing steadily as they approached the bottom.

"Give me a hand with this thing." Jon indicated the clamshell.

"What do you want to do with it?" Jeremy asked, leaving his father alongside the stairs to step around the circumference of the pond.

"Take it off."

"*Off*? But what about the crane. That crane will come."

"It's not the crane population I'm looking to cull," said Jon.

And together they removed the clamshell and, for lack of a more permanent option, pushed it in under the sundeck where it would live for the longest time, far longer than even the raccoons themselves would then. Jeremy looked down at the suddenly naked pond, then over at his father, then sat down on the sundeck stairs and opened the letter from his brother.

POSTED BY LUCY @ 4:11:49 A.M. 5/11/2007   72 COMMENTS

ACKNOWLEDGEMENTS

With thanks to Sidney Shapiro and Andrée Beauchemin for their design and editing skills respectively, and to my wife, my parents, my brother and his wife for their enthusiasm and ongoing support. I would also like to thank Stephanie and Danielle Needham for, among other things, refusing to take my seriously. And lastly, this book owes a tremendous debt to Sharon Purdy, without whose letters it would simply not exist.